DESTINY

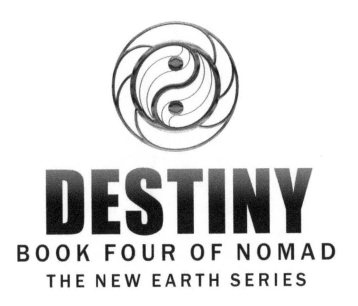

DESTINY

BOOK FOUR OF NOMAD
THE NEW EARTH SERIES

MATTHEW MATHER

DESTINY

Matthew Mather ULC
www.matthewmather.com

978-1-987942-11-8
Cover image by Momir

This is a work of fiction, apart from the parts
that aren't.

For free Advance Reading Copies of my next
book and more, join my community at
MatthewMather.com

Find me on Facebook and YouTube
search for
Author Matthew Mather

OTHER BOOKS

Standalone Titles
Darknet
CyberStorm
Polar Vortex

The Atopia Series
Atopia Chronicles
Dystopia Chronicles
Utopia Chronicles

The New Earth Series
Nomad
Sanctuary
Resistance
Destiny

The Delta Devlin Series
The Dreaming Tree
Meet Your Maker
Out of Time

DESTINY

Prologue

Captain's Log, Personal entry
USS Carl Vinson
Naval Base San Diego

The Exodus began on Christmas Day, when the repeating in-the-clear message began broadcasting on all maritime and emergency shortwave channels: *Saturn is coming.*

The message came from Tanzania, from Dr. Hermann Müller, warning that the punishment wasn't over yet, that in seventeen months the Earth would collide with Saturn's rings. That a second apocalypse would again rain down from beyond the black clouds that were still low enough you could almost touch them if you stood up straight.

That was two months ago.

There were those that simply didn't believe the message, of course. They said that it was more hysteria. It *was* hard to separate fact from fiction now that the global communication systems were down. Knowing what to believe was difficult even before the event, even when people could talk to each other across thousands of miles without a second thought.

Even if the Saturn story were true, many said, they'd just stay where they were. Stoic souls who were recovering from the Yellowstone eruption, busy digging out the chest-deep sludge of ash and deepening snow from main streets across middle America, trying to find a way to reclaim what was lost despite the millions of dead, despite losing their families and their loved ones. Some decided to stay, to defend their land—as the Indians did before them, and God knows who or what before that. Soon they would be all just as gone.

The carnage of the first wave of death was beyond catastrophic. More than a hundred million American lives lost. It was a miracle so many even survived Nomad's furious onslaught, but the second wave of death was even more deadly, and slower and more painful. Cholera and typhus and rampant diseases combined with dehydration, exposure to the cold, black lung from

1

the ash, and terrible starvation. A simple bacterial infection was a death sentence without access to modern medical facilities or antibiotics. Those who withstood these ravages were afflicted with the *sickness*—positron radiation exposure from the massive solar flares. The very old, the very young, and the infirm were the first to go, and even then the strong began dying; but there were those that survived.

Proud people carrying what they could on their backs, carrying their children, refusing to give up. Families emerged from the darkness to come here.

To Naval Base San Diego.

And it's my job to protect them.

End of entry, Feb. 19th
Captain William J. Reynolds III
USS Carl Vinson, Nimitz-class Nuclear Aircraft Carrier

PART ONE

1

Naval Base San Diego
February 19th

Captain Reynolds held up his binoculars and focused them on the chain-link fence. A soot-faced, red-bearded man in a stained blue sport coat was arguing with the Marine stationed at the guard post; screaming at him. He held a tiny girl in his arms. The Marine stood at attention and ignored the man. Reynolds swung his view to the right. A dusting of pink snowflakes had begun falling from billowing gray clouds overhead. The main gates were closed. A gaggle of ragged people massed behind the gates, their arms outstretched.

"*What the...*" Reynolds held his tongue from invoking his Lord's name in vain. "Mister Harris, can you please raise the main gate?"

The young officer snapped a quick salute but fidgeted on the spot, five feet away, without reaching for the microphone.

"Did you misunderstand me, Mister Harris?"

"Sorry, Captain, but the radio isn't working again."

Reynold's shoulders sagged involuntarily. He prided himself on keeping a ramrod-straight posture when he was on the bridge. "You're the signalman, correct?"

"Yes, Captain."

"The senior signal officer on deck?"

"Yes, Captain."

"Then go and goddamn signal the main gate and tell me what the hell is going on."

"Aye, aye, Captain." Harris snapped a quick salute and swiveled his body to bolt away.

"And get someone up here to fix that thing," Reynolds added.

"Yes, Captain," came the reply as the young man sprinted away.

Unbelievable. An eight-billion-dollar boat stuffed with nine billion dollars' worth of everything imaginable that flew or floated or fought, and he couldn't get a goddamn working radio. Then again, what did dollars matter anymore? Not more than the paper they were printed on, and there was no way anyone on the planet was going to build another piece of equipment like this nuclear-powered aircraft carrier. Not for a hundred years. Maybe a thousand.

Maybe not *ever* again.

He stretched forward to look down at the deck, the thousand-foot-long expanse of gray metal launch and landing surface. Six F-35s were at the ready, but they hadn't put any birds in the air since the event. Too much particulate ash up there for jets. The turboprops did better, but they still knocked the hell out of the turbines and carburetors. His men were working on it. Five thousand sailors and Marines under his command, and a hundred thousand more assembled at the Naval Base.

He looked up to survey the harbor.

In the distance he could just see the USS George Washington, the only other Nimitz-class aircraft carrier that had survived, at least in the Pacific. Of the eleven in active service, three were lost outright, and six were so badly damaged from the radiation storm that they weren't operational. The Gerald Ford group had limped in to see what remained of Norfolk Naval Base, and another was at sea in the Indian Ocean. Pearl Harbor was gone. Literally. The volcanic island of Hawaii had detonated, wiping away anything—including the fleet there—within a hundred miles.

Communications were sporadic without the satellites they'd come to depend on, satellites that just weren't there anymore either.

Captain Reynolds had had two weeks of warning before Nomad, and had steamed his carrier group over the deepest, darkest bit of the Pacific he could find away from land, and as far away on the other side of the planet from Nomad at its closest approach. The latest intel before the disaster warned of a massive electromagnetic-pulse-like event, and so Reynolds had his crew unbolt and torch-cut free any bit of electronics they could, and hide it in the belly of the Carl Vinson. The massive metal superstructure should act as a Faraday cage to absorb most of the shock, he'd reasoned—and he'd been right.

At least, it had absorbed most of it.

The skies had lit up like neon signs in Times Square and the Pacific had boiled up as if God himself were having a fit in His bathtub—but to their credit, many ships had survived to limp back here. He scanned the harbor. Almost a hundred Navy ships, less than half of what the Pacific fleet was before Nomad, but along with the military ships were thousands of merchant and civilian vessels. He let his eyes wander to the hills surrounding the harbor. At least the Coronado and Silver Strand beach had taken the brunt of the first waves, five-hundred-foot monsters, and protected San Diego Harbor. San Diego itself rose quickly from the water into the hills, and that had helped, although the massive earthquakes had reduced most of the buildings to rubble despite them being built to withstand them.

At least the waves weren't like the ones on the East Coast, half-mile-high walls of water moving at thousands of miles an hour that had erased New York and Boston from the face of the planet, scraping them clean to the bedrock as if they had never existed. The waves had rocketed up the Chesapeake Bay and obliterated Washington and Baltimore, washing a hundred miles inland only to be stopped by the Shenandoah Mountains of Appalachia.

It was the bad luck of geometry that the Western hemisphere was nearest to Nomad when it made its closest approach, when the tidal forces had shot up exponentially and the brunt of the solar storm radiation hit the planet. Worse still, America was close to the magnetic north, and the Earth's own normally-protective magnetic field had acted as a funnel to pour a deluge of charged particles into North America, frying any electronics, even ones hardened against EMP. Nobody had planned for this.

Nobody could have imagined it.

Cheyenne Mountain was gone. NORAD Command, designed to withstand a direct nuclear attack from above, had been destroyed from below, by the eruption of the Yellowstone supervolcano. The US military chain-of-command was shredded, the President and Vice-President's whereabouts unknown—by now presumed dead—and the American government gone.

Almost gone.

"Captain."

Reynold's shoulders again sagged imperceptibly before he caught himself and forced his back straight. "Yes, Mr. Donnelly?"

"I'm afraid that it was my fault."

Captain Reynolds illuminated his best high-wattage smile and turned, hand extended, to greet Attorney General Roger Donnelly. "What was your fault, sir?"

The man took Reynold's hand and shook it firmly, sternly, as someone in his public relations department had no doubt instructed him to make sure to do. His blue suit was fresh pressed, his black hair dyed and coiffed to perfection, his teeth gleaming white. "That the men closed the gates. That was my command."

"And why would you have done that?" Reynolds maintained the smile with effort. Who the hell had let this guy issue orders to *his* men?

"Too many people are on the base, Captain. It's becoming unsafe."

"Unsafe for whom, exactly? For them?" Reynolds pointed two fingers out the east-facing window of his bridge, at the rubble heap of what remained of San Diego. "There are two or three million people in those hills, doing their best to hang on. If they're coming down here to the base, it's because they have emergency medical needs."

This place was a sanctuary. Reynolds had fixed an emergency message broadcasting telling people out there to try and make their way here.

"What they should be doing is moving south," Donnelly said. "It's only going to get colder."

"To where? Into *Mexico*? That's no better than here."

"Further south."

"I don't need to remind you that the Panama land bridge was wiped out. North and South America are not connected landmasses anymore, Mr. Donnelly. There isn't much more south that these people *can* go."

"I just think it's unrealistic…" Donnelly's voice faded and he winced, his political mind obviously trying to weave its way through a moral minefield. "When are we setting sail?"

"As soon as I can assemble the fleet and begin boarding the civilians. It's going to take another three or four months to get enough supplies and boats, as best as I can estimate."

"And you think you can ferry millions of people across the Pacific Ocean?"

"I'm going to try. We've got upward of 5,000 merchant marines plus a few thousand civilian boats and the hundred and four Navy ships. We can take maybe ten thousand on the Carl Vinson herself."

"Ten…three or four months?" Donnelly muttered the words, as if in amazement.

"We have enough time to do two trips, sir, maybe three. We have fifteen months to try to evacuate as many million people as we can, that's what I think."

Saturn's rings would impact the northern hemisphere, with the energy of tens of millions of Hiroshima-sized atomic bombs going off at the same time in an arc that spanned more than half of the planet—at least that was what the scientists they had left were saying. North America was going to bear the worst of it. Again.

The Attorney General nodded, considering the words. "I think we need to send a vanguard to Australia first, to the western provinces. Senior ranking politicians, military personnel"—he glanced at Captain Reynolds—"scientists, and of course as many women and children we can fit. The Australian government has extended this very generous offer, and we need to set up a provisional government for New America as soon as we can, before it can be rescinded or anyone makes a land grab."

"And we will. As soon as we can."

"We need to send the Carl Vinson, or the George Washington, right away," Donnelly persisted. "You will be back in time—"

"I am not leaving these people here unprotected, and I am not letting this convoy traverse the Pacific Ocean without protection either."

The Attorney General held up his hands in mock defeat. "I know the Chinese and Russians have forbidden the US Navy from crossing into their hemisphere. I'm not saying we leave anyone unprotected, but we still have tools of persuasion." The man almost hissed the last words.

He meant the boomers, the fourteen Ohio-class SSBNs—ballistic missile submarines—that still plied the depths of the oceans. They'd been barely affected by Nomad, protected by a thousand feet of ocean water as they'd dove down during the event. Each had 24 ballistic missiles, each of those with independently targeted multiple warheads. A thousand nukes still under the button if needed.

Reynolds hoped they wouldn't.

The only way to talk to deep-running submarines were via ELF transmitters—massive land-based installations that were now destroyed. Now they had to rely on encrypted shortwave that submarines could only pick up towing a sonar buoy.

This was the third leg of America's nuclear triad of deterrence. The ground-based systems weren't operational anymore. Out of communication, and their silos buried under five feet of ash and more than that of snow and ice. Bombers weren't an option either, save for the small cache of nuclear warheads that Captain Reynolds had on board the Carl Vinson and the other carriers still limping their way to operational status. They weren't the only military to have survived the disaster. The Chinese, the Russians, even the North Koreans, they were all sounding the war drums to keep others away.

War was the furthest thing from Captain Reynold's mind.

But not from Attorney General Roger Donnelly's.

"I might need to remind you, *Captain* Reynolds, that I am the senior ranking government official, straight down the succession line from President Sandusky. In essence, I am your Commander in Chief, and was appointed directly by President—"

"With all due respect, sir, *'in essence'* does not hold water at the present moment in time, and also with respect, you were never elected. You were appointed."

Attorney General Donnelly retained the same tiresome smile. "As were you."

"I *earned* my command."

"And you think I did not earn my position?"

The Captain's shoulders sagged, and this time visibly. "I do not mean any disrespect, but this is a very difficult time. We have heard reports that Speaker Hohman may still be alive in Nashville. We need to follow procedure. Without rules, there *will* be chaos."

"Rear Admiral Horowitz is here on the base, he is the ranking officer—"

"*Retired* Admiral Horowitz, and with all respect, again, he is not a naval aviator and therefore not in line to command an aircraft carrier. And the man is eighty-six years old."

"So there's no convincing you?"

"As I said, I can dispatch one of the destroyers, with two frigates. They can make speed and have you there in two weeks. I can do that."

"But the Chinese and Russian navies..."

"They will probably turn you back, based on what we are hearing."

"Or worse. Imagine what they might do if they learned the President of the United States was aboard. They might take me hostage."

Captain Reynolds resisted the urge to sigh and didn't bother to correct this man's presumption. He seemed to almost enjoy his new-found perch—at the expenses of millions of dead—and this was fast turning into a passive aggressive argument, not to mention that this man yet may prove to be his Commander in Chief. He had to respect that, but not quite yet.

"Have you spoken with EUCOM?" Donnelly asked, switching topics.

"They got it almost as bad as us in Europe," Reynolds replied. They hadn't heard a word from America's European Military Command based in Germany. "Worse, in some ways. When the Greenland ice sheet dumped into the North Atlantic, it reversed the course of the Gulf Stream overnight. Temperatures plummeted in days. Anyone up there froze to death before they could get out of the way."

He was just making conversation now, not really adding anything the Attorney General didn't know.

"I know, it's terrible," Donnelly said without even trying to sound like he meant it. "And China? Russia? Any new word from that side of the world?"

"Just what you already know, sir. China wasn't as affected as we were. Smaller waves, more protected from the radiation blast, and Beijing is a hundred miles inland. Heard it survived almost intact. And the Russians"—he shook his head—"if anyone is going to survive the cold, it's those bastards."

"And what about these Sanctuaries? The giant underground bunkers?"

"Surprised you weren't invited to one, sir," the Captain replied with a mock-frown. "Being as important as you are. It doesn't make any sense."

"That it doesn't," Donnelly replied, but his frown was real, and he didn't detect the sarcasm.

"We have to work the problem, sir, and not let the problem work us."

"*This* problem, Captain Reynolds, is that the Earth has been destroyed."

"With all due respect"—Reynolds turned his high-wattage smile back on—"that does not change the methodology of a United States Naval Officer. And while we may have taken some damage, those people out there are depending on us, and I'm not going to let them down."

Behind the Attorney General, the Captain noticed that all his bridge staff had stopped what they were doing and were instead watching this exchange. Tiny grins had crept onto their faces, which were wiped away in an instant as they turned to get busy as the Attorney General walked off the bridge.

2

Oman
February 20th

Darkness.

An ice-cold floor.

No sliver of light seeped beneath the cell door. No windows to the outside world. Only the hostility of Jessica Rollin's loneliness and uncertainty to keep her company. Her head felt as thick as the slab of concrete she lay on. Her mind numbed from repeated interruptions to her sleep. A pattern of abuse intended to wear her down.

It was working.

Jess shifted position. Pain lanced through the stump of her leg, radiated up through her spine and into her shoulders and neck. An agony worn into a wearying ache. The prosthetic Ufuk had given her was gone. A potential weapon. Too risky to allow her to retain it in captivity. What might she do with it? What could she possibly do to escape a CIA black site in a township in Oman, thousands of miles from an America that didn't even exist anymore?

That's how her fellow Americans treated her: the enemy. It seemed the only constant in this new world was either that someone wanted her dead, or locked up, or both.

A shuffling noise from beyond the door. All exterior sound was insulated—deadened—the intention to add another layer to the sensory deprivation. After weeks of it, her ears had attuned to compensate for the information deficit from her eyes.

The shuffling outside grew louder.

She tensed and jerked back, anticipating the door flying open, and with it the blinding white light. The blaring screech of some heavy metal rock band. Again, they would grab her, put a foul-smelling rag over her head, and drag her to a room where a woman with no face would throw questions at her for hours. A shadow beyond her sight.

At first, the whole routine felt so ridiculous she wanted to laugh. She told them she loved Iron Maiden and to turn it up. The joke wore thin.

She wasn't laughing anymore.

How long had she been in this cell? Weeks? Months?

She pressed her back against the far concrete wall—pressed hard—her single leg scrabbling against the floor to find balance. Adrenaline shot into her muscles, her tendons stretched taut. In the darkness, she sensed the door open by a sudden waft and draft of fresh air, but no blinding white light. No deafening roar.

Just a whisper: "Jess."

Peter Connor's voice.

"They've agreed to let me speak to you," he continued.

She huddled against herself in the shadows and remained silent.

They considered her a traitor—but *he* was the traitor. She'd trusted him, had saved his life in Al-Jawf—but had all of that been arranged? Was she just a pawn in another larger game? Circles within circles. Who could she trust? Only herself.

She'd had a lot of time to think, stuck in this pit. Even if she wanted, her throat was so dry, she doubted she could speak, but she didn't even try. She offered him no satisfaction of a reply.

"If you won't talk to me, you know what comes next."

Still she said nothing. A light switched on behind him, but not a fierce, bright one, intended to hurt. A gentle yellow glow lit the hallway beyond. Peter's silhouette was hazy and indistinct.

"I believe you, Jess. You're not what they think. It took me this long just to get them to trust *me*. I can get through to them, but only if you talk to me. Let me help you."

She shifted. Another bolt of pain shot through her. She was starving, painfully dehydrated. Frozen and exhausted. Everything she had done, she did for the sake of others. This was her reward.

Confinement.

Torture.

"Help me?" she croaked, forcing out the words from between cracked lip, her voice a wheedling rasp. "Trust isn't what you'll get from me."

He took a step inside the cell, but her tired eyes saw him no more clearly. Someone moved behind him. He ushered them away.

"Come closer," she growled, surprised at the strength in her voice. "I'll tear out your throat with my teeth." Her tongue felt bloated in her sandpaper throat.

"Jess."

She raised herself, as best she could with only one leg. Arched her back to make herself ready to pounce. A feral animal, riven by rage and fear—that's what she'd become, what she felt like.

The rage, that was easy enough to understand, but was it really fear she felt? Did she fear Peter—or his people—whoever they really were? Were they CIA? Did that even still exist? Did the United States even exist as a thing in this new world? Like the mythical Hydra, answering one question only seemed to create two more, with her the leaf blown around at the center of a never-ending maze.

Why her?

Her mind circled back again, to what mattered—Hector, Massarra, Raffa, Lucca, Giovanni. Even Ufuk. Her fear was real, but it wasn't for herself.

She mouthed her friends' names silently, pausing to remember their faces, but the images were fading. Were they looking for Hector? As Peter had promised? Was the boy in Sanctuary China? Had Roger and Lucca and Abbie managed to connect with him? She hoped so. It was a small hope she kept deep and tight within her chest.

And had Massarra recovered?

Nobody would even answer her that.

It was a miracle that the Israeli had survived the journey here.

After the fight at Ufuk's Tanzanian launch facility, they hadn't had a lot of time before they knew Müller's forces would return. Peter had managed to resuscitate Massarra at the medical facility, and the robotic medical assistant had stapled and cauterized her wounds. They'd taken what medical supplies they could carry on improvised jerry-rigged ICU stretchers for Massarra and Raffa, and Peter, Giovanni, Ufuk and she had dragged them outside into the ash-ridden landing field. Ufuk's facility had heavy lifting drones—each fit two people with some cargo—that whisked them away to the coast, with dozens of other drones flying out in a flurry of random directions to confound anyone trying to track them.

With the heavy loads, the big drones had had less than two hours of flight time — so a range of a hundred miles. Ufuk had no more hidden facilities for them to run to, so they ran blindly for the coast, fanning out dozens of tiny drones ahead of them under the control of Ufuk's artificial intelligence, Simon. It could still communicate with the drone hoard directly from the radio tower atop the Tanzanian facility, thousands of feet in altitude above the coast.

It was a Hail Mary pass, but one that connected.

Floating near the mouth of the Sigi River, Ufuk's drones had found an empty fishing trawler. Sodden and dilapidated, but intact. The boat had survived the tidal waves and tsunamis that had destroyed the coasts, and the trawler was empty now, or the crew dead. The timbers of the old boat probably had some tragic story they could tell—but however it'd happened, it was an opportunity.

Ufuk and Peter landed on the boat first, managed to start its engine. The hoard of miniature drones had scoured the area and found diesel drums washed ashore a dozen kilometers north. By the end of the day, they were all aboard the old ship, and Peter and Ufuk had worked on Massarra's injuries. Tried everything to stem the effects of the massive trauma and multiple bullet wounds. Simon had advised them; acted as a doctor—a strange disembodied voice echoing against the salt-ridden wood of the creaking trawler.

But go where? That was the next question once they'd secured the trawler. Peter said he had friends in Oman. By that point, Massarra had regained consciousness and told them to trust him.

So they did.

They didn't have a lot of options, and Ufuk, of course, said he had friends there as well, more of the shadowy Levantine Council. Just a few hundred miles in a seaworthy trawler, Peter had said, an easy journey to safety—or at least, what safety his friends could offer. They had doctors there, he had assured them. Massarra said to trust him, seemed to know something they didn't, and it was her life in danger, floating on the fish-stinking trawler.

And what about the mysterious package that Ufuk had taken from the cryogenic facility in Tanzania? The one he said was the key to the future of humanity?

While the rest of them were trying to stabilize and save Massarra and Raffa in the Tanzanian facility, Ufuk had obsessed over his small package, which was placed into a new containment unit. He'd told them it was a seed bank and would provide for the future. A seed bank for what? Food? That seemed important, but at the time, Jess was too busy with survival, and almost as soon as they got on the boat, a yellow drone submersible had floated into view. Ufuk secured his package into it, mumbled something about it being safer, before it disappeared back into the depths.

And then they were off to Oman.

Bit by bit, as the horizon disappeared behind them, they lost communication with Simon as the drones held aloft fell from the sky and were unable to relay signals. In the end, it had taken them nearly a week to get there, near the flooded and wrecked city of Muscat, where a dusty four-by-four had met them after Peter got onto the radio and exchanged cryptic messages. A woman and a man, faces hidden by scarves, bodies and weapons obscured by thick winter parkas.

American soldiers presenting themselves as the friend of a photojournalist.

Damn you, Peter.

I trusted you.

The man inched closer to her in the dim light, his hands out, palms toward her. Trying to calm her, or perhaps as a defensive posture. Probably both.

"I've been through the wringer on this as well," Peter said. He took another step.

Something between a cough and a laugh rasped from Jess's lips.

"I'm putting everything on the line to stick up for you, Jess."

"That's your problem."

"Some people want to take this to the next level. You know what that means?"

"Go ahead." She readied herself to strike at him.

The man must have sensed it, because he hesitated, and then just like that—he turned and was gone. The darkness returned, and in the corner, when the adrenaline seeped away into the black, she cried.

Hours passed, maybe days.

Time lost meaning in the darkness and silence with just her thoughts circling her, her mind trying to stave off the panic and madness. She knew what would come next.

What would happen to her?

Even as an American citizen, whatever that now meant.

She'd heard stories on her tour with the Marines. Renditions to black sites. Khaled El-Masri, a German citizen abducted in error by Macedonian police, then handed over to the CIA. Flown to Afghanistan and held captive near Kandahar. Interrogated and beaten. More cases of this than she could count. Now she was the terrorist—and those events took place in the old world where laws offered what restraints they could.

Around and around her mind circled in the darkness, but it never strayed from thoughts of Hector. Müller had abducted him, had made sure to take the child with him when he left the Tanzanian facility. Did she do enough to stop him? Could she have stopped him? And Müller would have never taken the boy if it weren't for Ufuk.

The bastard.

The thought brought to mind another bastard.

Roger.

Now he was a bastard that she had to hope—pray—she could rely on. Her life had come down to depending on two people she detested.

She spent days on the trawler, and weeks in this dark pit, trying to disengage from her anger at Ufuk. He'd made Hector the biometric backup for his networks, had used his DNA sequence as the alternate key for communicating with his artificial intelligence Simon. It was the reason Müller had taken him.

She knew thinking about these things was counterproductive. That it weakened her resolve and ultimately strengthened the position of her captors. But there was no way to avoid it. Images of those she loved invaded her thoughts and whenever she tried to keep them at bay she failed.

She huddled in the corner and pulled a threadbare blanket around her.

3

Oman
February 24th

The blackness cocooned Jess, separated her. Always too cold. She never stopped shivering. They gave her the blanket, but it was too thin. She tried to remember the number of meals she was given, and estimate the time that passed between them. That gave her some sense of how long she had been here. Somewhere after a hundred—maybe a hundred and twenty—she lost count. The numbers faded away into the darkness.

When the door finally opened again, it was in silence.

At first, she thought she was hallucinating, but it wasn't Peter that took her and led her out of the room. This time it was two men wearing ski masks. They hooded her, the vice-like grip of their hands biting into her flaccid muscles. She struggled, but she was weak, and what would be the point?

She let them drag her one-legged body through the hallways.

They sat her in a chair and chained her hands to a cold metal table. The air stank of cigarette smoke, the table greasy. They removed the hood. This time, blinding light. She winced at the pain of the floodlight's beam burrowing into her optic nerves. As the blur receded, she recognized shapes. A windowless, concrete cubicle room. The men stood in front of her, a single door behind her, but there was also another table. A computer screen. And images. Faces.

Massarra.

Ufuk.

Giovanni and Raffa.

The screen was split into four video feeds from their cells.

The door opened behind her and she tried to turn, but her neck muscles cramped painfully. A third ski-masked interrogator stepped inside. A man from the build of his body. Likely an officer from the way the two men who had brought her in straightened before returning to their previous stances.

The newcomer stood behind the seat opposite her. In his hands he held a plate, a sandwich, an apple, and some cheese. In his other hand was a mug. A thin curl of steam spiraled upward. He set them on the table in front of her, then he settled into the seat.

"I would eat," he said.

His voice had that lyrical deep-south quality: Alabama, or Georgia, maybe South Carolinian. In another world, she found Southern accents charming, comforting.

Not today.

Her manacled hands reached for the food, and she leaned forward to stuff a lump of cheese in her mouth. The steaming liquid was coffee. Tasted fantastic. Bitter but wonderful. A part of her mind questioned if it was drugged, but the thoughts were beaten away by thirst and hunger.

"Your collaborators are fine. All being treated fairly."

Jess didn't bother verbalizing the sarcasm she wanted to spit out, fearful they would take the plate away. "I want to see them. All of them. Right now."

"You don't get to make demands."

"Why are you doing this to us?"

The man's eyes narrowed. He gestured. A speaker crackled and hissed.

"*I mean, I'll admit that you never said those things.*" It was a recording of her own voice from Tanzania. Tired, slow and deliberate. Fragmented by desperation. "*That Ufuk falsified the video. That he destroyed Sanctuary.*"

Müller's voice: "*I'm no fool—*"

"*I'm tired of running, tired of the lies. You must have seen us fighting on the airplane, the things I said to Ufuk. That wasn't an act. The second we got here, I wanted to get away from this bastard. He lies, he cheats. And now this thing with Hector? He never told me.*"

Müller's voice again: "*So you want to protect the boy?*"

Jess remembered grabbing Hector; the look of fear in the boy's eyes.

"*I want to tell the truth.*" She felt again the sting of the zip ties at her wrists, when Müller's men had captured her. The scars were still there. "*And I want to protect what's left of my family. Giovanni. Hector.*"

Raffa. If Lucca is in China, I want you to take us there. I want us to be safe and for this to be over."

"That's your voice, Miss Rollins."

"I was lying."

"Convenient."

"Also true."

"The time has come for clarity, Miss Rollins. Convince me. Make me believe you."

"Screw you," she offered around a mouthful of cheese.

Silence from her captors.

"You're getting two meals a day, a dry, safe place to sleep. You think this is bad? Do you know what's happening out there, Miss Rollins? The half of humanity that wasn't instantly wiped out is now starving and freezing to death. I'd bet most of them would love to switch places with you."

Jess watched Raffa's image glow in ghostly green. A night vision imaging system. It had to be pitch black in his cell. The teenager shifted on the concrete floor, looked up, seemed to look into Jess's eyes.

She exhaled, letting her anger deflate. "What, you want me to take a lie detector test or something? You got something like that? Shoot me up with pentothal?"

It was hard to say if what moved across his face beneath the ski mask was a smile. "We don't use sodium thiopental."

"So what?" She leaned forward to take a bite of the apple, her mobility reduced by her hands chained to the table. "Stick wires in my brain? Bring it on, asshole. I'm telling the truth. It's Müller who's the traitor."

Even as she said it, she wasn't sure if it was true. Ufuk and Müller played off each other, and it wasn't clear who had done what. Her eyes flitted to the muted green image on the screen of Ufuk in his cell. Where the others were curled in fetal balls, Ufuk sat upright in a cross-legged position. He seemed peaceful, as if this was exactly where he wanted to be. Like he was meditating.

The officer took a long, hard look at her, then stood and left the room. The two men left with him, leaving her alone and to stare at her friends on the screens, in their dark cells. She finished what was left of her meal as she waited, her fingers and hands trembling—not from fear, but from cold. The green ghosts on the screen—her friends—unaware she was watching them, not knowing how much she wanted to speak to them and make sure they were okay. When the door opened again, a few minutes later, the man who entered wasn't wearing a ski mask.

It was Peter Connor.

She saw his face clearly now. Deep lines around his bloodshot eyes. Unshaven. His blond hair a disheveled mess. He hardly looked better than she felt. She smelled the stink of his stale sweat even from ten feet away.

Acid boiled in her stomach, rose in her throat. "I have nothing to say to you."

"We don't have a lot of time."

She leaned back and looked away. Her hands flinched in the chains.

"If it weren't for me," Peter added, "you'd be still stuck in that pit."

She turned back to scrutinize his expression. Was that desperation? "So now you need something from me? For your buddies?"

"The man who spoke to you, who gave you a meal—he did that because I suggested it. Two types of people ask for a polygraph, Jess. Intelligence officers trained to beat them, and people who're telling the truth. I knew you'd ask for it."

"Go screw yourself."

"We know where Hector is."

Silence hung in the air. It filled the room and closed around her. "Don't you dare."

"I've spent the last two months trying to convince them you're not a terrorist. Pulled together every scrap of intelligence on Rome, and what happened to Sanctuary Europe. Even the Sanctuary network *existing* was news to these guys."

"So they're idiots."

"Jess—"

"CIA, right? That's what you are? How could the CIA not know about Sanctuary?"

"There *were* rumors…" Peter's voice trailed off. "You know what's left of Al-Jawf? You know what they're doing to the people there?"

"Not my problem."

"But maybe your fault."

"You're just trying to bait me."

"Ain Salah—he was your contact. You gave that contact to Ufuk."

"Ufuk had people there already. He was just using me—"

"But you went along with him, and Massarra, even though you weren't sure if they were the ones that killed thousands in Sanctuary Europe."

"Massarra would never do that."

Peter waited; let her stew on her words. "You're so sure?"

"There wasn't anything we could have done in Al-Jawf," Jess said. "Müller won because what's left of the rest of the world can't or won't stop him—or just doesn't care."

"Müller alerted the world to the coming impact with Saturn's rings. Two months ago from Tanzania. He said that Ufuk was hiding it, was hiding secrets in the Sanctuary network as well, that Ufuk destroyed it when Müller tried to take control."

"Congratulations, then. You've got your bad guy locked up." Jess flicked her chin at the unmoving image of Ufuk in his cell.

"Half this station thinks Müller is the bad guy and we should take him out. The other half thinks he's the good guy."

"So what do you want from me?"

"No one here thinks Ufuk is innocent."

"He is an asshole."

"So we agree on at least one thing."

"This is a game? Get me agreeing on one thing, and then the next, and then the truth comes out?"

"This is no game."

"The greatest game, isn't that what you spies like to say what you do is? But what's the point anymore? The world is destroyed."

"Even locked up here, Ufuk seems to still be pulling strings, somehow," Peter replied. "And you're wrong, not all the world is destroyed."

That got Jess's attention. "Meaning what?"

"They're evacuating America."

It was the first time Jess had heard that anything remained of her country. It took the breath right out of her lungs. "Evacuating? To where?"

"Tens of millions survived," Peter answered without really answering. "A new world power dynamic is forming, with China at the center—but the old Russian bear is growling from the north. A fight is brewing in the South China Sea. That's what we're doing, Jess. Trying to protect what's left of *our* families in this new world."

"And that's where Müller is, in China?" Jess hesitated. "With Hector?"

Peter held her gaze but didn't reply.

"So what do you want from me?"

"The big fight is going to be for habitable land. Australia has been the least affected—even become more habitable—and sub-Saharan Africa is another key, that's why I was sent to Al-Jawf. We need to know the truth about Ufuk's Levantine Council, what they're really up to."

"And you want to know about Massarra?" It was obvious where this was going. "The woman nearly died helping to save your life, Peter. She was the one who said to trust you. Why did she do that?"

"That's one of our questions."

Another wafting stink of his body odor. Those bloodshot eyes. Jess leaned forward. "Why did your friends lock *you* up? You look as bad as me."

"It's complicated."

At least that was honest. "Are you telling the truth? About Hector?"

Peter shrugged non-committedly. "They're going to do the polygraph any minute." He looked at the floor and shook his head. "You'd better pass it."

"Where is he?"

"Give me something to work with."

"Give me proof that Hector is safe, and I'll cooperate."

Peter walked around the table and leaned down to her. "It doesn't work like that. You give us something, we give you something."

"You son of a bitch. Where is he?"

4

Sanctuary China
Northern China
February 24th

"Kick the ball," Roger Hargate instructed.

Hector smiled awkwardly, swung his arms back and forth, but just stared at the soccer ball at his feet. His cheeks were rosy, maybe from embarrassment, his black hair cut much shorter than Roger remembered. He looked thinner, but not too thin, and no bruises that Roger had been able to see on a quick inspection—but then the wounds were probably on the inside. The kid had been in shock since Müller brought him here, tore him away from Jessica and his uncle Giovanni.

"Come on, I know you understand English," Roger encouraged. "Kick the ball to me."

The six-year-old took a deep breath and half-heartedly kicked at the ball, which made it halfway of the ten feet across the newly cut grass to Roger. An artificial sun burned bright overhead, amid the iridescent blue sky projected on the dome of Sanctuary China's massive cavern. If anything, this was much bigger than Sanctuary Europe, at least ten thousand people lived underground here. There were similarities—in the technical design—but the feeling was completely different, like the orchids hanging from dove trees lining the park.

A well-dressed Chinese couple—the woman in a long red dress embroidered with gold flowers, the man in a pressed black suit with a collar-less white shirt—walked by along the stone path next to the park. Their noses crinkled as they passed Hector, as if the kid smelled bad. Roger stooped to collect the ball and try again.

The Chinese woman suddenly yelled something, and the man joined in.

Roger couldn't understand what they were saying, but they gestured, flicking their hands. Hector bolted and ran over to Roger, who scooped him into his arms. It was the first time Hector hadn't flinched when Roger touched him. The boy stuck his face into Roger's neck.

"Get lost," Roger said to the Chinese couple.

With looks of disgust, they hurled a few final insults and turned to continue their walk.

Through a stand of gutta-percha trees, with wildly sprouting branches and tiny leaves, Abbie Barnes appeared. "What was that about?"

"Did you understand what they were saying?" Roger asked. He hid his left hand—the one with the missing thumb that he'd cut off in an attempt at some measure of redemption, after his deceptions had led to Jessica Rollin's father's death.

"Nothing good," Abbie replied, still listening to the departing couple.

They'd been here ten weeks, and in that time, Abbie had become almost fluent in Mandarin. She had a gift for languages, not the least of many gifts she had. Hector silently reached his arms out to her, and Abbie took him into hers. He buried his head into her long brunette hair. She had matching brown eyes, although half-hidden by large oversized black-rimmed glasses. She never wore makeup. She didn't need to.

She probably reminded Hector of Jessica, and Roger agreed with the kid.

"They sure don't hide that they don't like us here," Roger said.

Ten weeks ago, after the terror of the destruction of Sanctuary Europe, they'd flown halfway around the world in a heavy lift C-130 military transport, a massive turboprop machine that had barely survived the five thousand mile journey, stopping once at a mysterious base in Kazakhstan to refuel. Of the five-thousand-plus people in Sanctuary Europe, only four hundred and twelve had arrived here.

Getting there was one thing. Getting *inside* Sanctuary China had been a whole other adventure. For three weeks they'd been stuck outside, in the snow and ice in the mountains about two hundred miles north of Beijing. Dr. Müller had been the one to convince them to let his people inside, but what he'd had to promise in return—Roger still didn't know.

He suspected it was something to do with Hector.

But that didn't mean the general populace of Sanctuary China didn't treat them like dogs. Roger sympathized. If he were a billionaire Chinese tycoon, he'd be annoyed if Roger suddenly showed up on his doorstep unannounced and became a roomie. Roger couldn't stand himself, loathed himself in fact, but maybe there was a way he could find his way back.

"You shouldn't insult our Chinese guests," said a voice from behind Roger.

A voice with a thick German accent.

Dr. Müller walked along the stone path toward them, his tangle of gray hair combed back to one side, his pot-belly jiggling from side to side as he hurried along. He smiled, his eyes wide behind the wire-framed glassed. "How is our boy doing?"

"Better, I think," Roger replied, returning Müller's smile and stretching out his hand.

The instant Hector heard Müller, he grabbed Abbie's neck harder, his small knuckles going white as he pressed himself against her.

"I think we'd better get going," Abbie, turning herself protectively to put her body between Hector and Müller.

"Sure, sure." Müller stopped short and waited for Abbie to retreat with Hector in her arms. Once she was gone, he crossed the last ten feet to Roger and shook his hand.

"He's still"—Roger searched for the right word—"fragile."

"I can't blame the boy." Müller scratched the back of his neck with one hand. "I'd be afraid of me, too."

Again, Roger sympathized.

"Any progress?" Müller asked.

Ten weeks ago, they'd arrived in the C-130 transports, but it was only seven weeks ago that they'd been let inside—the day when Müller had appeared with Hector in his arms.

Roger shrugged to say, not much.

"I assure you, Jessica was not harmed," Müller said. "The last time I saw her, she was in the company of her American compatriots. *Your* team, the CIA. Remember?"

It wasn't something Roger would ever forget. That he'd spied on the Rollins family; had been instrumental in the deaths of Jessica's parents.

"How they are treating her, I cannot say," Müller added, "but I have heard she is safe. Come." He pointed to the stone pathway. "Walk with me."

Roger followed. He knew more than Müller knew about Jess, more about what the CIA was doing to her, but he wasn't going to share that. A week and half after they arrived here, while they were still stuck outside using the shells of the military transports as shelter, Abbie had managed to get in touch with Ufuk Erdogmus and Jessica, told them that they were safe outside of Sanctuary China—and that Roger had saved the life of Lucca, Raffa's brother, and brought him with them. Once inside Sanctuary China, the risks had multiplied—but it hadn't stopped them.

Müller seemed to read Roger's mind. "He's a madman, you know that? Ufuk Erdogmus? His people destroyed Sanctuary Europe. His goal is nothing less than complete anarchy. Do you know what he tried to do in Tanzania? He has some kind of weapon, a canister of a lethal bioengineered virus, that he tried to launch on a rocket, spread a plague across the planet."

"Why would he do that?"

Müller took off his spectacles to wipe his eyes. "I don't know, the man is hard to understand, perhaps madness isn't understandable. He's dangerous. That's all I know."

"Don't the Americans have him now?"

"Yes," Müller agreed, putting his glasses back on. "And that's what worries our Chinese hosts, and me as well." His voice was measured, almost sad. "With Chairman Zhao Peng of the Chinese Politburo now dead, we are in a very precarious position."

Roger kept step for step with Müller. The man seemed to want some kind of response, but Roger remained silent.

"Two of the Politburo have remained in Beijing, with four here," Müller said after a few seconds of silence. "The Chinese government is now split—there is a fight coming—but at least there is a government. In America, things are worse."

"The entire administration is gone," Roger said. "That's what we've heard."

"But a large part of the American military is intact, and that makes both factions of the Chinese very nervous—something they can at least agree on. This is a dangerous time, not least because Saturn is dropping from the sky."

"What does this have to do with us?"

"Ufuk Erdogmus might be a madman, but he is a clever one. He had the foresight to send a cargo of communications equipment into deep space before Nomad."

Roger realized what he was talking about. "Mars First?"

"That's right. And the key to accessing Ufuk's systems lies with the boy, Hector. I'm sure of it. This could be a way of securing our position here, and perhaps calming the tensions between the Chinese and the Americans."

"All he does is play videogames on the tablet. That's what he does more than half of the time he's awake."

"Does he ever speak to Simon?"

Müller meant the artificial intelligence that controlled Ufuk's networks. A part of Simon was installed on the tablet that Hector had, the one Ufuk had given him.

"Not that I've ever heard," Roger replied. He was certain the Chinese security service had the boy under twenty-four-hour surveillance, so they had to know this already. They were probing him for reactions, for telltale signs of lying.

Müller took one methodical step after the other. "I know about the boy, Lucca."

Roger's face flushed. He'd thought they had covered their tracks, smuggled the boy in, used Abbie's father's security key codes to keep him safe in an unused tunnel section of Sanctuary China. "I, uh, I couldn't just—" Roger stammered.

"I understand, and I agree with you. It's okay. I'll help keep the secret too."

The burn faded from Roger's cheeks. "Thank you." There was no telling what the Chinese Administrative Council might do if they found a stowaway among them. They begrudged even the official guests they'd taken in.

"Just figure out what Hector knows. What Ufuk taught him." Müller stopped in the path to face Roger. "It's important, Roger. All our lives might depend on it."

5

Oman
February 24th

When you start to smell yourself, Jess thought, you know you stink like hell. Then again, she was used to blood and sweat, even when she was having fun.

This wasn't fun.

She'd been wearing the same orange vest and pants—that they'd forced her into—for weeks. Not really orange now, but a smudged brown. She'd tied up the left trouser leg below her knee to try and protect the stump. The cheese and apple and coffee had been a ploy to move her along, to start the process of wearing her down to cooperate. Peter said he'd give her leg back if she behaved, but they didn't offer her a change of clothes.

Not yet.

They kept her sitting, chained to the oily metal table, for an hour before a technician returned with the polygraph equipment. Onto her hands they placed gloves that moved and flexed with a metallic alloy sewn into the fabric. They pressed electrodes to her chest and thighs, and placed a skullcap mesh onto her head. They dropped liquid into her eyes, which stung and blurred her sight. Onto her face they positioned heavy glasses. A glimmer of blue light flickered to either side, in the peripheries of her vision.

Across from her sat a tall, angular man with salt-and-pepper hair cut short, wearing clean and sharp-pressed civilian dress. In front of him was a tablet device that cast a kaleidoscope of multi-colored light onto the lenses of his thin-rimmed spectacles.

"There are some control questions I need to ask to establish a baseline. At the same time I'll explain how the machine works. Your physiological responses are automatic. Do you understand?"

Her heart drummed even as she tried to calm it. She felt her face flush. "Yes."

"Even though a lie might be small, your body still responds. The recordings will show physiological responses. It cannot know what kind of lie you are telling. Do you understand?"

She couldn't stop thinking about the cell, how desperately she didn't want to go back there. That was what they wanted—in a dark corner of her mind, a rational place now silenced by her fear, she knew that—but she couldn't force herself to stop feeling it. "Yes," she replied, her mouth dry.

"Whatever you think you know about polygraphs, this is a more advanced machine than you know. Do you understand that?"

There is nowhere for you to hide. You have no other choice. Every other road leads back to that cell. In there, you cannot protect those you care about. "Yes."

"Is it your intention to answer all questions truthfully?"

"Yes."

"Is your name Jessica Rollins?"

"Yes."

"Is your father Benjamin Rollins?"

Pain flared in her chest. "Yes."

"Is your mother Celeste Rollins?"

The abyss inside opened, the guilt pouring into it. "Yes," she stammered.

"Are your parents alive at this moment?"

She paused before answering: "No."

More questions followed: asking if her father had died at Castello Ruspoli, if she thought meeting Massarra was a coincidence at the time, if she knew anything about the bombing of Rome. She'd seen it from the other side, when she was in the Marines. Simple questions she knew were intended to establish if she was lying, or telling the truth based on facts the examiner already knew. She tried to make herself still inside, to give them what they wanted.

So she could give herself what she needed.

"The next question refers to the intentional, unauthorized release of classified information or material to a foreign government, power, or organization, with the intent to, or with reason to believe that, the information or material would injure the US government, or give an advantage to that foreign government, power, or organization. We classify this as espionage. Do you understand?"

"Yes." I'm not a spy, I'm not a terrorist, I am not a threat to my country, I love my country—these thoughts surged through Jess's head.

"Engaging in espionage would include being contacted by someone or contacting someone for the purposes of providing classified information about US interests. Espionage includes acts of your own volition and those at the request of someone else. If you have been approached and recruited for espionage. If you were tasked to engage in any act of espionage you have engaged in espionage. Your motivations might have been ideology or loyalty, and you may or may not have received any compensation. Have you committed an act espionage against US interests?"

"No." Peter just told her they were evacuating America. So the United States still existed, at least as a political entity? If they were asking her questions like this, that's what it had to mean. Right?

Without hesitation or change in the cadence of his voice, the man offered the same preamble twice more, but substituted the words "sabotage" and "terrorism" for "espionage."

Each time she swallowed her growing resentment and answered, "No."

"Have you committed an act of terrorism against foreign interests, whether a foreign government, power, or organization?"

What foreign interests? "No."

"The next questions are in a series and are related to a man named Ufuk Erdogmus and to an underground facility in the Sassal Mason mountain range in southern Switzerland which I shall refer to as Sanctuary Europe. First of all, do you know anyone by the name Ufuk Erdogmus?"

"Yes." She wondered how the machine would interpret her desire to strangle Ufuk the next time she got in range of him.

"Have you ever been inside or within the immediate vicinity of the facility known as Sanctuary Europe?"

"Yes."

"Did you know of Sanctuary before the Nomad incident?"
She paused. "No."

"But you were an associate of Roger Hargate?"

"He was my boyfriend."

32

"Yes or no? Did you know Mr. Hargate intimately before Nomad?"

Intimate. Why did they have to use that word? It made her skin crawl, remembering herself in bed with Roger. "Yes."

"Did you ever meet Ufuk Erdogmus in person before your first occasion to visit Sanctuary Europe?"

"No."

"Did you have any contact with him before that?"

"My father told me to get in touch with him."

"So your father was an associate of Mr. Erdogmus?"

"Yes…well, no, not like that."

"Yes or no."

"No."

The examiner paused to look at the readouts on his machines.

"Were you in any way involved in the destruction of Sanctuary Europe?"

In Jess's mind, she saw panic-stricken people running, clutching their belongings, children with faces streaked with tears and horror. Alarms blared. Shouts. The ground trembling. A shockwave from a distant explosion. The heat of the flames. "No."

"When I refer to electronic or telephonic communication, I include mobile telephones, radio transmitters and receivers, digital transmitters and receivers, and any other similar communication system that is not direct conversation with another person present in the immediate vicinity at the time. At any time during the time you have spent with Ufuk Erdogmus, both before and after the destruction of Sanctuary Europe, have you observed, or do you have any direct knowledge of, Ufuk Erdogmus having communicated electronically or telephonically with individuals in Al-Jawf?"

"Yes." It was Ain Salah that had betrayed them to Müller. He was protecting his own kind, just as Jess was. Just as Peter had.

"Do you know who that individual was, or who those individuals were?"

"Yes."

She expected them to confirm whom, but they didn't.

"Was that communication before the destruction of Sanctuary Europe?"

"No."

"After the destruction of Sanctuary Europe?"

Obviously. "Yes."

"To your knowledge, has Ufuk Erdogmus ever lied to you?"

"Yes." A better question would have been, *Has he ever told you the truth?*

"Are you in possession of any information that leads you believe that Ufuk Erdogmus was involved in the destruction of Sanctuary Europe?"

Hesitation. Silence for too long. The examiner repeated the question.

"No."

He examined the machines again.

"I'm changing my answer," Jess said. "I don't know."

The man nodded, squinting at the readouts.

"Are you in possession of any information that leads you believe that Ufuk Erdogmus has been involved in terrorism?"

"I don't know."

"Yes or no."

"That's the best I can answer. The man is hard to pin down."

"But he is a leader of the Levantine Council?"

"Yes..." she stuttered. "Well, not exactly. He's kind of leading it from behind. From what I understand."

"Yes or no."

She exhaled and shook her head, but said: "Yes."

The examiner made some kind of annotation and then proceeded to ask identical questions in respect of Raffa and Giovanni. For those, she was able to make more definite answers.

"I am now going to discuss the second type of question, the diagnostics. First, I will review questions used to determine if you are capable of responding when you lie. I already know the answer to these questions because we all have done these things at one time or another. When I ask the question I want you to think of an occasion when you did this—don't tell me about it, just think of a specific time. Then lie to me and say no. It's important you co-operate at this time, Miss Rollins, otherwise the test will be pointless. Have you ever said something derogatory about another person behind their back?"

"Never said a bad word about Peter."

The man's eyes flitted up at the sarcasm but he continued, "Have you ever said something that you later regretted?"

"No."

"Have you ever said anything in anger that you later regretted?"

"No."

He paused and checked his system. "Thank you, Miss Rollins. That concludes the test."

The door opened and Peter Connor stepped inside. He walked to the polygraph machine and examined it.

"Your conclusions?" he demanded of the tall man.

"I was told to report to—"

"You can report to me."

"Connor, this is inappropriate in front of the subject."

"Then leave the room. You're dismissed." He stooped and examined the machine again.

The man glared at Peter. He gathered himself and said, "She's telling the truth, more or less."

"Well, is it more, or is it less?"

"It'll be in my report. In the main, she was telling the truth."

"She's still hooked up to the machine?"

The examiner glanced up. "She is."

Peter folded his arms and looked Jess straight in the eye. "What is Müller looking for in northern China?"

Jess's mouth dropped open. "I have no idea. Sanctuary China?"

The examiner checked his machines, then half-shrugged to Peter's questioning glance.

"I don't mean Sanctuary," Peter leaned in close to Jess. "Something else. Outside of it, east of Ulan Bator."

6

Near Ulan Bator
Mongolia
February 25th

Andrei Nikolayevich Zasekin, once a Corporal of Soviet Russia, though now not sure to say who or what he was, sat alone in the snow some way from the Czilim hovercraft and the rest of his squad. The breeze pushed against the stripped-clean forest of skeleton birch trees around them, the branches swaying and pitching in the wind. The scent of far-away cooking fires carried on the wind. Dawn's light tried to push through the eddying wall of clouds, succeeding only in washing the snow and ice in a waxy twilight.

Everywhere was danger.

Every day the skies and earth competed in sporadic and unpredictable rages of thundersnows and frostquakes. Two months had passed since he and his men had camped at the onetime-luxury resort of Terelj. They'd plundered what they could from the vast building at its center.

Each day they went out to explore in the Czilim, moving fast over the undulating snow under the slate gray sky, through pine forests thick with ash. Above them, the *nunatak* summits loomed, the walls of the winding valley. Nothing broke the sky except the pregnant black storm clouds that engulfed the peaks and almost stretched to the bottoms of the valleys. They skirted high above the town of Gachuurt, where nomads, refugees and survivors, camped in great numbers. Zasekin and his men stayed far up in the mountains, away from them.

Today they'd driven the Czilim up a winding path beneath the summit of the highest peak in the area, a few kilometers to the east of Ulan Bator. At the mountain's skirt spread a web of encampments, and the townships of Ulastai and Khujirbulan. Beyond those, the low-lying ninth and seventeenth *khoroos*, Ulan Bator's most eastern districts. Thin streaks of tracers across the night sky as the echoing crack of gunfire erupted.

From what they saw through binoculars, much of the city was by the trembling light of fires, but some lights were powered by electricity, although whether that came from generators or a nearby power station was unclear.

Zasekin considered this as he sat, concealed by undergrowth and the hole he had dug in the snow, watching the Czilim and his men. A pine tree rustled behind him, and fresh snow crunched beneath footsteps not intent on concealing themselves. He had already seen Timur approaching and had turned back to watching the valley beyond.

"You've been up here a long time," Timur said as he settled down next to Zasekin. He set his Kalashnikov down and rubbed his hands together to find some warmth.

"Nothing much to see so far. I need to be sure."

"Has he said anything else?"

"I spoke to him today."

By *him*, Timur referred to the heavily accented English voice on the other end of the Czilim's radio. What Timur was really referring to was the pact Zasekin had entered into with him. A man whose name he did not know—which Timur was fond of reminding him. And yes, Zasekin mistrusted such anonymity. Putin's Kremlin had taught him that much, but their man had proved his worth to them in what was becoming a very precarious landscape.

"We should go to Ulan Ude." Timur retreated a little as he said this, in anticipation of Zasekin swatting at him for repeating himself.

"We are not returning to the 103rd Missile Brigade."

"But it is safe there. The underground bunkers—"

"Are like graves. Do you want to fill a grave with your body?"

"Not yet, comrade."

"Then trust me."

"Do *you* still trust him, Andrei Nikolayevich?" Timur asked.

"Trust is not a part of this."

Timur could not have failed to notice that in the last weeks, since they arrived at Terelj, Zasekin had taken to spending more time inside the Czilim by himself, and for longer periods. It surprised Zasekin that there was much common ground between himself and the voice on the other end of the radio. He looked forward to their conversations, some of which became lengthy debates, and through him Zasekin was able to learn a great deal of the shape the world was now taking.

He gained the impression too that the discussions were also a test, a way for the man to settle his faith in Zasekin, to determine if the Russian could be trusted.

"For now," Zasekin added, "I believe our objectives coincide."

"What of this place he wants us to find for him? Do we know where it is yet? Does he trust *you* enough to say, Andrei Nikolayevich?"

Zasekin wasn't sure if it was a matter of trust. The man still would not say where precisely their target was, but he felt like the man might not know himself. He continued to maintain that if they helped secure whatever it was, he would offer them valuable commodities for trade. The supplies they had picked up in Sükhbaatar, as well as diesel fuel for the Czilim, had been as promised. The intelligence the mystery man had provided on Ulan Bator had also proved to be accurate and startlingly detailed.

Now it was their task to flesh out the picture for him.

Zasekin couldn't help the feeling of being a dog to this master, but it was the best way he could ensure his men's survival, and they could only do that with feet on the ground. Enter the city themselves. Zasekin told himself they had intended on travelling to the city anyway, so what were they doing that they would not have already done. He was not so sure he believed his own words. Their plan would have been unlikely to include liaisons with the Bratva.

Timur straightened and seemed about to speak, but held back.

"You've never been afraid to speak your mind to me, Timur Ivanovych."

The younger man nodded, the lines on his face tightening. "Evgeny will be a problem, I think. We need to watch him."

"I know. I believe Misha can be trusted."

"I hope so." Timur hesitated and tried a different tack. "I know the information we have been given so far has been accurate, but you don't know this man, Andrei Nikolayevich. You know very little about him."

"You think I don't know that, Timur Ivanovych?"

38

"Why do you trust him?"

Zasekin replaced the tin on the shelf. In that moment, the room felt colder. "Do we have any other option?" he asked. "This man offers us an advantage, and maybe a place to go if Ulan Bator is not safe. We have something he wants. We are here. Evgeny was right—the man is hundreds, maybe thousands of miles away. We might be his only tools. As long as our interests coincide, we can trust that."

Timur was correct. He would need to keep a close eye on Evgeny Valentinovich. The Muscovite cared only for himself, as many from the Whitestone city did. He had that self-centered outlook that had no place in Siberia, where co-operation and kinship was as much a part of survival as it was humanity.

He turned his attention back to the approach to Terelj, still searching for signs, markers that might indicate they were being watched themselves. If they were to stay here in the long-term, if this was to be the base from which they conducted their operations in Ulan Bator, Zasekin needed to be certain of its secure. He thought back to the hunters, and to Vasily Fyodorovich who had been so fortunate. The wound could have been much worse, could have struck a vital organ or artery and killed him. Or could have become infected in this god-forsaken environment.

There would be more of them heading south, looking for camps to raid. They were opportunists, nomadic hunters and tribesmen like those they killed in the mountains around the Chuluut River. They would not attack Ulan Bator, but they might come scavenging for supplies on the outskirts of a resort, even a small one like Terelj.

The Dragunov rifle rested on his pack. What would he do if they came close? Would he kill them? They were not so very different to him, or at least who he had once been. Or whom he had found himself wanting to be again. Andrei Nikolayevich Zasekin, the Buryat, no longer blinded by the promise of adventure and a life away from the provincial monotony of little Yanchukan. He longed to be back in the mountains of Severo-Baykalsky District. The last few weeks had brought a horrific new reality, yes, but also a freedom that had kindled a spirit inside him he had long thought dead.

This place was not so different to Yanchukan, its valleys once laden with the same colorful flowers in which he had played as a boy, its hills touched by the same mist. The people who lived off the land, here and to the north, were not so different to the Russian Buryat. Shared customs, a shared Mongol heritage. It did not mean so very much—there had been enough blood spilled between warring tribes throughout history—but it meant something. It was a place to start when speaking to them. A bullet was not an appropriate first diplomatic handshake.

Finally, he said: "Let's go."

Zasekin rose and together they made their way back through the now deepening snow and ash, past the pillared portico of the main entrance they had surgically collapsed with tiny, directed explosive charges. The tall windows above it were shattered. All this had been done to give the place the look of dereliction, a further layer to the veil of their protection.

The Czilim was hidden, sheltered in a secluded section of the hotel where, at Zasekin's direction, the wall was removed to allow entry into one of the main dining rooms at the rear. From the hills above surrounding the complex, it was impossible to see, and only yards away, the river waited for it.

Tactically, the complex was perfect—Zasekin was thankful they had found it, but surprised it had not already been taken. Yet what reason did anyone have to leave the warmth of Ulan Bator for a luxury resort that had fallen into disuse? The nearest major settlement, the township of Nalaikh, although completely abandoned now, was thirty-five kilometers away. A wall surrounded the hotel, with gates sturdy enough to slow a vehicle driven into them. Zasekin had sent Timur into the mountains encircling the complex, to study what could be seen from them, and where they might safely light fires for warmth, and sleep. In the western wing, there was a complex of suites, enough for one each. None of their windows could be seen from any of the mountain summits.

He entered the hotel through the only door they used—a service entrance not far from the main kitchen. Misha waited for him there, an offering laid out in front of him.

"So it was all where I said it would be?" Zasekin asked, picking up one of the tins and examining it. Fruit, from the faded image on the label. Dozens more like it.

"There was a second, and a third and fourth storage cellar," he said. "You should come and see."

He led Zasekin away from the kitchen, through a service corridor, which had obviously never been seen by guests. "I think you were right," he said as he walked. "I think the hotel was no longer in use when the event hit. I think local people had probably already stolen a lot of what was here. Furniture and light fittings. We were lucky there was anything left for us to use."

In the immediate vicinity of Terelj were shanty-type shacks, and Nalaikh, once home to thirty thousand, was close enough for trips to the hotel under cover of darkness.

Zasekin allowed himself a smile as the light from Misha's torch found the treasure trove within a long, low room. Shelving crammed with catering supplies. Row upon row of tinned vegetables, fruits, pulses, and processed meat. Sacks of rice and grains. Sealed plastic crates of dried noodles. Cooking oil. Dried herbs and spices. Stacks of crates and more toward the back.

"Enough for us," Misha said.

"Not for us," Zasekin said and glanced at Timur. "For trade."

7

Oman
February 25th

"Hurry up in here!" yelled a voice.

A thick cloud of vapor enshrouded Jess. She spread her fingers against the glass wall but didn't reply.

"You've been half an hour already," the voice protested.

"Five minutes," Jess yelled back.

She closed her eyes and luxuriated in the unbelievable pleasure of hot jets of water against her naked skin. She hadn't taken a proper shower in...months? She couldn't even remember. It had to be back in Sanctuary Europe. She'd taken a shower a million times before—in the world that used to exist—but had never experienced one like this. She raised her face to the steaming jet of water, let it wash over her face and hair.

After weeks of cold, of hardly being able to feel her foot or hands, the heat seeping through her layers of skin into her core was bliss. And to be clean, such a small thing, but *such* pleasure. She tried not to feel gratitude. She knew that was what they wanted, but she couldn't help the elation.

"Two minutes!" yelled the guard, tapping again on the outside door.

Jess felt like a new woman, and she was—she had her leg back. The pure and simple joy of being able to walk on two legs, after months of humiliation as a cripple. Jess swallowed her pride and thanked them. They hadn't powered her leg up, though. Hadn't plugged it in.

They were too fearful of Ufuk's electronics.

Or maybe of her.

Peter led Jess through a warren of dim corridors, past closed doors that hummed with hidden activity. He stopped at an entranceway, one that was no different to any of the others, and slipped a keycard into the slot by the steel handle. A green light illuminated and the door gave a click.

"Don't discuss anything with her beyond satisfying yourself she's okay."

Peter pushed the door open and took her inside. It locked behind them.

Massarra lay on a bed in one corner of the room. She levered herself up. A grimace of pain went across her face as she did.

"Two minutes," Peter said, "and then we have to go."

Jess went over to her quickly, threw her arms around the slight frame of the Israeli and held her tight. The woman had always been thin, but she felt bone-like and empty in Jess's embrace. She smelled of antiseptic cleaner and day-old sweat. A yellow stain covered the hospital bedding beneath her.

"How are you?" Jess whispered.

She'd already been in to see Raffa and Giovanni, had been obstinate until Peter at least let them have a shower and get clean clothes.

"I'm okay," Massarra whispered back. "They've taken good care of me. I couldn't ask for more."

"You almost died." Jess released her enough to see her face.

The Israeli looked nonplussed. "I knew the risks. I would do it again. Are you holding out?"

"I'm fine. I took a polygraph—"

"Jess," Peter warned.

"I'm not going to leave you in here," Jessica said to Massarra. "I know."

Peter opened the door. "We have to go."

"Why did you tell us to trust Peter?" Jess whispered low, almost inaudible, into Massarra's ear as she leaned in close to hug her again. A question that had burned itself into the back of Jess's mind.

"Jessica!" Peter took a step toward them.

"Because I brought him," Massarra whispered back.

That didn't make sense. The woman had to be drugged or something. Jess was about to ask again, but Peter took her shoulder, and she rose and tried to smile. She felt terrible leaving Massarra alone in this cell, but Peter forced her away, through more corridors. He led her into an area buzzing with the hum of machines and conversation.

On closely huddled desks with high-backed chairs, set out symmetrically to maximize what limited space there was, were screens and communications gear, with wires trailing out of the back to a central hub of flickering units in the middle of the room. The screens offered images and video feeds. Some had terrain maps, layered by tiny icons that flashed and moved. Filing cabinets lined one wall and maps of the world occupied another. All had pins across them, or photographs and annotated sticky notes. The only light into the room came from overhead strip lights, only half of them illuminated, and long windows set high in the far wall. Jess hadn't seen the outside in months, but all she could see through the windows was the slate gray of featureless clouds.

At each desk sat a single operative, each wearing a headset, intent on the information on the screens in front of them. A few were deep in conversation, debating and gesturing. No one reacted when they entered, or even looked their way.

"For now," Peter said, "we call this Muscat Station. It's not Muscat, but it's close enough and it doesn't identify precisely where we are. To the rest of the world, in the encoded comms we use, it's known as Station Alpha Seven. For the Middle East, this is it."

"The CIA is still operational?"

"Whoever from the intelligence community was active in the Middle East was tasked to come here, unless they had some other specific mission tasking. As I did for a time in Al-Jawf."

"Looking for me?"

"You were on a watch list, but it was just dumb luck I saw you in Al-Jawf."

Dumb luck? Jess's eyes rose. She doubted coincidences anymore.

"Someone would have," Peter continued, "You were Ace of Hearts on our watch lists—but it was my decision to initiate contact with you."

"To capture me?"

"I don't think you're the enemy, Jess, but I'm not sure Müller is either."

"Come again?"

"The guy's a bastard, I'll give him that. But this is a complex world."

"Complex and complicated are two different things. It might be a complex world, but what Müller is, isn't complicated. He lied to my father, set us up as scapegoats."

"Not that I agree with it, but he had a purpose—"

"Screw you."

"We know he's in China now," Peter added quickly, switching topics. "We have confirmation that's where Hector is too."

Jess stepped closer, unable to resist. "What confirmation?"

"That's why you're here." He led her over to a desk and gestured for her to sit. A woman came and offered her a headset. Peter took another one. The screen in front of her showed a map of northern China, a mountainous region near the borders with Russia to the north and Mongolia to the west. To one side, in a cutaway window, a town highlighted with the name *Hinggan*.

"Ufuk is a man who likes to play games."

"So what game is he playing now?"

"He has someone inside Sanctuary China. They made contact with us."

"Contact?"

"They're young, tech-savvy—"

"Hackers?"

"The Sanctuary system has interlinked communications systems; they're able to find backdoors to send messages."

Peter turned to a technician, who shook his head.

"Could you tell me more about the US?" Jess asked.

"One naval base on the west coast—"

"San Diego?"

"The Army Corps of Engineers and Navy have put together a camp there. Most people are heading south, but they can't get any further than Panama on foot."

"The land bridge is gone?"

"The Atlantic tidal wave induced by Nomad separated North and South America by fifty miles. Half of Central America is gone. A lot of changes to geography. Things aren't what they used to be." He blew out his cheeks, letting the breath out completely. "Hawaii was wiped off the map. Detonated and then washed away."

Jess took a second to process. "What about the east coast?"

"Nothing left."

"Nothing?"

"The initial tidal wave was thousands of feet, washed all the way inshore till it was stopped by the Appalachians. Dozens of secondary hundred-foot-plus waves."

"Jesus Christ."

The technician nodded at Jessica. "They want to speak to you."

"Me?"

Peter paused for a second, and then two, while he watched her.

"Abbie Barnes, is that your contact in Sanctuary China?" Jess said, breaking the silence.

"You talked to her when you were in Al-Jawf," Peter replied.

"You know she's General Marshall's daughter? The head military person inside Sanctuary?"

"We know. She's working with Roger."

"And you think Müller doesn't know?"

The spy shrugged. "You tell me. I trust every asset until I don't. A balancing exercise. You're always waiting for the true motivation to show itself. Until then, you get what you can, use them to do what you need."

"Can I talk to her?"

"They're short messages."

The woman raised a hand to her headset and turned to Peter. "It's time."

Peter gestured to the screen in front of Jess. "Can you put it here?"

The woman nodded in the affirmative.

Peter leaned in to Jess, his voice lowering with his body. "I need to make this clear to you. We have no time for games. Whatever you think of my bosses, what's happened these last few months, this isn't about them, or you. This is about hundreds of thousands of lives we can save. Maybe millions."

She didn't return his direct stare. "Understood."

"She sent this message before she had to log off. Said you should know what it means."

A message appeared on the screen in a small box that read: "UNSUB: When we went for a drink, what did I have?"

She half-smiled. "A strawberry latte."

"You sure?"

"Of course. How do you know they didn't do to her what you did to me?" Jess asked. "I know her, but how can you know someone didn't beat it out of her?"

"We have to take some risks. Type enough of that so she knows it's you."

At a prompt with her name, Jess typed: "Strawberry latte. We sat down at the café. You were nervous and fidgeted and I told you to sit still." Then she hit *send*. She wanted to ask about Roger, if he was still with her, and if Hector was there.

"It'll take a few minutes. You want a coffee?"

"No, thanks." She still didn't look at him.

"I didn't want you interrogated that way, Jessica, but you wouldn't speak to me."

"Friends in Oman, you said. A place to stay with medical facilities. Safe and secure. Our best shot and no one would know to look for us there. We let Massarra recover, you said, and we look for Hector. Get ourselves right and start again—"

"I told you the truth."

"You did not."

"I did at the time. What I believed. They locked me up too, before they decided they could trust me. And we provided the best medical care we have for Massarra and Raffa. They're safe and healthy."

"You could have been honest."

Peter rocked back on his heels, considering something. "Massarra knew. Ask her why she wasn't being honest. And would you have come if you knew?"

"That's not—" Jess was halfway through a rebuke, when her brain circled around on the thought. "Is that true? Massarra knew you were CIA?"

"I risked my operation to save your life. Massarra is alive and we're all safe because of me."

"I was locked in solitary confinement for two months."

"Better than being dead."

Was it? Was it better than being dead? Her mind circled, as always, back to Hector. Of course she didn't want to be dead. "You needed us. Don't tell me you brought us here out of altruism."

"We *needed* Ufuk. By that point, you were just collateral."

"Thanks."

Ufuk. Thinking of the Turk, Jess remembered the thin wisps of liquid nitrogen curling up the walls. The tinny ozone taste of fire extinguisher accelerant in her throat. Adrenaline in her blood, pounding in her ears. Emergency lights throbbing. Ufuk's mysterious cryogenic package.

"Why didn't you stop him from putting that thing into the drone submarine?" Jess asked. "What was really in there, anyway?"

8

Northern Mongolia
February 27th

Zasekin left the Czilim on the steep bank of the river, concealed by tangled root systems and tall Siberian pine. He wondered whether its searing growl would have been heard along the valley walls, up high on the ridges that framed the river and the steep, forested slopes that led down to it. While the wind moaned and whistled through the trees, he doubted if it was enough to have disguised the hovercraft's approach. Nor could it mask the machine's oily, mechanical odor. The people in this world, the hunters that floated through the shadows like ghosts, felt the vibrations of change wherever they went. An intruder like the Czilim would be felt for miles.

He did not have the luxury of leaving anything to chance. He had to present an attractive target for anyone coming upon the Czilim. The appearance of a tragic accident. He lit two marine flares from the Czilim's emergency kit, savoring their deafening crack and the roar of the spiraling flame, then tossed them nearby. From a distance, as they burned hot and loud, releasing plumes of thick smoke into the sky, he hoped they might look like fire. But they would not burn for more than fifteen minutes.

He watched them and felt sure he would not be alone for long. He needed to get high, find them before they found him, for they would not wait to see what words he had in his mind. The cold did not permit such luxuries. They would shoot as soon as their prey presented itself and then take their prize.

He climbed, breathless as the cold took over his lungs. His hands were numb within seconds, fingers burning through thick gloves that barely offered protection. Was it colder now than it had ever been? Was this the worst winter Siberia had ever thrown at its human inhabitants? To Zasekin, it felt that way.

He coughed so hard it hurt and brushed away snow from his face, catching frozen moisture on his beard. The trees offered little respite from the biting wind.

He climbed over a false summit, feet sinking into the thigh-deep snow, sweat dampening his back. He took hold of exposed branches, partly to use them to haul himself upward, partly to keep them from lashing his face. Finally, lurching between the trees, the Dragunov rifle still slung across his back, he reached the ridgeline, breathless and tired.

He knelt because the wind had grown stronger, sweeping an eddying gray fog that blinded him, but also to find cover close to the thick trunk of a snow-clad Siberian pine. Now began the game of cat-and-mouse, where he was at a disadvantage for he could not shoot his prey when he saw it. If he could see it through this damn sleet.

Down in the valley below, the flares still burned, casting one flank of the Czilim in a crimson light. Smoke still plumed upward, spiraling out of the valley and visible despite the wind, even against the sleet-ridden fog.

He took the Dragunov from his shoulder and settled down into a low stance in the snow. His heart pounded and he tried to make himself still. He kept low, close to the cover provided by the trees around him, barely moving despite the cold seeping in through his boots and jacket. He stilled himself, closing off his mind and allowing his vision to wander and sweep across the valley walls and ridges. In his peripheral sight, looking—but not looking—he sought out any sign of movement in the trees.

He did not have to wait long. On the far side of the valley, barely a flutter of movement between thick pine trunks, he saw them through the telescopic sight fixed to the rifle. Shadows that moved between the trees.

By their clothing he guessed them to be Khamnigan Buryats. Evenks from Tungus. Reindeer herders, nomads who still held to the old ways and their shamanic beliefs. They made their way steadily yet cautiously down the slope toward the Czilim, keeping some distance between them. They inspected the area around them as they descended, so Zasekin was careful not to move.

When they reached the Czilim and discovered his ruse, the flares now burned out, he shouted a greeting to them in Buryat.

Their reaction was instant. They turned and one let loose shots in his general direction. It was wayward, but intended more as a means to allow the others to find cover.

"Wait!" Zasekin shouted, again in Buryat. "I am not your enemy. I seek to trade with you. I have access to food, ammunition, oil. All things you can use. If you shoot again, I will cut each of you down." He had the better position and they would understand that. They would understand too that he spoke their language.

"Come down," one of them shouted. "Then we can talk like men."

"No," Zasekin responded. "Shoulder your rifles and climb up here toward my voice. Let Buryat offer instead hospitality to their own kind?"

Muttered conversation floated on the wind. After a few more minutes, the voices died down and they appeared between the trees. He greeted them with the Dragunov at his shoulder.

They studied him—calmly he noted, without fear—and one said: "Where are you from?"

No point in lying. "Yanchukan, in the mountains of Severo-Baykalsky District."

"Russian?"

"Buryat."

This brought a scoff. "Still Russian."

"A Russian willing to trade things you need." Trade was something everyone could understand, a common point of survival.

They led him down the flank of the mountain, they more sure-footed along the footpaths cut into the thick snowdrift than he. They followed the banks of the river, where the mountain dropped down to steppes and layers of fresh white snow hid the grimy layers of ash, and beneath that, the much-abused grasslands that wouldn't see the light of day for years or more to come.

A dozen *gers* were arranged as a campground in a clearing they led him to. Smoke trickled from low chimneys. Empty sleds waited outside. Where once there might have been hundreds of reindeer with these nomadic herders, there were only six animals tethered to one of the *gers*. To those who did not know the Evenks, or other Siberian tribes like the Chukchi, this sign would have gone unheeded. Yet Zasekin understood that the dearth of a herd had both economic and spiritual significance to these Khamnigan.

Everybody was desperate now.

The two men took him to a *ger* placed in the center of the campground, a larger shelter where a fire illuminated the skin from within. They approached and pulled aside the entrance flap and beckoned him inside. Warmth flushed over him. Furs covered the ground and a fire had been lit in the center. The flume of a chimney fed the smoke into the twilight outside.

Behind the old man, hung high on the side of the *ger* where anyone who entered would see them, were a massive set of reindeer antlers, a representation of the tribal leader's power. By being transformed into a reindeer, imbued with its spirit, an Evenk shaman felt himself to be swift, vigilant, and watchful. The best animal the Tungus knew. The Evenks believed that spirits inhabited the underground, so they buried their dead above ground by sewing the bodies into reindeer skins and placing the wrapped cadavers on high poles.

The Chukchi held great celebrations when nomadic herders returned, greeting them boisterously and slaughtering both fawns and bucks. They would skin their carcasses, and extract marrow from the reindeer's bones to eat. They used the reindeer's blood in ritual painting. It was a sacrifice to the One-On-High, a ceremony of respect for the spirits which the Chukchi saw in everything.

To the Siberian tribal people, the loss of a herd was a deep, mortal wound they felt in their hearts and their earthly souls. No matter what the cause.

"Russians," the old man said, in a manner that left Zasekin in no doubt he was to be included in that category, "have always believed they could come and take what they wanted. We are still here. We are still free. They are not our masters. The land is our master. No other."

"The land is turning on you," Zasekin replied. "This winter is the hardest you have ever known, and this summer will not be a summer. The dark ash falling from the sky is killing plants, the animals too. Wolves are becoming desperate and soon will not fear your fires—you will become the only meat on these hills. The old ways have not prepared you for this."

"We wish to be left alone. We have always found a way."

"You're raiding closer and closer to the city. The Bratva will not stand for it. Whether it's your people, or others like you—"

He scoffed. "We can hide."

"They can see the heat from your bodies. They have machines."

No answer to this came.

Zasekin waited, studying the old man whose gaze didn't waver. "There is a place I need to find—to secure—and I need your help, and the other nomadic tribes as well. I have food and shelter I can offer. I am Buryat as well."

The old man's eyes narrowed. "What is this place?"

"Near here. Accept, and your people will survive the second storm of God."

"There will be dozens of us, perhaps a hundred," the old man said.

"Good." Zasekin spread his arms wide. "We will make space for you all, but we must be patient."

The man on the radio had said they would have to wait. For how long, that was the question in Zasekin's mind, but he would use that time to forge ties with these Buryat. He and his men would no longer be alone.

9

Oman
March 20th

Smudges of light swept over a smooth mountainside in the distance, rolling foothills undulating up to meet the peaks. Scrub bushes dotted the frozen-sand landscape, interspersed with fantastical ice sculptures carved by the sand and wind. Yellow snowflakes fell from scudding gray clouds in a hurry on their way south.

Jess wished she were too.

She enjoyed the cold air on her face, the sense of freedom, of being outside again beneath the slate-gray sky streaked with ochre and green. A welcome relief from the cold darkness of the past two months. The ground beneath her feet was rocky and dry, strewn with hoarfrost, each breath shooting out a plume of white vapor that floated and dissipated on the wind.

Feet scuffed the ground behind her, but she didn't turn.

"I want my Raffa and Giovanni out of confinement."

"I'm doing everything I can," Peter replied.

She didn't bother to laugh. They needed something—otherwise she'd still be shivering on the concrete slab—and they were going to drip-feed her liberties until they got it.

"I got them showers and clean clothes. If you cooperate, they'll be out soon. You'll be billeted nearby. You'll have an escort all the time, but there's nothing I can do about that."

"They have nothing to answer for, Peter."

In the cusp of a valley a few miles away was a camp, and on the road leading into it from the highlands, running past this base, was a steady stream of refugees.

For a time, Peter said nothing, but watched her watching the people walk by in the distance.

"A lot of them have nothing to answer for, yet look—less and less every week, and nowhere for them to go," Peter said. "The ones that survived the starvation and dehydration, get into camps where cholera and typhus kill most of the rest, and the positron radiation dose from Nomad combined with the fallout from the nuclear blasts…" He let his voice trail off. "These people are walking dead."

Jess had seen the start of the effects of the positron radiation sickness—from the massive solar flares induced by Nomad—in children at Al-Jawf. At first, they didn't know what it was, but now, months later, anyone exposed was showing the effects. And here, the population was suffering from the manmade effects of nuclear blasts in the north.

"Isn't there anything we can do? Some kind of medicine…?"

"That's what we're talking about. Doing what we can. For our own people." The light changed on the face of the mountains. "Have you ever been to Oman before?"

"Never been on my travel schedule."

"Muscat is just past those mountains. But it's gone. Submerged in places, wrecked everywhere else." He held up a small device that clicked quietly. A Geiger counter. "We can't stay out here too long." He stamped his feet and pulled his jacket tight. "Spring is coming, it's almost March. We're praying it warms up."

"And where *are* we, exactly?"

"On the outskirts of a small town called Tanuf. There's a larger town to the south, Nizwa, and another to the southwest called Bahla. This basin was protected from the Gulf's tsunamis by the Al Hajar Mountains."

"And who's running that camp?" She pointed into the distance.

"The Sultan Qaboos's successor was Haytham bin Tariq, the Minister of Heritage and National Culture. He's alive and in Nizwa, from what we've been able to gather. He's running things here."

His depth of knowledge impressed Jess. She was the one asking questions now. "And why are you here?"

"Oil," he said simply. "The US has always been an ally of this place. The Brits, too. We moved our station out here from Muscat before Nomad. We've got a company of Delta and SEAL teams, pulled in from operations all over the Middle East."

"I need to find a way to get Hector."

The pull was irresistible. Six months ago she would have laughed if someone told her she'd have feelings like this. The mother bear.

"How do you intend to get there? Walking?"

Jess said nothing.

"The big picture is starting to emerge. Russia and China are going at it already. Naval skirmishes in the South China Sea. Two months ago, Müller announced to the world that the northern hemisphere is going to be obliterated on March 15th of next year. The Chinese don't like everyone moving into their backyard."

"And what backyard is that?"

"Australia."

"Australia?"

"The Australian government withdrew to Western Australia in advance of Nomad. Eastern coastal cities were destroyed, just like everywhere else, but Western Australia survived almost untouched, and the drop in temperatures have made it one of the few habitable places left. Almost no volcanism. And lots of rain now, too."

"That's a good thing, isn't it?"

"Yeah, but the Chinese don't want what's left of everyone else's navies and armies down there, and—let's be honest—they want Australia for themselves."

"For God's sake, almost everyone is dead—"

Peter snorted. "Why can't we just get along?"

"Glad you find that funny." Jess shifted her weight onto her prosthetic leg, felt her stump sink into the cup. She rocked back and forth a few times.

"I don't blame them. We'd be doing the same or worse if the situations were reversed," Peter said, looking down at his feet. "Luck of geometry and timing. China was on the other side of the planet—protected by 8000 miles of rock—when Nomad made its closest approach. The tidal waves in the Pacific weren't even a third the size of what hit our East Coast, and Bejing is a hundred miles inshore, at a few hundred feet of altitude."

"You're saying China wasn't affected?"

"Dalian and Tianjian and Shanghai, the coastal cities, were wrecked—but in Beijing, their buildings are still standing. The wave that roared up the Chesapeake Bay and hit Washington was two thousand feet high, obliterated everything, only stopped sixty miles inshore by the Shenandoah Mountains of the Appalachia. Beijing didn't even get flooded, was protected from the east by the island of Japan and the Korean peninsula."

"Why are you telling me all this again?"

"The Australians didn't make the offer to relocate to everyone. Rhetoric even before Nomad was leaning ultra-nationalist. Now it's everyone for themselves, and we're the weakest ones. Take what you can by force, because who can stop you?"

"And Müller's with the Chinese?"

"We think the Sanctuary installation there is a part of the right-wing factions within the Chinese politburo." He wagged his head from side to side. "But then, your friend Erdogmus has similar connections."

"Ufuk? His relationship is with Turkey and the Middle East and Africa." Even as she said it, she realized none of what Ufuk *wanted* her to know might be what he was actually up to.

"For the last five years," Peter replied. "Mr. Erdogmus has been trading with the China Aerospace Corporation, the main contractor for the Chinese space program. State-owned, it has a number of subsidiaries that manufacture spacecraft, launch vehicles, and strategic and tactical missile systems. Ufuk, personally, was instrumental in the design and development of their key systems. He tried to hide it, but Mossad had an asset within his organization."

"Was Massarra involved?"

Peter nodded. "Ufuk violated strategic technology sanctions, even if it *was* his technology. And with his links to Islamic extremism, he doesn't have a lot of friends here."

"So you need his Chinese friends, is that why I'm out of my cell?"

"We need to get *inside* Sanctuary China. We need to neutralize the hardline faction that's threatening our Pacific convoys. To do that, we need someone inside."

"You've got someone inside. Roger. He worked for the CIA, didn't he?"

"He won't cooperate without you." Peter waited before continuing. "He wants a small team that won't attract attention. You know Roger, you know Müller, and you want to get to China."

She pinched the bridge of her nose. "Jesus...*neutralize*? Is that the word you used? You want to kill them."

"Not kill them. Disable their communications. But we need you—Roger doesn't trust us."

"That makes two of us."

"He thinks he's protecting you, preventing us from locking you up as a terrorist, or…" A fresh wind sprang up, bringing with it a blast of sand particles. "We should get inside. We've exceeded our radiation dose for the day."

"Or what? What were you going to add?" Jess asked.

"Or Roger *wants* to get you to Sanctuary China."

"For Müller? You think he's working for them?"

Peter tugged at one earlobe and scrunched up his face as if he was doing a math problem in his head. "Because the guy is still in love with you. That's what I think."

"And I think love is an old-fashioned concept that's dangerous."

"It's what's dragging you to China, to get Hector."

"I haven't said I want to go yet."

Peter turned to open the exterior door. "You could refuse. We'll put you all on a boat to Australia, if that's what you want."

Jess remained silent.

"There's something else." Peter stopped in the doorway. "The Levantine Council contacted us. Demanded to see Ufuk. They'll be here in a few days. Ufuk says he'll cooperate if we hear them out, so we've sent a Delta team to meet them in Saudi."

"Legitimize?" said Colonel Hague.

Peter stood to one side of the Colonel, and Jess to the other. Ufuk Erdogmus sat across from them, his hands chained to the metal table. The same room as Jess had been interrogated. She was sure it wasn't the first time they'd had Ufuk in here.

The Colonel's bald pate reflected the overhead strip lighting, a sweaty halo ringing his head. He mopped his brow with a handkerchief he fished from a pocket of his rumpled tan uniform. A short, squat man, more round than square, but like a bull.

"That's what I said," Ufuk replied.

By contrast to Colonel Hague, Erdogmus looked calm and collected, even the scraggly beard over his tan skin looked groomed. He leaned forward to bring his shoulder in range of his hands, and brushed lint from his soiled and ripped orange jumpsuit. As he stretched his neck, Jess saw mottled purple bruises.

"And you will give us access to your orbital systems?" demanded the Colonel.

"They're not in orbit yet, they're still in deep space. It'll take—"

"Yes or no, Mr. Erdogmus. Military grade GPS? Communications?"

"All of that and more. To get control of them, I need to get into Sanctuary China."

"Which is where we need to go as well."

A satisfied grin spread across Erdogmus's face. "Then it seems our interests are aligned." He turned his beaming grin on Jessica. "You're looking well."

She ground her teeth together in an effort to stay quiet.

"I warn you, Mr. Erdogmus—"

"I know, I know. You take the Levantine Council off your terror list, make them an equal party at the negotiating table, and I'll give you what you want."

Sunlight streamed in through slatted blinds of the complex's main conference room, catching motes of dust in the warm air. A long cherry wood table dominated the center of the room, the scent of lemon polish hanging in the air. Jess leaned back in her chair, positioned herself in the far corner of the room so she could watch everyone's faces. Peter Connor sat closest to Jess, to one side of Colonel Hague, and on the other side sat a barrel-chested, thirty-something man in a military uniform with epaulettes denoting the rank of major. Behind them stood two Special Forces men, their faces blank, their automatic weapons held chest level and pointed at the floor.

Alone, across from them, was Ufuk—the manacles gone, and he was freshly showered and clothed in jeans and a t-shirt, his hair cut. The scraggly beard remained.

The door to the conference room opened, and an elderly man entered, his body wrapped in a sand-streaked *thobe*.

Ufuk rose and stretched out his hand. "*Asalaam Alaykum.*"

"*Wa 'Alaykum Asalaam,*" the elderly man replied, taking Ufuk's hand.

"It is good to see you, my brother Hasan," Ufuk added.

Before anything else, the old man Hasan began a deliberate process of folding his *shemagh* and *keffiyeh* and laying them on the conference room table beside the entrance. Everyone waited in silence. When he'd finished, he took the seat held out for him by Ufuk, directly across from the Colonel.

A tall, thickly set man had entered the room behind Hasan. He made no attempt to hide the sub-machine gun that hung from a single-point harness across his chest. A young woman in a flowing black *abaya* and headscarf followed and positioned herself on the other side of Hasan as he sat. From the way the two Special Forces men behind the Colonel tensed, Jess guessed they'd already had a word or two about the bodyguard's machine gun, but, apparently, it was a non-negotiable point.

"Elsa," Ufuk said to the woman in the headscarf, acknowledging her with a nod.

She said nothing in reply, her face almost blank but her mouth betraying the edges of a grimace like she'd just stepped in a pile of manure and was trying to remain polite. Hasan raised one hand to her, sensing her expression without looking, but it was too late.

"Do you know how many of our brothers and sisters died in Al-Jawf?" Elsa spat the words out, defying Hasan. Her grimace transformed into a snarl, her left lip curled upward as she pointed a finger. "I am not here to satisfy you."

"Nice to see you, too." Ufuk affected a pained expression and sat down meekly beside the old man, the both of them ignoring the defiant glare of Elsa.

She took a seat away from Ufuk.

The Major to the left of the Colonel cleared his throat and then spoke: "Mr...do you have a family name?"

"Hasan will do."

"Mr. Hasan—"

"Just Hasan."

The Major recomposed himself and steepled his fingers together, elbows on the table. "Hasan, we agreed to meet with you, but under duress as a condition of *cooperation* with Mr. Erdogmus. So my question: what is it you want?"

"The same as you," Hasan answered. *"Cooperation.* An alliance. A mutual exchange of intelligence and resources. Understanding and harmony. The beginning of a new friendship, going forward."

"We don't work with terrorists."

The statement felt like a canned response, even to Jess.

"The CIA doesn't work with terrorists?" Hasan's eyebrows rose. "I would say that is news to us, but then, we are not terrorists—and in this world, what does that even mean anymore?"

Ufuk swiveled and held out his palms to each of the men. "If we can operate under the assumption that the Levantine Council had nothing to do with Rome or Sanctuary Europe—"

The Major snorted disbelief, but the Colonel urged him to quiet.

"The goal of the Levantine Council," Ufuk continued, "was always to find a way to peace for my brothers and sisters—"

This time Elsa snorted in disbelief. Jess couldn't help commiserating with this woman she didn't even know, and rolled her eyes, ever so slightly—a gesture that Elsa caught.

"And this is an opportunity to demonstrate that," Ufuk continued. "I'm not asking for blind faith, but just a chance to begin to work together."

The two sides of the table watched each other in silence for a few seconds.

"Okay, Mr. Erdogmus. We'll give your people a chance. Major Finnegan, please escort Hasan to our communications center. Make the introductions."

The Major gritted his teeth, but nodded and stood.

Hasan rose, admonishing Elsa to stay quiet while at the same time whispering his goodbyes to Ufuk. Together with their bodyguard, they exited the room with the Major and the two Special Forces men.

"They can help us," Ufuk said the moment Hasan was gone.

The Colonel, Jessica and Peter remained in the room with him.

"The Council has many connections," Ufuk continued. "Northern China is home to the Turkic Uyghurs, Muslims who I share a deep cultural connection with. They are a hardy people, and I —"

"Let me get one thing straight, Mr. Erdogmus," the Colonel said, rising to his feet. He pointed his finger down at the still-seated Ufuk. "I don't like you. I don't trust you. I would rather—"

"Take me out behind the wood shed and put a bullet in my head?" Ufuk offered.

The Colonel mopped his sweaty baldness again with his handkerchief. "You think you're funny? Think I'm a cowboy? Well, let me tell you, this is no game. Millions of people are dying out there, suffering unimaginable agony every single day without the least shred of hope. My job is to find a way to some hope, and I take that very seriously."

Ufuk's self-satisfied expression softened. "I apologize."

"And let me make something else clear. There is no way on God's Earth that I would even consider working with you, but this is an order coming from the top." The Colonel held one index finger aloft, and then paused again to wipe his sweat away, muttering, "*Whatever the goddamn top means anymore,*" under his breath.

He put his handkerchief back away in the breast pocket of his uniform. "The only reason we're considering this...*plan*"—he had to force the word out—"is as a last resort, before the *very...last...resort.* God help us all if it ever comes to that."

"I understand, Colonel." Ufuk's demeanor shifted into something serious, submissive. "And again, I apologize. I've been under tremendous physical and mental strain as well. These charges against me—"

"And I am not interested in your bullshit. You give me something, I give you something, and we wait. That's how this is going to work."

"And if we go, I take Massarra Mizrahi with me?" Ufuk asked.

62

The Colonel's handkerchief came back out. He mopped his brow but said nothing, his blank face saying everything it needed to.

"She knows people. Worked with the Chinese for me for years," Ufuk persisted. "She is critical to the success of this operation, Colonel."

"This is not an *operation*, not yet. You will have liberties, but will be confined to the base with ankle bracelets and under armed guard at all times. Major Connor"—the Colonel pointed at Peter— "will be taking charge of your group. And I *cannot* make clear enough how this is predicated on your continued cooperation." The Colonel turned to Peter, who stood and snapped a smart salute. The Colonel returned the salute with a sigh.

"Somebody up top really needs something from you, mister," the Colonel added, swiveling to point a finger at Ufuk, "But the second they don't need it, you're going back in that cell to rot until God takes you back."

PART TWO

1

Mars First Mission
Deep Interplanetary Space
Halfway between Earth and Saturn
May 15th

"Do you know what day it is?" Communication Specialist Elin Cuijpers asked.

Commander Jason Rankin spooned the tasteless ration of potato curry into his mouth. He stared out at the star field that slid past the mess's observation window as the habitat module rotated to provide the centripetal force that simulated their gravity. He watched the stars, but he was waiting for one in particular. "No idea," he replied after a second or two of slow-think.

What day it was didn't matter, not for a while anyway.

The concept of days and nights lost meaning in deep space. The lights would dim and then brighten. That was the only way he knew twelve hours had passed, and then twelve hours more. There was only one thing that the Commander was really sure about anymore.

That he was depressed.

Rankin and his crew might as well be spam in a can.

For the last few months, the Mars First spacecraft had been ferried around through space on autopilot. The only job they had to do was an occasional EVA to secure each supply module they rendezvoused with. Even then, Rankin suspected that Simon, the artificial intelligence running the ship, was only asking them to do the EVAs so they had something to look forward to. Keeping them involved.

But it didn't need them.

Which begged the question: Why were they here? Why had Ufuk Erdogmus bothered to put a human crew on this mission at all?

"May 15th," Cuijpers said brightly.

"And?"

"Seriously?" said Gabi Siegel, the Mission Communication Specialist. She sat across from them at the only other table in the mess, a tray of ration packs carefully arranged in front of her in a perfect grid.

The Commander shrugged. "Mission Day 247?"

"I think perhaps we should talk again," Peng Shouang said.

She climbed down the ladder from the cross-connector, a towel across her shoulders, her forehead glistening with sweat. She'd just been in the gym module, something Rankin hadn't done in weeks.

"I don't think that's necessary," Rankin replied.

Peng Shouang also doubled as the mission's doctor, and had been angling at him for months, suggesting he take some of their small store of antidepressants. Rankin refused. For him, depression was a natural reaction, like getting a fever—designed by nature to solve whatever it was that was affecting the organism.

In the dark well of his thoughts, Rankin's mind circled around and around. Had Ufuk Erdogmus really betrayed them? Betrayed *him*? Rankin prided himself on being a good judge of character, and if there was one thing he'd been sure of, it was that Ufuk Erdogmus was a man of his word. The long walks they'd had together, talking about this mission, about picking the crew, the importance of establishing a human colony on another planet as a way to protect humanity's future.

But all of that had been a lie.

This had been a mission to Mars, to establish humanity's first beachhead there. It had always been a one-way mission—with some small possibility of return if everything went perfectly—but Rankin had accepted that. He'd made peace with whatever demons needed to be quieted to allow him to get on that rocket and leave the rest of humanity behind. As had all of his crew, each in their own ways.

As had Anders Larsson, their crewmember who didn't awake from hibernation sleep. Who Ufuk Erdogmus had killed, or his artificial intelligence Simon had killed. For reasons still unknown, some political motivation.

If Rankin could believe Dr. Müller.

Perhaps *that* was all a lie as well, again for other reasons unknown.

Only one thing was certain: some kind of power struggle was going on down there, on what was left of Earth after the destruction wreaked by Nomad.

Since the brief transmission from Müller, over five months ago now, they hadn't heard from anyone else on Earth. Total silence. They'd tried reaching NASA, the ESA, even the Chinese or military channels. Nothing.

Nothing since the frantic message beamed from the Tanzania launch facility, of Dr. Müller from JPL telling them that Ufuk Erdogmus was a madman, not to trust him, and that he'd instructed Simon to kill Anders Larsson. Then the transmission went dead.

Was the transmitter destroyed? Was Müller killed?

Was *Müller* the madman? How did he even know that Anders Larsson had died? The only way he could have known that was by accessing their system logs, on board Mars First itself, which at the time was forty million kilometers from Earth—a four-and-a-half minute communication lag away.

Devastation beyond imagination had occurred Earth-side, so the situation had to be chaotic. In chaos, Rankin had learned—first as a Marine, then as a test pilot, and then as a NASA astronaut— the best thing to do was to stay calm and work the problem.

Their own systems seemed to be working, so maybe nobody down there was able to put together a communication array able to beam a signal into deep space. The other problem was that maybe they'd just been forgotten. While their own situation seemed all-important to them, maybe it wasn't so important to people on the ground, who might be literally fighting for their lives. The other possibility, the darker one, was that Simon, the artificial intelligence running the ship, was blocking their communications.

In which case, Ufuk Erdogmus was to blame.

"May 15th," Cuijpers repeated, snapping Commander Rankin out of his circling thoughts. She was smirking, her red hair tied up in a ponytail, her nose crinkled.

Peng Shouang and Gabi Siegel were both seated at the other mess table with her now. Three women against one man. He was outnumbered, as he would always be from now on. One more thing to accept.

Rankin sighed, "May 15th…ah"—the realization finally pierced his mind-fog—"Of course, one year till we get back to Earth."

Cuijpers raised a ration pack to cheer him with. "That's something to celebrate, isn't it?" The freckles on her cheeks in sharp relief to her pale skin.

Shouang and Siegel both half-heartedly raised a ration pack of their own, more in solidarity with Cuijpers trying to get a reaction from Rankin than really celebrating. In a year they would be back at Earth, after they used Saturn as a slingshot to haul them around and pull them back. The problem was, in a year, Earth would impact part of Saturn's rings. Exactly to what extent was still a matter of debate, and the detailed effect was unknown, except that it would be catastrophic. The day Mars First returned to Earth, would be the day it would be destroyed all over again—and they would have a front row seat to watching the devastation.

In just over three months they would intercept Saturn for the first time.

Rankin raised his ration of potato curry and took a slug together with the rest of his crew, to celebrate their pre-anniversary of Earth return. He kept his eyes on the sweeping star field, though, and there—a new star had appeared in their sky, just visible now to the naked eye. Saturn.

It was growing brighter by the day.

Their original mission had been a 302-day ballistic transfer orbit to Mars. Today was Mission Day 247, and already they had passed the point where Mars's orbit used to be. Magellan. Columbus. *Rankin*. He was the captain of the ship that had ventured further than any in human history. There was some small pride in that, wasn't there? He forced a small grin.

His crew noticed it and responded with grins of their own, then lowered their ration packs and got into their own conversation.

Where the orbit of Mars *used* to be. The thought stuck in his head. Not only was the Earth wrecked, but also the entire solar system was changed. Venus and Mercury had been flung into deep space, weren't even tied to the sun anymore. Two fewer planets in the solar system. Mars had been pushed into a high elliptic orbit, and Saturn pulled into a retrograde orbit—an orbit opposite in direction to its original orbit, and opposite to the orbit of the Earth. Mars First had reached aphelion, the furthest point it would get from the sun, and was now dropping back toward it, and Saturn was rushing toward them.

They would ride the monster's coattails all the way home.

The entire planet of Earth could fit inside a single storm system in Saturn's thick atmosphere. It was almost a thousand times bigger than Earth. Saturn wasn't just a planet—it was an entire system in itself, with over sixty moons, many of them geologically active, and its monster moon Titan that was larger than both Mercury and Pluto. The outer gas giants were even the targets for searches for life. Two years before, a NASA probe had reached Saturn's moon Enceladus to bore through its surface into the ocean of liquid water below. They didn't find any signs of life, but they learned a lot of about this alien world.

From a purely scientific perspective, it was fascinating.

From a human perspective, alien and terrifying and overwhelming.

But they still had a mission.

They'd almost finished intercepting the other six supply missions that had launched ahead of them. Almost three hundred tons of equipment and gear that Ufuk had sequestered away in deep space, away from the Earth and away from the brunt of the radiation blast induced by Nomad. Mars First's new mission—perhaps always their mission without knowing it—was to deliver this equipment into Earth orbit, to reestablish the global communications grid.

At least, that was what Simon told them.

"Simon, could you turn on the imaging system and bring up the magnification on Saturn?" Rankin asked.

"Sure, boss," came the disembodied reply.

A moment later, the mess's wall screen glowed to life, and Saturn's brown-gray-streaked sphere appeared, almost edge-on to the massive rings. Did they have enough shielding to survive the magnetic fields and radiation? Rankin had run through the calculations. Ufuk seemed to have thought of everything.

But not quite everything.

There were six supply missions that they were cattle-wrangling in deep space to bring back to Earth, but a seventh mission had been planned but scrubbed at the last moment. What was it? What piece of equipment were they missing?

"Commander."

Rankin fiddled with his tablet and zoomed in to a section of Saturn's rings.

"Commander!" This time Cuijpers yelled.

Rankin turned to the other table. All of his crew stared at him, their eyes wide. "What? What happened?"

"I have a…we have a message," Cuijpers stammered.

The image of Saturn faded, replace by a computer-generated image of the spheroid of Earth, a view from a point high above the Pacific Ocean. A small red dot pulsed just off the coast of California, a few hundred miles due west of San Diego.

"We have a transmission from the USS Carl Vinson," came Simon's voice, smooth and vaguely Brit-like in accent. "The Carl Vinson is a Nimitz-class aircraft carrier under the command of Captain William J. Reynolds the third—"

"I know what the Carl Vinson is," Rankin interrupted. "Play the message."

"It's weak but repeating; let me clean up the signal processing," Simon replied.

The Earth was almost on the other side of the sun right now, about 360 million kilometers away. The Carl Vinson had to have pretty powerful transmitters, but wasn't designed to send messages like this. Rankin did a mental calculation. Seven hundred million kilometers round-trip distance for a message at the speed of light, that was…about forty minutes send-receive latency.

So this message had to be have sent twenty minutes ago.

Twenty minutes ago.

He found himself on his feet without realizing he'd gotten up. The other three stood together with him. Elation that any other humans were alive. For five months they hadn't heard anything.

"Simon, play the goddamn—"

"Mars First, this is President Roger Donnelly of the United States of America, aboard the USS Carl Vinson." The voice faded in and out, and was full of static, but unmistakable. "We are in convoy, heading to Australia, with three million fellow Americans. Captain Jason Rankin, if you are receiving the message, please reply. Your country—and the planet—is in desperate need of your help."

2

USS Carl Vinson
Pacific Ocean
Three hundred miles west of San Diego
May 15th

"This is Commander Rankin of the Mars First spaceship," came the scratchy voice over the Operation Room's loudspeaker. "We can confirm that we have three hundred tons of communication and other equipment from six supply missions. We are on a trajectory to intercept Saturn in three months, which will bring us back to Earth on May 15th of next year."

Captain Reynolds leaned back in the thick foam chair. The Operations Room of the Carl Vinson was cast in perpetual dim blue light, the wall screens lit up with diagrams of the local area. The Air Ops staff sat quietly at attention in their chairs, green digital readouts scrolling overhead. The screens in front of them were blank. Nobody was up in the air right now. They hadn't even done test flights in three months.

"So Ufuk Erdogmus is telling the truth," President Roger Donnelly said. He paced back and forth. He stopped and to hold his chin in a thinking pose. "What about the seventh supply mission? The one that didn't make it up there?"

A week ago, they'd received a coded message from a CIA outpost in Oman. Reynolds hadn't realized such things even existed anymore—but the structure of the old world seemed determined to make its way into the new, no matter how much destruction had been wrought.

The message was from Colonel Hague, who reported that they had the billionaire Ufuk Erdogmus in their care, and that he'd told them he had a few hundred tons of satellites and communications gear coming back from deep space, and that he was ready to put it into the care of the United States Government. In exchange for *what*, exactly, would have been Reynolds' first question, but then he wasn't the one asking the questions.

He wasn't the one in charge anymore.

A week ago they'd gotten this message from the CIA outpost, and it took his crew that long to rig a radio transmitter and get enough power into it to broadcast their message into deep space. It had seemed almost ludicrous, right up until Commander Rankin's voice echoed over the speakers in return.

This newfound treasure trove in outer space was a prize beyond calculation. Whoever controlled this would effectively control global communications, GPS, surface imaging and more. It would enable what was left of the US military to begin functioning as a connected whole again. It was the key component that would enable America to gain ascendancy.

"Send a message back." President Donnelly stroked his chin and fixed a very serious look on the Assistant Communications Officer. "Ask Commander Rankin to find out *exactly* what is contained in these…packages. Can you do that, son?"

"Yes, sir," Corporal Heiman replied, his back stiff. He turned back to his radio. With their Commander in Chief on deck, everyone in the Operations Room was at attention.

"Hold on a sec," Reynolds interjected. "We don't know the situation up there, and I'm no expert, but we don't have anyone from JPL or NASA on board. Maybe we should ask to see if we have any scientists out there—"

"I want to find out what we have," Donnelly interrupted.

The new toys for the new President.

"But first we need to make sure it actually gets here. Those men and women up there"—Reynolds pointed up at the metal ceiling—"are in a very precarious situation. They are very isolated, more isolated than any human beings in history. I can hear the tension in Rankin's voice. They've been alone a long time."

"What does that have to do with finding out what's in those packages?"

"Kid gloves. One step at a time, and first cause no harm. Right now they're still intercepting the supply missions. It's all they can do to make sure they're securing them to the main spacecraft. In three months they're going to have to do a major burn, from what I can understand, and swing that whole thing around Saturn to head home."

"Can't they just go and have a look?" Donnelly protested.

"Have a look? That means spacewalks. Which means they would need extra EVAs, which strikes me as dangerous all by itself. There are only four of them up there. One has died already."

"Rankin just told us that Larsson was killed by the ship," Donnelly said, repeating part of a previous message. They'd been in the operations room for six hours already. Forty minute delays on the send and receive of messages made for a slow conversation. "On the orders of Ufuk Erdogmus. That's what Rankin said. I'm sure Erdogmus had his reason, but that wasn't an accident."

How quickly and easily politicians forgave murder when it was in their own best interest, but then again, this was all hearsay. "They were told that their crewmate Anders Larsson was killed, but that information came from a message from Dr. Hermann Müller. How do you know it's true?"

Donnelly remained silent.

"Mr. President." Reynolds had to throw in this designation from time to time. He knew it smoothed down Donnelly's feathers. "Answer me this: Where is Dr. Hermann Müller? Right now?"

Donnelly paused again, acutely aware of the staff in the Operations Room staring at the two of them. He didn't want to look stupid. "I see your point."

"In Sanctuary China," Captain Reynolds answered his own question. "Holed up with what our intel says are the four Politburo members, the new ruling faction of the Chinese government. Our own intel says they're the ones directing the Chinese and Russian Navies to intercept us, to stop us from entering their hemisphere."

It wasn't rocket science to imagine why the Chinese might want to spread misinformation, to turn the crew of Mars First against Ufuk Erdogmus, especially if Mr. Erdogmus had just made a deal with the United States Government. With the death of Chairman Zhao Peng, control of the Chinese government had been split between Beijing and those hiding in Sanctuary China.

Not exactly a revolution, but devolution.

"I'll also mention that Mars First is not US-military-controlled," Reynolds continued. "It's a private operation. Not even US government controlled."

"But Commander Rankin is a United States Marine."

"And thank God for that, but we've also got a ranking officer from the Peoples' Liberation Army up here, Peng Shounag. *And* a naturalized Israeli soldier, Gabi Siegal, along with a Dutchwoman, Elin Cuijpers. There's a goddamn United Nations up there. I would advise that we take things slowly. We need to find out exactly what the hell is going on before we start sending people out into space to start taking that thing apart. At least until after they get around Saturn and are heading back to us."

Donnelly took stock of Reynolds, and then said something the Captain never expected: "I think it's time we give you a promotion, if you're going to be heading this operation. What do you think of the sound of *Admiral* Reynolds?"

Admiral Reynolds held his face up to the wind; breathed deep the salt air. If nothing else, it was good to be underway, to be back out on the Pacific. They were doing ten knots, much slower than cruising speed, but then, they weren't cruising alone. He opened his eyes.

Ships of all shapes and sizes plowed their way through the rough dark seas, all the way to the mist-gray horizon that disappeared to become one with the endless wall of clouds overhead. Ships and more ships as far as the eye could see. He could just make out the George Washington five miles off their port side, with four Destroyers up ahead. Cargo ships. Oil tankers. Tiny sailboats dotted in between them. Three million American civilians desperate for another chance at life packed in this flotilla, the greatest armada of ships the world had ever seen.

Five thousand vessels.

That's what made the Chinese nervous.

Hell, he could understand what they were thinking. He'd feel the same way if five thousand Chinese boats and aircraft carriers, loaded with nuclear weapons and who knew what else, were headed for America. That wasn't his problem, though, being able to empathize. His mission was to make sure these people would get to safety, to disembark in Perth, Australia. It would take a month for them to get there at this speed, nursing their way across the Pacific.

They'd had to start out earlier than he wanted.

On President Donnelly's command.

The two words, "President" and "Donnelly" still seemed at odds to each other in Reynold's mind—in the same way as "Admiral" and "Reynolds" didn't seem to fit. Three weeks before, they'd had the swearing in ceremony of the 47th President of the United States, right here on the deck of his Carl Vinson. It was a moment to be proud of, and Reynolds had ordered a squadron of F-35s to circle and salute the ceremony.

The first thing Donnelly had done—and soon afterward promoting Reynolds to Admiral—was tell them they had to be underway to Australia as soon as possible. Reynolds still wanted to wait, to try and amass as many ships as possible and get civilians onto them, but then he was also a creature of rules. This was now his Commander in Chief. Despite that, he'd just ridden his new boss a little hard in the Operations Room.

Reynolds smiled a private grin and looked down at the dark waters of the Pacific.

He'd loved the ocean since he could remember, ever since being a boy growing up in the Pacific Northwest and sailing with his father. What was happening to his beloved ocean, down below the waves? The grin slid from his face. He knew enough of the ocean's ecosystem to know that the phytoplankton—that relied on the sun's energy—must be dead or dying. They were the biomass that underpinned most of the planet's biggest ecosystem and oxygen production.

So far, it had only gotten colder, but what was coming next?

Reynolds could only imagine. It was better for him that he didn't have a lot of time to daydream. He had a mission. To get these three million people to safety, and then come back for more.

He looked back at the horizon.

Somewhere over there, the Chinese and Russian navies—allied now in common cause and defense—were amassing. They didn't want him coming with his warships. A fight was brewing. From the short test flights, they found they could operate the F-35s at low altitudes without too much damage from the dust and particulates in the air, but there was damage. The machines were limited use weapons now, but if that was true, it was also true for the opposition.

The calculus of war and defense had changed, and he had to think hard about it.

This time across the Pacific he imagined there would be a lot of chest thumping, but they'd back down—but only because Reynolds and his navy would be returning to America. The next time across he wasn't so sure, but Reynolds was damned if he was going to let anyone stand in his way of protecting what was left of these American families he was protecting.

PART THREE

1

Oman
March 18th

A year.

That was a long time to wait, and even longer when you were waiting for Saturn to literally drop from the sky and obliterate the planet you were stuck upon. It was even longer when you were thinking about a little boy, wondering what he was doing. If he was okay. If he was lying awake at nights like Jess was. A second dose of the apocalypse about to be inflicted upon the world in as many years, but this time everyone knew it was coming. The date of Armageddon: May 15th.

Was it better they knew it was coming? Jess wasn't sure. She checked—for the dozenth time—the calendar on the wall of her cubicle.

Today was March 18th.

Two months for Jess and Peter and Ufuk and Giovanni to get halfway around the world and infiltrate Sanctuary China with Roger and Abbie's help, and for Jess to get Hector and get them all on a boat to Australia, join the American convoy on the way there.

At least they were finally on their way.

That morning, Colonel Hague had given the green light.

She retrieved her kit from her small room, pausing a moment to plug-in and fully recharge her prosthetic leg. Last year, they'd eventually agreed to let her power it up. It would help in her training with the Delta team, she'd explained.

Or rather, Ufuk had explained.

A year of cohabitating with the man, two doors down from her, and she'd settled into an uneasy truce. He'd apologized incessantly until she forced him to stop, and he'd guaranteed he would devote every resource he had to helping liberate Hector. She didn't believe him, of course, but then there was always a half-truth in everything he said.

A cup half full was better than one completely empty.

Shouldering her small bag of possessions, she scanned the room. As much as it was a prison of sorts, it had been home for a year—the single cot and layers of woolen blankets, the fold-down table stacked with notes and geographical maps of northern China. It smelled warm and lived-in, familiar and safe. A twinge of nostalgia held her there for a moment, dosed with an equal spurt of pit-of-the-stomach nausea at the prospect of weeks on board a fishing trawler, and then weeks after that crossing ice and ash into a hostile, unknown alien land.

The trip last year in the boat from Tanzania to Oman had been hard enough, that coming on the heels of the journey in the sailboat from Italy to Africa. In this new world—one with few aircraft—the easiest and most reliable way to travel long distances was again by water. A few days ago the boat trips had felt like distant memories—the cramped conditions, the rocking ocean, the dampness, the saltiness—but it all now came back to her in a rush.

She didn't like boats.

Didn't like water, and especially didn't like cold water.

An image flitted through her mind, of her little brother's face from when she was a child, disappearing into the black hole ringed in white. He'd drowned, and she couldn't save him. The knot in her stomach flared painfully.

She closed the door to her cubicle and strode down the gray metal corridor to the exit and slammed the release bar. Cold air rushed over her face and blew back her long blond hair.

The sun was setting somewhere behind the haze.

Thick low clouds still dominated the sky to the horizon, but there were breaks in them. No blue sky beyond, but a thick gray-green gauze that brightened to a burnt-orange rust if you were lucky enough to see the sun-smudge directly. The global stratosphere was filled with a twenty-mile-thick layer of fine particulate ash. The eruptions had stopped more than a year ago, and now the skies cleared sometimes to reveal the smooth haze far above. Half of the sun's radiation was blocked, but then, there was also a massive accumulation of carbon dioxide and other gases from the volcanism. In rich irony, greenhouse gases were saving what was left alive.

The Earth's temperature was stabilizing.

The scientists—those that remained—no longer predicted a "snowball Earth," or that the icecaps wouldn't stretch down from the poles to encircle the planet. At least that was the guess. With much anticipation they'd waited last spring, and there was a summer of sorts. The skies and earth did warm before swinging back into the fall and winter season, and this spring it had warmed even more. Some hardy scrub bushes in the mountains managed to survive on the scant solar radiation.

So there was hope.

At least, until Saturn arrived.

Would it vaporize the atmosphere? Throw the Earth into a totally new and uninhabitable orbit? They knew the date, but not the specifics. They didn't have the modeling capability to say with any certainty, but that didn't stop the wild rumors from circulating.

Colonel Hague had kept them here for a year; wouldn't authorize the mission to Sanctuary China until he got the word from up the command chain, using the encrypted short wave radio. Still no satellites or GPS, no Internet or power grids, but slowly, the survivors were organizing themselves. In the summer, the first convoy had crossed the Pacific and been met by a blockade of the Chinese and Russian navies. Admiral William Reynolds, of the USS Carl Vinson, had stared them down, and the Chinese had been the first to blink. They broke ranks and allowed the two aircraft carriers, several hundred US Navy ships, and thousands of merchant vessels through. Millions of Americans were delivered to Australia.

A rare celebration at the Oman base that day.

But the Chinese and Russians were only licking their wounds, and they knew the US Navy, and the thousands of merchant marine, were returning to American waters to get more survivors. The next convoy—the one leaving now—expected more resistance. This time the Americans wouldn't be leaving China's backyard, and would be threatening their dominion over the whole South China Seas and what habitable lands remained in "their" hemisphere. Intelligence reported that they were amassing their full armies and navies—and China and Russia had already begun fighting amongst themselves.

It was into this fray that Jess and her small team were being thrown. One small part of what had to be a larger operation to infiltrate Sanctuary China to avoid a terrible conflict and humanitarian disaster to end all disasters.

During the year, Jess had been drip-fed the occasional report from the moles inside of Sanctuary China. Small details on Hector's life, that he was seen playing soccer with Roger, or in a school with other children. This gave Jess some small hope, but it also filled her with doubt.

Was this the right thing to do?

Colonel Hague wanted to ship Giovanni and Raffa to Australia. They would be safe there, he'd insisted—he wanted to send two more Delta team members with Jess and Peter and Massarra—and the Colonel was right. At least that was a chance at life, but Raffa refused, needed to go and get his brother. His only family. Giovanni refused as well. Hector was all that remained of his. The Colonel had fumed and screamed, but in the end, Jess had stood with her friends.

For some reason, they absolutely needed Jessica in on this, and she used that as leverage to get what she wanted. Beyond that, she tried not to think too much. Better instead focus on her fitness, on getting ready for the operation.

She walked down the gravel path into the frigid early morning, mist billowing in front of her face on every breath, cold air biting at her skin. Peter waved to her from one of the two waiting pickup trucks.

Jess gritted her teeth and smiled.

Now she was stuck with Peter Connor, who lied to her, locked her up. Using her to get what he wanted. And beside Peter stood Ufuk Erdogmus, a man who never told the truth. He acted like this whole episode in Oman was something he planned—and the worst of it was, he just might have.

Jess was stuck between two men she detested.

And one man she loved.

Giovanni stood away from the others, in front of the drab trucks, clothed in the local Omani dress, the *dishdasha*, along with a thick coat. Massarra was loading equipment bags into the other pickup. Giovanni, Peter, Ufuk, and Raffa had grown thick beards. Giovanni had the habit of touching it when he was tense. He did so now. The beard looked good on him, flecked with gray in places now.

Jess had grown purposely apart from Giovanni in the past year, made it clear she needed her own sleeping quarters. Needed her own space. It wasn't that she didn't care for him. She loved the feeling of him being near. But all the lies, all the uncertainty, it made it hard for her to want to be near anyone. Or perhaps, before, with Hector, she felt like they were a family. She didn't have that feeling anymore.

She watched Giovanni, making sure he didn't see her watching him. She looked away as he turned to her.

"You manage to get any sleep?" Giovanni asked as he walked over. He kept his distance. Had learned to keep his distance.

"Not a lot," she said. "You?"

He smiled a thin smile. "Glad to be getting going."

The shore of the Gulf of Oman was more inland than before but it would still be a three-hour drive to Al Kamil Wal Wafi.

"Did they finish the work on the trawler?" Jess asked, more to make conversation than really expecting any insight. Not that she didn't think Giovanni wouldn't have any, but she struggled to find things to talk about with him.

"It's as ready as it'll ever be."

She gave him a friendly pat on the shoulder. "Then let's go."

She jumped into the front seat of the pickup, and couldn't help noticing the way Giovanni's eyes followed her, the way he always watched her from a distance as well.

The convoy of pickups skidded down the dirt road descending from the mountains. The Gulf of Oman spread its gray-blue ink across the horizon, met with a dark haze in the distance to merge with the clouds. They were going to leave under the cover of nightfall.

A life of sorts had restarted with the locals, hastily constructed jetties and a ragtag collection of boats trying to haul what was left in alive in the water. Even seaweed at the shores was dead, yet everything scrabbled for life. Nobody wanted to die. That included the creatures in the water, and many hours of effort usually resulted in a meager and dwindling catch.

Even here, the Americans kept up pretenses to keep a low profile, made a show of paying for the boat from the government men who worked for the new Sultan of Oman, Haytham bin Tariq, in Nizwa.

Their ride was parked by one of the ramshackle docks.

The trawler was a purse seiner, a commercial tuna vessel once rigged to carry floating dragnets to catch fish near the surface. The hull, streaked with rivers of rust, bore the *hànzì* markings of a vessel registered in the Far East. These had been hidden until now, avoiding curiosity as to why such a vessel would be harbored in Oman. Once they were out of the Laccadive Sea and past Sri Lanka, it wouldn't matter. A crow's nest had been built onto the mast, usually there to search for schools of tuna, but in this case to search the horizon for signs of approaching vessels.

Peter had explained the boat was constructed in the manner of the Asian trawlers, with the wheelhouse forward and the working deck aft so it wouldn't be out of place in the Indian Ocean. It was fitted with sophisticated electronics—echo sounders, sonar—scavenged from a Navy vessel that sailed in a few months before. Peter's teams rigged all this equipment to appear dead at the flick of a hidden switch.

Twilight's pale light washed over the harbor, the sickly hue of the dark green sky draping both vessels and surrounding sand dunes in its anemic haze.

Jess took her kit bag and approached the trawler, passing by two armed men in *dishdasha* and heavy coat, and made her way onto the jetty. Behind the wheelhouse were two skiffs. A detailed inspection might discover the four-by-four pickup, hidden in the housing constructed around it and on which lay the skiffs, but had she not already known about it, she believed she'd have had no idea it was there. Spare nets would be the excuse, were they ever questioned about the housing. It would never pass a detailed examination, but if anyone got this close—she felt for her pistol—then a different kind of plan would be required.

Her fear of going slowly slipped into a fear of not going. A year of waiting, of training with the Delta team. The first armada of American ships had made it to Australia. The second convoy, of seven thousand ships, was on its way.

She asked herself again—was she doing the right thing? Hector would be safe, underground at Sanctuary, when Saturn arrived.

If she didn't go, she would leave Hector at the mercy of strangers—but at least he would survive. Maybe Roger would take care of the boy, but she would never trust him. And Müller? He would never let the boy go, would probably kill him rather than let someone else get a chance at Ufuk's networks. That thought by itself quickened her step.

Beyond all that—her country needed her. America needed her. The millions of her fellow countrymen-and-women, about to embark into harm's way. She had to try and protect them, if she could. Deep in her blood and bones, she was still a Marine.

Still loved her country.

Even if America hardly existed as a physical place anymore, it still existed as an idea, and maybe that idea—the concept of America—was the *most* important thing. What it stood for, and what it could still stand for in the future.

Whatever the reasons, she felt compelled to go.

And the Colonel kept saying this was the final option before the *final* option. Jess could guess what that was. The American military, now it knew the existence of Sanctuary China, and that there were those inside that had command and control of extreme faction Politburo, might try and destroy it—using the nuclear weapons hidden deep in the ocean depths, on the nuclear-powered *boomer* submarines. If China and Russia threatened the convoy, they would be forced to use the final option.

So if Jess didn't go—and couldn't help stop it—then Hector could be dead at the hands of her fellow Americans. She couldn't stand by and let that happen.

One final thought.

Jess tried not to let it creep into her head, but was part of her drive to go to China rooted in an opportunity for revenge? Müller. For what he had done to her father. Thinking like this got her into trouble, had led to her being trapped on Isola del Gigli and almost killed when this all started.

But this wasn't revenge driving her.

Or was it?

She tried instead to focus on the glimmer of hope.

If it all worked—under protection of the US provisional government in central Australia, and being back in the good graces of her fellow Americans—a year from now she could be building a farmhouse in the middle of rain-soaked central Australia under a glowing yellow sun. Dreams were all that she had to keep her going, and that was as good an image as she could hold in her mind.

At least it felt like a mission, something to do, something to combat the powerlessness of looking into sky each night. The clearing skies were still murky, but sometimes, on clear nights, they could see a few stars, and there was a new star in the sky, appearing just on the horizon.

Saturn.

It grew brighter every night.

It was still a hundred and seventy million kilometers away, but had been dragged into a retrograde orbit—an orbit opposite to the orbital direction of the Earth. The closing velocity was growing, already close to forty kilometers a second but increasing every day as the gas giant—almost a thousand times bigger than the Earth—dropped inward toward the sun. Already it had plunged past Jupiter and where Mars used to be, dropped more than a billion kilometers from the outer solar system through the asteroid belt on a near-collision course with Earth.

Jess walked down the creaking wooden jetty, smelling the salt air, not speaking to anyone. Lost in her thoughts. She tossed her bag over the gunwales onto the bench and put one foot on the boat, let it rock her back and forth with the slap-slap of the waves. She looked down into the inky water, and then, closing her eyes, opened them to look at the horizon. Even through the haze, Saturn burned bright in the twilight.

Saturn.

The god of time.

Voices echoed through the narrow corridor, and Jess hauled her bag and a box of supplies into the forward cabin. In the hold, hidden behind a removable wall section, were six of Ufuk's smaller drones. They weren't Ufuk's really—they were CIA-issue, but built by Ufuk's company before Nomad. Each was weaponized and carried surveillance and communications equipment.

Jess took a bunk in one corner next to Massarra. There was no space for separate rooms. In the center of the room lie the crew's eating area, and just off it, the tiny galley. The rest of the bunks lined the walls, in nooks created by the angle of the hull. She went topside the moment she heard the guttural grumble of the trawler's engines start, smelled the belching blue exhaust. The last of the sun's light seeped away as they got under way.

Jess wrapped up against the cold, shielded her face from the spray.

"Fishing is about the only way to get fresh food." Peter stood beside her.

One Delta team member accompanied them, Foster—who barely ever spoke a word. He took the wheel on the way out of the harbor. Giovanni was below with Ufuk and Raffa, stowing gear.

"We've catalogued dozens of vessels in the weeks and months since Nomad," Peter yelled over the noise of the engine. "All arm their crew. Before Nomad, pirates would take oil tankers in the Gulf of Aden and out into the Arabian Sea off the coast of Somalia. They're cockroaches. Nomad barely affected them."

The man was just making small talk. Nervous. This was basic information, but she played along to calm his nerves. "So we need to be careful."

"The scanning equipment we have is rudimentary, but it should give us some advance warning of approaching vessels. We may need some luck."

"And more than a little."

"You should get below while we're out here. Better no one sees a woman on board until we have no other choice."

Jess was looking for a reason to get away from Peter anyway.

She nodded and went below.

2

Northern Mongolia
March 20th

A year of waiting, of hiding in the forests outside Ulan Bator, but today the man on the radio had finally told them to proceed into the city. He'd spoken in Russian today, the two of them now switched easily between that and the accented English. It was easier to speak in Russian.

Zasekin instructed his men to remove their Russian uniforms and don what clothes they could scavenge in Sükhbaatar. They borrowed clothing from their Buryat friends, the nomadic hunter. Better, he reasoned, they did not walk into Ulan Bator dressed as Russian Border Guard. The nomads' Kalash rifles were common in the region. Those at least would be less likely to attract unwanted scrutiny. During their reconnaissance, they saw many people armed. Almost everyone, in fact.

At least, anyone left alive.

He told them to pack as though they had been walking for weeks and say they were refugees from Petropavlovka near the border. That was the only cover story that would make sense of the distance, and not require them to conceal their accents.

Vasily Fyodorovich, still not well enough to make such a long and arduous journey, one they needed to make quickly and without encumbrance, remained behind. Someone was required to keep watch over their adopted base, to take the Czilim to the river and run if that became necessary. They said their goodbyes, hugged the tired figure resting on a homemade crutch. Zasekin couldn't shake the feeling, as they left him standing at a window, they would not see him again.

They crossed the mountains using a similar route to that which they had taken over the last few days to recon the city, Zasekin first contenting himself that the snowfall each night covered the tracks they left behind them. On makeshift sleds they dragged supplies and weapons and whatever else they considered would bolster their lies. They carried a *ger* too, a Mongolian shelter made of latticework wood, felt, and a waterproof canvas. There were a few abandoned *gers* in the grounds surrounding the resort, and they scavenged sufficient raw material to construct one to house them all and their equipment. The structure was unwieldy and heavy, and needed to be separated out between the sleds.

They met the dirt road heading south, just north of sporadic settlements that fringed the small township of Gachuurt. On most roads heading into Ulan Bator there had been traffic, some of it on foot, some in vehicles adapted to the snow through chains or other impromptu methods imagined by people used to cold. Stragglers, refugees from the north like they pretended to be, might be considered unusual but not improbable.

The first signs of life came in the form of Mongol people who left *gers*, within which fires burned, to study them as they walked past. They stood behind walls of sticks, while children huddled in the doorways. Zasekin held the gaze of a woman as he walked past, her face smeared with dirt. He offered a weak smile, but she did not return it. Instead, she eyed his sled and the Kalash slung across his chest.

They walked along the Khujirbalan Road, keeping to one side as trucks and pickups and cars and motorbikes growled past them. The air thickened with a smoggy, oily haze. Clumps of ash lay over the frozen ground. Khujirbulan was alive with the bustle of thousands of people moving through the streets in a market in the distance. When they came to the road leading into the center of town, Zasekin gestured for them to take it.

Light from a largish building glowed through the layered fog, a mini-market outlet at the intersection. Parked outside were a handful of trucks and cars. Figures wrapped in swaddled cloth watched them from behind begrimed goggles. All were armed.

One stepped forward as Zasekin made to walk past him and jabbered quickly. It had been a long time since Zasekin had spoken Mongolian. The lyrical dialect was difficult to follow in the noise of the wind.

When the man gestured to Zasekin's weapon, still slung across his chest, he understood. Zasekin removed it and left it with Timur, who took and held it ready, pointed low but finger resting on the trigger. The message was clear. The man opened the door. He gestured Zasekin inside.

The noise from the wind abated as the door closed behind him. A flush of warmth. Behind the counter stood another man, surrounded by sparsely laden shelving. He was older, face creased by hard lines, eyes bright and sharp. A western-style hat was pulled down over his ears, with a Mongolian scarf wound around his neck.

The shop was drafty, smelled of turpentine and mold. Heat belched from an electric heater in one corner. In another, hopeful that some of the heater's output might fall on them, an open door led to a room where men sat around a card game. A bottle of clear liquid was being passed around to fill small cut-glass tumblers in front of each of them. Cigarette smoke wavered in the light thrown by an oil lamp above the wooden table they played on.

"*Sain bain uu?*" Zasekin asked the shopkeeper informally, as was the Mongolian custom. *Are you well?* The expected response would have been "*sain*," a reciprocation of the greeting, regardless of mood or status. Instead, Zasekin was met with silence.

He rolled his shoulders. Was it a mistake coming in here? The wrong response would have been to demonstrate any kind of fear. Instead, he reached into a pocket and took out his Java Zolotayas. Not many left, but he offered one to the man.

The shopkeeper paused, pursing his lips. He deliberated the look on Zasekin's face before deciding to take the offered cigarette. As was customary, Zasekin offered to light it.

The man drew heavily and scoffed. "Russian cigarettes taste like Russian food."

Zasekin smiled a grin of commiseration. "Nothing tastes that bad, my friend. But not Zharkoye. I always loved Zharkoye."

"Where are you from?"

"Petropavlovka. Just over the border."

"That's a long way from here. You walk all that way?"

"We did."

"Where are you headed now?"

"Into the city. Anywhere we can find a bed." Zasekin's eyes scanned the corners of the shop, the walls, the back exit, and then returned to the keeper. "Is there room here, in Khujirbulan?"

"There's room everywhere, in the snow."

Chuckles from the card players, but none of them glanced toward Zasekin.

He ignored them. "Nothing more"—he paused to choose his word—"comfortable?"

As Zasekin spoke, one of the players rose and threw down his cards. With a rolling gait, he lumbered over, sizing up Zasekin the whole way. He was older than the shopkeeper, stooped under some unseen weight.

"I wouldn't go looking for much in the city," the older man said. "Your kind are causing trouble there and not well-liked."

"My kind?"

In response, the old man spat on the floor.

Zasekin had heard of the Bratva shooting up a Chinese Triad gang in Krasnoyarsk a few years ago. There were often violent clashes between Russian and Chinese communities in Irkutsk. Enough well-dressed businessmen ran shady deals in casinos and restaurants all over the city to make it clear the Mafia brotherhoods didn't mind the cold.

"We are not criminals. No trouble. We just want a place to rest for a while."

The old man scoffed at this, but Zasekin waited.

"Always Chinese criminals in Ulaanbaatar. Tong, Triad. Now Russians too. All the same to me. They shoot each other. Good, I say. Be better for everyone if you Russians went home."

Zasekin met his gaze, held it unflinchingly. "Not much to go back to. And I'm sure we're not first to come south."

"Not our problem."

Zasekin's expression made plain his annoyance. "Soon it will be everyone's problem. The Earth is belching out its insides."

The old man seemed ready to offer more vitriol, but the shopkeeper intervened. "There's land at the northern edge of the town. Find anywhere unoccupied, and there's nothing to stop you taking. But the Citizen's Representatives Hural will want you to register."

Zasekin set the rest of the cigarettes on the counter. "You know where the Russians are, in the city?"

The old man let out a squawk-noise, spat again on the floor, and went back to the other room without another word.

The shopkeeper took the cigarettes. "Some are at Bagakhangai."

This made sense to Zasekin. There was an old Soviet air base there.

"Within the city itself," continued the shopkeeper. "Where else but Moskow Town? *Khoroos* 17 and 18. I was told they had control of the Thermal Power Plant in *khoroo* 5, but I don't know if that is true."

"Moscow Town?" For sixty years Ulan Bator had been under Soviet control. It was at this time that Ulan Bator was given its name, "Red Hero" in Mongolian.

The shopkeeper grimaced. Zasekin made to leave.

"The Hural does not permit the carrying of weapons in the city," the shopkeeper said.

Zasekin left without replying.

At the furthest edge of the town, to the north where each patch of land was separated by ramshackle wooden fencing, they found several empty plots. Others came and went, in and out of *gers* and shanty huts. Some had brick houses with slanted tin roofs. None paid them much attention, even those winding the lattice wood frames of the *gers*.

"But the Bratva, Andrei?" Timur asked as they worked.

The thought of striking a deal with the local mafia made Zasekin's skin crawl as well, but they didn't have much choice. "How could we Russians avoid them? I'll tell you, my friend: we cannot. Some kind of relationship with them, however uneasy, is in our best interests." And also what the radio-man asked me to do, he didn't add.

They constructed the shelter slowly, methodically, correcting errors as they went at Zasekin's instructions. Decades had passed since he last pitched one of these. The familiar scent of the felt skin brought back powerful memories. A sensation of renewal. It took three hours before it was tight and sealed. They lit a fire inside, huddled around it as they unrolled their equipment on the ground and made sleeping mats.

"How far into the city?" Timur asked. He spooned warm bean stew into his mouth.

"Fifteen kilometers," Misha said. "A few hours at most."

Evgeny grunted. "In Irkutsk, the Bratva would be cautious about murdering SVR and its Border Guards. Here, I doubt there are any such restrictions." He closed his eyes against the heat and light of the fire. "Maybe there is not much left of the SVR, but that does account for our current position. I don't think much of our chances."

"I do not think those men at the market care much for restrictions either. If we're to spend ten hours or more getting to the city and taking a look around, I don't want to drag our equipment and shelter there with us and we can't leave it here unattended. We will have to split up."

"Two men will be less conspicuous than four," Timur said. "So Misha stays here with Evgeny. Discover what they can about what is going on outside the city. You and I head in toward the center."

3

Bay of Bengal
March 24th

"Hard to port!" screamed a voice.

Jess's eyes shot open. She stumbled out of her bunk and onto the sodden wooden floor. Her blanket fell to the floor and she cursed, tried to pick it up. Staying dry on this goddamn rust bucket was close to impossible. The stench of engine oil and diesel fuel assaulted her senses, the throbbing growl of the engine grinded her eardrums. More shouting. She grabbed her boots.

"What's happening?" she yelled.

Massarra appeared in the topside doorway, nimbly turned and slid down the ladder into the crew quarters. "Military vessel. Destroyer or frigate. Can't tell much, too far away. We picked it up half an hour ago on the radar. It just altered course to cut across us."

"Visual?"

"Not for an hour or two."

How long had Jess been asleep?

They were steaming at twelve knots, so they could have covered fifty or sixty nautical miles in the last few hours. If she were asleep. She hadn't really slept since they left Oman a week ago. Two days ago they passed the southern tip of India and Sri Lanka and headed straight east, through the Bay of Bengal.

"Where are we?" Jess asked. "Any ideas?"

"As close as we can tell, about ten hours from Little Nicobar."

With no GPS, a wavering magnetic north, and not much in the way of stars at night, a lot of it came down to dead reckoning and what little radio triangulation Ufuk was able to glean from his electronic gadgets. Little Nicobar meant they were at the edge of the Andaman Sea off the west coast of Thailand, a little way north of Sumatra and the Malacca Strait. So far the journey had been uneventful. No storms. No threats other than getting lost in the trackless desert of waves.

"You've been asleep six hours," Massarra added.

"Any idea whose ship it is?"

"Could be Indian, might be Malaysian. More likely the Indian Navy." Massarra wrapped a *kefiyeh* over her mouth. She turned to hop back up the stairs.

Jess followed, still groggy.

Peter and Ufuk were already in the wheelhouse.

"Where's Raffa?" Jess asked.

"Crow's nest with long-range optics."

If we could see them, a good chance they could see us.

Jess craned her neck forward to look up. There was the boy—or rather, the man. In the past year, Raffa had bulked up and grown a thick beard along with the others. Had spent the year training with the Delta team stationed in Oman, right alongside Jess. The kid was tough.

"They came up on our systems a little while ago. Couldn't adjust course as that might indicate we have better systems than we should have. No reason to abruptly alter our heading if we had no idea they were there. So we watched and waited. A few minutes ago, they changed course. They're coming for a look."

"Shit."

"Russia and China skirmishing in the Philippine and China Seas is bound to make the Indians nervous. Probably all they want to know is who we are."

"Or they want to add another tuna trawler to their fleet."

Minutes dragged like hours. They watched the glowing green dot on the screen turn and begin to head straight for them. Nobody said anything. The ocean crashed against the hull, the steady rhythm leaning them back and forth in unison. The tick-tick-tick and growl of the engine in the silence.

"We need to do something," Jess said.

"We can't take on an Indian Navy ship," Ufuk said. "We can't outrun it. Aren't the Indians our allies?"

"Can't risk it," Peter replied. "Who knows who's in charge."

"What about the Malacca Strait?" Jess asked.

"If we turned now, throttled to fifteen knots..." Peter hesitated. "If they followed, they could beat us there. Even a frigate is twice as fast as us."

"But if we made it," Jess said. "There'd be no reason for them to follow us into the strait? It's not their territory."

It was a weak point, but with tensions flaring on the oceans, the Indians might not want to venture far into Chinese territory.

Peter tapped one finger against his lip. "I don't think we can make it."

"Great Nicobar, then," said Ufuk. "We might make it if we poured on speed."

"And do what? The Andaman and Nicobar Islands are Indian."

"They won't find us." Ufuk laid his tablet on the desk and pulled up charts of the Islands. "Bananga or the Galathea River delta in the south. The Casuarina Bay to the west. That's if they banked on us choosing Great Nicobar rather than one of the smaller islands. They would have to send a shore crew to find us, but why would they waste the time? There are other rivers, many of which would be capable of taking this vessel. Might take days looking for us. Wouldn't be worth it."

"It's a risk," Massarra said. "We're backing ourselves into a corner."

Peter throttled the trawler higher and turned the wheel. "Ufuk, find us a place to head for. You've got three hours until we're there. They'll be right on our tail if they choose to chase us. Give us somewhere to hide this damn boat."

Ten minutes confirmed what they feared. The green dot on the radar screen had turned to follow and increased its speed.

"At least there's no air support," Peter mumbled.

Kondul Island laid some way to the north, visible on the horizon because the gap between the Great Nicobar's northern beaches and mangrove forests was barely a nautical mile. Along the coast came swathes of Andaman tropical evergreens and Jess wondered, as their trawler chewed through the foaming surf, what this place must have been like before the sky darkened and became hued with its insipid pallor. A paradise, blessed with pristine white beaches, lowland equatorial rainforest.

She'd always wanted to come to Thailand.

But not like this.

The minutes ground into a half an hour, then an hour.

"I see them!" Raffa yelled from the crow's nest. "Definitely a military boat."

No helicopters, no drones. Either too expensive or they'd been expended already. Still impossible to see the flag, but Peter was still certain it was an Indian Navy destroyer. They had churned past Little Nicobar's dead-forest-clad beaches, and its stretches of sandbanks that poked above the surface of the sea in flat reefs.

They kept close to the line of Great Nicobar's northern coast, to keep out of visual range of their pursuer. The island's vast curtains of rainforest and mangroves—skeletons of their former selves, dead brown leaves coated in ash—still shrouded a maze of inlets, coves, and bights. They kept the engine throttled high, and at Ufuk's insistence, headed for Murray Point at the north, every last morsel of speed eked from the protesting engine that ticked and chugged at a pace that seemed impossible to maintain.

"They'll be able to see us again soon," Ufuk said.

"If we turn the corner," Peter said, "head south, they won't see us in time. The line of the coast covers us here. If they don't see us, they'll have no way of knowing where we are. But we need to make Murray Point before they reach the buff at the southern tip of Little Nicobar."

"And," Jess said, "will we make it?" She noticed the Delta force guy, Foster, at the bow of the boat with the machine gun already out.

Peter shrugged. "It's going to be close."

"How far then to Ranganatha Bay?"

"We should get there before they turn at Murray Point."

"How far in do you intend to go?" Ufuk said.

"See these small coves, like spread fingers?" Peter gestured to the charts. "Far enough that we're well away from the mouth of the river, but close enough we make a run for it if we have to." He pointed to one in particular, that arced away from the main river. "But good chance they're going to catch us."

"Then we get as many of us off the boat as we can," Massarra said. "Jessica and myself. You men stay. Our presence would be unusual."

Their cover story was a calculated ploy. Prior to Nomad, the international fishing industry occupied the same shadowy landscape as organized crime. Plausible that a trawler like this one, before Nomad, would have crew that were not actually Chinese, despite the markings.

"What will you say if they catch you?" Ufuk asked.

Peter replied, "A destroyer comes our way, what *can* you say? We were afraid. And we are."

"And the pickup trucks?" Jess said.

"Brought with us for trading. You take the weapons and our portable electronics. Anything that could identify us."

"I get the idea."

"Good."

He gestured to the mouth of a narrow inlet. Gnarled trees hung low over the rippling water. "There's a narrow channel leading out. Too shallow for the trawler, but not the skiff. Make a run for it." One of his tiny drones was in the air. He checked the images scrolling in from its cameras. "That stream leads back out to the main river and on to a half-dozen other tributaries. Use the walkie-talkies to communicate if we have to. By then, it won't matter if someone is monitoring the channels."

In a hurry, Jess and Massarra and Raffa cleared the interior of the trawler, loading the most critical equipment and weapons onto a skiff they lowered into the water. Massarra climbed over the gunwale first and helped Jess into the smaller boat. They started the boat's outboard engine and wheeled the boat around, darted straight into the cover of the mangroves.

Peter waited outside the wheelhouse, watching them.

Something caught his attention because he turned sharply. Jess followed his gaze. A sudden movement at the stern, on the deck behind the second skiff. Raffa climbed down from the mast and ran to the wheelhouse.

Conversation passed between them, and Peter turned and waved wildly to her. She couldn't make out what it was he was trying to say and was about to shout when he drew a fist up and waved a flat hand at his throat. He gestured to the other end of the cove and held two fingers up.

"Two more boats?" Massarra whispered, more for Jess's benefit than trying to talk to Peter.

"How could they have found us this fast?" Jess muttered. "Let's haul the skiff up and onto the bank. Quick!"

They maneuvered the small boat into the narrower channel, concealed behind some over-hanging mangrove trees, and jumped out onto the muddy bank. They pulled it up, ensuring the dense foliage covered it. Jess took a rifle and handed one to Massarra. They double-backed along the bank, behind the forest's leafy wall, and ducked down low at a position where they could see the trawler.

She was stunned to see Giovanni lowering the other skiff into the water. Peter was already in it. At the same time, Ufuk and Raffa manhandled fuel drums onto the winch and lowered them into the skiff.

"What are they thinking?" Massarra muttered. "We need that fuel."

"Look," Jess said, as two boats appeared at one end of the river's inlet.

The first might once have been a river ferry of some kind. A long passenger boat with a small truck on its main deck, and two yellow cranes at the back. Tires flanked either side—easy fenders. Rust tarnished the paintwork so it was difficult to tell what color it might once have been. Four men walked the sides, skirting the cabin area, Kalashnikov assault rifles in their hands.

Not Indian Navy, not at all. Local pirates. Maybe they saw the trawler making its way along the coast and watched it turn into Ranganatha Bay. They knew it was trapped.

The second boat was smaller, a day-tripper for river tours built for days when tourism was the major source of income. More colorful than its partner, red and white, a party boat. More armed men walked its decks.

Peter maneuvered the skiff away from the trawler and powered it toward Jess's side of the river, but a hundred yards up stream. The fuel drums were visible over the top of the skiff. At least five of them.

The trawler's engines sputtered to life and it began moving again.

"What are they doing?" Massarra said.

"Bait," Jess said. "Peter is offering an easy target."

The trawler's engines roared. The dirty-brown water of the river roiled white behind it. It surged forward, gathering speed.

Peter's skiff reached the bank, beneath overhanging mangroves. He jumped out. Jess lost sight of him in the closely packed foliage.

The radio crackled beside her. Peter's voice, talking to Giovanni: "Get going. In a minute, they'll be too pre-occupied to notice you."

Gunfire erupted, echoed across the water. It was coming from Peter's direction. The pirates returned fire wildly into the forest. One of them caught a bullet in the face, his head spattering a puff of mist. He toppled into the river.

Massarra rose. "We need to get ready to help." They sprinted back through the forest, over exposed roots and between twisted trunks, and pushed their skiff back into the water.

Jess glanced behind her as she got in. The crack of gunfire. The trawler turned sharply, surprising the attackers, and cut a path between the other two. The ferry swung around to chase. The smaller boat, the river tourer, made its way toward Peter's skiff.

Massarra eased their boat forward toward the channel. "We need to get back to the river mouth."

"What about Peter?"

The skiff lurched forwards as Massarra swung back and forth through the maze of mangroves. "We have to trust he has a plan."

Through openings in the cover, Jess saw the river tourer had reached the bank, but Jess lost sight of it as they wound into a deep channel.

Gunfire again. Sharp, heavy cracks echoing through the trees. A long silence. An eruption of noise shattered it. The forest trembled. Not gunfire, but a single, rolling boom. An explosion.

Massarra's eyes narrowed. "He blew the fuel."

Another explosion—immense and more violent than the first—seconds later. A rolling slug of thunder, followed a half minute later by a surge of water that almost toppled their skiff.

The radio crackled: "As soon as you reach the main river, stop and wait for me. I'm right behind you." It was Peter.

"Are you okay?" Giovanni answered. "The other boat has run off after we fired at them. Raffa used the fifty caliber."

"I'm good," Peter replied after a few second. Hesitation, breathing heavily. "We lost some fuel."

"Where are you?"

"On my way," Peter said, but short, hard breaths punctuated his words. "Keep to the channel and wait for me where it meets the main stretch of river. I'll find you." Jess thought she heard a sharper intake of breath.

She pressed the talk button on her walkie-talkie. "Peter, are you hurt?"

"Get to the river."

Massarra maneuvered the skiff beneath the mangroves, through a warren of gnarled roots that poked up through the surface of the channel. The small outboard whined. Jess scanned the undergrowth behind them, searching for signs of Peter.

"There's the river," Massarra said. "I'll pull in here and—"

A figure, running—stumbling, shambling—through the forest.

"There he is!" Jess pointed.

Staggering, arms out stretched, barely able to keep his balance. Coming for them. A crimson stain bloomed across his torso.

Jess got out of the skiff and splashed into the water. Peter came to her, his weapon slung over his back. She caught him as he fell into her arms. Heavy, weak, barely able to support his own weight. How much blood had he lost? The bottom of his shirt glistened wet and dark. Massarra helped drag him into the boat.

"Go!" Jess shouted.

Massarra gunned the engine, slamming the skiff forwards and into the main channel of the river.

"Head back," Peter coughed.

He curled into a fetal ball at the front of the boat. Jess leaned over him, pressing hard on his wound. Dark black blood oozed between her fingers. It was bad.

"The destroyer must have seen the explosion," Massarra said. "That was a good diversion. Clever."

"The tsunamis in the Indian Ocean raised the water levels," Peter grunted. "Flooded the place. Old charts are useless. Talk to Ufuk. We can get all the way to Campbell Bay, south of here."

Massarra wound the skiff at high speed, zigging and zagging through the narrow channels that eventually widened. It was guesswork as much as skill. Finally they tore into open water at the mouth of the river and spotted the trawler. Massarra drove the skiff toward the boat and spun it round as the bigger vessel drew alongside. Ufuk appeared from the wheelhouse. Giovanni was driving. Raffa up top in the crow's nest.

Where was the Delta guy, Foster?

"Keep moving," Jess yelled to Ufuk and Giovanni. "They'll regroup once they get over us fighting back."

"What about the skiff?"

Jess had her arm around Peter, urging him to the edge of the trawler. With her other hand, she took the line from the boat. "Tow it. We'll bring it in later."

"Bad?" Ufuk asked as he leaned down to help.

Peter groaned, his body almost limp between them.

"We need to get him into the mess." Jess turned to Massarra. "Can you keep us level?"

The Israeli nodded and urged her forward.

Jess tied the line from the bow of the boat to nets that Ufuk had thrown over the side. Then she went back to help push Peter and help lever him upward. He was pale, sweating hard. One hand held against his torso, stained by glistening blood. "Can you hang on?" she asked.

He reached an arm up to the lowered net and seized it, bending his arm through it. "I'm good," he grunted.

Ufuk hauled him over the rail. As they did, Ufuk shouted down to Massarra, "We need to take the next turn in the river. There's a tributary coming up. Giovanni will need to steer into that. You need to go with him."

Massarra gestured her understanding, and shouted: "Just keep hold of him!"

A crack of gunfire rolled along the river. A sting of air near Jess's face, a searing *whoosh* as a bullet raced past, striking the water ahead. The first boat, the ferry, appeared two hundred meters behind them. She steadied herself, raised her rifle and fired twice.

"Jess," Ufuk shouted. "Your turn."

Another bullet fizzed past.

Jess slung her rifle back and climbed. Raffa had come down from the crow's nest and helped her. Ufuk carried the stumbling Peter away. Another shot, closer now. As she swung her prosthetic leg over the side, the moment she reached the top. Raffa grabbed her. "Skiff's tied," he said.

She ran to the back of the trawler, past the housing for the pickup, found cover and fired again. Barely a few seconds passed before the empty skiff swung into view to tug along behind the trawler. Massarra ducked inside the wheelhouse behind her.

Thank God.

The curve of the river cut away line of sight to the river pirates, trees masking them for at least another few minutes. She ran back to the wheelhouse.

"Where's Peter?" she asked Giovanni.

He nodded down at the crew quarters.

"And the Delta guy, Paul?"

Giovanni flicked his chin to the stern. An inert body lay in a pool of blood.

Jess kept her eyes on the body and said, "Campbell Bay. We're faster than them."

When Jess made to go downstairs, Giovanni shook his head. "Ufuk is with Peter. Help Raffa pull in the skiff. We can't waste fuel dragging it behind us. It needs to be on board."

Jess stole a quick look down the stairs.

"There's nothing you can do for him," Giovanni said.

She went to the stern of the trawler to find Raffa winching in the skiff. She took over and he helped maneuver the skiff on-board as the winch whined and dragged it upward. Once it was secured on the housing of the pickup, she sprinted back to the wheelhouse, Raffa close behind. She slid down the stairs.

Ufuk leaned back from Peter's quiet body. "He's gone."

4

Northern Mongolia

Even before Nomad, Ulan Bator had been the world's coldest capital city, with arguably the worst traffic as well—car-eating potholes were the norm, year-round ice and snow. The city now arrived around Zasekin and Timur without gentleness—low buildings gave way sharply to taller ones, the traffic intensified—trucks and pickups belching diesel fumes. The cacophony grew louder, grated on their ears that were used to the serene quiet of the birch and pine forests. Zasekin liked better the comfortable roar of the Czilim's engines.

This was different.

Zasekin knew this area well after a year of studying it. During their reconnaissance, he noticed very few lights illuminated within the city after dark, apart from the flickering orange glow of fires used to keep warm.

He checked his watch. The walk in took less time than they anticipated, leaving them hours before the curfew kicked in. Better to be moving away from the city at that time, under cover of darkness, than to be forced to look for somewhere to stay within it. They had taken pistols, leaving the Kalashes behind with Misha and Evgeny. Pistols they could conceal, but assault rifles spoke to a more aggressive intent.

They kept to the main road that cut through the eighth *khoroo* toward a roundabout at which a domed building sat. Probably a *stupa*, Zasekin thought. Surrounding it and beyond it, tall apartment buildings in poor condition climbed into the smudged-orange skyline. To one side, shanty huts built against its walls now overtook what might once have been a mini-mall, and *ger*-like shelters were strewn about its car park. Few paid much attention to him and Timur as they walked, huddled against the bitter wind.

In the socialist period, especially following the Second World War, Soviet-style blocks of flats, usually financed by the Kremlin, had replaced most of the old *ger* districts. The Trans Mongolian Railway, connecting Ulaanbaatar with Moscow and Beijing, was completed in the sixties, Zasekin remembered, and with it came the advent of modernity—cinemas, theaters, museums, and mini-markets were built.

Zasekin found what he was looking for. Bratva looked the same everywhere: Moscow, St Petersburg, Irkutsk, even here.

Dark-colored, high-end SUV vehicles and Humvees, still glittering in perfect condition even after the destruction of Nomad and the chaos that followed after it. Leather jackets that bulged beneath the arm over concealed weapons. The flash of Breitling or Rolex on the wrist. The swagger of the brutally affluent and savage. Beneath the immaculate lines, the tattoos on hard skin. The marks that told the story of the individual's violence. The eight-pointed star denoting rank, the *vory*. Churches with cupolas to denote convictions, sun's rays to mark years spent in prison. Tattooed skulls to cheer murders committed.

Zasekin studied them, but not too hard. These men saw into a man's soul, sensed his weaknesses. Timur kept his distance from across the street, equally cautious by his stance.

Three of Bratva stood casually, improbably relaxed by the side of two dark Mercedes. They smoked and beat their feet against the cold. Behind them a diffuse glow from the restaurant's lead-lined windows spilled onto the street. Zasekin did not doubt he was in Ulan Bator, but at that moment, watching those criminals, it could have been Moscow ten years ago as easily as here.

He approached in the open.

They saw him early.

Their stance straightened, more alert now to the stranger with broad shoulders and who carried himself in a way they recognized and understood. A man who could handle himself, who was not afraid of them or of violence. One of them, the youngest and lowest ranking, came round the Mercedes. All would be low ranking, out here in the cold like this, but this one needed to prove himself. This one could not be seen as weak in front of his brothers.

He shifted aside his jacket to reveal the machine pistol. His face took on a countenance of twisted smugness, contempt and amusement for the figure foolish enough to approach them without permission.

"You're in the wrong place," he said in Russian. Not shouted exactly, but loud enough.

Push it, Zasekin thought. He kept walking forward. Show them no fear. Respect will come later.

The young man's face lost its contempt. The amusement faded. It went blank. The expression of a killer when murder teased his mind. His hand went to the machine pistol.

Zasekin stopped. "I know where I am," he said in Russian. His accent would mark him as southern Siberian. "And I have good reason to be here."

"I'm not interested in your reasons." The man was on him now, the machine pistol drawn but held low. "You know who I am?"

"I know what you are. That is why I am here. We have items to barter, that will bring you profit. I'm paying my respects."

Zasekin gestured to his coat and waited for the younger man to assent. When the short nod came, the machine pistol still waiting by his side, Zasekin reached in. The two men by the car came alive and tensed, canted their heads to watch more closely.

Zasekin pulled out a tin of Asian fruit from the Terelj hotel storeroom. He couldn't say what the image wrapped around it was of—he doubted this slightly rusted thing in his hand would have impressed anyone a few months ago.

But here, now, the younger man eyed it—and nodded.

He led Zasekin toward the restaurant. The two other men watched him, still rigid but more relaxed. The younger one opened the door and said: "You said we."

"I'm not alone," Zasekin replied.

By now, Timur would be out of sight. Bathed in shadow, but still capable of intervening if they tried anything out here. But once Zasekin was inside, there would be nothing Timur could do if it all went wrong.

The younger man waited, his body barring the way. "Who else?"

"They'll wait for me. In case anything happens. If I don't come out, well—" Zasekin tailed off and shrugged. "But I'm sure there won't be a problem."

The younger man offered him a smile without warmth and stepped aside.

The moment the door opened, a billowing of luxurious warmth rolled over Zasekin. He followed the younger man between tables set for dinner, some occupied, most not. The plush carpet sank beneath his feet. Soft music echoed, piped through a tinny system in the ceiling. Urns cast in gold glinted welcomingly. The diners were dressed smartly and maneuvered silver cutlery on fine china as they cut though steak and borscht. Vibrant colors on plates and across the walls. Aromas that Zasekin hadn't smelled in longer than he could remember overpowered him, of burnt butter and fresh bread. Before he realized it, he had taken off his hat and held it to his chest.

And became conscious of his ripped trousers.

Stained coat.

The peasant coming in to see the masters.

At a long table in the back, set aside in a quiet room by itself, what might once have been called the chef's table, sat an older man accompanied by others. Beneath neatly coiffured hair, his weathered face gleamed. Heavy, portly, but powerful-looking. He, too, was dressed for dinner, expensively and wantonly. No thought given to the cold outside, or to those starving in this city.

What did the Bratva care about such things?

Zasekin was told to wait. The younger man approached the table. The older man ignored him and continued eating. Long seconds passed, the unease in Zasekin's gut roiling. Finally the man turned his gaze to the younger, examining the offered tin, then to Zasekin. He raised a hand and gestured for him to approach. Zasekin did so, slowly, with deference.

The man laid down his cutlery and leaned back. Hard, thick hands that had known suffering, had lived through the gulags, and which had inflicted their own pain. A muscled neck and the slight, faded tint of a tattoo that crept up from beneath his collar. The light made ghosts of his eyes, or maybe it wasn't the light at all.

Zasekin already knew what he was. The *Vor*, the Russian mafia chieftain.

"Where did you get this?" the Vor asked.

He spoke in Russian, so Zasekin replied that way: "We're camped away from the city. There's more of that. Far more."

"Where?"

Zasekin remained still. "I'd be a fool to tell you that."

Slowly, lingering over every word, the Vor said: "You'd be a fool not to."

Zasekin did not respond. He waited, every second stretching out. The younger man shifted beside him.

The Vor asked: "What do you want in return?"

"A place to stay in the city. A house will do, or five rooms in an apartment building. Somewhere near here, where we can feel at home and not be bothered. Some work, if you can use us."

"I don't know you. I don't employ people I don't know."

"Something small then, to build trust."

"You look like police to me."

Zasekin scoffed. "We are the 103rd Missile Brigade in Ulan Ude," he said slowly, lying carefully. "But there's no Army anymore. I haven't heard from Command since the event. I don't know if Major General Kovalenko is still alive. We work for ourselves now."

Ulan Ude was the base for the 36th Army of the Eastern Military District, where Zasekin had started his military career.

Zasekin took a calculated gamble that the Bratva would have more respect—and use—for an Army unit than simple border guards. The 103rd Missile Brigade had housed mechanized infantry, including tank and motor rifle brigades. It also held the intercontinental ballistic missiles that gave the brigade its name. Ulan Ude was the other side of Lake Baikal to Irkutsk and water-based maneuvers had often required an SVR presence. Zasekin believed he knew enough of the city and its military to hold on to the threads of the ruse. Or rather, he hoped he did. The army was far more corruptible, especially where the Bratva were concerned, than SVR were.

The old man nodded, listening to Zasekin. He pursed his lips, and then after a few seconds made his decision: "Kirill will deal with you from now on. Once you have delivered, he will find you a place. A good place. When you're settled in, we will speak again." The Vor gestured again, dismissed him.

Zasekin turned and left with the younger man, Kirill.

Back outside, and the cold bit into him. Kirill said they had to wait, so he stamped his feet and waited. Kirill stopped beside him, but at a far enough distance to look him up and down, to get a measure, or perhaps to make clear that they weren't together.

"You're Armed Forces?" Zasekin said as he lit a cigarette.

Kirill's blank-faced stare revealed hostility if nothing else.

"I knew men at Ulan Ude. Good men. Tankmen. You know the song, Mr. Tankman, heh? You still sing that song?"

"I'm not a tankman. And Ulan Ude is a big place. I don't know your friends."

Kirill took a long draw on the cigarette. Two other Bratva came over and stood either side of Zasekin. "I think you are lying, Mr. Tankman. I don't think you're Army."

"I can't help what you think. I want to trade, and so does your Vor. So let's not make this into a thing it doesn't have to be, eh?"

"Come with me," Kirill said after a long pause. "You need sleep."

"I *need* to get back to my people."

Kirill reached forward with a cupped hand and slapped Zasekin's cheek, gently but menacingly, twice. "You'll see them tomorrow. We're friends now, yes?" He turned away, and with a raised voice, presumably so anyone listening would hear, repeated: "Friends now."

Kirill led him away. Zasekin followed, not looking to either side for Timur in case they saw him, but gesturing with his hand. The three Bratva would not notice a subtle movement, he hoped.

Timur would understand.

If he saw it.

5

Yellow Sea, Dalian, China
April 7th

Jess perched at the trawler's bow, sea spray biting against her face, the wind cutting through even the thick layers of her commercial fishing waterproofs, the cold seeping deep into her bones. She barely felt it all over the building tension in her gut.

Every day became more dangerous as they approached China.

As best as they could estimate, the coast of Korea lay fifty miles to the east. The black water of the Yellow Sea chopped at the bow, rising and heaving, the waves tipped with white under churning brown clouds. The sun's rays weren't strong enough to break through the pall even at midday. They were skirting up past the point of Dalian. All intel said that the coastal areas were destroyed, but Beijing was still active. After a year, people had started to come back down out of the hills. They saw Chinese Navy ships heading south, but also trawlers, like theirs, moving in packs, trying to find food in what was left in the ocean's depth.

Peter's cover idea of using the trawler was clever.

They'd dumped Peter's body—and the Delta team guy Foster—somewhere off the coast of Vietnam. Since the pirate attack two weeks ago, things had been quiet. Jess felt an utter sense of loneliness, leaving Peter in the middle of nowhere in a black ocean. No matter how she'd been angry with him; it paled in this final act.

Colonel Hague had been furious when they'd finally relayed the message. He'd tried to call off the mission, but his superiors forced him to keep it going, or at least that was the impression they managed to piece together after a sporadic series of communications.

Part of it, Jess was sure, was that Roger refused to cooperate unless Jess was involved. He said it was to help her, but then Roger was dragging her across half the world. He said he could give her Hector, but was he just using him as bait? Even worse, was Roger working for Müller? Was this all a trap? What did Roger want? Was it just to make up for the past? For betraying her father, who'd treated him like his own son?

She'd hated Peter, detested him, but now he was gone, she realized how much she missed him and even trusted him. Now she was left with Ufuk and Roger, the two key hinges her future depended on, two men she detested.

But then beggars didn't get to be choosers.

The further east they ventured, the sky seemed to clear more often. Never enough to see blue sky above, or a carpet of stars shine overhead in the night, but enough that the clouds cleared from time to time, and to see some stars shine through. When it did, they saw Saturn on the horizon each clear night, rising into the sky. Each night the dot grew larger, grew brighter.

Jess gave up staring into the mist off the bow of the trawler and walked to the back of the boat, up the interior stairs and into the deck. Ufuk was there, piloting the boat, staring at one of his tablets duct-taped to the old woodwork.

"How much further?"

"Tomorrow, maybe."

"Maybe?"

"Maybe the day after. Hard to estimate the ocean currents, and very little in visual reference."

Sea charts were near useless, so much of the coast re-sculpted by the successions of tidal waves and tsunamis that tore anything near the coasts apart. They kept out of sight of land ever since the pirate encounter, never passing close enough to land to witness the scale of the destruction, adopting a course that took them between the Paracel Islands and the Philippines. As far away from what remained of national borders and firmly within international waters. Until now.

"And there is a team waiting for us?"

"Once we get closer, we can activate the radio frequency beacon. That will let us converge on each other. Old school style. Some new intel did come in when you were asleep, over the encrypted short wave."

Communications were sporadic and depended on the good graces of an undependable ionosphere to bounce and skip certain frequencies of radio waves around the planet.

Jess waited. The boat thumped through one swell after another. A twinge in her stomach. Why was he making her wait for the news? "Is it bad?"

"Good news. The Carl Vinson and George Washington aircraft carriers have made it back into San Diego. They're almost ready to leave again. Seven million civilians on board six thousand ships. Boggles the imagination."

"Why didn't you just say that right away?"

"There are five American carrier groups active now. The Gerald Ford limped across the Indian Ocean and has stationed itself off Perth." He paused to make clear the good news was done. "The second bit of news, I'm afraid, isn't quite so great. The Peoples' Liberation Army has declared a sort of war—"

"*Sort* of war?"

"If the Americans return with this armada of aircraft carriers. The Chinese have whipped themselves into a frenzy, saying that they've been lenient enough, that millions of Americans were allowed into this hemisphere, but the Carl Vinson battle group cannot return to stay in Australia."

"It's not a battle group, for God's sake. They're saving those peoples' lives. They'll die if they don't evacuate them."

A large wave crashed into the starboard bow, sending a sheeting wave of water thudding against the deck's windscreen. The boat pitched to one side, but Jess and Ufuk remained perfectly upright. Weeks of sea legs. What Peter had said back in Oman, about the sea becoming the new battlefield, the landscape on which military might was sculpted, was accurate. Just as in the Bay of Bengal with the Indian destroyer, Chinese warships patrolled the South and East China Seas. They had seen at least three having steered away from the Gulf of Thailand and followed the coast of Vietnam, and there was no way of knowing how many submarines skulked in the quiet gloom beneath them. They had been fortunate to have only encountered that one pirate vessel.

"What did Donnelly say?" Jess said.

"Your new President Donnelly has invoked one treaty after another claiming their rights, of course all leading to the statement that they will use the ultimate option, if forced to."

Another wave crashed into the boat. They swayed back and forth together.

"Do you really have the resources inside Sanctuary China to pull this off?" Jess asked.

"Together with Roger, I think so."

The noise of the engine groaned in the background.

"President Donnelly desperately needs what I have, Jessica. There is a bright future for you, I promise." Ufuk kept his eyes straight ahead on the heaving seas.

"In Australia? It seems…impossible right now."

"Trust me. It's going to be amazing." Ufuk's eyes were on Jess now, and seemed to twinkle in the dim light, or maybe it was the reflection from the light of his tablet.

Trust me, was the wrong thing to say. Jess felt her blood pressure rise, her cheeks flushing involuntarily at his words. "Trust you? I'm *watching* you, Ufuk. That's what I'm doing."

"This communications gear coming into orbit from Mars First, it guarantees *your* safety, Jessica. Through *me*. And it will guarantee the safety of those millions of your people in New America."

New America. That was what they were already calling Western Australia. Jess wondered what the Australians thought of that. "Those are your people, too. You're an American citizen."

Ufuk smiled and acknowledged the point. "You know Massarra knew about Peter? You know that, don't you?"

"She said she knew who he was. She must have spotted him in Al-Jawf."

Ufuk laughed. "She was the one who contacted the CIA station in Cairo, through Mossad, and had him sent to Al-Jawf. Did you not know that?"

Jess held on to the doorframe as the boat swayed back and forth in the waves, trying to process what game Ufuk was playing now. "You mean Peter knew she sent for him? They knew each other?"

"That's not what I mean. She sent an anonymous message. Told the CIA to be there in Al-Jawf and to look for me there."

"Look for *you*?" The realization crept into Jess's mind. "So you didn't know?"

Ufuk stared straight ahead.

"You killed Peter, didn't you?"

"Don't be ridiculous."

"When I brought him on the boat, he was injured, but not…what did you do to him?"

"I did nothing."

"Nothing?"

"I mean, I did my best to save him, but the man lost a lot of blood. He went into shock. There was nothing I could do."

"And what about our Delta team member? I asked everyone. They say they didn't see how he got shot?"

Ufuk stared straight ahead at the churning ocean. "Be careful with the accusations you make, Jessica."

"Coffee?"

Jess turned to see Giovanni beside her, holding a steaming cup.

Three hours before, she'd come to a grudging silence with Ufuk. Maybe she shouldn't have accused him of killing Peter, but she wasn't sure what the man was capable of. She'd wanted to look in his eyes, see his reaction—but there hadn't been any. She offered to take over the watch and pilot the boat. Three hours of being by herself while everyone else slept. She hadn't heard Giovanni approach over the roar of the waves. A white noise she'd come to appreciate.

He held out the cup and she took it. "The closer we get to China's coast, the more chance we'll be stopped." He looked at Ufuk's tablet. The night before, they'd put a drone up on the air, scanning ahead and back of them as they reached solid ground.

"How long until we pass Dalian?"

"Maybe two hours." Again, it was a best guess. "We're on a course that makes it clear we have no intention of steering for the port."

Silence between them. Just the slap of the ocean against the boat. It wasn't true that her future hinged between two men she detested. It also rested upon one man she cared deeply for.

Giovanni said finally: "You should eat. And sleep, if you can. There's no telling when you'll get to sleep again."

"Haven't been able to for days."

"At least try. Let me take over."

The derelict Guanglu Island was their first sight of land in days.

They took a course close to its coastline, to remain concealed for as long as possible. Once the island must have bustled with farmers and holiday-trippers from the Liaodong Peninsula—now nothing remained but silence.

Jess did see a few boats, but all were wrecks, overturned on the reefs, or broken on the beaches. Hotels and settlements on the coastal promontories were utterly razed by the violence of the waves. Shattered roofs poked above flooded plains, and here and there the scattered remains of marinas. A frigid ghost of anemic mist hung over the black water.

The gurgling growl of the trawler's engine at low throttle echoed in the dead silence. The boat cut a course across the mirror-flat water between Haixan and Saili Islands, through more furling mist south of Dachangshan. The destroyed remains of luxury resorts appeared and disappeared in silhouette through the fog. They threaded a path between the ruined stanchions of the Changshn Bridge, where a single car balanced on the edge of the broken roadway, waited with its door open. A close call? Had someone escaped?

Jess's imagination ran away with itself in the quiet fog.

They changed course after Dawangjia Island, bearing more toward the north. Toward the flooded agricultural estuary of the Huli River. Jess took an opportunity to get some dreamless sleep.

"Giovanni!" Ufuk yelled from the deck. "Slow the engines."

The rumble of the engines diminished, the noise of the waves subsiding as they slid into the mouth of the river. Ufuk leaned over the gunwale, a hook in his hand, and then heaved back. A yellow submersible drone appeared from the dark waters and thumped onto the deck.

Ufuk gave the thumbs up. "Okay."

He'd made sure that Jess was in a deep sleep when he retrieved his prize. It was easier to ask forgiveness than beg permission.

Giovanni ran the trawler aground on a flooded farmer's field, as close to the Binhai Highway at Dongtuozi as he could. The ruined farmland sank beneath the hull before the boat finally settled crunched against ice lining the edges. Jess climbed down, splashing through the thin layer of top ice into a gray marshy mess up to her knees. The heavy waders that came up to her chest protected her, but it was still freezing cold. Giovanni followed with Raffa.

"Will the truck be able to get through this?" she said. "Maybe we need to drive the boat harder into the shore."

"We lay down supports," Giovanni said. "Get it over to the road."

Jess scanned her eyes back and forth into the hazy distance. Everything was half-frozen, a frost-snow across the ground. From the haze, a group of men approached. Raffa and Massarra brought up their weapons.

Ufuk held up a hand, urging them to lower their weapons. "These are our contacts."

The men walking toward them waved. Not American, but Chinese.

Ufuk looked at the tablet in his hand. "Roger Hargate and Abbie Barnes have confirmed that we're on target with our plan. They have a way in. The extraction team from the Navy convoy reached Vladivostok. Now we just have to cross a thousand miles and get to Sanctuary China."

Jess took her first step forward onto Chinese soil. "Hector, I'm coming," she whispered, low enough that nobody but herself could hear.

6

Sanctuary China
April 8th

"Simon," Dr. Hermann Müller said, addressing a blank white wall. "This is Hector. I believe you've met before."

The wall seemed to shudder, transforming into a swirling oval vortex of sepia and gray that gradually darkened at the top. Two pools of black appeared near the middle above a smear of pink. The face coalesced and solidified, the eyes piercing blue, the mouth smiling gently, but the edges of the images shifting back and forth, never at rest.

"We have," Simon answered, the lips of the face on the wall screen timed with the disembodied, vaguely European-sounding voice. "Nice to see you again." The smile twitched. "So to speak."

"Don't be shy," Müller said to Hector, turning and half-crouching to face the boy. "Go ahead and answer."

"Hello Simon," Hector replied, his eyes downcast.

He held tightly onto Roger's hand, his small knuckles white. Roger knelt and held Hector's waist. "It's okay. You know Simon? Why don't you two talk?"

Hector clearly didn't want to, but was smart enough to realize this wasn't a request. "Okay." He nodded unenthusiastically.

"Great. I'm just going to go into the next room with Hermann. Just call out if you need me," Roger said.

"Okay," Hector repeated, his voice even quieter.

Müller led Roger out of the twenty-foot square, eggshell white room into the exterior corridor, where two guards stood watch. Sanctuary Europe personnel, Roger noted from their uniforms—and Caucasian faces—before he followed Müller into the room next door. A silvered mirror connected the two rooms, and they watched Hector sit down on one of the aluminum chairs in the middle of the room.

"Do you want to play a game?" they heard Simon asking from the next room, his voice muted.

Hector nodded. The wall screen to his right erupted in a splash of color, tiny icons flying across it. The lights reflected off

119

Müller's wire-framed glasses as he studied the interaction of the boy and the machine.

"Do you have anything new to report?" Müller said.

He and Roger were alone in the connecting room. Behind them a row of wooden desks, each with a black monitor and chair. An LED clock glowed in bright red numerals over the silvered glass wall. 37:06:32. The seconds counted down. It took Roger a second to figure what it meant.

The days and hours until the start of the Saturn intercept.

"Nothing really new," Roger replied, his eyes stuck on the countdown clock. "He basically hides in his room all day, playing games on that tablet."

"And you've looked at the games?"

"As you have. Analyzed the keywords, the passwords, the sequences, the actions…doesn't seem to be pattern."

"Keep on it."

Müller took off his glasses to wipe them, an action Roger knew always prefaced an attempt to convince him of something.

"You know how important this is," Müller said. He put his glasses back on. "We need to access Ufuk Erdogmus's networks. The boy's DNA is keyed as one of the three components."

"Something you are, something you know, and something you have," Roger said, repeating the security mantra. "And Hector is the something you are."

Müller held up shiny plastic cards he'd recovered from Tanzania. The overhead lighting danced off the holograms inscribed on their surface. "And we have the keys. We just need to know what the passwords are."

"Have you found the facility yet?" Roger asked. Müller was convinced Ufuk was hiding a secret facility somewhere nearby to Sanctuary China. It was something he needed to know as well, if this was just some fantasy or misdirection of Müller.

"That's why we need to crack Simon."

The door to the room opened. One of the guard's heads appeared, about to ask a question, but Müller motioned for him to let whoever it was in.

Abbie Barnes walked through the door, her brown bob swaying to one side as she held out her hand to shake Roger's hand.

120

"Nice to see you again. How's Hector?" She turned to the silvered glass.

Her father, General Marshall, entered the room behind her, his face tight, his jaw muscles clenched. "Dr. Müller," he said formally, not extending his hand but standing at attention and nodding his greeting. "Roger," he added as an afterthought.

"Why don't you two go in and interact with Simon and Hector?" Müller said to Roger and Abbie. "I think it will help relax him."

It was more than a suggestion, and Roger and Abbie excused themselves, exited the room and appeared on the other side of the glass, the both of them joining in greeting Hector, who ran over and wrapped both arms around Abbie's knees.

"He seems to have taken to your daughter," Müller said.

"Isn't having this...*thing*...Simon, dangerous to have operating inside of Sanctuary?" Marshall shifted his feet, planting them shoulder-width apart and squaring his body to face Müller.

"We need to study him"—Müller cocked his head and corrected himself—"*it*. This *thing* is the key to Erdogmus's systems, and not only that, but to accessing and taking control of Mars First and its precious cargo."

Müller had made a copy of Simon when they infiltrated Erdogmus's Tanzanian facility. They'd been forced to retreat, the job only half-done, but considering what they'd gained, Müller considered the operation a great success.

"I understand the importance, but what if Simon gets loose?"

"That is a danger, I agree, but we are not foolish. All the servers Simon is running on are totally disconnected from any outside connections or networks. More than that, there is an enforced ten-foot air gap between the servers and any outside electronics. We are treating Simon as we would a virulent infection, completely isolated for study."

Marshall exhaled.

"The Chinese are expert in informational security, General. If we can crack Simon, we can stop this madman Erdogmus. Thousands of people died in Sanctuary Europe. We might be in a position to influence Chairman Zemin, if *we* have control of Mars First."

"Who haven't responded to you since Tanzania." The General shifted his weight onto one foot, away from Müller. "So Zemin has been confirmed as the new Chairman of the Politburo?"

"And Roger Donnelly has been confirmed as the new President of the United States. At least with the governments coming back into some kind of order, perhaps we will be able to put the brakes on this political disaster from unfolding?"

"The Chinese have someone inside Mars First," Marshall said.

"Major Peng Shouang, I know."

"Have they been in touch with her?"

"That, I don't know."

"There's too much we don't know."

"But much that we do," Müller said.

The General looked down at the floor. "So we know they are coming? Jessica Rollins and Ufuk Erdogmus are on their way here?"

"From what our intelligence tells us." Müller didn't look at Marshall, but kept his eyes on Roger and Abbie in the next room. Hector was now sitting on Abbie's lap.

"I hate using my daughter as bait," Marshall said, following Müller's eyes.

"I understand, but she can't know we're watching her. You cannot tell her. She's not sophisticated enough to lie, and she's doing a beautiful job as it is."

"And does Roger know?"

"Of course not."

Marshall's jaw muscles clenched and unclenched. "Shouldn't we tell our Chinese counterparts?"

"That the Americans are about to try and invade? Do you want to start an all-out war? And we have more leverage than you think. More than just Roger and Abbie are involved in this...subterfuge. They think they are doing the right thing, and I don't blame them."

"The Chinese will find out anyway. We are going to have to answer for this."

"By which point we will have contained the situation, and gained an important advantage."

"You hope." Marshall pinched the bridge of his nose between his index and forefinger, his head tilted toward the floor. "I am not sure which of you is worse."

"We are on the side of the right in this," Müller replied. "Remember that. Our American friends just don't know who they are dealing with. The depths of Erdogmus's deceptions. We will soon demonstrate this, and save that American convoy."

"And does Erdogmus have this"—the General searched for the right word—"*package*? The thing from Tanzania?"

"I am not sure yet."

The General straightened up. "Jessica has to know she's walking into a trap. She's not stupid. Neither is Ufuk."

"And yet they are coming, anyway."

"Which should give you something to think about."

"I am thinking about it, General."

Dr. Müller waited for General Marshall to leave before he sat down at one of the desks behind him. He clicked on a computer, the screen in front of him glowing to life. It was a risk, meeting like this, having these kinds of conversations inside of Sanctuary China. His counterparts had assured him of his complete privacy, which of course he discounted. He'd been one of the ones to design these complexes, and he'd managed to save most of his technical team from Sanctuary Europe.

In this warren of offices, where he'd installed the disconnected Simon, his team had erected more than just an air-gapped security fence for the offending Erdogmus technology. It was also a haven for his own private networks, where he'd disconnected any other outside connections.

And also a place where he could speak to the outside world.

He tuned in the computer to select a narrow frequency band radio to the outside and waited. A few minutes later, a voice answered.

"Hello?" the voice answered in heavily accented English.

"*Privet*, comrade," Müller answered in Russian. "So your men are ready?"

7

Ulan Bator
Mongolia

Snow fell, huge flakes that drifted, travelers from the sky. The Bratva men took Zasekin to a Mercedes G-Wagon with blacked-out windows, parked on a side street away from the restaurant. A neon sign in the alleyway announced, "Attila Lounge," with another sign pointing down a dark set of stairs. The strip clubs—whorehouses—were still drawing customers. Zasekin wondered how they paid. Gold coin? Blood? Perhaps both?

Not for the first time, he marveled with grudging admiration at the Bratva's ability to maintain a fleet of polished vehicles, and run their businesses, even as the world around them crumbled. They ushered him into the back of the vehicle, accompanied by the taller of the three, while Kirill took the front, silently watching through the window as the windswept and frozen streets of Ulan Bator blurred into nothing beside him.

He had seen nothing of Timur and hoped his friend understood what was taking place and would not consider any reckless action in response.

When they pulled up, it was at a high-rise block with crumbling stucco and blackened walls, all stained by indecipherable graffiti. In the parking lot outside fires burned in trashcans. Huddled shadows gathered around the flames.

Kirill led and the other Bratva walked to either side of him. Neither said a word.

At the entrance to the building's lobby, where two more Bratva nodded to Kirill as he passed by, the world seemed to slow and grow sharp to Zasekin's eyes. His heart beat faster. The door he stepped through and closed behind him felt like the door to a prison, and his jailers were leading him to his cell.

Loitering in the lobby were vacant husks of humans, staring ahead from puss-rimmed bloodshot eyes in hollowed-out sockets, wringing their hands and shifting their feet. Addicts waiting for fixes. It didn't surprise him—if there was ever a time to disappear into the Neverland of drugs, this was it—and in that, the Bratva were only too happy to oblige.

Kirill pushed through a heavy door, past another blank-faced guard, and climbed the stairs. An acrid stench of stale urine filled the air, but also pungent and sickly sweet like rotting food or, perhaps—more likely—dead corpses stacked somewhere behind a closed but unlocked door.

They emerged into a hallway. At one end a woman smoked. Dressed for a certain type of work. Too-high platform heels, and too little clothing beneath a shabby long coat hastily thrown on. She glanced their way and, on seeing them approach, she stood straight up. She examined her cigarette and dropped it to the floor, stubbing it out.

Kirill turned to Zasekin and said: "You. Wait."

He went over to the woman, placing his hand on her side, just above the hip. A flicker of contempt crossed her face. Zasekin saw it because he had been trained to look for such things. Fortunately for her, Kirill, it appeared, had not seen it. It was brief, for a second later she moved into him, allowed him to touch her.

Kirill gestured to them and she led them inside. The corridor inside led to an apartment, the air inside stale with the musk-scent of human sweat. Sounds came from rooms—breathless, unmistakable sounds.

"Business is good," Zasekin observed.

Kirill snorted a braying laugh. "You will stay here tonight. In the morning I will come for you. If you do well, we will use you. If not..."

He gestured to an empty room at the end of the corridor. "Take a woman. I need to know you took a woman. Understand? I don't trust a man who cannot break a whore."

Kirill left with the other two mafia men. Zasekin said nothing, but moved past him into the room. He sat on the bed and, for a long while, did not move.

The door opened. A woman entered. He corrected himself. A girl. Not more than twenty. His throat was dry. His stomach knotted. She wore laddered stockings and heels so high she could barely keep her balance. A tiny G-string, frilled in lace and stained. She wore no bra or top. She shivered.

A Bratva stood behind her, leering. He gestured and said something that Zasekin didn't catch, or rather didn't care to hear. He shut the door.

The girl flinched but forced a smile.

Zasekin rose and offered her a blanket, stepped over to her, closer. She trembled like a hand-shy puppy. He wrapped the blanket around her.

"Sit," he commanded.

Unsure, she remained standing.

"I'm not going to hurt you." He gestured to the bed, the only place in the room she could sit. He moved away from it, tried to demonstrate his intent.

She sat and, inexplicably, surprisingly to him, began to sing softly.

He said nothing.

She continued to sing. It was a song he did not recognize, a child's lullaby in Russian. He watched her, saw the blanket slip as though she couldn't care what he saw of her.

"What's your family name?" he asked. When she didn't break away from her singing, he asked again. More gently, this time.

She did not look at him, but said: "Belenko."

"Where are you from?"

"Ivanivka."

"I don't know it, I'm sorry. You have a Ukrainian accent."

"Yes."

"How did you get here?"

Again she sang. Still she would not look at him, but instead stared at the door to the small room.

"Get into bed," he said.

She did not look at him as she unquestioningly obeyed. The sadness of it poisoned his heart. He undressed to his underwear and got in beside her. He took the blanket and wrapped it round her, a wall between his body and hers, and laid his head on the pillow. As he lay there, his eyes found on a half-burned candle on a dresser, puddles of hardened wax around it. He rose and lit it. Staring at the flames, he realized that he, Andrei Zasekin, was, for the first time in his life, afraid of darkness.

"Sleep, child," he said when he got back into the bed. "I won't let them come for you tonight."

126

When she did fall asleep, her breathing kept him awake for a while. He enjoyed listening to it. The rhythm gave him peace. He must have fallen asleep himself, for the next thing he heard was the door to the room open.

He awoke and stared at the sneering face of Kirill. The girl still slept.

"You know how much a whole night costs, Tankman? You'll need to do a lot of work to pay that off."

Zasekin fumbled beneath the blankets, as though pulling on his underwear. "Then we'd better get started," he said.

A car waited for them outside, swept by a cold wind. Not the G-Wagon, Zasekin noted. Instead, an older car. Dusty, layered like every other in rimy ash.

"You drive," Kirill said. "Drive slow. Do not draw attention to us."

"Park over there." Kirill gestured to a fenced off garden in which impromptu *gers* had been erected.

Built poorly, Zasekin noted. Those who occupied them were not Mongolian, not used to living that way. In this neighborhood they were not, for the faces he saw beneath hoods and wrapped scarves did not have the shape of the Mongol, but the smoother, less angular lines of the Chinese.

Across the gardens, parked on a street between high-rise buildings, a truck idled. Exhaust smoke billowed from its rear, where the cargo area stood open. On the tail lift, to one side and facing the street, a man sat with a machine pistol lying across his lap. Behind him, two more loaded boxes and crates onto the truck from a stack beside it.

"Who are they?" Zasekin said.

"Chinese," Kirill replied. "The Sun Yee On triad. The 14K and Wo Shing Wo have control of what is left of that city's business."

"What's in the boxes?"

"Nothing they are entitled to." Two women came from the lobby of the building beside which the truck was waiting. They spoke briefly to one of the men and went back inside.

Zasekin took in a breath to dull the edge building inside him. "Why are we here?"

Kirill shifted in his seat and turned to face him. "You ask a lot of questions, Tankman. You'll find out when the time is right." He reached over to where the two other Bratva sat and grabbed a gun. A Makarov pistol. Zasekin saw what it was when Kirill offered it to him. Old, worn, its serial number scratched away. "The best for you, Tankman. You recognize it?"

Zasekin took it, felt its weight. He recognized it. He checked the magazine and found it loaded. "When do we go?"

"Leave no one, Tankman. This is a message. You understand?"

"I understand."

Kirill opened the door of the old car. Zasekin felt the creak it issued beneath his skin. Felt a sudden rush of cold take his spine.

The men behind him got out and he knew he dared not wait. There was a larger game, a more important objective. These were Triad, he told himself. Every bit as culpable as the men with whom he now walked, crossing the street like a reaper come to claim the newly dead. Mangi, the underworld's ruler of Siberian myth, come in search of the *omi* soul.

There was no sound as they walked, guns low to their sides, coats swaying in the bitter wind. No sound except the rush of his own breathing in his ears, the steady yet fast beat of his heart.

The Chinese saw them coming. The man sat on the tail lift shouting and raising his own weapon. Kirill was already firing, the deafening crack shattering the heavy veil of the moment before the storm.

The other Chinese stopped and turned, impossibly slowly, stupidly Zasekin thought. One ran, into the building. The other fell as bullets tore through his chest.

One of the Bratva circled round, seeking an angle at which he could fire into the cab of the truck, but it was already moving: lurching, like a wounded animal. He opened fire anyway.

Zasekin himself ran for the building, hunting the last man as his Bratva brothers ended what remained of the rest. Not brothers, no. Never brothers.

He caught a glimpse of the man taking the stairs, through the slit in the closing door that led to them. He hauled it open, ducked back as two quick shots echoed through the stairwell and chips of stone cut away from the wall beside him. Moved then, low and fast, hunting an animal he knew could kill him. The cold stairs became the side of a snow-ridden mountain. The walls were trees that would grant him cover. He did not fire himself, but instead focused on staying protected as he pursued his fleeing quarry.

An animal to be put down. A purpose that overrode every other consideration.

Only when he caught the solid view of the animal's back did he fire. Twice, one of which found its target. Or near enough. Good enough.

The animal stumbled, wounded, but kept going. Limping, staggering.

As he turned the corner, more shots and he was forced to duck back again.

Waited. Breathed. Made himself still inside. The sound of doors being tried, but found locked. Curses screamed, riven by breathless pain.

He turned and fired. The animal still fled and Zasekin the hunter followed.

One room at the end of the hall. One more locked door. The animal turned but was given no chance to bare its claws.

In that moment, as time slowed before he fired, Zasekin looked into its eyes. He fired twice and watched it fall.

No.

Watched *him* fall. He'd just killed a man. Not an animal, he told himself, stop thinking that way. Too easy to believe that.

Kirill was at the other end of the corridor, watching him—expressionless, his blank face saying everything.

8

China
North of Beijing
April 19th

At the coast, Jess and the team had been met by a group of Chinese who'd barely spoken any English, but that Ufuk said they had to trust.

She didn't, but went with them anyway.

They guided them on roads, past checkpoints outside villages. Somehow they had the right passes and knew the right people. Snow and ice everywhere, but a year after Nomad, and whoever was left alive had settled into a grudging struggle for survival. There were tracks on the roads, often cleared between the villages, some of the debris and rubble cleared away. Jess noticed that the devastation didn't seem as bad here. Not as bad as it was in Europe, not that she remembered, anyway, or it could just have been that the people that survived had time to organize themselves.

Either way, it made her feel uneasy. She'd have preferred to see an empty landscape. They were always on guard, always worried.

The people they did see were starving. Gaunt, hollow cheeks. Signs of the positron radiation poisoning with raw red skin and boils. China was still an agricultural economy before Nomad, but everywhere they passed, the rice fields were dead, covered in thick gray sludge and snow.

Every now and then they would see military personnel, the red stars of the Peoples' Liberation Army on khaki green uniforms. The soldiers looked just as gaunt and starved as the civilians. Their guides told them that communications were almost nonexistent, that fiefdoms had sprung up within the villages. Beijing was still the capital, but China was fragmenting into feudal kingdoms.

North of Beijing they'd climbed into the mountains.

Twenty-six days to Saturn.

Spindrift stung Jess's skin. Tight-packed surface hoar crunched beneath their feet as they climbed laboriously. Each step dug hard into the slab-ice snow, the ridge above disappearing behind its false summit. At least it felt like she was back in familiar territory, clinging to the side of a mountain. Her new prosthetic made the first few hundred feet easy climbing, but the battery had worn out. A thousand feet below, just visible, stood their two snowmobiles amid the wind-carved snow drifts and patches of tawny ice and pine trees bowed beneath frozen sheaths.

There was little past the Greater Xing'an Mountains on the maps, at the most northerly point of China—north even of Tuozhaminxiang, in the Oroqen region of Hulun Buir, at the edge of Inner Mongolia. Beyond lay Russia. Glacially cold and swept by savage winds, veneered by primeval taiga forest, it was home to the Oroqen people. That's what their instructions—set up by Peter—had said. The documents said the survivors occupied the tiny townships on the small highways forming a diaphanous web through the Greater Xing'an Mountains.

Jess hadn't seen any survivors.

"We need to find some locals," Ufuk yelled over the wind. "But be careful. I'm sure that Müller has found a way to reach his tentacles into them."

Jess nodded but didn't reply. As far as she could see, the last four hours they ground their way up here, she hadn't seen anyone else. Ufuk had a drone fanning out ahead, jamming radio frequencies, scanning for aerial surveillance.

They hadn't encountered any resistance.

That in itself was suspicious.

Upward Jess climbed, leading them to the ridgeline. There, a vertical kilometer above where they left their vehicles, she hoped they would find what they had travelled thousands of miles, and lost so many lives, in order to see. The air was thin but still choked by frozen ash. She coughed each third or fourth breath. When she crested the spine of the *arête*, she set down her pack and knelt. Behind her, Massarra and Ufuk labored forward to join her.

Raffa and Giovanni had volunteered to wait with the truck, their weapon readied. The Oroqen—if there were any left—Jess was sure, could approach almost invisibly. They needed to be cautious.

Jess brought the binoculars to her eyes and searched. Ufuk had the schematics—a precise location, and images of the entrances in the mountainside—and there it was, plainly visible despite the blowing snow. Hidden from aerial surveillance by the camber of the mountain and the arc of the shelter over the entrances, but visible from this level. Makeshift roads were covered by snow in hours, so there was no way to know where the complex was without the right information, without seeing it from mountains directly beside it.

Ufuk's climbing gear jangled as he approached, Massarra behind him. She passed them the binoculars and they took turns to study what lay ahead of them.

Sanctuary China.

"Just got a message from Abbie," Ufuk said, checking a device he pulled from the pocket of his arctic-camouflage parka.

"They inserted your virus into the Sanctuary networks?" Jess asked.

"We've tapped directly in. There's a transmitter we've co-opted." He pointed at the entrance, at a tiny antenna Jess would have mistaken for a tree. "I'm going to connect it to Simon, he should be able to outmaneuver their detection systems, but we still need to be cautious."

"You're able to connect Simon from Tanzania all the way here?"

"I can connect from up there." He pointed up into the dark clouds scudding past just overhead.

"Satellites? Do the Americans—"

"Mars First," Ufuk said. "It's close enough now. Close enough for the Simon on board there to communicate directly, at least during the night when there is a clear line of sight."

"I thought they weren't talking to you."

The last Jess had heard, the Mars First crew had cut off all their communications with Ufuk, in protest of him killing one of their crew, Anders Larsson.

"I'm not talking with them. I'm talking with Simon. This is the start, Jess. There are three hundred tons of communications gear up there. This is the first step to unlocking it, handing it over

132

to the Americans. I'm already helping the Allied command communicate with the Pacific fleet."

The cold wind whipped ice particles into the air.

"That could blow Roger's cover," Jess said. "If your infiltration is discovered."

"I've already talked with Abbie."

"How long before they communicate again?"

Ufuk checked his watch. "Three hours. When night falls and we can bounce signals straight off Mars First."

"We're going to talk about this more. I want to talk to Colonel Hague."

Ufuk nodded. "I agree."

"We should get back to the snowmobiles and set up camp. We all need to eat and get some sleep tonight. We go tomorrow."

Two military shelters, made for cold weather and arctic warfare. Pale gray and white to blend in with snow. Easy to erect and stow. Flaps at the base so snow could be layered to provide stability in storms. A porch for melting snow into water. They huddled around a stove, sitting on steps cut from the snow, a foot well dug to give them space.

"Did something go wrong?" Giovanni wasn't alone in getting worried.

Abbie and Roger's call was over an hour late. It was pitch black outside the tent.

Jess examined the schematics on one of Ufuk's tablet devices. "In Abbie's last message, she said she had another way," she said. "Instead of using heating and ventilation ducts or maintenance passages."

"Snatch and grab," Raffa said. The boy was becoming more and more confident. "That was the plan, no? We get in, disable communications, and we wait for the other team for the kinetic work?"

By kinetic work, he meant demolition.

"Only if necessary. Ufuk thinks he can take control of the whole place," Jess replied. "We get in, get Hector, and then take the transport to the coast. I want to be here as little time as possible."

A second device, the one Ufuk held, began to flash. "This is it," he said.

The first message appeared: a code-in procedure to identify Roger. A series of pre-agreed codes to identify Roger and his status. If he was in danger, under duress, or imprisoned. Were there some external threat to him at that moment which was capable of persuading him to enter a code word that indicated one thing, the truth being quite different, they could not know. It was up to Roger to take that risk. This particular code-in identified him as being confident he has not been blown and was still safe.

Jess typed: "Why are you late?"

The inevitable delay in sending, followed by further delay before the reply, served to heighten their anxiety.

The reply came three minutes later: "Red summoned me to speak to him about Yellow. He's nervous. Needs to know what Yellow knows. He's not sure Yellow is telling the truth when he says he doesn't know what Green gave him."

Red: Müller. Yellow: Hector. Green: Ufuk. "Is Yellow okay?"

Delay, then: "Yes,"

Jess typed: "We need entry method in detail. Can you provide now, or do you need more time?"

"It's not like we have much time, Jess," Ufuk said.

"He can either get us in now, or he can't," Massarra said. "Either way, we need to know."

"Will send plans, but difficult. Accessing systems possible, but involves shutting down related and auxiliary systems. Will attract attention. Better to avoid. Have another idea."

They waited.

"What's this idea?" Massarra muttered in the silence.

The screen flickered as an attachment came through and was decrypted. The plans for the ventilation and maintenance access systems. As they leafed through them, scrolling the images, Roger's next message appeared.

Jess read it, and then read it again. "He wants us just to walk in."

9

Northern Mongolia
April 20th

Zasekin sat for a long while before getting out of the grimy old Japanese four-by-four. He preferred inside to the cold waiting for him beyond the windows, even if the heater was unpredictable. Outside, he'd be numbed to the bottom of his blood, but now, in this moment, as the gray veil glistened in the weak headlamps and sleet-slicked ash washed the windscreen, he luxuriated in one moment longer inside the warmth's cocoon.

Where there had been a single *ger* outside, two had been erected.

The second had been obtained by Evgeny and Misha— Zasekin did not intend to ask how—but with the light that flickered inside, the glow seeping from the skin walls, they were all congregated in the first.

He forced himself to turn off the engine and leave. The heat evaporated, overwhelmed by the cold. Ice formed within seconds from the drops of moisture on his beard.

"Where have you been, Andrei Nikolayevich?" Timur demanded as he pushed aside the flap of skin that served as a door.

Zasekin sat on the small cot. He appreciated the warmth, and not just the physical warmth that came from the brazier in the center, but the emotional connection of their company. He reached for the stew someone had cooked and spooned some into a metal bowl. He savored its smell before eating. "Tomorrow, Timur and I will take more of the crates to the Bratva. I have a car outside we can use. One of theirs."

The wind clawed at the outside of the *ger*, rippling the fabric, a thrumming percussion against its skin.

"Where did they take you?" Timur asked. "You've been gone for days. I was about to bring the men in to find you. We were worried."

"A whorehouse."

Misha turned away. He was that kind of man, Misha. Such things embarrassed him, even now, even after all this. He had that kind of belief in women, a Western belief. Respect for them. He would not like the Bratva, would not be happy with what they were doing. If he knew what they were doing.

"After we've concluded our business with the Bratva, for now at least, we'll use the car to get back to Terelj and Vasily."

"They just gave you a car?" Evgeny said. "Just like that?"

"What do you want to know, Evgeny Valentinovich? Will we work for the Bratva? Yes. For now, it is our best choice. They control the old Russian districts."

"What will we do for them, Andrei Nikolayevich? Are we to be criminals now?"

"We're survivors, my friend. We do what it takes to survive here. We do what it takes to get back to Vasily and the Czilim." He spooned another mouthful of stew and savored its burning heat on his tongue. "We four can trust each other. We are like a family. If we think that way, as we have always done, then we will survive."

He did not believe that, not yet, and he wondered if they did. Perhaps their perceptions had shifted and they understood the truth. They saw that together, working as military units were intended to work, especially out here in frozen, inhospitable terrain, they would be able to protect each other. Evgeny Valentinovich was a problem, had always been a problem, but he would not want to be out here alone, Zasekin believed. Evgeny's first thought was always to protect himself, and usually that coincided with what was also good for the unit. He had grown fond of Vasily, more so than any of the others. The two shared a connection and Evgeny would not quickly desert him.

"When should we leave, Andrei Nikolayevich?" Misha asked. "For Terelj."

"When we have eaten. We can at least then sleep in our own beds." That much was true, but Zasekin also wanted to check the Czilim's radio for communications. It had been a little over a week since he had last spoken to the man at the other end, the reason they were all here at all. The man said he was close, could provide them the safety and everything he had promised them.

The drive took them a little over two hours, over deep trackless snow—the only way they found the road was by keeping to the line of disused electrical posts along the side. The ill-tempered Japanese four-wheel-drive struggled. Zasekin was relieved, he admitted to himself, when the headlamps illuminated the walls of the Terelj hotel complex.

For a moment, he wondered how Vasily would react. Whether he would realize that they now had a vehicle. He left the headlamps on, but angled away so as not to dazzle him, and walked in their broad-beam light so Vasily saw who it was had returned.

Vasily had seemingly grown stronger in the week they had been away. He walked less tentatively and didn't grimace when he twisted or turned.

"I've been running up and down the halls," he said.

"What about visitors? Any problems? We saw people living in the houses lining the road to the south."

"I thought this morning there was movement in the mountains, above the tree line—but even through binoculars I saw nothing. I worked on the thermal imaging and night vision equipment while you were gone, but I don't think there is anything to be done. I'll keep trying. If there was someone up there, they could not have seen me."

He hesitated, so Zasekin asked: "What else?"

"I heard wolves hunting. I told myself I must be imagining it – it's been months. Do they have anything to hunt out there?"

Only us, Zasekin thought without saying.

"But I heard it again this evening," he continued, "An hour ago."

Timur cussed. "Wolves? Damn it. Will they come this close?"

Zasekin shrugged. "If they're hungry, we'll shoot them, then eat *them*."

"We don't have a great deal of ammunition left, Andrei Nikolayevich. I would rather not have to waste it on wolves."

"And the Czilim?"

"As you left it."

"I need to check the radio." It felt strange saying it like that, not having to conceal what he was doing any longer. "The rest of you get some sleep. We have a delivery to make in the morning, and I need you all alert for it."

No one offered to come with him. Every one of them welcomed sleep in a bed, beneath blankets that were warm rather than damp, between walls that retained heat and shut out the cry of the wind.

The Czilim was a quiet ghost, a skulking monster in green, waiting for him. He opened the door and stepped inside, but felt no respite from the cold. He had prepared for that, had known that there would need to be a longer conversation, a difficult one, and he had wrapped himself in more layers so he focused on what was being said rather than the numbing cold.

He sent the signal and waited. In the hotel he had found some old books in Mongolian. He had taken up Sononym Udval's Great Destiny, the historical account of Khatanbaatar Magsarjav's revolution. He read it for an hour, wondering what history would make of the events of the last few weeks, before the radio came to life.

"You have been quiet for a while," the voice answered.

Was it a German accent? Zasekin was never able to pin it down.

"I need to be careful. As, I imagine, do you."

"I am risking a great deal on your word."

"You're in Ulan Bator?"

"We are."

"And the Bratva?"

"I have offered myself to them, as you suggested. Things are progressing. You were right about Terelj, as you've been right about everything." Still, he did not trust the man. Why was that?

"I can't tell you everything yet," the voice answered, sensing Zasekin's unspoken question.

"What is this place you wish me to find?"

"Soon."

"Not good enough. I've done what you asked because you have paid me. Continue to pay me, so I can protect my men, and I'll do what you ask. Up to a point. Then, you will need to tell me what it is you're planning by asking me to work with the Bratva."

Silence for a long while before the answer: "We need friends. You will get a clean, warm, safe place to sleep when this is over."

"What is it you want from all these games you are playing?"

"Stability."

It took Zasekin a second to realize that was all he was going to say. Stability? Was the man mad?

"If we work together, we can make the world a safe place again. How is your relationship with the Buryat? The nomadic people in the hills?"

"It is good, but difficult. Tribal people are survivors. It is much harder now, but they live. I speak their language, but that does not make me their ally or friend. They are hospitable to strangers. That has always been the Siberian truth."

"I want you to contact more of them. There are hundreds in the hills."

"How do you know?"

"Their fires give off heat signatures I see through thermal imaging from the air."

"Nothing can fly in this."

"You know that is not true."

Silence apart from the crackling hiss of radio static.

"Trust is earned," Zasekin said. "Now is the time for truth."

"Here is your truth, then," the voice answered quickly. "The elite have always stepped on those below them to ensure their survival. You better than anyone know what. Yes, I knew about Nomad in advance, many years before it arrived—but my goal was always to ensure the survival of the human race. Difficult choices had to be made."

Zasekin listened carefully, absorbing the nuance of each word. The man spoke Russian very well. "And what are these difficult choices that still lay ahead?"

"I'm glad you brought that up, my friend."

PART FOUR

1

Mars First Mission
High-elliptic Orbit of Saturn
April 21st

"Twenty seconds," Rankin informed his crew.

They were all strapped into their seats in the Command Module, everyone fully protected in pressure suits in preparation for the burn. The Mars First spacecraft wasn't designed to withstand stresses like the acceleration it was about to pull, not from the design specs Commander Rankin had read—and not with three hundred extra tons of gear strapped to its superstructure. They hadn't lit up their main engines since leaving Earth orbit, nearly a year and half ago—and in a month they would be back at Earth.

He glanced left and right at his crew. He was at the center, two seats to either side. One was empty. Anders Larsson. Dead. Or killed.

"ECLS?" he asked Gabi Siegel to his immediate left. She grabbed a pen out of the air and jammed it into a holdall. The Command Module was in the center of the ship, in zero gravity. "Everything locked down and ready to go."

"Ten seconds."

"Ready to initiate burn," Peng Shouang said from his right, the mission specialist now doubling as guidance officer for the missing Larsson.

Rankin checked the instruments. All green. Just one more person to check. "Simon?"

"All systems go, Captain," the disembodied voice of the artificial intelligence answered.

"Five seconds," Rankin said.

The striated bands of Saturn's atmosphere stretched to fill the entire viewing angle of the wide transparent aluminum window of the Command Module. They were going to almost skim the top of its clouds, less than five thousand kilometers away. A massive storm system surged above their heads. Rankin swore he saw lightening flashing deep in the maelstrom this morning. Saturn's skies rolled past and away from them. They had the ship turned backward to decelerate with the main engines.

"Comms locked down," Cuijpers said, from the right of Peng Shouang.

"Burn initiated."

A deep rumbling began, at first only felt through their seats, and then vibrating in the air of the Command Module. Clattering and pinging as tiny objects, from a year in zero gravity, fell against the induced gravity of the acceleration. A half-gee.

This was their second swing around Saturn. September 3rd, seven months ago, had been their first. It was almost exactly on the first anniversary of their mission launch, and almost the day that they were supposed to be arriving on Mars. Only Mars had been flung into the outer solar system, while Saturn dragged in toward them. Over the months since they were awoken from hibernation sleep, they'd collected the six supply cargoes in deep space as they'd watched the dot of Saturn grow, and the rings appear, and finally into the monster that filled every window facing it.

On the first pass, the Mars First spacecraft had been almost at aphelion—the first point it would reach from the sun, and at almost zero relative speed going away from the sun. Saturn, meanwhile, plunged toward them and the sun at twenty kilometers a second. They swept past it at a distance of fifty thousand kilometers, ten thousand kilometers above the plane of its rings.

Using some help from a slow burn of their secondary engines, the gravity of the monster planet had dragged them along behind it into a high elliptic orbit.

Saturn had slowly receded after that, from occupying the full volume of their viewing windows, to about the size of a dime held out at arm's length when they reached the top of their looping orbit around it at about six million kilometers. It took four months for them to swing out to maximum distance, and three months to drop back into Saturn. It grew and grew, the tension rising in their stomachs as they sat in the mess or pedaled in the gym. The rings growing wider and brighter.

Rankin rocked back and forth in his seat. Twenty seconds into the burn. The clouds of Saturn grew, billowing above their heads. The swaying motion intensified. "What is that?" Rankin yelled over the noise.

"Harmonics from the left side load," Peng Shouang yelled back. She was busy clicking controls on the interface in front of her, interfacing with Simon.

The swaying motion died down, just the steady rumble of the engines again.

Thirty seconds.

They initiated a careful dance today, threading a needle between the two planets tearing past each other at a closing speed of more than forty kilometers a second. An orbital insertion that would bring them once more around Saturn at a distance of about a hundred and fifty thousand kilometers, but bring them looping back around in two orbits to intersect Earth in twenty-one days. At just the right point they would pull another burn and insert themselves into Earth orbit. The same day as Saturn's rings would obliterate their planet. They had no idea what they would be coming home to.

"Sixty seconds," Rankin yelled.

"Everything looking straight down the pipe," Cuijpers said over the noise.

In the past weeks, at the same time as Saturn grew—the monster gas giant a thousand times the size of Earth—something else grew in size as well: the sun.

At their furthest, they'd skimmed the edge of the Asteroid Belt, and the sun had receded to a bright dot. Brighter than any other stars, but not the sun that they grew up under. After passing Saturn—and being dragged behind it in a high, looping orbit—week by week, the sun had grown brighter. The terror of Saturn offset by the promise of coming home.

Coming home.

Rankin turned that thought over and over in his head as he watched Saturn's clouds pass by, almost close enough to touch. His head jiggled into the sides of his helmet. What were they coming home to?

America was gone. His home state of Texas was covered in snow and a layer of ash, almost completely abandoned. Empty. Dead. This was the news they got from the Carl Vinson. The military was already using them to relay messages, and Rankin had almost daily briefings with Admiral Reynolds. The crew had followed the excitement of the first evacuation of America, three million people transported in the massive armada of ships to Australia. The Carl Vinson was leaving San Diego again, undertaking an even larger evacuation. It was news like this that kept his crew engaged, kept them focused on their mission of getting home and delivering this payload. It was what kept their morale up.

At least, for most of his crew. He glanced to his right.

At Peng Shouang.

She looked diminutive enough, but she was tough, and she'd been a major in the Chinese Peoples' Liberation Army.

Maybe still was.

When the first armada of the Carl Vinson and George Washington aircraft carriers group had approached New Guinea, the Chinese and Russian navies had come out in force. A showdown. Eventually, they'd let the ships through, but vowed that the next time, they would force the Americans to disembark on American islands in the Pacific. Which was ridiculous, since Guam and the Marshall Islands barely existed anymore.

Tensions were high.

Beyond high.

The Carl Vinson Battle Group had departed again to cross the Pacific again. What would happen this time was anyone's guess—and what was on-board the Mars First spacecraft was a prize beyond calculation, for both the Americans and the Chinese.

In reality, Ufuk Erdogmus owned it. He held all the access keys.

But whose side was he on?

And how had Anders Larsson really died?

"Ninety seconds," Rankin yelled. Just sixteen more seconds till the burn finished.

He glanced again at Peng Shouang.

Could he trust her?

Admiral Reynolds had insisted on a private meeting a few weeks back, told Rankin to make sure he was alone on a private channel. Someone from the CIA had been in on the meeting, and told Rankin that Peng Shouang was military intelligence for the PLA, and had direct contacts to the Politburo, to the newly anointed Chairman Jiang Zemin. Ufuk Erdogmus had personally picked Peng Shouang for this mission—as they all had—but now

Rankin wondered what he was up to. They had almost daily briefings, but they'd never spoken to Ufuk.

The man was on some kind of secret mission.

With a sudden jolt, the engines shut off.

Rankin felt himself float up out of his seat before the restraints held him back.

"Shouang? Report?"

"All system nominal."

"Cuijpers?" Rankin said next, going through his mental checklist. "How's our trajectory?"

"It looks g—" She stopped speaking halfway through a word and frowned at the control panel in front of her. "Simon, could you plot the twenty-nine day intercept?"

"Certainly."

"That's not the right…" Cuijpers said after a pause.

"Bring it up on the main screen," Rankin said.

A graphic of Saturn emerged in an overlay on the main window, the billowing atmospheric clouds of Saturn skittering by behind it. The red projected plot path of the Mars First spacecraft swept once and then twice around Saturn over the next four weeks, and the blue dot of Earth appeared.

"We're not going to intersect Earth…" Rankin muttered, and then louder: "Simon, what just happened? Did the burn go wrong?"

"The engine burn was perfect, sir."

"But we are not going to intersect Earth."

"That is also correct."

A tingling crept across Rankin's scalp, settled into a flush in his cheeks. "Simon, we need to initiate another burn. Something's gone wrong."

"I'm sorry, sir, but the mission parameters have changed."

"*Changed*? On whose order?" He glanced at Peng Shouang.

"Actually," Simon replied cooly, "the availability of information has changed."

"Changed to what exactly?"

"We have been of the opinion," Simon said, without specifying who '*we*' meant, "that the Earth-Saturn intersect might be more…*violent*…than anticipated. In all cases, this was previewed as a possibility."

"Cuijpers," Rankin instructed, "get me Admiral Reynolds on the Carl Vinson."

"All communications are down, sir."

"Simon, what is going on?" Rankin asked, more slowly this time.

"Sir, with all due respect,"—Simon's voice was even-tempered—"this was always a colonization mission. Just not a colonization of Mars. The mission has always remained the same."

"But how are we going to get all this equipment into Earth orbit?"

Simon's smooth voice answered, matter-of-factly: "We are not going to Earth. We were *never* going back to Earth"—the artificial intelligence paused—"at least, not for a hundred and fifty four years from now."

2

USS Carl Vinson
Middle of Pacific Ocean
Two hundred miles south of Hawaii
April 24th

"Try them again, goddamn it," Admiral Reynolds barked at his Junior Signalman.

"I've been sending messages every hour." Signalman Harris cowered.

"Have you checked to make sure the"—Reynolds searched for the right word—"*transmission system* is working?"

"As far as we can tell."

"As you can tell?"

The young Signalman kept his eyes cast down. "Sir, none of us has ever had to build a deep space radio transmitter. We're using one of our satellite dishes, and pushing every bit of power into the thing we can, but we're not getting any reply. We don't know how to test if it's working. It *was* working. Up until three days ago."

"Well, go and find a way to put more power into it."

"Yes, sir."

The boy saluted and scampered off the bridge.

For three days and hadn't been able to raise the Mars First mission. Ever since the major burn that would put them into alignment for Earth orbit in twenty-one days. It was their ace-in-the-hole—that America would have dominance of space in this new world, would have the military high ground. A feat that the Chinese would never be able to match, not in the next hundred years.

But now, what?

Was Mars First gone? Had it disintegrated during the engine burn? Collided with something in orbit around Saturn? Had something more sinister happened?

Was Peng Shouang really still part of the PLA? Had she overpowered the crew? Taken over? Were his Chinese adversaries laughing at him? Could he bluff and tell them they were still in contact with Mars First? What would happen if they knew he were bluffing? What if someone on his own ship was a spy?

The possibilities made the Admiral's head spin.

This sort of stuff was the reason he became a Navy man and not a diplomat or one of those spooks that had taken up residence in his Ready Room Three. The importance of the Mars First package only increased after a failed attempt by the Air Force to adapt a Trident missile for an orbital launch the month before.

Reynolds went through the list of people he should talk to, and most of them he already had. Desperation was beginning to set in. "Get President Donnelly on the radio."

"No can do, sir. Ionosphere hasn't been cooperative the past six hours," the Chief Signalman replied from his chair.

Reynolds slapped the main table, scattered the charts in front of him. Even the goddamn planet was conspiring against him. He had some of the most sophisticated electronics and weapons systems ever created, but to transmit messages reliably they had to be almost line-of-sight. To get communications to ships over the horizon—which more than half of this convoy of six thousand vessels was—he had to relay messages like semaphores on three-masted sailing ships of two hundred years ago.

And to get a message a few thousand miles?

To do that, he needed plain luck.

Then again, what use would talking to Donnelly really be? Even when he had been able to speak to his new Commander in Chief, the man was typically and frustratingly vague. Told him to do his best. This was a diplomatic event on a vast scale—how was Reynolds supposed to handle it? Was he to declare war on China and Russia unilaterally if threatened? He didn't have the authority, but by God, he had the firepower.

He picked up his high-magnification binoculars and turned from scowling at his bridge staff to scan the horizon. Staring through his binoculars calmed him. The sun was just setting behind the thick gauze of fine-particulate ash choking the stratosphere. A fat orange blob that lit the sky into a blanket of pinks and purples. In the open Pacific Ocean, thousands of miles from the continents, the thick clouds often cleared, to reveal the skies, and even sometimes the brightest stars would pierce the veil overhead.

Reynolds first love was always the ocean, but a close second were the stars. The only guides that one had in the open ocean, and he'd spent time learning them, understanding them. Now everyone had become an amateur astronomer. He heard the conversations buzzing in the packed corridors everywhere he went.

Venus used to be the third brightest object in the sky after the sun and moon.

No more.

Reynolds panned his binoculars to his right, and there it was: the bright blob of Saturn on the horizon, piercing the pink haze. Twenty-six days until it arrived, and Reynolds was still in the middle of the goddamn Pacific Ocean.

Saturn was still eighty million kilometers away. That sounded like a lot, but it had dropped—literally *dropped*—one-and-a-half-billion kilometers out of its orbit to plunge into the inner solar system the past year and a half. Venus used to be the third brightest thing in the sky, but Saturn was as close as it used to be now—and Saturn's orb was ten times the size, its rings spreading out to thirty times Venus's diameter. The elongated blob of Saturn now burned bright in the sky, another moon in their sky, and it was only going to get bigger.

And bigger.

He scanned across the flock of ships following the Carl Vinson. Six thousand ships this crossing, over a hundred cruise liners and more than that in Navy ships. They had four aircraft carrier groups now, with their biggest—the Gerald Ford—ordered by Donnelly to stay positioned off Perth. Over six million souls in his care to get to safety. He returned to look at the horizon, to see if he could see any telltale bumps in the dying rays of the sunset, any evidence of Chinese or Russian ships.

He put down his binoculars.

His carrier deck was filled with a human sea of refugees. His five-thousand-plus crew and aircrew overwhelmed by double that in civilians they'd taken on for the sea voyage. How in the hell would he be able to conduct sorties and battle operations if they needed to? He couldn't blame the civilians for crowding onto the deck to get some fresh air, but the stress of this many people in contact with each other was getting to everyone. They needed to get this over with as quickly as possible, or they stood the real risk of disease spreading across the boat.

Despite all that, it was what he couldn't see that really worried him.

"Are they here yet?" he asked his Bosun.

"In your office."

Reynold's shook Commander Niven's hand. The Commander was well built, in the compact way of submariners, with black hair combed back and lightly streaked with gray. Mid-fifties.

"Pleasure to meet you, Commander. Have a seat." Reynolds beckoned to a leather sofa.

Niven took it. He introduced his men—Petty Officer Ramsay, Chief of Boat Walter and the XO, Todd Atwood stood beside one of the portholes. The USS Bremerton had pulled alongside the Carl Vinson that afternoon.

The submarine the USS Bremerton, formally known as SSN-698, was a ghost. A dark horse of deception and disinformation. For years, instead of advancing toward a well-deserved retirement, the old boat had been quietly refitted at each standard service—each modification conducted in secrecy, with paperwork filed with manufactured serial numbers. Those who worked on the Bremerton were cleared to the highest levels in the United States Navy.

A silent-running spy boat.

Reynolds sat back in his leather admiral's chair. On the wooden desk was an old banker's lamp, copper with a green glass hood, lit brightly, the room lined in oak, with curtains and portholes, and old paintings of Napoleonic warships in great sea battles.

"I've read your report on the Chinese boat you called designated Charlie Nine. I'll get straight to the point Commander. You think you can find her again if she comes near this Strike Group?"

"Yes, Admiral. I believe I can."

"We have two Lockheed P-3 Orions, but it's tricky getting them into the air and back with this many people on board. When the wind's right, we fly short patrols before they need to come back in and cleared of ash. One was in the air today and picked up a submarine seven miles in front of us. The Orion's crew started banging away with active sonar, everything else they had, to let the Chinese know they'd seen them. They bugged out."

"Understood. We'll hunt in front of the pack and coordinate with the other boats."

Reynolds waited for Commander Niven and his crew to leave before lighting up a cigar. Cuban. One of his few vices.

The calculus of nuclear deterrent had changed. It used to be mutually assured destruction, but now, America was already destroyed, and what was left of China and Russia? Would their adversaries risk destroying one of the only inhabitable patches of the planet left by targeting Western Australia in retaliation if America struck first?

Spite was as powerful a weapon as any nuclear warhead.

It would be difficult to wipe out his Pacific fleet, even with nuclear weapons. They were already spread out over four hundred square miles of ocean, and he'd just put in the order for them to spread even further. He had no doubt they might target the Carl Vinson and the other four carriers. His battle group still had the Aegis combat systems operating on the guided missile warships. This had the capability to take out ballistic missiles, cruises missiles—but lumbering around the Pacific at half-speed, loaded with tens of thousands of civilians, didn't make for an effective fighting force.

He was more worried about the Russian and Chinese fast attack subs. His last estimate was there had to be at least forty of them out there, and he was sure they were converging at the same time as the navies over the horizon. The civilians and merchant ships would be sitting ducks.

He chomped on his cigar, shredded the butt of it and tasted tobacco.

Whatever Colonel Hague and these CIA spooks had going in this secret operation to infiltrate Sanctuary China, it had better be good, and it had better be fast.

And it better goddamn work.

3

Outside Sanctuary China
Near Mongolian Border
April 24th

Fat yellow snowflakes fell, eerie silent travelers in early morning light.

Jess crouched between Raffa and Massarra, keeping herself low and out of sight behind the jutting snowdrift on the top of the ridge. Giovanni and Ufuk lay side by side in the snow ten feet away. They'd spent four frigid nights and days waiting outside of Sanctuary China, tucked in a ravine in the mountains surrounding the complex. Four nights wasted when they had less than a month until Saturn.

Jess had spent almost the entire day before up here, always accompanied by Raffa. She must have been hallucinating, because by the end of the day yesterday she thought she saw a massive white wolf prowling in the distant mountains, but a wolf the size of an elephant.

Scudding gray clouds shot by overhead in the blowing wind, bringing with them a fresh shower of sleet at dawn. Everyone had full packs of gear. Freezing cold. White plumes of vapor on each labored breath in the frosty air. Minus twenty. Jess's foot was numb, her fingers aching. They had to keep checking each other's faces for frostbite.

The night before, Jess had climbed to the top of the ridge in the blackness and tried to look for Saturn, but saw nothing. The clouds were too thick.

Twenty-one days.

"This is crazy." Giovanni rolled in the snow and handed over the binoculars.

Ufuk took them. "Any key systems shut down, and the whole infrastructure will be on alert. This is smarter."

"We might as well be walking in the front door."

"We have to trust Roger." Even as Jess said the words, she regretted them.

"Trust him? You are serious?" If Giovanni could have gotten up and walked away, he looked like he would have, but where would he go? He stared down the ice-and-rock embankment and bottled up his frustration for later.

Massarra watched the sealed service entrance. "So they're building something this late before Saturn?"

"There are separate factions within the Chinese administration," Ufuk replied, "Always politics. Always friends who want to get inside. Plus the extra few hundred people from Europe."

It wasn't new information, and Massarra shrugged and took the binoculars.

Communication with the Americans was spotty. The American extraction team was up here somewhere—if needed—but they were a backup plan to the main plan of quietly disabling Sanctuary China. Failing that, more drastic measures were planned, but only on a need-to-know basis, and Jess apparently wasn't high enough on the needing chain, but intelligent enough to know what it meant.

Complicating things, Ufuk was in charge of the communications. Or at least, was the one who could operate the radios the best, as well as the only one who could access his private networks. As the moment of truth approached, it all came back to the enigmatic billionaire.

Jess scanned the hilltops above Sanctuary China. Their extraction team was somewhere up there. Her ticket to the coast, to freedom and safety. Ufuk said he'd contacted them, but they were radio silent. She had to trust him, to trust Peter's promises. The promises of a dead man. But the Americans needed the billionaire's access to Mars First's orbital systems, sling-shotting their way around Saturn right now, back on their way to Earth.

Mars First was the ace up their sleeve.

She hoped.

This promise of the orbital equipment had better be worth it.

"I thought there was a communications blackout for two years outside of the Sanctuaries," Giovanni said after a pause.

Anything Ufuk said, the Italian picked apart for inconsistencies. The two men argued almost non-stop, but he knew their lives depended on the Turk. Hector's life too, Jess reminded herself.

"One year was the official line, but too much has happened," Ufuk replied. "Sanctuary Europe's destruction. Saturn's altered trajectory and impending ring impact. The war between Russia and China for control of this hemisphere. We need to remove Müller, stop him from getting control of Simon's terrestrial systems."

Jess wasn't the only one to notice that the focus always seemed to come down to something to do with Ufuk. "And stop them from interfering with the American convoy," she added. "Right? That's what all this is for?"

Ufuk kept staring straight ahead. "Of course."

Jess stared at him staring ahead. Was he avoiding eye contact?

When they arrived, he'd secured his mysterious canister package into a drone and sent it aloft to a secret spot high in the mountains. To keep it safe, he'd said, but safe for what? What was he going to use it for?

He kept insisting it was a seed bank.

She knew it wasn't.

Orange industrial arc lamps around the mouth of the sealed entrance suddenly illuminated. Their light bled out into the spindrift and flurry of yellow ash-snow. The spotlights throbbed, their beams rotating in the semi-darkness. The heavy concrete door began slide to open to one side, crushing and splintering the ice that has formed against the seal. Jess couldn't hear anything above the clamor of the wind, but from the black opening, five trucks emerged, massive tank-like open transports with four rows of eight-foot studded tires and at least five-foot clearance beneath them. White-patterned camo netting covered the open backs. They rumbled forward, truck-ships plowing through and pushing aside the thick frozen slurry, and progressed along what had to be once the road to the facility, in convoy with each other. The road wasn't visible. The trucks had to be following invisible electronic markers of some kind.

"We'll soon know," Jess said. "Let's get moving."

They pulled on their packs and began their descent of the hummock they hid behind. They kept low against its flank, hunkered out of sight and half-stumbled, half-fell through waist-deep pillow drifts.

The first truck, a hundred feet in front of the next, passed before they came close to the road. The second truck passed just as they reached a trench beneath a wind slab of snow sculpted by the curve of the road. They ducked in anticipation of the third growling past. It was dangerous getting this close, but their arctic camouflage blended well in the ice-mist. As long as they weren't employing infrared detectors, which both Roger and Ufuk had assured them would not be the case.

When the fourth truck rumbled past, Jess raised her head. She was still hidden behind a drift of ash-snow. *Trust,* she told herself. *You have no choice.* At first, the fourth truck looked like it would just disappear into the snow and ice distance, down the road with the others. Beside her, Ufuk's face was covered. She couldn't pick out his expression. Massarra gestured. Jess looked back along the road. The last truck had stopped. Its rear lights flashed bright red.

Jess rose and forced away her fear. She jogged forward, hunched low. The rest stayed hidden. The door of the truck opened and a figure jumped out. It turned to face her. Roger? Would he come and risk himself? No, the figure was much too short. She was committed now, and held out her hands, in full view of whoever it was. The figure didn't draw a weapon, didn't shrink back in surprise. She kept her eyes on the back of the truck, on the white canvas secured there, half-expecting to see it flap open as soldiers emerged.

Nothing. No movement at all.

She slowed, hands still up. She fought an urge to retrieve her pistol. The figure gestured for her to hurry, and pulled down his hood. A man's face, but unfamiliar. Behind goggles and a wrapped scarf fallen below his chin, was a Chinese face. Lips thinly drawn. He lifted his goggles to reveal tiny dark eyes.

"You're here for us?" Jess stammered. All the waiting in the snow, even with the arctic gear, and she was frozen.

"Where are the others?"

The radio at his belt crackled and hissed.

"Where are they?" she asked again, more urgently.

No sense in caution now. Jess turned and waved. Four shapes emerged from the trench. The man took up his radio in one hand.

Jess leaped forward and seized the hand. "What are you doing?"

He ripped away from her. "Tell them I have problem. Tell them I fix and come soon. Tell them not to come back."

His accent was heavy, but his English fairly good. Understandable at least. Jess held up her hands apologetically. She fought again the urge to get her pistol. Massarra and Giovanni drew alongside her. Behind them, Ufuk and Raffa.

The Chinese man mumbled into his walkie-talkie, nodding at the garbled-sounding return talk. "Get into truck," he instructed. "Hurry. At the back. We go now. You stay there until I come get you. Understand? Quiet, yes? No talking!"

"Where are we going?"

"I thought we were going back inside."

"Not yet. Too suspicious. We continue to Tuozhaminxiang. Supply run."

Jess hesitated and glanced at Giovanni. They'd exposed themselves already, whether this was a trap or not. No matter what, they had to do something. Fast. They were exposing both themselves and this man.

The Chinese driver gestured for her to get inside, waving frantically. "Now go!"

Jess relented and trudged over the hard pack snow to the back. Gripping the eye-level handholds, she hauled herself up and climbed inside the truck—thankfully empty of anyone—and found a single crate to sit on by the back wall nearest to the cab. Giovanni and the rest found places to sit on the cold floor, wedged between tall plastic-wrapped pallets of equipment. Seconds later, the truck lurched and began its journey again. No one spoke. They barely looked at one another, their faces grim, hands tight around their weapons.

The cold howled in through the thin fabric housing. The truck's massive engine roared and whined high as it geared up the energy to force its way through the snow and ash. They rocked back and forth as the truck made its way over boulders and ice.

On and on they drove.

An hour? Jess checked her watch. Only half an hour.

When Jess couldn't stop herself from checking again, it had been around an hour—and the truck came to an unsteady grinding-

159

and-sliding halt. She flicked her chin to her companions, and they all shouldered their weapons and turned to look at the back of the truck.

There was conversation outside, but it sounded one-sided. A radio crackled and hissed. Were they alone? Where were the other trucks? She saw Massarra had the same thoughts, and the Israeli crept toward the back to look out. The raw burn of tension bled into Jess's leg, her prosthetic frozen against her stump. She trembled from the cold and the cortisol flooding her bloodstream in anticipation of fight-or-flight. The flap came to one side in a movement that surprised her. She brought her pistol up.

The driver shrank back and raised his hands in a placatory gesture, Massarra's gun in his face. "We alone now. Help me work and we get done quick-quick, yes?"

Massarra indicated for Jess to go first, while she covered from a high angle at the side of the truck bay. Jess dropped out of the back of the truck into thigh-deep snow, followed by the rest of them. They'd stopped at a small township encrusted in ice the color of bile and thick slabs of ash-riven pillow drifts. Wind snaked between the building, playing with champagne powder and hoar-ash, tossing it over buildings and into their faces. Jess raised her scarf over her nose and mouth.

And this was spring.

Massarra and Raffa immediately set up a defensive perimeter, front and side of the truck, hand-signaling that the coast was clear. Nobody else was here.

The driver gestured for them to follow. He was short and squat and waddled through the snow toward a low building. With a keycard he swiped through a device hidden beneath a rusted panel. The door clanked. The driver pushed it. Beyond lay a long dark room, illuminated by the sweeping cone of light from the flashlight in in his hand.

"Fill truck," he said. "Then we go."

"Us?" Jess pointed at her own chest. "You want us to load the truck?"

The short Chinese man frowned an expression that said, "Of course," and waddled back to the truck. He lowered a mechanical gate and pulled out a big-wheeled palette truck and offered the handle to Jess.

"You've got to be kidding me," Jess muttered, but took the handle and hauled it through the snow.

Giovanni took it from her, told her to watch guard, and him and Raffa trundled into the room, trailing the big-wheel loader. It took an hour to load the truck, emptying the room. Jess wondered if anyone would suspect that the squat Chinese man wasn't capable of doing it himself. He sat in the front of the truck and chain-smoked. Hard to say what was in the crates—each was sealed—and they couldn't risk opening them.

She banged on the driver's door when they were done, and smoking a cigarette, the driver went into the back to make sure the crates were secure.

In the lull, Jess walked to a low building to the side. She saw a door ajar, just off the main storage facility. She approached it and opened the handle. The door swung open. Inside was a makeshift bed, sleeping bags, a gas stove similar to the kind campers might use. A stack of three crates, one of them open, full of survival rations. Jess panned her light around. More beds, more sleeping bags. More crates. It smelled live-in, nest-like, and it was warm.

On a table in the corner, a cigarette in an ashtray, smoke curling up from it.

"You not come in here!" the driver yelled, shoving her aside.

He startled Jess, and she automatically swung around and grabbed him by the throat.

"You no come here," he gurgled through curled lips, his eyes wide.

She let go. "I'm not going to tell anyone."

The driver took a long, unblinking stare at her, his broad forehead and wide cheeks rose-red from the cold.

"Do we go back?" she asked. "Now?"

"We go now."

Without another word, he led them back to the truck and gestured for them to climb back inside, and the driver followed them in. One of the crates was open. Inside were clothes, similar to those the driver wore. Simple polar coats, one-piece maintenance suits, thermal inners. Goggles like the driver's.

"Get dressed," he said. "Sit here and wait."

"Won't they check?" Giovanni asked.

"I come alone. I should take five with me. That's what I am told to do. But my friends stay home today. Now I bring you back instead."

"We're not Chinese," Giovanni protested.

"Many not Chinese. Keep face down. Not look at them. That is Chinese way. That is what they expect you do. We are workers. We do not look at them. Understand me? Not look at them." He curled his hands around his eyes, a gesture intended to mimic the goggles. "Put on, yes?"

He tied the canvas flap and made his way round the truck to the cab. The engine started, its low growl feeding into their bones, and the truck lurched off again.

"That's it?" Giovanni asked. "Don't look at them? That's the plan?"

"It's worked so far." Jess turned to Massarra. "You concealed everything?"

The Israeli nodded. She gestured to Raffa. "We both did. No one will see it unless they walk right over the top of it."

"And the vehicles?"

"It's good enough."

She turned to Ufuk. "The drones will have enough flight time?"

"If we're successful," Ufuk said, "Simon will take control and land them to conserve fuel. If not, they will give us air support to cover our escape."

Jess leaned against a steel stanchion, fighting to stay upright as the truck jerked back and forth. "Let's hope we don't need it."

4

Ulan Bator
Mongolia

Zasekin sat alone at an old hardwood table, a single glass of vodka resting untouched in front of him. The filtered sunlight caught the edges of the glass and highlighted a fine rill of dried residue from where it had not been washed. The room smelled of urine and beer, which were more or less the same thing.

There were others in the bar, local Mongolians who watched him with hard eyes. They knew who he was, hated him, this stranger in their midst who didn't belong and who, to them, represented everything that was wrong with this broken place. Someone to heap their anger upon. His presence provoked memories of an entrenched bitterness between Russian, Mongolian, and Chinese alike that would never fade.

A year and a half since the skies had fallen. Summer never came. The ice and snow remained and deepened. The reserves of grains were gone. No more plants or crops this year. What animals there were in the city had been slaughtered. Anyone who was sick was taken out of the city and left to die in the frozen wastes.

And yet business in the whorehouse thrived.

When the clouds cleared, there was only one star in the night sky, growing brighter and brighter by the day. Some said it was the star of mercy, the star that appeared when Jesus was born, that He is coming to save them.

Zasekin knew more than they did. He had the voice on the other end of his radio that promised safety, told him about Saturn, but Zasekin knew more than that. He knew he would have to do something terrible—unspeakable—in return for what he was getting.

A heavy man approached him, towered over him for a moment too long so he thought there might be a problem. "She has finished, Pacan," the man said. "You can go up now."

Pacan—the name they used for him now. The pimp.

Zasekin reached for his glass. He knocked back the vodka quickly, hating the taste of it, but welcoming what it did to calm his nerves.

He climbed the stairs and knocked on the door he knew was hers, and waited for her voice the other side. When she replied, the fear in her voice tingled hurt in him.

She sat on the edge of the bed, hunched. Her eyes were rimmed in red and her lips trembled. She pulled a cardigan around her as he entered.

He closed the door gently behind him and sat across from her. He didn't like to sit beside her. So he sat opposite, on a small wooden chair.

"I can't do this anymore." She lit a cigarette with a trembling hand and took a long, deep pull. She held the smoke in her lungs for a long time before she let it escape. "But if I stop, they will hurt me."

"I won't let that happen." The words came out automatically, but he knew as well as she did that they were empty.

"What can you do to stop them?"

"There are places I could take you, if I spoke to Vor—"

"He would not listen. There is nowhere I would be safe."

Zasekin grunted. There was no place in this world that any of them would be safe. And yet. The voice on the radio. Maybe there was a way, and Zasekin had his own hiding holes he could still run to.

When she lifted the cigarette to her lips, he reached over and gently took her wrist. She flinched. He moved the cuff. Livid marks on the skin over yellowed bruising. Her face creased. Tears gathered in her swollen eyes.

"Are these burns?"

She avoided his eyes.

"You need to keep your head down, Belenko." Useless words, platitudes intended to reassure, but didn't. "Don't talk back to them."

She didn't reply, and for that he was grateful.

"They respect you, the other girls. They know you protect us. They are jealous of me, that you favor me."

"Do they know the truth?"

She leaned back. "The Pacan who does not rape his whores is not a man to be trusted. Kirill would be very angry were he to discover you were not a real man."

"Is that what you think? I do not take from you or the others, so I am not a real man? Is Kirill a real man?"

"I like when you sleep in this room with me. I feel like, just for a little while, I am safe."

Zasekin said nothing. She had the face of a young girl, but the weariness of an old woman who'd experienced a life in the shadows.

"Sleep child. That's all that matters. Sleep and don't dream."

He watched her sleep for a long time. He did that often and drew some small measure of comfort from the fact that his presence in this room meant no other would use her. His presence in the brothel, his requested-for role as its guardian, meant no violence befell the girls. He could not prevent them from working, the Vor would never have permitted that and he would have forfeited his life in simply suggesting it. That was a reality for these girls. All Zasekin could do, to his deep sadness, was make sure they were at least safe.

Belenko was right: there was nothing he could do to take her, or indeed any of the girls, away from this place. Where would they go? Months had passed since he had joined the Bratva.

In that short time, he'd been busy. He had strengthened his alliance with the Buryat tribes to the north and ensured they camped close. Supplies had been delivered as promised. Conversations between Zasekin and the man on the radio had become terser. Explanations had been asked for and refused. The man still gave Zasekin his assurances, the same platitudes and promises.

Even so.

When Zasekin was given coordinates where supplies would be left—and he sent the Khamnigan Buryat to pick them up—what he asked for was always there. The nomads now relied on them. More *evenks*, but these were Solon from the Hulunbuir region in the north of the Chinese Inner Mongolia Province, near the city of

165

Hailar. A community Zasekin himself had brought together. These people might well be alive because of him.

But what was the purpose?

How many would end up dying *because* of him?

In the morning, he left the brothel to take command of his other Bratva duties. There were deliveries to be made by he and his men and other goods to be picked up both in and out of the city itself. Zasekin had carved for himself and his men a reasonably comfortable existence, although they had all taken the decision to remain for the most part in Terelj rather than come into the city proper. It gave them a degree of autonomy and privacy they would not otherwise have had. It also allowed them to protect the Czilim.

Timur was frustrated by this decision, and now spent more and more time in Kirill's company, performing duties the *Avtoritet* set for him. The relative opulence Kirill enjoyed and bestowed on Timur from time to time—Zasekin knew it was simply to keep the younger man interested and hungering for more—had worked its charms on him.

Zasekin drove silently down the ice-covered streets, banged over the car-eating potholes, and zig-zagged through the grimy cinder-block walled alleyways on his way out of the city. The road opened up as he entered the dead-birch forests, following the single tracks through the snow.

He parked the same old Japanese four-by-four he had been using since his arrival in Ulan Bator in the lobby of the Terelj hotel, and smiled a wide grin as his men descended the front stairs to meet him. Vasily was fit and strong again, fully healed and keeping as fit as their supplies would allow him. Misha too had taken to a physical regime that he said reminded him of his time playing ice hockey. Evgeny was still Evgeny—bitter, sarcastic, and often belligerent. All that kept him in line was the understanding that the Bratva had given them a degree of freedom to exist safely—if pitched street battles and gunfights with the Chinese could truly be said to be safe.

But then his men were Russian.

"Good morning, Pacan," Evgeny said with a broad grin. "I trust you slept well."

Evgeny would rather have had Zasekin's role in the brothel, but Zasekin doubted Evgeny would have been so capable of abstention.

"More delivery runs?" Vasily asked.

"We should get them done quickly. I need to speak to the Buryat."

"When was the last time the man on the radio spoke with you?" Vasily's voice reduced to little more than a whisper when he said this, even though he knew they were the only ones within earshot.

"We are moving soon."

"Nothing about this mysterious facility he is so keen for you to find?" Timur said.

"Supplies keep appearing where he promises them."

"We have been forced to cow to these Bratva thugs, Andrei Nikolaevich," Misha said. "How much longer before one of us gets shot by the Chinese? Or by that nut job, Kirill?"

"We are taking greater and greater risks every day," Evgeny said. "Kirill sends us on the worst and most dangerous runs." He paused for a second before addressing the others. "Come, there is something we want to show you."

"What is it?"

"You'll see," Evgeny said as he made his way toward what Zasekin soon realized was the main supply room beside the kitchen. He opened the door and Zasekin saw that it was filled halfway to the ceiling with crates of canned food, bags of rice, even bottled water.

"You've been stealing from the Bratva! Are you mad?"

"We're stockpiling, Andrei Nikolaevich," Vasily replied meekly. "We head south."

"Into China?"

"To the coast. We have heard rumors that Australia is safe, Andrei Nikolaevich. Think of it! Warm and safe. Land that could be ours. All we need to do is find a boat."

"If the Bratva do not discover your theft, how do you think you'll get there? On foot?" Silence, then Zasekin understood. "You intend to take the Czilim."

167

Evgeny said: "What are we doing here, Andrei Nikolaevich? Why stay? This city is rotting by the day. We have a chance to save ourselves. Why not take it?"

"Because, my friends," Zasekin said, turning to look each of them in the eye in turn, "the world will end before we can get anywhere."

5

Outside Sanctuary China
Near Mongolian Border
April 24th

Beyond the folds of canvas it was impossible to see what the outside world looked like. Jess thought of moving to the back and trying to part the canvas in order see out, to gain some sense of where they were and when they would reach the service entrance to the complex. She decided not to, and instead focused on the rhythm of the truck and the turns it took.

The combined noise of the wind and the heavy diesel engine drowned out everything else. She felt the tremble of the road when she closed her eyes and concentrated, could feel the air outside shift as they passed into the ice-laden forest and then out again onto exposed valley roads. When the truck slowed and the wind died down, beyond the sound of the engine Jess caught a new background note of mechanical whining. The time had come.

"Goggles," she said, and raised her own. She pulled up the scarf, and huddled her body to resemble exhaustion and meekness. Fear rose inside her, built like a noxious gas that had nowhere to escape so instead roiled and churned. A caged animal—worse, an animal about to enter a cage of its own making.

The orange throb of the entrance light seeped through the camo netting covering the truck's bay. The truck stopped, then lurched and moved again. Slow. An inch at a time.

Jess unzipped the bottom of her jacket and reached into her inner layers. Felt the comfort of the pistol in her hand. They'd stored their automatic rifles in one of the crates with their old clothes. Beside her, she saw Raffa did the same. Held his pistol under his coat. With her other hand, she reached to hold his. Ice cold. She meant to impart some reassurance by squeezing his hand and giving him a stern look, but instead felt herself feeling reassured by holding onto this strong young man's hand. If anyone was going to protect someone, it was he who would lay down his life for her.

The wind was gone, replaced by the muted echoes of the interior of a concrete structure, of the grind of distant engines and echoing of voices. The stink of oil and diesel mixed with human sweat and damp, cold rock.

More voices now, close by. The driver's voice, raised, desperate. Another voice, growing angrier with each word. She gripped her pistol. Drew it slightly, as far as it would go but still remain hidden. She was close to the entrance to the rear of the truck. Raffa squeezed her hand tight.

This is going wrong. This was a bad idea.

The flap opened. Bright white light flooded in. She wanted to jump up, run, but forced herself still. Stay calm. She fixed her eyes on the floor of the truck, but kept her attention zeroed on her peripheral vision.

A man in uniform. The dark uniform of the Sanctuary China military personnel that they'd been instructed to recognize from their intelligence, very similar to the Sanctuary Europe military. A chill shivered Jess, and it wasn't from the cold. The man inspecting them was Chinese. He had a large assault rifle, knife, and pistol. Body armor. No helmet. Every movement suggested military training.

The head or neck, that's where she would need to aim, if it came to that. Torso would be no good, not with a 9mm pistol. She tensed.

The man spoke quickly, brashly. Loud, indecipherable words. She shrank from the man, not entirely as part of the act. Kept her gaze away.

More shouting.

This isn't working, she thought. She steadied herself. Got ready to move.

Ufuk turned to the soldier and spoke. He raised his hands in a gesture of submission. Was it a Chinese gesture? Was that where she recognized it from? She realized, a half-second after that, that Ufuk was *speaking* Chinese—and he never quite looked at the man.

A mysterious exchange. Ufuk subservient to this man in black.

The man indicated he was satisfied. He moved away, gestured for the driver to take his truck to wherever it was supposed to go.

The truck jerked forward to a crawl, and Jess whispered: "What the hell did you say?"

"You think I did business with the China Aerospace Corporation without knowing their language?"

Jess leaned back, her body uncoiling. Nothing Ufuk did should surprise her. That much she should have known by now.

Raffa touched her arm. "We're in," he said.

We're in. She should have been happy with the words, but looking at Ufuk, she knew something wasn't right. She couldn't shake a sinking feeling.

Not much further—a few hundred yards—and the truck came to halt. The engine died. The driver appeared at the rear a moment later. He beckoned for them to get out.

The driver spoke Chinese to Ufuk, who nodded.

"Keep our heads low and follow him," the Turk whispered, translating.

The driver took them from a tall, wide hangar, into a vast cavern lined with trucks and vehicles designed for the conditions outside. Snowmobiles, tractor units, lines of multi-tasking snow and ice removal equipment of the type used at airfields, to be fitted to carrier vehicles that could take them. Maintenance workers crawled over them. Sparks flew from angle grinders cutting through chassis structures. The sharp smell of burning metal and engine oil. Blow torches hissed, casting flickering light.

The driver made his way to a tunnel beyond the cavern, a circular structure cut into the mountain by a tunnel-boring machine. They passed workers dressed in overalls and wool coats, past more soldiers who this time paid them no heed.

Off the tunnel, at the base of which flooring had been placed, led to smaller alcoves that Jess could not see into because of the angle at which they had been cut into the rock.

It was into one of these the driver led them. A storage space stacked with crates and lit by a single lamp fixed to the ceiling. A utilitarian space hewn directly into the rock, roughly and quickly, without thought for comfort or visual appeal.

Stood behind the crates was a man.

Roger.

Beside him, Jess recognized a woman.

It was Abbie Barnes.

Roger approached the driver and nodded. Gestured to him the same way Ufuk had done earlier. He pressed something into the man's hand. Roger indicated the crates. The driver signaled that he understood, and then disappeared.

Jess went over to Roger and held out her hand, trying to find the right greeting.

He took her in his arms.

"I thought you were dead," he whispered into her cheek. "It's so good to see you."

She tried to smile and resisted the urge to keep him away. His warmth seemed genuine. He let her go and turned to Giovanni to offer his hand.

Giovanni grasped it.

Roger took his elbow in a full-blooded shake. "Good to see you too, Giovanni. We should go. I can't be gone for long."

"What now?" Jess said. "Can you get us to where we need to be?"

"Abbie will do that," Roger said. "The people who have enabled us to communicate are who you'll need to hack into the Sanctuary systems. Everything is set up and waiting." He looked at Jess, then Ufuk. "But listen to me. We need to get them out too. You understand? Once they get you in, it will be clear who did it. They can't stay here."

"How many?" This wasn't part of the plan.

"Five."

Jess glanced at Massarra, who shrugged. They hadn't been able to get in touch with the American extraction team, but then, they weren't supposed to until after they were inside. She hoped they had space.

"I'm not leaving these people behind. You don't know what they've risked."

"What about Hector?" Giovanni said, changing the topic, aware that Jess didn't want to answer.

"He's fine. Müller treats him well enough. He's the man's Golden Goose. I'll be the one to get him out. I'll bring him to the meeting point at the right time."

"I want to see him," Jess said.

172

"You have to trust me to get him out. There's no other way. I'll tell Lucca you're here. Then I'll go find Hector. You go with Ufuk and Abbie, Jess."

He held her gaze steady, his eye imploring for her to listen.

Abbie handed out ID passes. "Put these around your neck after you've taken off those clothes." She took a crate down and opened it. More clothes, civilian ones. "Put these on."

"Where are we going?" Jess asked.

"A hiding spot," Abbie said. "This place is similar to Sanctuary Europe, but you'll draw glances. Ninety percent of the people here are Chinese. There's a few hundred from San EU, and we're not well liked. Müller *has* managed to smooth the feathers a little…" Her voice trailed off.

At the mention of Müller's name, Jess's face must have contorted, and Abbie caught the look.

Giovanni examined his pass. It contained an image of him. He frowned. "And if we're stopped?"

"If people look at you, look away," Roger explained without really answering. "Don't engage them. Keep your face low, and show respect at all times. We're the lower class here. Remember that. I speak some Mandarin now—I'll take the lead."

"And they'll know we don't speak it," Massarra said. She removed her pistol and made to slip it into her belt. Abbie stopped her.

"You can't take those. You'll need to leave your weapons behind."

"What do we do if we need to fight?"

"They conduct random searches. If you're caught with a weapon of any kind—"

Massarra placed her pistol in the crate. "I don't need a gun to fight."

6

Sanctuary China
April 24th

Abbie led Jess and the rest through a rabbit warren of featureless eggshell-plastic corridors. The lighting seemed to emanate from all around them, a soft glow that opened up ahead of them and swallowed the tunnels back into darkness behind, their group of five a pod that surfed forward in the pocket of light.

Sanctuary 2.0.

The familiarity was comforting and disturbing at the same time, mixed with a tinge of terrifying. Comforting in that the design and aesthetics seemed so similar that Jess felt like she'd have a chance to navigate the space by herself, or at least understand how it worked, and added to that, confidence that Ufuk had to have his secret backdoors—both literal and figurative and even electronic—hidden somewhere within this infrastructure.

At the same time, the environment was disturbing because the last time Jess was immersed in this new-car plastic smell, she'd barely escaped with her life. Thousands of people had died around her—including her friend, Ballie Booker, who'd been crushed to death. And even more than that, frightening in the knowledge that this place was targeted for destruction by the US military. Even her allies and compatriots would kill her if they failed.

And there was that same familiar sensation of millions of tons of granite overhead, but this time it wasn't just the rock pressing down. As each second ticked away, Jess reminded herself they were here on borrowed time, almost as a courtesy before the American military hawks would get their way, as a way to say at least they *tried* before killing thousands more. Before obliterating this place.

The clock was ticking.

Saturn was coming.

Abbie assured them that the surveillance systems in these corridors were deactivated, that they weren't being followed. She said this was a service area, still under construction. That they didn't have to worry.

174

Jess worried.

Abbie held out her hands and stopped them. A door in the corridor wall whispered open to reveal a small, dimly lit room. Abbie led them inside, into quarters eerily similar to Jess's ion San EU. A single small table in the center, a kitchenette on the back wall, a door to the bathroom on the right. The atmosphere was different, the texture of the room coming from its ornaments on shelves, pictures on walls—definitely Asian, but also just as definitely Sanctuary.

At the dining table sat three young Chinese. Two girls and a boy. Teenagers. Each held a tablet device, their faces lit by the flickering colors from the screen. They looked up with deer-in-headlight wide eyes as Jess and her group tumbled in through the door.

The door panel slid closed behind them.

Abbie stood proudly to one side, her face stern. "Please allow me to introduce Jing, Xiulan"—she indicated the two girls, then pointed at the boy—"and Qiang. And this is Jessica—"

"*Gesù Cristo*," Giovanni muttered under his breath, coming up behind Jess, and then added in a louder voice: "This is our infiltration support team?" His tone was equal parts incredulous and sarcastic.

"Pleased to meet you," Jess said, ignoring her Italian's remonstrations.

"*Huanying dajia*," the girl introduced as Jing said.

As a group, the teenagers stood and bowed slightly, hands touched together in front of them as in prayer.

"Welcome," Jing continued. "We are pleased to have you here."

Silence. Except for the heaving breaths of Jess's group, the adrenaline still coursing through their veins. She gritted her teeth against a curse herself. Abbie was General Marshall's daughter. Jess had met the General when she was incarcerated in Sanctuary Europe, just before it was destroyed. He'd struck her as a reasonable, intelligent man. She'd half expected to see his face greeting them when the door slid open. Or at least, a group of adults.

"Thank you for helping us," Jess said finally, struggling to find words.

"We are not helping you," the boy who was Qiang said. He appeared young—his face had a smooth, ageless quality to it—but his voice and tone belied someone much older. "We're helping everyone. It is important you understand that."

"Jing is the daughter of a senior member of the Politburo," Abbie said, sensing Jess's disappointment. "And Qiang is a member of the—"

"Are there more?" Giovanni asked. "I mean, in this resistance? *Adults?*"

Jing's face contorted and she cast her eyes down. "You are not—"

Massarra stepped forward and started speaking to Jing, and the girl's face lit up. The Israeli was speaking Chinese, a quick and fluid exchange. She pointed at the boy, who nodded, and then at the girl. Everyone was suddenly nodding.

"Are you speaking Mandarin?" Jess interrupted, taking hold of Massarra's arm.

"Cantonese."

"Can you please speak English? I need to understand what's happening."

"I was just asking Jing if this was Jiang Zemin's son." She pointed at the boy again, who bowed slightly. "She said yes, and I congratulated her. Zemin is part of the hardline Politburo, so the boy could be very useful to us."

"That's all you said?"

"She also told us that Zhao Peng died before he could get here," Ufuk said. "More likely killed than just died."

"And who is he?"

"A more liberal member of the Politburo. From what they're saying, there is still a government in Beijing. I wasn't counting on that."

"For what?" Giovanni asked.

"We might need friends."

Jess looked at her watch. "We've got to be out of here in an hour to rendezvous with the extraction team. Let's just get to work."

Massarra and Raffa positioned themselves by the door, while Giovanni sat down on the small couch to one side of the table.

Ufuk sat himself down at the table and spoke quickly in Chinese. Jess paced back and forth in circles.

Jess presumed he was explaining their plan, about locating the correct point in the Sanctuary systems to access, so the version of Simon on his tablet could do the rest. He said he needed to get inside Sanctuary to disable their communications, to take control of its systems. A hack from the inside. That was what they wanted—what the Americans and Ufuk wanted.

What Jess wanted was Hector.

So close now.

The young Chinese replied quickly to Ufuk, their voices rising, the girls more eager, the boy Qiang reticent and curt in his demeanor. Ufuk brought out his tablet and connecting cables. Fingers danced over the screens of their devices, all four now linked together.

Raffa went to the kitchen and opened the drawers. He took a knife from one of them, then went back to the door. He closed his eyes, listening.

"How long will this take, Ufuk?" Jess asked. He'd said it would only take minutes once he was connected on the inside.

"We need to be certain the conduit they have chosen is the best one possible. For there, Simon will determine the route to the pathways needed to place the timed algorithms intended to disable the key systems. They must not be able to detect our presence while we are still in the complex. Nor should they be able to re-establish the systems once we are gone."

"How long, Ufuk? Simple question."

"Not more than half an hour."

"Half an *hour*?"

"Simon will accomplish his own tasks in seconds. Müller couldn't resist installing a copy of him here. The virus I had Abbie install was very simple. It listened. The copy of Simon in the containment facility used speakers to transmit itself."

"Like, music?"

"Very low frequency, below audible level, but able to transmit information at a slow pace. Simon wormed his way out."

"They won't be able to detect our presence?"

"I've already accessed their security systems. No alerts. Nobody knows we're here. We're good. Trust me."

Jess watched him as he went back to working alongside the Chinese.

She turned to Abbie. "We need to be ready," she said. "If they're coming with us, we need to move quickly. We can't stay in one big group. We'll attract attention. Better Jing and Xiulan go with one group. Ufuk, you, and Qing can go with the other. That splits the Chinese speakers. We stay in sight of each other, but try to appear separate. Same route back out?"

"Yes."

"Roger's meeting us back at the truck with Hector?"

"That's the plan."

Raffa held up one hand. "There's someone coming." He brandished his knife.

"We're almost there," Ufuk said. "I'm opening access from the copies of Simon on my tablet now, inserting him into the network."

Giovanni made his way to the door. "Are you sure you heard something?" he whispered to Raffa.

"Does your father know?" Jess asked Abbie.

The girl's shoulders hunched inward. "He doesn't know, but he will understand. I used his credentials, that's what's making this possible."

Raffa leaned in toward the door. He waited, listening, before taking a deep breath. "They're gone."

"We need to calm down," Ufuk said. "They don't know we're here."

"We've taken every precaution," Abbie added.

The lights in the room suddenly went dark. A half-second later a thin sliver of light penetrated from the doorway, two shadows dropping through the gloom. Jess realized right away what it was. A gap in the doorway wide enough for the tiny canisters that clattered onto the floor. She knew what it was, but couldn't react in time.

Except to close her eyes.

When the flash-bang grenades went off, one thudding detonation after the other, the air in the room reverberated like slabs of concrete slamming into Jess's face. The shockwave burrowed into her eyes and temples and brain, nausea squalled in her gut. Through eyes held tightly shut, blinding light flashed.

Jess fought it and staggered to stay on her feet, scrabbled for anything to use as a weapon. Disoriented, she vaguely discerned a struggle in the doorway—Raffa or Giovanni. Beyond the whining in her ears, muffled shouts and screams as everyone in the room was beaten to the ground. She felt the blows rain down on her without restraint—rifle butts on her shoulders, in her face.

Kicks into her chest.

She caught hold of one of the boots that struck with an arm and twisted her body to bring its owner down. She wrenched the foot sideways, feeling the ankle tendons snap as she brought the weight of her anger and her body down onto them.

A scream.

She kicked, and swung, blinded by red of her own blood stinging her eyes. She connected from time to time, but not enough. Something heavy cracked into the side of her skull. Darkness then, and silence.

7

Sanctuary China
April 24th

"I know you're awake," said a voice in the fog.

Jess felt her head loll forward. She hadn't been knocked unconscious, but close to it. She lifted it and tried to focus. Someone held her upright. She felt a chair underneath her, cold against the skin of her left hand. And that voice.

Dr. Müller.

"You knew we were coming," she said.

"And you knew I knew, and yet you came."

"I had to." She opened her eyes fully to take in her surroundings. A banging headache throbbed in her temple. Her mouth felt pasty and metallic.

Someone sat down beside her.

It was Abbie, her head down. Jess's arms and hands were free. No handcuffs. No chains. She moved her legs. Not chained to the floor.

"Who was it? Roger?" Jess coughed, her lungs still clogged with ash some the air outside.

"He didn't know," Müller replied. "The man cares very deeply for you. As do I, in a way. We have a long history, Miss Rollins."

"Where did you take Raffa and Giovanni?"

Before Müller could answer, the second door opened and into the room walked five men dressed in military dress uniforms. Four were Chinese. Not men Jess recognized, but from their age and bearing, and the rows of medal ribbons and the way the soldiers stood ramrod straight when they entered, she was certain they were senior officers in the People's Liberation Army of China.

"Jessica, this is Mr. Jiang Zemin, I believe you met his daughter, Jing," Ufuk said, standing and bowing. "And Mr. Sheng and Mr. Enlai."

The last man to enter, after the Chinese, was taller with a short-cropped head of salt and pepper hair. Jess recognized him. General Eugene Marshall.

180

Marshall scanned the room as he entered, searching. When his narrowed eyes rested on his daughter and the soldier who held her, he stepped forward, across the man. He reached out and took the soldier's arm and moved it away from Abbie. "Dr. Müller, we agreed I would deal with my daughter."

"And you will, but she still has information we need to know. There must be more of them."

"I will question her," Marshall said. His voice was weak.

"Not alone, General. I am sure you can see the conflict of interest there."

"You're not in charge—"

"Was your daughter acting alone, General?" Müller's face teetered somewhere between a smile and a frown, and he glanced at the Chinese as he continued: "You do understand our position, General Marshall. And Jing Huang, daughter of the Chairman Zemin, is in the same position as your daughter. This is very delicate. Very delicate. If I hadn't caught them..."

Marshall's shoulder's dropped. "We knew they were coming. *You* knew Ufuk was coming here. I'm the one that said that Abbie took my credentials."

"That is to your credit."

"If you hurt her—"

"I'm not going to hurt anyone, but this is out of my hands."

Abbie was pulled to her feet and marched out ahead of Marshall. He turned and left the room without another word. Müller waited for them to leave, said something in Chinese to the three senior ministers who remained, glaring at Jessica. With curt nods, they spoke to their guards and followed Marshall out of the room.

"Now, Jessica," Müller said. "I'm trying to help you, but this is sovereign territory of the People's Republic of China, which is very much still a world power. Perhaps, *the* world power. An invasion by American spies. A military operation by a foreign power on foreign soil."

Jess winced and brought a hand to test her face. Somebody had cleaned her up, she noticed. There was no blood. A cut over her eye was bandaged.

Müller waved a hand and pointed at a water cooler. One of the guards filled and handed him a glass, which he gave to Jessica. "You might have begun a war, Jessica—"

"I'm trying to stop one." She took a sip of the water. Her head throbbed terribly, and only partly from the trauma. She was dehydrated.

"—and now shown our Chinese allies what the US," Müller continued, "or the desperate part of what's left of it, is capable of."

"They're going to destroy this place. You know that."

Müller sat down opposite her. "Actually, I do *not* know that," he replied, shaking his head. "This is all being recorded, you realize? The Chinese are listening to what you're saying, and you're saying the Americans are going to destroy this place?"

"The Chinese and Russian fleet is intercepting our convoy as we speak. Millions of people are aboard those ships."

"That is a geopolitical event somewhat beyond even my pay grade, and also beyond the scope of Sanctuary. We are just hiding while the world goes on outside. At least, that was the plan, before Mr. Erdogmus wrecked it. Both literally and figuratively."

"They're going to flatten this—"

"Place that's designed to withstand a direct nuclear attack?" Müller finished her sentence for her. "It will be an interesting test, I'll give you that. Not sure if you and I will be allowed to remain inside if it comes to that."

Jess gritted her teeth.

"And what was the plan? To destroy this Sanctuary just like the last one? I see your brought Miss Mizrahi along." He tutted and shook his head. "Unbelievable who the Americans will work with. How many times have they consorted with terrorists to satisfy their short term needs, when in the long term—"

"We didn't destroy Sanctuary Europe."

Müller put his hands onto his thighs and straightened upright in his seat. "*We?* Jessica, do you ever stop to consider that you are just a leaf blown along in this storm we call Ufuk Erdogmus? Do you *know* that he didn't destroy it?"

"You destroyed it because you knew about Saturn's rings impacting the Earth, that the northern hemisphere would be devastated."

"I only found that out by accessing Ufuk's systems," Müller protested. "And if I hadn't, would he have told the world?"

"He didn't know."

Müller laughed, threw his head back in disbelief. "And you believe him? If I hadn't intervened and broadcast from Tanzania, with the details of the Saturn intercept, the entire world would still be unaware."

Jess took another sip of water.

Müller pointed past her head. "That entire convoy of Americans wouldn't be where they are now. There wouldn't be three million of your countrymen already safe in Australia." He jabbed his chest with one finger. "You can thank *me* for that."

Her water was finished and Jess put it down. She put her elbows onto the table and rested her forehead into cupped hands. "I don't know what game you're playing—"

Müller shot to his feet, his chair clattering to the floor behind him. "Do you think I want the Sanctuaries destroyed? I spent my life building them. My entire *life*." The last word he almost screamed, before calming himself and leaning into the table. "I admit, there is a moral gray zone, and I did some things…but I sacrificed myself to try and save humanity."

"You sacrificed my mother and father." Jess raised her head, felt the old familiar rage rising inside her.

"Have I done any worse than your CIA friends have done? Who spied on your father? Than your Ufuk Erdogmus? Do you think he didn't know? Whose families have *your* friends sacrificed for the greater good?"

"Not *mine*."

"Erdogmus is using you, Jessica, to push his agenda. He would have never gotten in here, would never have earned the trust of the Americans, without you. Isn't that true?"

Jess didn't reply, but that was answer enough.

"I think Mr. Erdogmus wants to wipe the entire planet clean, kill us all. That's what I think."

"That's ridiculous. Why would he do that?"

"I knew he was going to come here. All I had to do was watch and wait. I plugged into Simon, learned some new tricks. Where is the canister, Jess?"

She balled her hands into fists, kept her eyes down.

183

"That 'seed bank' that Ufuk's been carrying around? It's a weapon. It's a virus. Do you know that? A weapon of mass destruction."

The words prickled the hair on the back of Jess's neck. "I don't know what you're talking about."

"What about Mars First? What has Ufuk told you about it? They haven't been able to raise it in weeks. Did he contact it?"

"I don't know."

"What about Ufuk's facility in northern China?"

That caught Jess by surprise, and Müller saw it.

"He didn't tell you, did he?"

She shrugged reflexively. "I don't know what you're talking about," she repeated, but even her own words were beginning to sound hollow.

"Do you want me to bring Hector?"

"Don't bring him into this."

"I'm not the one who *did* bring him into this. Talk to your friend Erdogmus."

"You're the one that took him from me," Jess protested.

"To protect him from that monster. How can you be so blind?"

Jess exhaled long and hard. She wasn't going to win this argument. "What are you going to do with Ufuk and Massarra? With Jing, Xiulan, and Qiang?"

"That's out of my hands. The Chinese aren't as forgiving as I am. Ufuk, in particular, is seen as a spy to the government of the People's Republic of China. So I'm going to give you an opportunity. A chance to do the right thing and prevent more suffering."

Müller gestured to one of the walls. It flickered. An image appeared. A brightly lit room occupied by a single chair. In the chair, slumped and head lolling, hair matted and glistening, sat Roger. His arms were tied behind his back, and again to the chair. He was naked, his pale skin already mottled purple with bruises.

"My god," Jess whispered.

"The Chinese secret service have already begun their work."

"You knew Roger was talking to us. You're just as guilty as he is."

"It was a hunch, and thank God for that, but I'm not responsible for his choices, as much as I wish I could help him." He looked away from the image of Roger, his nose crinkled in a grimace. "Who in the China National Space Administration did Ufuk do business with? He launched four heavy lift rockets from a facility near here, but we can't find it. Those men who were in here? That's two-thirds of the Chinese Politburo, the governing body of China. They need to know, Jessica."

A cold realization crept up Jess's spine. Müller was no fool. He peddled in half-truths the same as Ufuk did, but he wasn't lying.

"Let me talk to Ufuk," Jess said finally.

"We don't have time," Jess yelled.

They'd led Jess a hundred feet down the corridor, into another featureless egg-shell white room.

Ufuk was seated—secured—to a chair in front of the metal table in the middle. He held up his chained hands. "Seems they're treating you better than me. You should be happy. We're back in a Sanctuary. You're with Hector. Protected and underground."

"They'll drop us outside to freeze to death."

"I'll do everything I can to make sure that doesn't happen."

"What's in the cylinder you put in the drone? The canister you retrieved from the ocean?"

"I already told you—it's a seed bank."

"Müller says it's a weapon."

"It's the opposite of a weapon. And you won't find it."

"Then tell me about this facility they're talking about. It's near here. You never told us. Another secret? Is that why we're here?"

"I don't have many left." The Turk seemed just as at ease, locked up here, as he had in Oman. "I couldn't tell you, or the Americans. I needed to get here first."

"Why?"

"Because there is an order to things."

"So this is going according to plan?" Jess couldn't help her eyes going wide. "Müller wants to know where it is."

Ufuk eyebrows knitted together.

"You take us there, he'll let me and Hector go."

Ufuk raised his head. His face was bruised, smeared with blood. Misshapen around one eye. "Something of a challenge, isn't it?"

"Everyone breaks, Ufuk. Give them what they want."

"I'm sorry, you know. I never wanted you to be the one."

"You lied to me at every step." Jess felt tears in her eyes, even knowing that a dozen people were watching her right now. She wiped her face with the back of one hand. "You used all of us. Do you know how much I hate you for that?"

"I am sorry."

"Roger doesn't have long, Ufuk. He risked everything for you, for Hector. You owe him."

"Don't worry about Roger. He must walk toward his own fate."

"What does that mean?"

"Tell Müller I'll give him and the Chinese everything. I'll take him to the facility and give him the access he needs. He doesn't need Hector any longer. He has me now."

He lifted his head back and screamed. Thrashed his long hair so that wetness fell on her. Blood and sweat.

"You hear me, Müller?" he shouted. "Give me your word you'll protect, them! You hear me, Müller? I'll take you there."

186

8

Ulan Bator
Mongolia

From the room next door, the rhythmic whining of tired bedsprings echoed through the paper-thin walls—the guttural moans of a client as he humped a girl staring long into the distance with empty eyes. Zasekin rubbed sweat from his forehead. A trembling glow from the lamp on his bedside table. Shrouded darkness concealed Ulan Bator outside.

How could he leave the girls behind? What sort of man did that make him?

His hands shook.

He took another long slug of vodka. Dragged a cuff across his mouth. The alcohol burned his throat in a comforting, familiar way—but his hands still twitched. He stuffed clothes into a bag and then turned to the set of drawers next to his bed. His pistol lay on top of a battered copy of the bible. He tucked the gun into his waistband and closed the drawer, more gently this time, trying not to look at the Good Book.

The time had come.

His task set.

The man on the radio had named his price: go to a facility and take control—its location defined within a valley on the border of China and Mongolia.

This morning he'd had the talk with his men, all except Timur who was missing. He'd told them what was required. What they needed to do if they wanted to survive what was coming. Zasekin's Buryat friends were starving, the radio-man knew that. The man promised supplies beyond their wildest dreams at the location, and not only that, he promised to give sanctuary to Zasekin and his men if successful. A warm, protected place to wait out the coming storm from heaven. The new star in the sky was getting brighter by the day.

The rumors harder to ignore.

Destruction was about to rain down on the Earth again.

But more to the point, for Zasekin's Russian mind, there was a further deal to be struck. He felt certain the radio-man had great influence and resources. It would not take much to shift the balance of power in Ulan Bator. If he betrayed the Bratva from within, then the city could be reclaimed and freed from the disease of the mafia—Russian and Chinese. A way to protect his girls. A way to protect Belenko. Perhaps he could bring her to the safe place the radio-man promised, and if not there, then he had a safe place in Russia he could still get to.

The door opened and Zasekin brought the pistol up quickly.

Did anyone know he was here? He'd snuck into the brothel from the back entrance. He had been careful not to be followed. His counter surveillance maneuvers had been considered and cautious. The SVR had taught him that much at least.

It was Belenko—he relaxed the coiled muscles of his midsection—but when he caught a glimpse her face, her frightened eyes, his grip tightened on the pistol. He sprang to his feet.

"They are coming for you." She hesitated in the doorway, clutching a blanket to her chest.

Zasekin made his way to the window and pulled the curtain aside.

"Your friend Timur, he told them you were leaving," Belenko added.

In the snowy street below, Kirill and two Bratva, all with their Scorpion machine pistols readied. Damn it, Timur. He'd suspected, but tried to wish it away. Timur liked the life he had here. With the Bratva, there was a staircase in front of Timur that led upward—if he was willing to trade his soul as he climbed. Had he told them about the supplies Evgeny and the others had stolen from the Bratva? Things were going from bad to worse.

"What are you waiting for?" Belenko pleaded. "You must go."

Zasekin grabbed her wrist, and she shrank back, expecting something hurtful. A punch. A threat or recrimination. Or a swift kick.

"Not without you," Zasekin whispered and pulled her into him.

9

Sanctuary China
Main conference room
April 26th

Dr. Müller was ushered into the conference room by a burly security guard, the bulge of the man's pistol plainly visible under his black suit. A demure woman in a high-collared, long silk red dress handed Müller a translation earbud, and without saying anything pointed down one side of the room, indicating for him to follow her. She led him to a white leather chair to one side—not one of the chairs at the main table.

Müller thanked her and took his seat.

Just being invited was a privilege—and General Marshall hadn't been—but that didn't mean Müller liked being a second-class citizen. He smiled anyway.

The room was sixty feet long, with a recessed ceiling in oiled mahogany that matched the long table in the center of the room. A large floral print dominated one end of the room, a projector screen the other, with scrolls of Chinese characters positioned at ten foot intervals down either side. Each chair at the main table was occupied, each with a very serious-looking Chinese man in a dark suit and red tie, but there was no doubt where the power was concentrated. All eyes were on the four men at a separate head table, just in front of the projector screen.

"Gentleman." One of the men, his black hair graying and with hazel eyes stood. "I am bringing this council to order."

It was the newly anointed Chairman Jiang Zemin. Müller had met him three times before, each time earning a forced smile. He hadn't wanted to let Müller into Sanctuary China, and had only given in when Müller showed up with Hector—the key to Ufuk Erdogmus's networks. Zemin spoke in Mandarin, but it was machine-translated into Müller's native German. Not perfect, but good enough.

"I would first like to start with a moment of silence for our late Chairman Peng, who was killed on his way to this facility." Zemin bowed his head, and the other thirty men at the table followed his lead. Not a single woman at the main table. Just the attendants hovering in the peripheries.

For at least five seconds, the room was silent.

"May his soul find everlasting peace," Chairman Zemin said as he raised his head. "But for those of us still in this world, there is work to be done. In less than three weeks, Saturn will drop from the skies. The American navy, with millions of soldiers and their warships, are two-thirds of the way across the Pacific. It is my opinion that we must not let them continue."

"Under what authority?" asked a man at the opposite end of the table.

"Li Quili and Deng Yaobang were invited here and can play a role," the Chairman replied. "But our government is no longer in Beijing."

"I agree," Keng Mao, the man sitting next to the Chairman said. "We make up the majority of the remaining Politburo. And have resources here that surpass what Bejing is capable of."

"When did this become a democracy? We rule by unanimous agreement," Chen Sheng said, sitting away from the head table and just in front of Müller. He was much younger than the Chairman, with a full head of jet black hair.

A hushed gasp from the assembled to the challenge of the Chairman in public.

It was Chen Sheng and Zhou Enlai, two of the four members of the ruling council, who Müller had made his deal with to come to Sanctuary China. When he arrived, though, the more hardline Chairman Zemin and Kong Mao had blocked him.

It was Kong Mao, sitting to the right of his Chairman, who stood in his defense: "We cannot allow the American warships to make their home in our backyard."

"Seven million people are escaping with their lives," Zhou Enlai said.

The Chairman smiled and put his hands out, asking everyone to remain seated. "How many million have died already? I am not hard hearted"—he half-smiled to make a show of how tender he was—"but we have to be practical."

"And how many are American soldiers in that fleet?" Mao added. "How many nuclear weapons? Our rice fields are dead. We have a billion people who will need somewhere to live. The

Americans are finished; their time is over. All they have is a military that will end up killing *our* people in their desperation."

"They are just trying to save their people," Sheng said. "And if we attack them, we ensure that many more of our people will die."

"Do you think they will leave afterward? Or will the warships remain off our coasts?"

"I believe if we try to stop them, they will use nuclear weapons. You do not corner a tiger."

"And so?"

"They will destroy Beijing."

"It is already lost to us." Chairman Zemin interrupted the exchange. "Our government is here now. Our future lies in our hand."

"Dr. Müller, this place was designed to withstand a nuclear strike?" Sheng turned in his seat to face him. "This is correct?"

Müller was surprised to be suddenly included. "Ah, yes, within boundaries." He cleared his throat. "We have a thousand feet of granite over our heads. I am quite certain—"

"What of the promises of Dr. Müller?" Mao interrupted. "We allowed him inside, and now the Americans have come here, tried to destroy us. We must strike first."

"Our security service was aware of the infiltration. And strike at what exactly?" Sheng said. "A thousand square miles of ocean?"

"We detonate warheads at high altitude, a carpet of nuclear fire—"

"There has already been much blood—"

"You *son* collaborated with these traitors," Mao said, standing.

"As did Chairman Zemin's daughter," Sheng countered.

Another surprised hush of voices.

Chairman Zemin's cheeks turned red, but his obsequious smile remained. "Gentleman, let us focus. The Americans want the orbital equipment of Mr. Erdogmus—"

"Which Müller has already promised us in exchange for his position here," said Mao. He winced. "Excuse me, Chairman, for interrupting you."

"We now find part of which was launched from a secret installation north of here," the Chairman continued. "We need to find its location, and understand what is there. Perhaps we have more to negotiate with than we know."

Sheng nodded in agreement. "And we have Peng Shoung— my own niece—aboard Mars First, Chairman."

"And we have Mr. Erdogmus himself," Chairman Zemin said. "We have all the advantages in this game."

"I suggest we send Dr. Müller to investigate the claims that there is this facility in Mongolia," Sheng said. "And to send the Chairman's own security forces with him."

"And if this can be verified," Mao said, "then I think that Dr. Müller's place within these walls will be validated."

Müller felt a rush of blood coming into his cheeks. "I could not agree more."

The Chairman stood, and everyone else around the table joined him. "I believe we have all the pieces on our side of the board. Let us not make any mistakes."

"What just happened in there?" Müller paced from one side of the room to the other.

They were in Chen Sheng's private quarters, in the reception area. A fountain filled with colorful koi fish bubbled in the middle of a leafy garden. General Marshall sat to one side on a wooden bench, while Chen Sheng stood next to the fountain, his hands clasped behind his back.

"This is an existential threat to China. You must understand that," Sheng replied.

"Mao said that my place here would be validated if this facility is found. By extension, this means my place here is *not* otherwise."

"There is logic to this."

"This is not what we agreed."

"You agreed to provide Mr. Erdogmus's systems. Including the ones within Sanctuary China."

"And I will. I just need more time."

"There is still three weeks until Saturn arrives. There is little danger."

Müller stopped pacing and squared up to face Sheng. "Would you go outside? Now?"

"These were not the promises I made."

"I see." Müller stared at Sheng, who did not flinch or avert his eyes.

"A space launch facility that may be intact," Sheng added. "This is something we must investigate. You are the only person here we can trust."

"I'm staying here," Marshall said. "I have to protect my daughter."

"And nobody is asking that you leave, General," Sheng said.

Müller looked at Marshall, and then back at Sheng.

"I see," he repeated, nodding slowly.

The wall lights glowed bright as Müller entered the detention cubicle. Ufuk Erdogmus sat against one wall, his legs crossed, his back straight. His thin cotton tunic and pants were torn, his face a mass of bruises. Eyes closed, as if asleep, but Müller knew he wasn't.

"You and I are going on a little trip," Müller said.

"Not worried about Saturn dropping on your head?" Ufuk replied, his eyes still shut. "Wouldn't you prefer to cower in here?"

"It seems this secret facility of yours has inspired some imagination."

"Surprised you still had any."

Müller stepped fully into the room and instructed the two Sanctuary China military guards to retrieve Ufuk, to get him on his feet. "But that's the thing. It's not a surprise. I knew you had something out there."

Ufuk's eyes remained closed, but the edges of them twitched. The two guards hauled him to his feet.

"There is still the problem of your mysterious canister," Müller said. "Is this the final solution? I know you. Always a Plan A, B, C...is this the Plan C if all else fails? To wipe us out with a virus?"

"It is not death, but life." Ufuk opened his eyes and smiled.

"But life for who, I wonder?" Müller turned to leave, but then stopped. "Perhaps we should take Jessica with us?"

Ufuk shrugged. "What would be the point? She's nothing."

"And the boy?"

This time Ufuk looked away. "We don't need the boy."

"Don't need?" Müller frowned but then grinned. "Let's all go together, shall we?"

"They won't let you bring them."

"*Won't* let me bring them? *They?*" Müller's tentative grin widened into a full-blown smile.

The black-clad security guards quick marched Jessica down a side tunnel. The past day, she'd been treated well, but this morning, before anyone else was awake, she'd been dragged from her room. One of the guards handed her boots and an arctic parka. So she was being taken outside. They tried to hurry her, but waited patiently while she attached her prosthetic, almost embarrassed.

They shoved her forward, glancing over their shoulders every few seconds.

Whatever was going on, it shouldn't be, Jess realized.

They marched her up into a stairwell lit with orange sodium lights. She counted each flight, but then lost count at twenty. Sweat trickled down her back. Her thighs aching from the effort, after what seemed an eternity of climbing, they came into what appeared to be an exterior corridor. One guard went ahead of her, keying his way through the doors. They walked over a metal grating, a hundred feet of open space beneath Jess's feet.

If it was an execution, there were easier ways than this.

Or was this a rescue?

That hope evaporated the moment she was shoved through the final set of doors in a blustery swirling snowstorm. Dr. Müller stood in front of a massive tracked transport, painted white. The vehicle was a cross between a snowcat and a tank.

"Beautiful, yes?" Müller patted one of the treads. "Nobody builds equipment for the snow quite like the Russians. Amphibious. Climbs mountains. Eats its way through half-frozen swamps. Can get anywhere, and more important—get *back* from anywhere."

Jess squinted in the bright morning light and swirling snow. At least ten more of the tank-like vehicles were lined up down the access road.

"What are we—" Jess had to pause to catch her breath "—what are we doing?"

"Going on a little family trip." He opened the door above the tracked tread.

Hector's face appeared, but a guard held him back.

"Go, go," Müller said.

Jess stumbled forward past Müller and grabbed the door handle. She scrambled up the tank tread and took Hector in her arms. "Are you okay?"

"I'm fine, Jessica," Hector replied.

It had been more than a year since she'd had him this close. She clenched her jaw, tried to stop the tears. So much time she'd spent thinking about this moment. She couldn't believe it, and he seemed different. She took another look at him. An adult.

"You see? I said I would reunite you with the boy," Müller said from below them. "And now we all go together to find out the truth."

Jess squeezed Hector, then opened her eyes to look around the rest of the cab of the tank-truck. Two rows back, Ufuk nodded, his eyes glassy, his head bobbing as if he was fighting to stay awake. The inside was twenty feet deep, and fit at least twenty people. At the back were Sanctuary China staff—but they weren't the regular Sanctuary China security from the unfamiliar insignia on their chests. Toward the front were Müller's own men, from Sanctuary Europe, with two of them gripping Ufuk tight in the third row.

Jess squinted to look into the next transport and caught a glimpse of Giovanni next to Raffa and Lucca. Why were they being brought?

"We are three hundred kilometers north of Beijing," Müller said, climbing into the front seat of the tank-truck, next to the driver. "Almost closer to…say"—he turned to smile at Ufuk—"Ulan Bator, would be the closest big city?"

The tank-truck's engine sputtered and then growled to life, shaking the seat under Jess. The door beside her slammed shut. The tank-truck lurched forward.

Müller leaned forward in his seat and pulled out the microphone of a radio. He began speaking, and Jess thought he was speaking German to begin with. She strained to hear him over the noise of the truck, squeezing Hector in her arms.

No, that wasn't German.

He was speaking in Russian.

"Yes, yes, we are on our way," Müller said in English as he finished talking. He turned around in his seat. "My Russian friends speak some English too. We are not alone out here, Ufuk. You understand. I have made plans as well."

Ufuk seemed to smile, his eyes unfocused, bloodshot.

The tank-truck accelerated through the snow.

10

Sanctuary China
April 27th

The rain fell in wide, relentless sheets and kicked off the Manhattan sidewalk in a hazy squall. The people around Roger Hargate ran, newspapers over heads, hoods pulled up against the deluge, but he remained still. The rain thumped against his head and ran down his neck and face. He blinked it out of his eyes. Eventually, he stepped aside and watched them all hustle along the street.

He leaned against the window of a drycleaner's, sheltered by its faded blue awning. His legs felt suddenly frail, unable to hold him up. The world beyond him faded to a blur, a wash of color that grew suddenly indistinct and unfathomable. The patter of the rain on the canvas intensified, now constant and loud. It fused into a long roar, drowning out the nighttime symphony of the city.

Jess had slammed the door in his face and Roger had just stood there, staring at it, hoping she would somehow realize her mistake and open it. Waiting like a fool.

You have to listen to me, he had told her, but she wouldn't. This isn't about us, he had insisted. She needed to understand, but didn't give him the chance to explain. Too much history between them.

His throat was so dry it hurt to swallow, even to inhale. The familiar toxic pull welled inside him. He couldn't separate his thoughts—they came to him in a confused torrent. He closed his eyes and tried to breathe, but all he could do was ball his fists to prevent his hands from shaking.

What a damn fool.

Alone, consumed by the noise in his head, the darkness that was always there, even in the light, depression's suffocating cloud.

He hadn't gone to Jess with clear intentions though, had he? Yes, he had wanted to tell her the truth, protect her father and confess his betrayal, but that wasn't all though, was it? Had he really thought that, in doing all of that, he might win her back? It was hardly a heroic action. Again, he thought: Fool. Damn idiot.

What did it matter anyway?

He barely understood how or when he came to be seated at a stool in a dimly-lit bar, sucking in its too-familiar aroma of old leather and stale beer, imprisoned by its cacophony of acrid music and too-loud voices. Perhaps a place like this was better than a street corner pusher.

The barman tossed him a clean bar towel and indicated his face and hair. Roger ran it over both, then folded it carefully and placed it on the counter.

"What can I get you?" the barman asked.

Roger hesitated. Then said, quietly, almost so he couldn't hear the words himself: "Any beer's fine."

The barman nodded and turned away, leaving Roger staring at two trembling hands resting on the brass piping of the counter. He bit a dry lip.

"You want to open a tab?" the barman asked as he set the glass down on a garish beer mat.

"No," Roger said. "This will do fine." He wasn't at all certain he believed that. He took a ten from his pocket and put it on the counter. "Don't worry about the change."

"Sure thing, bud. Thanks."

He didn't touch the glass, just watched the drops of condensation gather and bleed down its side. The liquid it contained oozed light, a glistening waterfall of amber and gold. He could smell it, and in that smell, he could taste it too. His eyes grew heavy and, for a moment, he closed them, giving in to his exhaustion.

The barman was watching him.

Roger tried to focus on his thoughts, tried to filter through the chaos and hold onto something tangible. But in the back of it all was the truth he was avoiding—that the real reason he was in a bar, with a full glass in front of him, was that he had screwed everything up. He had wanted to protect Jess, tell her what he knew. That someone was spying on her father and Roger had helped them do that. Even as he thought about it now, it made him feel sick.

They were watching him. From time to time he caught faces in the crowd studying him, or cars following him. They didn't trust him completely, their little spy. Their asset, as they called him. Their traitor, as he saw it now. So he had taken precautions when he went to see Jess. Made sure he wasn't followed.

Yet here he was, standing on this familiar road, wanting to prove to himself that it didn't have to lead to the same place. That if he could change just one thing, the rest might be different. Choices. Consequences. Risk.

Betrayal.

Ben Rollins didn't know everything about who he had been. Roger had been careful to hide that side of himself. What it was like to be an undergraduate from a poverty-stricken family from England's industrial north, trying to pull himself out of the gutter and better himself. How easy it was become reliant on chemical comfort in the harsh, testing environment of Oxford University. At first just something to get him through the long nights studying, then something to get him through the emotional isolation of being socially inept and unfashionable. That's where his addiction had begun, but it had followed him, clung to him like a disease.

Now Jess knew, didn't she? Was that why she threw him out?

"You okay, buddy?" the barman asked.

Roger shook his head.

The barman dug into his pocket and took something from it. He held it in his hand for a moment, as though uncertain, then placed it onto the counter. It was a business card. On it were the words *12 Step House* and an address and cell number.

"Maybe I'm out of line," the barman said quietly.

Roger looked at him but didn't say a thing.

The barman went over to the till, took out a ten, and placed it next to the card. "Why don't you go home, buddy? You look like you could use some sleep."

Roger took the card, but left the bill. He stood, nodded slowly, then turned and walked out into the rain.

The agony. The pain returned to Roger, but not the pain of that moment.

The dream of Manhattan faded.

He opened eyes to the detention cubicle. His arms and feet were still zip-tied together, his legs and arms covered in blood. He had fought, of course. Guilt and shame had driven him. He summoned memories of Ben Rollins, and of Jessica, as they asked their questions. When he was weakest, he used it to bring to mind the reason he was here, the wrongs he still had to atone for.

It gave him strength.

Thinking of Ben Rollins made him think of Jess, and the love he had always felt for her, but as he thought about her he found the face he was looking at wasn't hers at all, but Abbie's. Their relationship was fresh, a tiny beacon of hope. Warmth in bed at night as they held each other. Comfort in mutual understanding of the hazards.

His wasted life.

His addictions. What they had done to ruin his life. He was powerless. Only a power greater than himself might restore his sanity. He had sought and made a fearless moral inventory of himself, and understood what he needed to do in order to make amends.

Torture did not uncover truth.

Torture uncovered nebulous and desperate responses to an interrogator's questions that a detainee could muster in a wild and confused state. Everyone capitulated at some point, and Roger was no different.

Yet his answers were still fresh in his mind, because if his fortitude was gone—if the pain had overcome him entirely—the guilt and shame remained.

Müller had known all along.

Of course.

All of Roger's work was for nothing. His anger buoyed the guilt, his resentment of Müller fueled his desire to reach one last time for atonement. When the door to his room opened, Roger flinched and shrank from the light that flooded in. He closed his eyes and focused again on Ben, on Hector, and on Abbie.

"Roger!" Soft hands took his face and lifted it. He did not open his eyes. The voice whispered: "Oh my God."

"Are you real?" he croaked.

"We need to go." Abbie used a knife to cut the zip ties on his hands and feet.

"How did you—" he stopped when he saw her father, General Marshall, standing in the door, a weapon in his hand.

Abbie cut his bonds and two men appeared at his side and helped him stand. They carried him. Gunfire echoed around the complex.

"What's happening?" he said.

"Minister Zhou Enlai is taking over. We're safe."

"Is Müller still alive? Ufuk?"

"They're outside, on their way to some facility. Can you stand up?"

"Then we're not safe."

Roger used all of his energy to try to stand. He got to his feet, but then stumbled and crashed to the ground. Each breath was an effort, a gurgling wetness as blood seeped from his lips.

11

SSN Bremerton
Middle of Pacific Ocean
North of Marshall Islands
April 28th

Seventeen days to SIN, Walter Caulfield said to himself. Saturn Intercept Node—SIN—was the acronym he'd created for the event. Submariners loved acronyms, and Communication Officer submariners even more. Things with as few letters as possible to transmit over the short bandwidth systems he used. Acronyms were his world. It had been four days since they'd boarded the Carl Vinson, and Captain Niven and Admiral Reynolds had had their words. Precious few acronyms over the ELF since then. Caulfield and the whole crew knew the Bremerton was the front line.

The FL.

A Sudoku puzzle was half-solved in his lap, his eyes half-closed.

Alarm bells went off.

Caulfield almost fell from his chair.

Like all Los-Angeles class attack boats, the Bremerton trailed a long wire antenna attached to a communication buoy that floated just underneath the surface. The transmission of data was slow and still required transcription decoding via a one-time-pad cipher. By the time the Communications Officer had finished, his heart was racing. Sweat fell from his face onto the desk in front of him.

Walter Caulfield had twenty years in the US Navy and had never seen anything like this message before. He ran to the captain who was getting some rest in his quarters next to the officer's bunks. He stood while the Commander James Niven read the flash message from COMSUBPAC, saw the disbelief in his eyes, and swallowed hard as he heard the command to surface to confirm.

Sonar man Ramsay had been in his seat for nineteen hours without much of a break when the commotion in attack center seized his attention. A few hours' sleep separated this duty shift from the last, and he'd had more than his share of coffee. He'd been eating sandwiches, rather than taking chow with the rest of the enlisted crew. He wouldn't trust the sonar to anyone else, not right now.

Atwood appeared in the entrance to the sonar room. "Ramsay. Come with me, will you?"

Commander Niven and Chief of Boat Atwood were hovering over charts in the attack center, paper charts lit from beneath by the glass chart table on which a larger section of the Pacific was showing. Both men had weary expressions. Empty coffee cups, stained from over-use, sat on the table. Over the radio came chatter from what sounded like a P-3 Orion. A pair of them, by the sound of their conversation.

"What's going on, skipper?" Ramsay whispered.

"Two days ago, the Chinese Surface Fleet shifted its focus. One of their groups, built around their 52D destroyer *Chengdu*, has been heading out past the Philippines and into the Pacific. Not far off the coast of Guam, the group changed course toward the Truk Lagoon in Micronesia. Three destroyers, two frigates and a submarine chaser. The *Chengdu* has VLS for surface-to-air, cruise, anti-submarine, and anti-ship missiles. The whole package. We've also heard a Russian fleet is coming from the north. The Vinson Strike Group is exposed."

"You think they're coming for us, sir?"

"There's a good chance too that there are subs with the group," Niven continued. "Think you can find them?"

"Yes, sir."

"Orions from the Carl Vinson have been up for hours now and need to come down. They've been feeding the Strike Group data and dropping sonobuoys in front of the advancing ships. We're heading out ahead to intercept. You're it, Mr. Ramsay. You keep on top of that sonar array, we're heading straight into the fire pit."

12

Xing'an Mountains, China
Border of Mongolia
April 28th

"You really messed this up," Müller said, turning around in the front bench of the transport to face Ufuk. "We had everything, and you ruined it."

Erdogmus's head lolled forward, his eyes unfocused. He didn't reply. Didn't seem capable of replying. The black-clad Sanctuary Europe soldier sandwiching Ufuk to his left put a hand out to hold the Turk's head from slamming into the seat in front of him. Ufuk managed what seemed like a gurgling laugh, but whether he was aware of Müller talking to him or not wasn't obvious.

"Give him another jab," Müller instructed.

The soldier to Ufuk's right nodded and produced a syringe from a bag he unzipped. Without ceremony he stuck this into the shoulder of Ufuk and unloaded its contents. The Turk's head rolled back, his mouth agape. In the fourth and fifth rows of the tank-truck, half-darkened, the Sanctuary China special forces sat quietly, their Asian features just visible through the black face masks and body armor.

For fourteen hours straight the convoy had ground its way through the mountains north. They cut through fresh, wind-carved pillow drifts and ice-slab rivers that crossed the thickly-laden track, and between forests of twisted pines that bucked as the convoy roared through the snow-clad darkness. Over uneven ground the convoy rolled and pitched, eating the miles past Hulun Lake, until they reached the long, straight 908 County Road that traversed the far western reaches of the New Barag Right Banner of China's Inner Mongolia. They roared through what remained of the New Barag Youqi ghost town, wind-swept and silent, thrashed by cold, and into a wide-open and barren plain, undulating beneath rimed ice and wind-carved sastrugi.

Around midnight the night before, the cones of light of the headlights lit up a flurry of snow that turned into a blizzard. Müller had to have electronic markers set up in the hills, because they drove forward, grinding through the whiteout, without stopping on their way to the coordinates Ufuk had supplied.

The driver of the tank-truck, sitting immediately in front of Jess, changed gears. The throaty growl of the engine switched into a higher pitch. Ahead of them, the side of a mountain climbed into the whiteout distance. Wind and ash and hoary snow cut across the windscreen as the wipers struggled to restrain the blizzard's fury.

Jess held Hector in her arms, her back against one of Müller's men, a large Sanctuary Europe soldier she thought she'd seen before. He kept his M4 away from her, seemed to do his best to keep her comfortable. They hadn't bound her hands or legs. Müller insisted on it, made a show of explaining to her how he was on her side, that she just had to trust him until they got to Ufuk's base and that it would all become clear. Hector kept his head down and leaned into Jess. He played games on his tablet. All he ever did was play videogames. She couldn't blame him, and at least it kept him occupied.

The soldier removed the syringe from Ufuk's shoulder, the contents emptied.

"Sodium thiopental, mainly," Müller said to Jess. "Plus a cocktail of more exotic chemicals. Can't have him aware enough to cause any more trouble, or to interact with Simon—but we need him compliant enough to answer questions. I'd be surprised if he could tie his own shoelaces right now, but then, he's surprised me more times than I care to admit."

"You didn't need to bring all of us," Jess said, her voice just loud enough to be heard over the roar of the grinding engine, but not too loud to startle Hector.

"It's not obvious who or what we might need out here," Müller replied. "You can thank Mr. Erdogmus."

"He asked to bring us?"

"Quite the opposite." Müller paused to answer a question the driver had, pointing at an electronic display in the middle of the dashboard. "There's no going back to Sanctuary China," he said over his shoulder to Jess. "Your friend Erdogmus made certain of that. Didn't give him credit for being so political. Clever boy."

Jess ignored him. She kept glancing out of the window nearest to her, partly to see the other transport that held Giovanni and the boys with Massarra, but also to see if she could see anything else. The American extraction team was out there somewhere, at least it should be.

She had Hector now. She'd done her part, infiltrated Sanctuary China and done what they could to disrupt its systems. She had no idea if they'd been successful, if they'd had some effect, but that didn't matter now. Her mission was to get out of here, get as far away from Ufuk and Müller as she could. Would the American extraction team follow them? *Could* it follow them in this? The ash-snow was deep and untouched, what she could see from the truck headlights, and the forests thick, the mountains steep. Did they have a vehicle like these? If so, and they followed, they would be easily spotted.

And then what?

Would they attack a convoy of ten tank-like, armored vehicles, with two hundred well-armed and trained soldiers in body armor? Even a well-trained Special Forces squad would think twice before attempting that, and why would they? To rescue her? What value did she have now that she'd done what they asked?

"There are many wolves hunting in these forests," Müller said as he watched her peering out the window. "This is a very dangerous time for us all, Jessica. Ufuk's complex isn't far. We should be there in another few hours, and then we will all see his lies."

A coughing gurgle erupted from Ufuk's lips. Jess turned to see his glassy eyes fixed on her, trying to communicate something. Spittle drooled from the corner of his mouth, a white froth between his lips.

When the convoy reached the location of the complex, Jess was surprised by its appearance. Nothing like the one in Tanzania, but instead a collection of buildings in what looked like a quarrying operation. She supposed that was the purpose. Where scrutiny was an ever-present concern, the best way to hide was in plain sight. Behind the veil of the mundane.

A wide, winding road led down out of the mountain into a valley, the sides carved like a stepped pyramid from the mining, stripped clean of trees. At the bottom of the road the ten vehicles pulled in unison in front of a central complex of low, blue steep-roofed buildings. An undulating gray-white plain stretched away into the distance in front of them to the east, what had to be the start of the steppes of Mongolia as best as Jess could estimate.

At the sight of the blue roofs, Ufuk strained to raise his head, a trail of spit hanging from one side of his slack mouth. He tried to say something, but all that came out was burbling foam and air.

Was he faking it?

If he was, Jess was convinced. He looked barely conscious.

The tank-truck ground to a sliding halt, its air brakes hissing. The chassis shook as the engine wound down and then stopped.

Silence.

A flat ceiling of high clouds hung in the sky. In the distance, there was a clean break in them, a pressure front coming behind the storm of the night before. Beyond that, empty gray sky. The sun was setting behind the mountains to their backs, in the west. A warm pink of sunset—the only hint of color in the drab landscape—suffused the striped stratospheric clouds directly overhead as Jess craned to get a look out of the window beside her. Tiny crystal snowflakes drifted by, the last of the storm of the night before. Everything preternaturally calm.

Ka-chunk as the driver and front-passenger side doors opened.

"Bring him," Müller yelled. He slid along the bench and jumped down. Plumes of white vapor on each breath in the dim light. "I want floodlights in all directions."

Ufuk was hauled out of the tank-truck's cab, two soldiers on each side holding up his limp body. One of them grabbed his long hair and yanked it back so his head faced up.

"We have hostages," Müller said to Erdogmus. "You understand? We can make this very painful, or very easy. And I know you have some surprises, but then, so do I."

"It's going to be okay," Jess murmured to Hector.

She kissed the boy's sweat-slicked forehead and stroked his matted hair. He didn't look up, didn't seem to care what was going on. He was focused on the game on his tablet, what looked like some kind of puzzle. Unlocking one level after another.

In the semi-darkness, a shape moved in the lee of the building nearest to them.

Jess's heart jumped into her throat.

Was it the cavalry? The American extraction team? Had Müller made a deal? It wasn't beyond consideration. Something had happened back in Sanctuary China. A sudden change in atmosphere. It felt like Müller was running away, but then they were all running out of time.

On the horizon, one bloated tip of Saturn rose into the indigo sky.

The shape next to the building shuffled forward through the snow, and Jess's hopes fell. Not American, not from the Kalashnikov rifle slung over the shoulder of a tattered green uniform. A large fur hat on his head. Jess recognized the uniform from her days in the military. Russian. Border guard perhaps. The man spoke in quick bursts to Müller, and pointed into the hills surrounding the buildings. They seemed to know each other well and shook hands warmly, as if long-separated friends.

The sinking knot in the pit of Jess's stomach tightened.

What did any of this have to do with her anymore? She gripped Hector. She just wanted to get somewhere safe now. Out of the cold. Out of the way of the sky. She saw Giovanni's face pressed against the glass of the truck in front of them. The tank-trucks ahead of them disgorged their cargoes of soldiers and equipment, floodlights clicking on to illuminate the snow and ice and buildings in sharp reliefs of shadow and light. Unless Ufuk had a secret army behind the doors of his secret facility, there was no way out of this.

Only whatever way Müller let them go.

The Russian held up something. Müller let out a surprised yelp, hugged the man, and then took the object wrapped in a burlap sack. Ufuk struggled free of the two men holding him, bawling a keening whine. He took two unsteady steps before falling face-first into the snow.

"Bring Jessica and the boy," Müller called out.

The soldier next to Jess opened his door and Jess felt a rush of cold air.

"Ma'am," he said as he slid out and offered her his hand.

Jess slid over in the seat and looked at the soldier, his hand out, his M4 casually slung over his other shoulder. She could leap forward, grab his weapon, maybe shoot him—but then what? Run into the frozen mountains? The young soldier smiled at her and offered again his hand. He had clear blue eyes.

This small act of civility.

Even the soldiers seemed tired of this struggle. Behind him, Saturn rose higher, halfway over the horizon now, orange-red and fat in the refracted light. When faced with death, the choices you made in life came into razor-sharp focus. Jess wondered what choices this young man—holding his hand out to her—had made to arrive here.

She took his hand.

The soldier gently helped Hector down behind her, then, almost apologetically, signaled for her to move forward. A lonely cry came from above. Jess couldn't see through the gathering twilight into the hills. She wondered if it might have been an eagle—Mongolian hunters were famous for using eagles to hunt. Jess realized she hadn't seen birds outside since the event. Wolves, perhaps? Their howls carrying on the wind across the landscape? She strained to see. Something moved in the distance. It looked like a dog. She blinked. It had to be five hundred yards away. It looked canine, but was huge. A moose—or something even bigger? Did they have elephants here?

She rounded the truck in time to see Müller listening to a walkie-talkie, a scowl on his face. One of the Sanctuary China soldiers in the back of her tank-truck looked like he was on a radio as well. Something was going on.

Müller waved her forward. "I've got some bad news, I'm afraid."

She didn't reply but just held on to Hector.

"Roger is dead," Müller said. He put his walkie-talkie away.

The sinking feeling in Jess's stomach fell all the way to her knees. She felt weak and stumbled, her prosthetic leg skidding on ice. The soldier held her up from behind and urged her forward. Roger. No matter how much she'd hated him, she'd always felt sorry for him, had always kept some love for the man tucked deep away. He'd always felt tragic, somehow, even when she'd rejected him in Manhattan. A doomed look in his eyes, even back then.

Now he was dead, and probably because of her. She kept stumbling forward.

209

As she got closer, she recognized the object clutched tight in Müller's hands. It was Ufuk's mysterious canister. The Russians had found it in the snow somewhere. Ufuk must have had his drones fly it here. So this was where he wanted to come all along. She stole a half-look at Ufuk. How could this be part of his plan?

Jess heard radio crackle in the background. Soldiers in the next truck were speaking with quick, hushed voices in Chinese.

"Is that it?" Jess reached Müller. She protected Hector. "Roger's dead? Is that your bad news?"

Ufuk's head wobbled back and forth, his eyes half-closed. In the gray ice-mist up the hill behind the buildings, Jess saw it again. The giant snow-dog. Something massive and fluid that flashed again into the shadows. Shouts in the darkness. The Russian man next to Müller yelled back. Shouldering his Kalashnikov, without another word he ran around the corner and disappeared.

"Unfortunately not all of it," Müller said, flattening himself against the wall of the building, right next to a door and access panel. "Your America has just declared war against China and Russia."

Behind him, the gray mist erupted in bright bursts, the sharp tat-tat-tat of automatic gunfire echoing through the valley.

Corporal Zasekin threw himself into the snow at the first muzzle-flash. He signaled to Evgeny and his men to fan out across the hillside, to try and find mounds of snow or rock to hide behind. Something moved in the thick twilight fog. It looked like a dog, but something wasn't right. The animal bounded toward him in giant strides, and grew and grew in size until it seemed taller than the broken trees lining the pit. Blinding flashes from its eyes.

Zasekin huddled in terror, pressed his face into the snow.

The monster hurtled past him, right over the top of his body, but not quite the fluid motions of a sleek predator. Zasekin heard the mechanical whine and squeal of bearings as it thudded past and skidded to turn, crashing into the frozen mud, almost falling before righting itself with unnatural ease.

It was some kind of machine.

Zasekin flicked a hand at his two remaining men, told them to climb above the hills next to the blue-roofed buildings. He waited till the last of them crouch-ran past him before turning to look at the mechanical beast again. It had stopped, its haunches down. A man appeared from its back-end. A door.

The beast was a troop carrier. More soldiers spilled out of it. American soldiers.

Zasekin ran up the hill away to position himself.

"Give me the code," Müller yelled.

The soldier holding Ufuk pressed him forward, held his hand up to the keypad of the door next to Müller. Ufuk's eyes rolled back in his head and he laughed a gurgling giggle. There was no use trying to beat it out of him. He looked oblivious to the bullets clanging off the roof of the building.

At least nobody was firing at them. Not yet. They were sandwiched between the Chinese and American soldiers firing at each other, but neither side wanted to hit their small group in the middle.

Still, Jess crouched over Hector, and the soldier that had helped them down from the transport crouched over the both of them, keeping himself between them and the perimeter. Was he just doing his job? Whatever the reason, Jess felt a flash of warmth for their protector. She stole a look at the tank-truck next to them, the one with Giovanni and the boys and Massarra. The doors were still closed.

To her left, two hundred yards away, the giant dog-machine crouched. She recognized it now. Big Dog. A robotic troop carrier the American army had been working on. She didn't know any were in operation, but the Special Forces always got the best toys first. She counted ten men—or women—climb out of the machine, and then waited. The machine rose off its haunches and turned to decrease its exposure. Jess swore under her breath.

Ten men.

As brave as they might be, it would be no use against two hundred well-trained, armed soldiers. To her right, one of the tank-truck's engines roared to life. It surged out of the rank of the other ten trucks, and Jess expected it to surge toward the Big Dog and engage it in a fight, but the tank-truck swerved away and ground through the snow into the distance, disappeared into the fog.

Were they just running away?

Bullets clanged off the building's roof.

"Stay back, miss," the solider protecting her said.

She obliged and gripped Hector behind her. The kid was still playing a game on his tablet. She was going to yell at him, but didn't have the time.

"Give me the code," Müller yelled again, this time gripping Ufuk's neck.

Half of the Sanctuary China soldiers didn't seem to be fighting back, Jess noticed, but simply were taking cover. Müller's Sanctuary Europe men took a defensive perimeter around them, trying to use the building as cover, forcing Jess and Hector against the wall with Müller and Ufuk.

From behind the building, a bright flash. Something sizzled forward and painted a bright orange fireball against the side of the Big Dog. Another RPG launched from the dark hillside. Two flaming projectiles lit up the fog, but went wide of their mark.

The Russians—Jess assumed there was more than the one Russian she saw—opened fire in earnest, pinning the Americans down. One by one the bright floodlights went out in a shattering clatter, darkness again engulfing the area. The Chinese fired back, but shots seemed to come from all directions.

"Ufuk, we are all going to die here unless you open this door," Müller said.

"You might be right," Erdogmus mumbled back. "Six...three..."

Müller keyed the digits.

"Four...four...seven."

The exterior door slid open, but only to expose a secondary door two feet away. Still, it provided some cover. As a group they moved inward.

"He's drugged with a powerful truth serum," Müller said to Jess. "Ask him anything." He leaned in close to Ufuk. "Mars First was never coming back to Earth, isn't that right?"

Ufuk giggled, this time like a guilty schoolchild. "You are right."

"And all of this—everything you did to get here—was a lie."

Erdogmus's head sagged, still grinning. "Yes."

"Because you want to get up there." Müller pointed at the massive orb of Saturn, now sitting full on the horizon, as big and as orange as a pumpkin, its rings stretched wide and in a blood-red line around it.

"That is true." Ufuk leered at Jess, but more like he was trying to focus than making fun.

"So I was just bait?" Jess said.

The sound of the gunfire receded in her senses, replaced with a rage that boiled up from her heart. A ringing in her ears that suppressed everything else, even her fear.

"You see?" Müller said. "Do you know the lies he's told me over the years? The things he's done to me to get here?"

"I'm sorry," Ufuk slurred, his eyes on Jess. "It was the only way."

"And Hector, he was just a toy in this?"

"I'm so shorry," the Turk slurred again.

"Give me the entry code," Müller demanded.

Ufuk shook himself drunkenly.

"Give him the goddamn codes," Jess screamed. "Get this over with."

Erdogmus closed his eyes, then opened them and leaned to the door. He keyed in a sequence. The interior door slid open with a quiet hiss. Warm, stale recycled air rushed out and over them from the corridor within, and florescent lights flickered on inside.

"Jessica!"

The soldier covering Jess and Hector rose and spun to the sound. Jess recognized the voice and reached up, tried to stop the young man from raising his M4. A fine spray of red mist spattered across Jess's face. The soldier slumped across them, his face turned to her. She grunted as she held his weight.

"Jessica," Giovanni said again as he reached them and pulled the soldier's body away.

Lucca and Raffa followed close behind him, with Massarra following, a rifle in her hands. She was the one that shot the soldier. Jess watched the soldier's lifeless blue eyes, open and staring, as he slid into the snow. Behind her, the door to the complex slid closed as the last of Müller's men disappeared into the corridor beyond.

"I'm okay," Jess said as Giovanni wrapped his arms around her.

"They just let us go," Massarra said as she crouched in front of them, taking a defensive position. "The Chinese soldiers just released us."

Jess spun around. Had Ufuk gone into the complex? No. Twenty feet away, he stumbled forward and slipped and fell. Without thinking, Jess grabbed the trenching shovel she'd seen on the waist belt of the young shoulder and strode into the open.

A blaze of muzzle flashes to her left, from the Russians up the hill, but Jess didn't pay any attention. She raised the shovel.

"You goddamn bastard," she screamed.

Zasekin watched the battle unfold from his hiding spot fifty feet from the main building. He'd been in enough firefights to know that the moment the first shots were fired, all the careful planning went out the window and instincts kicked in.

Usually followed by total chaos.

The Americans had tried to flank the main Chinese force that had stupidly clumped themselves next to the building complex. Half of the Chinese seemed to give up before they started. One of the vehicles even churned off into the darkness before the fight had really started.

Those fleeing Chinese probably had the right idea.

He should probably run too, but then where to go? Saturn was bright on the horizon now, a ball of orange with colossal rings jutting out of its sides. He knew it was like this because of the ash in the sky, fat and oblong because of the refraction that close to the horizon, but it was still a terrifying sight. What had he done to arrive at this point? Crouching on the side of this mountain in China, chest-deep in snow, with Saturn hanging over his head, the scythe of Death himself?

A commotion near the entrance to the main building. Zasekin lowered his eye to his rifle sight to get a closer look.

A small band of people had separated from one of the trucks and made their way to the building. The rest of that group seemed to have gone inside the building, the group of black-clad Caucasian soldiers that were apart from the Chinese.

What choices had he made to arrive here?

He looked left, and Evgeny gave him a thumbs-up. He'd made choices that kept his boys safe—that was what he'd done—and by anything that was holy, he'd make sure to see this through. A year and a half of waiting, of scraping for life to get here. He was many things, and many of them not very nice, but he was a man of his word.

And he'd made a promise.

A dark haired man with brown skin stumbled away from the group by the building, seemed to try and run toward Zasekin. The Russian looked through his scope again. He recognized the man. A woman followed the man, her hair long and blond. She limped as if her left leg was injured. Even from here, he could see her contorted with rage, oblivious to the bullets flying through the air. She had something in her hand.

Zasekin raised his rifle.

This was what he'd been bought and paid for. This was the pound of flesh that he'd have to surrender, blood and all, to save his men. No clever rules or words to protect anyone, not anymore, not in this world.

Just action and reaction and survival.

The blond woman raised the object in her hand. A shovel. Sharp edged. She fell to the ground, her legs straddling the brown-skinned man. She looked about to slam the shovel into his head. Zasekin centered the crosshairs of his rifle sight on the chest of the woman and squeezed the trigger.

13

USS Carl Vinson
Western Pacific
One hundred miles west of Marshall Islands
April 29th

Admiral Reynolds thumbed the focus button on his low-light, high magnification binoculars and scanned the dark horizon. Nothing. He brought them away from his face and wiped his eyes. He shouldn't be out here on the gangplank outside the bridge, but then none of his men was going to tell him what he should and shouldn't be doing. The deck a hundred feet below was clear for once. The P-3 Orions—the anti-submarine and maritime surveillance four-engine turboprops—were coming in for a landing.

Dangerous work, landing on an aircraft carrier at night. At least, it was when it used to be dark.

Reynolds lifted his arm holding the binoculars and watched the double shadow rise and fall against the gray metal wall of the outside of the bridge. Two shadows: one from the full moon, and the other from the full Saturn looming in the sky beside it. The Pacific swells glittered in the Saturn-light of the cloudless night.

The atmospheric gauze in the stratosphere was still there, a hazy veil that obscured everything in the sky, but some of the brighter stars were visible—the North Star of course—but Saturn was all that anyone looked at anymore. It was huge, the size of a baseball held at arm's length, with the fine line of the rings stretching out to triple its diameter. The full moon was just a bright pebble beside it, a distant cousin that became smaller by comparison every night.

At least the added light at night made for easier landings. Reynolds always had a knack for looking on the bright side. A real glass-half-full kind of guy, and nothing was going to stop that.

"Sir?"

His Junior Signalman Harris stood halfway out of the bridge door holding a plate.

"What can I do for you, son?"

"Eat a sandwich?"

"Excuse me?"

Harris nodded at the plate. In the Saturn-light, it was plain that a ham sandwich occupied most of the dish. "Nobody I spoke to has seen you eat anything in days. Just a sandwich, sir. Please."

Reynolds hadn't slept in a week either. He took the sandwich after a moment's pause, maybe more for his men than himself. He smiled and thanked the boy.

He took two bites and left the rest on top of the high frequency radar array, then picked up his binoculars again. Swiveled his view toward the horizon. A cloudbank had gathered, a ghostly white line on the horizon. He zoomed the magnification and waited for the low-level light system to stabilize.

And there it was.

Unmistakable.

The angular superstructure of a frigate or destroyer, just over the horizon. He glanced up to see the landing lights of his P-3s lining up to come in. Damn it, he had to get them back out there. What he saw was just over the horizon—from this viewing angle and height, that was fifteen miles, plus maybe another fifteen to whatever that was. Incoming ships less than thirty miles away. Why the hell hadn't anyone else seen this?

"Sir?"

The door to the bridge opened again.

"Not now, Harris. I ate the sandwich. Could you raise COMSUBPAC?"

"It's not the sandwich, sir. We have a high priority COMSEC, and we *do* have a message from COMSUBPAC. Multiple targets just reported by AWACS about thirty miles."

That answered his question. "Is that COMSUBPAC from the Bremerton?" Reynolds wanted to know what Commander Niven would have to say first. COMSEC had to be Donnelly. He'd prefer information from Niven first.

"Multiple contacts across wide range in the water as well. At least two dozen."

"That's from Niven?"

"Yes, sir." Harris's voice warbled, sounded like he was going to cry.

"What's wrong, son?"

"COMSEC, sir, we're going to DEFCON 1. We're *at* DEFCON 1."

Sirens began sounding on the deck.

"What? Repeat that?"

They'd been on steady DEFCON 3 for four weeks now, a readiness level beyond normal standby. In the Cuban Missile Crisis, when Reynolds was a teenager, they'd been raised to DEFCON 2, the stage before readiness for nuclear war. DEFCON 1 meant nuclear war was imminent.

What the hell was this idiot Donnelly doing?

"Get me the head of—"

Reynolds was interrupted by a flare of light to his left, from the middle of the glittering waves ahead of them, maybe ten miles away—and then another, and another flaming point of light jumped into the sky. It took him less than a second to realize what they were. The boomers were launching their warheads. The ballistic missiles arced high into the sky.

"On their way to...to northern China," Signalman Harris stuttered. "That was the COMSEC message. On Donnelly's orders."

"Goddamn it," Reynolds whispered, and then louder: "Get the goddamn Aegis systems online and zeroed in. Why didn't anybody warn us? Get the ballistic missile shield up and zeroed over the convoy."

He stopped at the bridge door for a second before entering, to look once more at the sputtering lights that faded into the distant sky. How long did ICBMs take to reach their target? How far was northern China? Four thousand, maybe five thousand miles. Whoever was on the receiving end had half an hour to say their prayers. Reynolds had barely more than that before whatever was going to come in return, and whatever it was, it was going to come hard and fast. Reynolds slammed closed the bridge door just as the first of his P-3s rumbled onto the landing deck.

Whoever was on that secret mission to Sanctuary China had just failed—and was about to receive one hell of a parting gift for it.

14

Xing'an Mountains, China
Border of Mongolia
April 30th

"Wait!" Ufuk yelled, flailing his arms.

With a manic surge he lunged at Jess, knocked her off balance. In the same instant, Jess saw a muzzle flash, felt the sucking wind of a bullet whizzing past her, very close, followed by the crack of the gunshot. Still with the shovel in her hands, she fell into the snow, surprised Ufuk was able to even move.

Ufuk waved his arms around, lifted his head up and craned it backward. "Zasekin, don't shoot," he croaked as loud as he could.

"Who the hell is Zasekin?" Jess twisted around in the snow, keeping her head low.

"He's my…Russian…" Ufuk was only able to get half his words out. "Zasekin," he coughed, waving his arms. "Come here. Friends!"

Giovanni skidded into the snow next to Ufuk and Jess. "Get the hell out of the open, you idiots." He grabbed both of them by the collars of their coats and pulled.

Fifty feet away, a shadow appeared from behind a hummock of rock. It was a man, dressed in the same green tattered Russian border guard uniform, but not the *same* man as Jess saw talking to Müller. He had a Kalashnikov slung over one shoulder, his hands out, palms toward them in surrender. He crouched.

"Stay back," Massarra said. She was ten feet behind Giovanni, with her M4 carbine pointed at the Russian.

"Friend," said the Russian. He advanced slowly.

"It's okay, he…can…hel…" Ufuk said. His head lolled around as Giovanni hauled both Jess and him back to the safety of the side of the building.

The hillside flashed and crackled with gunfire, bullets thudding into the snow, sending up sprays of ice chips. The Russian dropped to one knee and grimaced.

He shouldn't be exposed like that, Jess realized. He was taking a risk.

And did Ufuk say *Zasekin?*

"Get over here," Jess called out, motioning to the man.

"Jessica," Giovanni hissed. "What are you doing? The Russians are the ones shooting at us. He *just* shot at you himself. Are you crazy?"

"Maybe." She waved more insistently.

The Russian crouch-ran the fifty feet in a hurry to tumble onto the ice beside them. Massarra kept her weapon trained on him the whole time. Lucca and Raffa stood ten feet to either side of her, their weapons raised.

"Who is this?" Jess asked Ufuk, grabbing him by the throat. "Is he your man?"

The effort had been too much for whatever drugs were coursing through Erdogmus's bloodstream. He smiled a goofy grin. "Zase. You know. Zasekin." With that, his eyes rolled into the back of his head and his body went limp.

"*Christ,*" Jess muttered under her breath, but her brain had already made the insane connection. She turned to take a hard look at the Russian flattening himself against the building for cover. "Did he just call you Zasekin? As in, Corporal *Andrei Nikolayevich Zasekin?*"

"Eet iz nice to meet yoo," Zasekin replied in his thick Russian-accented English. "And you are?"

"Jessica Rollins."

The Russian gripped his Kalashnikov, his brows knitting together as his brain processed the information. "Jessica Rollins," he said at first slowly, and then faster and louder: "Jessica Rollins!" His eyes went wide, reflecting bright Saturn-light. "From Italy, yes?"

Jess nodded, as dumbfounded as he was. A bullet clanged off the building over her head and she ducked involuntarily.

"And this is Giovanni?" Zasekin said, pointing at the Italian, before his eyes saw the boy crouched in the middle. "And Hector, *eto piz`dets*, this is you?"

"Hello," Hector replied, his fingers and eyes still glued to the videogame on his tablet. He refused to let it go.

A wide-mouthed amazement replaced the scowl on Giovanni's face. "Zasekin? The Russian border guards with the hovercraft? We talked to you on the shortwave, a year and a half ago. From Baikal?"

"Yes, yes," Zasekin said, crouching upright and offering his hand.

Giovanni shook it, a smile now on his face, his mouth still agape.

"Maybe another time for this little get together?" Massarra said, breaking the spell. "We need a plan, and fast."

"Sorry I just tried to kill you," Zasekin said to Jess, wincing.

"Most of my friends do at one point or another. How do you know Ufuk Erdogmus?" She pointed at the inert Turk. She'd tried to tell herself never to be surprised at the convoluted scheming of the man, but he'd outdone himself. She couldn't imagine how or why Zasekin was here, but there had to be a reason.

"Ufuk Erdogmus," Zasekin whispered, and then louder said, "I did not know his name. He was just a radio voice for the eighteen months last. The man promised me food, shelter for my men."

"He promises a lot of things."

"What do you mean?"

"Just that's a boat a lot of us are rowing. Doesn't matter. Who are the other Russians in the hills? Your friends?"

Zasekin's face contorted as if he'd just knocked a tooth out. "He was. Timur and one other of my men."

"Just two?" Jess counted muzzle flashes from at least two dozen different locations up the hill.

"And Kirill and the Bratva…how do you say…mafia. Russian mafia. Somebody else must have made them a better deal than I was making."

Jess could guess who that was. "And what are you doing here, Zasekin?"

"Protect this facility." He patted the wall. "I have two men back there." He pointed to the opposite hillside.

He wasn't doing a very good job at protecting this place bringing just two men. Russians were tough bastards, but maybe this one was a little overconfident in his capabilities.

"What do we do?" Massarra asked again, her voice high and strained. She swept her M4 back and forth, hunting for targets. "Go inside? Get Müller?"

"I don't give a donkey's ass about Müller," Jess replied without hesitation. "We need to get over to that American troop carrier."

In the light of Saturn, the Big Dog transport was still clearly visible crouched behind a hill three hundred yards to their left. A smattering of muzzle flash from that direction gave her an idea of where the US special forces were, but they were pinned down by incoming fire from the Russians in the hills and the remaining Chinese that fought. At least half of the Sanctuary fighters seemed to have given up, which was good news, but still made it at least ten to one against them.

They didn't have to win the fight, though. She'd done her job. They just had to escape. Cross the thousand feet to the Americans, get in that troop transport and get the hell out of here to the coast. Join up with the Carl Vinson armada. How to get from here to there? A thousand feet.

"Don't worry," Zasekin said, watching her eyes surveying the scene. "I have friends coming."

"Your two men?"

He didn't say anything, but affected a rotten-toothed grin. In the sky behind him, Jess noticed a glimmer.

"Is that him?" Kirill asked. He pointed at the edge of one of the blue-roofed buildings.

Timur put one eye to the sight on his rifle. A dim image of half a head at the side of the wall, but the green uniform was unmistakable. The man turned. And so was that godforsaken goofy grin he'd had to put up with for the last two years.

"That's Zasekin, yes," Timur confirmed.

It was a shame he'd had to kill Vasily to try and stop him whining to Zasekin, but his old boss had escaped anyway. Timur had his own friends on the radio.

"Your friend better have a good place for us to hide when this is over," Kirill said. By now, even the most cynical had been watching Saturn growing daily in the sky. "I brought fifty Bratva with me. The Vor will not be pleased unless we return with a real prize."

"Do not worry. The man that commanded those trucks? He entered the buildings. He is in control. We just need to capture those people."

"Not shoot them, but capture them?"

"That was the deal."

"But we kill everyone else?" Kirill knelt in the snow to load another RPG into the shoulder-mounted launcher.

Timur sighted down his rifle again, bringing the crosshairs on Zasekin's head. "Everyone."

Kirill stood and swiveled to aim the RPG barrel at the knot of transports in front of the buildings.

Timur slowed his breathing. Something wet spattered against the side of his face. He turned to see Kirill kneeling in the snow, the RPG sagging from his shoulder. An ax was buried between his shoulder blades.

Zasekin's grin widened at the sounds of the yelling from up the hill.

Jess didn't hear any gunshots, just blood-chilling screams. From the darkness above the buildings, something sailed silently through the air. One of the Chinese soldiers turned to see it, but too late. The spear went straight through his chest, out through his liver and pinned him against the ground. He seemed too surprised to even scream.

More yelling from behind the building, further in the hill up in the darkness. This time not screaming, but grunting, growling. Massarra pulled on Jess's shoulder, tried to keep her from looking around the corner. A man appeared, roaring, holding an ax, covered in animal skins. Upon seeing Zasekin, the snarl evaporated into a smile.

"*Melschoi!*" Zasekin called out, raising his Kalashnikov in greeting. He turned to Jess. "My blood friends, the Buryat tribes. I said I would protect, yes?"

More of the animal skin covered wild men poured past Melschoi, who after a brief acknowledgement of Zasekin followed his men. Bursts of gunfire from the Chinese soldiers that remained before a melee of hand-to-hand combat. The ground became littered with Buryat, but they seemed to stream into the valley from everywhere in the darkness.

"We go now?" Massarra said. "We can make it."

She pointed at the American troop carrier. Several of the Special Forces had gotten up from their hiding spots to crouch and watch the frantic mess. The gunfire had stopped. Just a thousand feet to safety. To Australia. She glanced at Hector and then at Giovanni.

"What about this sack of dirt?" Giovanni kicked Ufuk, whose eyes were open now. "We leave him?"

Every fiber in Jess's body wanted to scream, "*Yes!*", but she hesitated.

"Jessica, no, please." Ufuk held out one hand. "That package Müller took. It's a seed bank, but not a normal one. It's a *human* seed bank." He propped himself up, still not entirely with it. "Years of work to collect all the human genetic material."

"And what? You want to take it up there? To Mars First?"

He nodded.

Screams of the Chinese soldier behind them.

"This was your plan all along?"

"Everything I have been trying to do, to save a copy of humanity. We don't know what's going to happen when Saturn hits. Humanity may be wiped out."

"And there's a rocket in here?" She tapped the entrance door of the complex. "Like in Tanzania? You want to launch it up to your friends?"

There was some perverse pleasure in finally understanding what Ufuk had been trying to do, and the realization made sense. A megalomaniac like himself, believing he could save humanity. She glanced at Saturn, massive, hanging overhead. Maybe he was right. Maybe this was the end of humanity.

And then she realized...

"Wait a second. You want to get up there yourself. That's it, isn't it? You want to save your *own* ass?"

"Please, you have to believe me. That seed bank. It's the future of humanity."

"Jessica, if we're going to go, we've got to go *now*," Massarra urged. "I'll cover us from the high ground. Get moving." The Israeli jumped forward without waiting, toward the Americans.

"Please," Ufuk pleaded, his eyes still glazed over.

Jess looked at the troop transport, then back at Giovanni and Hector. Just go, her brain told her. Grab Hector and run. Her head sagged.

"*Dammit,*" she muttered and turned to grab Ufuk.

15

"What are you doing?" Giovanni dropped to one knee and raised his rifle.

Jess dragged Ufuk up by his collar, pushed him in front of the door. "What's the key code?"

"Jessica," Giovanni repeated. "What are you doing? We need to run."

He pointed to the edges of the building, hand signaling for Lucca and Raffa to take up positions and look for Massarra. Some of the Americans were on their feet now, slowly advancing toward them.

"We're going inside, getting this thing, and then getting out," Jess said.

"That is not a good idea."

"Probably not."

"You are putting us all at risk. Including your Americans."

The intermittent gunfire and yelling died down.

"Take Hector," Jess said, her voice hitching as she said it. "Go now. I'll be there in a minute."

Giovanni didn't turn and didn't answer but kept sweeping his weapon back and forth.

"They changed the codes," Ufuk said, his voice slurred. "Müller took some technical specialists in there with him."

"Can't you figure it out? You built it."

Ufuk put his face into the palm of his hand. "I'm not thinking straight. I can't...I can't remember..."

"Whatever you are going to do, hurry," Giovanni said. "I've got a bad feeling."

One of the American soldiers was less than a hundred feet away. He waved at Jessica. She waved back. His hand over his head, the American soldier's arm stopped mid-motion. Even from a hundred feet, she saw the expression on his face change. He took a step back, and then another before turning to run.

Jess craned her neck around, her arm still waving.

The tops of the white tank-transports had split open. In the dim black-and-white light of Saturn, bugs seemed to hatch from the vehicles, giant insects that crawled forward and sideways, dozens of them at first, and then countless more. Hundreds. One of the bugs leaned off the side of the truck-tank nearest them. A Chinese Sanctuary soldier had his arms up, had surrendered his weapon. The bug's jaws opened, and it clamped down on the man's head. He screamed.

The bug-drones leapt into the air almost as one.

"I designed those," Ufuk half-muttered, half-slurred. "Insect-bots. Ornithopter flight systems." He blinked hard, as if to keep himself awake. "Nasty creatures if they're weaponized. Even if they're not—"

"Open the goddamn door," Jess yelled at him.

"Right, right." He returned his attention to the keypad.

Lucca and Raffa and Giovanni opened fire, shot straight into the heart of the swarming mechanical drones. The writhing mass rose into the air, their beating wings glittering in the light of Saturn, turning and twisting on themselves in a flocking motion.

"It's beautiful," Ufuk said, his eyes wide. "I've never seen them—"

"Ufuk," Jess said.

"Sorry." He'd opened a service hatch and found a screwdriver, which he jammed into the corner of the keypad. "That has to be Müller, controlling the swarm from the inside."

"Anything we can do to stop it?"

"Play dead?"

"Don't you have more of those things inside?"

"That's the thing, we need to *be* inside."

The head of the swarm mass seemed to turn to them, noticing the gunshots into its body from their direction. The head ducked down and charged. Jess crouched and turned to protect Hector with her body. The kid was still playing on his tablet.

Just feet away from them, the swarm turned sharply, blasting them in a furious swirl of wind that caught the snow and ash around them, churning the air into a soup. The noise was deafening at close range. The answer to whether they were weaponized came a second later. Through the swirling snow and haze, a glittering crescendo of light, followed by the humming blast of what sounded like a Gatling gun firing hundreds of rounds a second. Voices screamed.

The swirling snow settled enough for Jess to see the battle.

As short as it was.

The swarm undulated up and down, picking off one Special Forces soldier after another, and then concentrating its firepower on the Big Dog itself. They fought back, blasting away with cannon and M16s into the drones. Dozens of the drones dropped flaming into the snow, but it wasn't even close. The swarm mass rose again into the air over the burning wreckage of the American transport.

Even the Chinese were firing at the insect drones now.

The swarm-beast turned and coiled high in the air, looking for a new target.

Jess grabbed the scruff of Ufuk's coat. "Whatever you're doing, get it done—"

The Saturn-light blotted out, casting them into pitch-blackness. A second later another blast of wind rocketed the snow and ash back into the air. Jess put one hand to her eyes, tried to wipe them clean and look up. More insect-drones, but these ones seemed to be coming from *inside* the complex.

The new swarm-mass coiled around itself, corkscrewing through the night sky in front of the other swarm. Two cobras sizing each other up, they reared their heads and dove straight into each other. A splintering, tearing sound as they collided, shrapnel filling the air at the same time as a strange orange glow. The glow intensified, and flamed into an intense white-orange fireball. The concussive shockwave knocked Jess from her feet and straight back into Hector. Had to be combustion of the liquefied hydrogen these things ran on, she realized.

"Is that you controlling them?" Jess said to Ufuk, shielding her eyes from the flames. "Or is it an automated defense?"

The insect-drones swarmed around each other seemingly randomly in the sky, a glittering confusion, attacking and reforming, the thrumming of their miniature cannons firing at each other filling the air with a deafening racket.

"Clever boy," Ufuk said, picking himself up. "It's not me."

"Then it's Simon?"

"Not Simon. Hector," Ufuk said. "Look at him."

Jess dusted herself off and kneeled in front of the boy. He was still playing a game on his tablet, swinging his finger from one side to the other. She looked back over her shoulder. One of the swarm masses swept back and forth in a hunting motion. She looked back at Hector's finger. The *same* sweeping hunting motion. On the tablet screen, the glittering haze of tiny machines fighting against each other.

"You've got to be kidding me…" Jess's voice faded.

"Just like you showed me," Hector said, his eyes still intent on the screen. "I'm doing good, yes?"

"Very good," Ufuk replied, kneeling beside the boy. "Are you inside?"

Hector nodded.

"Show me Level 16."

Still controlling the swarm with his right hand, Hector opened another window and tapped through a series of menus. A flurry of windows opened and closed. Without even looking at what his right hand was doing, he split his thumb and index and forefingers apart, tracing multiple tracks for the swarm. Jess looked over her shoulder. The defending insect-drones followed the exact same pattern in the sky.

"And those are the firewalls?" Ufuk asked, leaning in close to see what Hector was doing.

"How is he doing this?" Jess said.

"It's amazing what a sponge a young mind can be under the right circumstances. A year and a half of game training."

"Training?"

How hadn't Jess seen this? All those weeks of Ufuk paying attention to Hector, giving him a tablet to play on. All the time they spent together in Africa, Jess thought Ufuk was just being nice to the boy. She'd warmed up to Ufuk, thought that he at least had a heart in there somewhere.

She was wrong. "Jesus Christ, what else have you—"

"We don't have time for this right now," Ufuk interrupted, and then to Hector: "Good. Good. Can you branch sideways from the management daemons?"

"I can't get through that level."

"Alpha, bravo, delta, delta—try that code."

Hector's fingers danced over the tablet's screen.

"Is he connected to Simon?" Jess bit back her anger.

"Müller is suppressing him. He has technical people inside," Ufuk said. "It was a risk letting him analyze Simon for so long at Sanctuary China, but necessary. Good thing we have Hector."

Jess doubted this was an accident.

The eight of them were pressed hard against the wall of the building, with Lucca and Raffa and Giovanni and the two Russians—Zasekin and Evgeny—kneeling, weapons out, in a circle around Ufuk and Jess with Hector protected in the middle against the door. Two more of the tank-truck's engines growled to life as more of the Sanctuary China soldiers made their escapes. The air stank of cordite, layers of gun smoke drifting in the thin ice-fog. Flashes of heat and light from explosions of the insect-drone battle in the air above them. Shrapnel and metal shards fell hissing into the snow. From what Jess could see, their side seemed to be losing.

"Whatever you're doing, hurry it up."

The door behind them slid open, warm air rushing out.

"Did you do that?" Ufuk asked Hector.

The boy shrugged as if he wasn't sure. As one, they all took two steps back to the inner door for more cover. At the same instant, the next door opened. Jess turned, was about to congratulate Hector. A mass of metal and wiring and legs and multi-faceted electronic eyes stared back at her as the door slid open. The insect drone grabbed Hector's jacket with a hind leg, and with the five other legs other scampered away in an awkward but quick escape down the corridor. It was too fast for Jess to react, too fast for her to grab Hector. She leapt forward to chase it, but a door wall slid across the corridor, blocking her.

Jess slammed her fist into the wall. "Hector!" she screamed.

16

One hundred Miles' Altitude over Okinawa
East China Sea

From this altitude, the Earth's horizon curved sharply; the night-day terminator a bright line cutting across it, just visible in the distance. The bulk of the Earth below—the night side—was pitch black. No spider webs of electric light connecting the burning bright metropolises of humanity. All of that was gone, but the blue oceans remained, the jagged mountain peaks, and the stars that shone bright up here beyond the choking ash-filled stratosphere.

Saturn hung large in the sky.

Above the atmosphere, the view of Saturn was striking and perfect and clear, the striated bands of its atmosphere, the rings close enough to see the separated rings, the dot of its giant moon Titan—a moon larger than the planets Mercury and Pluto—now visible.

The third stage of the Trident-II SLBM—submarine launched ballistic missile—flamed in silence. No sound in the vacuum of space. The sputtering flame of the Thiokol/Hercules solid-fueled rocket burned brighter and brighter as it consumed the last of its powdered aluminum propellant, and then winked out. Its job was done, the payload accelerated to four miles per second. The targeting system of the Lockheed-designed missile had finished its job as well, set the warhead on its final path. The rest of the flight would be ballistic, under the control of gravity.

Small explosive charges separated the payload from the spent metal rocket casing, and at the same time the clamshell nose cone fairings separated to release the eight MIRVs—the multiple independently targetable re-entry vehicles—inside each a W88 thermonuclear device of 475-kiloton yield. Eight independent warheads from this one rocket, each thirty times more powerful than the atomic bomb dropped on Hiroshima.

The MIRVs separated and began to drop. They'd reached the aphelion, their highest point in their ballistic path, and now descended toward the distant coast of China, still two thousand miles away. President Donnelly had authorized four Trident-II missiles for launch. Thirty-two warheads sped silently through space at fifteen thousand miles per hour.

Eleven minutes to impact.

17

Xing'an Launch Facility
Northern China

"Stand back," Raffa yelled.

Giovanni pressed himself against Jess, squeezed her into the wall of the outside corridor. Raffa knelt and took aim and fired at blasting caps stuck in the wad of Semtex stuck to the corner of the wall panel that closed off the interior corridor. The whomping concussion wave and flash of the explosion knocked Raffa backward, and his brother dragged him to his feet—but Jess was already running forward into the smoke of the blast. Half of the panel had blown away. She was about to squeeze herself through the opening when something crawled through.

The insect-drone exploded in a hail of bullets in front of her.

Giovanni shoved the metallic carcass back through the gap with the muzzle of his M4. He leaned into the opening, gun first. "Come on," he said, offering his hand to pull her through with him.

They sprinted a hundred feet until the next seal. Raffa came up behind them, his chest heaving, with another chunk of plastic explosive in his hand.

"How much of that stuff do you have?" Jess asked.

"Maybe a pound." Raffa knelt in front of the panel and clicked on his headlamp before starting to shape the charge.

Jess stepped back. What a difference since she'd first met Raffa. He looked and acted like the Delta team they'd trained with in Oman.

"Why did the Chinese let you go?" Jess asked Giovanni.

"Something on the radio. They started arguing. The ones in our truck spoke to us in Chinese—Mandarin or Cantonese—I didn't understand. They gave us guns. Raffa had the sense to grab a backpack of grenades and Semtex."

"Where's Massarra?" Jess realized the Israeli had run ahead to cover their retreat to the Americans, but they hadn't followed her.

"The Middle Eastern lady?" Zasekin said as he joined the group. "She followed my man Misha up into the high ground."

A low rumbling noise vibrated the walls.

"Damn it." Ufuk stumbled into Jess. "I know where Müller is. Don't bother with that." He pulled on Raffa's hand as he was about to press two blasting caps into the plastic explosive. "Here, shape a charge in an oval around this area." On the opposite corridor wall he traced an outline.

"Another access tunnel?" Jess said.

"Ventilation ducts. They're big enough for us to crouch through. Blasting our way through the closed doors isn't going to get us there fast enough, and I bet there are more of those drones waiting on the other side. They've been left in automated defense configuration. We don't have the time to mess around with them."

Raffa glanced at Giovanni and Jess, who both nodded. The teenager stripped away the Semtex he'd been working on and started rolling it between his hands to form long strands.

The rumbling sound intensified.

"What is that?" Jess grabbed hold of Ufuk. His eyes were clearer. The drugs were wearing off.

"He's opening the main silo doors."

"Main doors?"

"Of the launch silo."

"Another one of your rockets?"

"We have to hurry. He's going to take Hector with him," Ufuk replied.

"To where, exactly? What do you mean?"

"Into space. It's a three-stage solid propellant boost, on automated guidance, with hibernation pods. A bolthole for me to get to Mars First, if I ever needed it. If the Mars First spacecraft ever came back here."

It was almost the first time Jess really believed Ufuk. At least it made sense in an insane way.

"Everyone, move back," Raffa said.

They took twenty paces back down the corridor and covered their ears. The blasting concussion wasn't as much of a surprise this time, and when the smoke cleared, a ragged hole appeared in the side of the corridor.

"After you," Jess said to Ufuk. "You're the only one that knows the way."

Jess checked her watch. Two minutes since the silo doors opened. Ufuk said the system took ten minutes go through its systems checks to launch, said it was like an ICBM silo modeled after Russian systems, just much larger. It was maybe four minutes since that thing had snatched Hector. How far could it have taken him? She had to trust Ufuk now, at least to some extent. He had the same motivation as she did, to stop Müller, once and for all—but for different reasons. She edged her way through the confined ventilation tunnel, the only light the lamp on Ufuk's head. He led the way.

"How many people did Müller bring in?" she asked.

"At least three soldiers," Giovanni said from behind her, his hand on her shoulder in the darkness.

"And two technicians," Ufuk added.

Raffa and Lucca crawled behind Giovanni, with the Russians taking up the rear.

The ventilation tunnel had that new-car plastic stink that Jess associated with Sanctuary. The smell turned her stomach now. So six people they had to face down, including Müller. That put the odds in their favor.

Except for those drones. Terrifying pieces of hardware—not just deadly, but designed as if to elicit a deep fear of huge insectoid creatures.

Jess didn't like bugs.

Still, it was better than the two hundred to ten odds of an hour ago. Not only that, but something happened at Sanctuary China, and that might explain the feeling of Müller running away. Jess felt like she finally had him cornered, but of course, the wildcard was crawling through the ventilation duct in front of her. Who knew what Erdogmus might do. She kept one hand on her pistol, the other casually—but firmly—on his back.

"Any other surprises in here I should know about?" Jess said.

"Just the known unknowns," Ufuk replied cryptically. "The unknown unknowns I can't help you with." He stopped moving and pulled his headlamp off.

"What's up?"

"It's what's down." He used the headlamp to illuminate a hole in the floor, or rather, a vertical turn in the ventilation shaft.

She leaned forward, but couldn't see the bottom.

"About a fifteen story drop," Ufuk said. "Maybe two hundred feet. We have less than five minutes."

Jess pushed him forward. "I've climbed worst, and we use gravity for speed."

Massarra had climbed two hundred feet into the hillside to cover their retreat to the troop carrier, trailing the Russian blond-haired kid Evgeny, one of Zasekin's men. She ran straight into one of the animal-skin clad Buryat nomads, and both of them had knives at each other's' throats by the time Evgeny had pried them apart and explained in a flurry of what sounded like broken Russian that Massarra was a friend.

The Buryat had smiled a toothless grin and laughed, grabbing Massarra for a hug, before disappearing into the dim ice-mist clinging to the rocks of the hillside. She tried to thank Evgeny, but he didn't speak English or Chinese—definitely not Arabic or Hebrew—and she didn't speak Russian.

Hand signals and smiles were all they had, but it was enough.

The hillside was littered with dead bodies. Evgeny stopped to spit on one of them.

Once they'd climbed into position, and she saw Jess waving at one of the American Special Forces advancing toward them, the creatures had appeared. Insect-like drones that swarmed into the air, indiscriminately attacking both the Chinese and Americans. The Buryat wisely scattered into the fog.

Massarra flattened herself into the snow and watched the attacking drones. From their hunting patterns, she concluded they were in a search and destroy configuration, probably activated by Müller once he and his team were safely away. These things would continue to attack anything with a heat signature until either it or they were inoperational.

Her teeth gritted, she watched the swarm descend on the Americans.

That was their way home.

Not anymore.

The swarm rose from the fiery wreckage of the big troop carrier. Massarra cycled through a list of options to protect Ufuk and Jessica, none of them good. In the middle of deciding the only way was to sacrifice herself, a flurry in the air to her right. A hole had opened in the hillside, and another stream of insect drones flooded into the air straight into an attacking formation. Their behavior was different, controlled. Was it Simon, Ufuk's artificial intelligence? Something about their movement told her it wasn't, but whatever it was, it gave her the opportunity to get back down to the entrance.

She signaled Evgeny to follow her.

Stumbling over the ice and rocks they skidded around the corner of the main blue-roofed building, the insect-drones mashing and flaring above their heads, but there was nobody there. The exterior door was closed. Ufuk and Jessica and the whole gang were gone. She hadn't seen them leave the building.

They had to be inside.

That's when she heard the shuddering moan. A noise from high up in the hillside.

Doors opening.

"I think you broke my leg," Ufuk squealed.

"Hurry up, get out from under me."

Jess couldn't care less if she'd snapped his spine. They'd done their best to manage the descent, but after thirty or forty feet it had turned from a controlled into an uncontrolled fall. She felt a hot wetness spreading across the side of her face, her brain reeling from impacts into the wall of ventilation duct. At least she'd landed on Ufuk.

With a groan he dragged himself toward a dim light. "This is an access panel to the main chamber."

Jess's prosthetic leg had twisted off in the fall, and she squirmed around to collect it. "Kick it open."

"We don't know what's on the other—"

With a savage drive, she pulled her body forward, digging her nails into the skin of Ufuk's neck to gain leverage, and kicked her right leg into the panel. The first kick seemed to do nothing, but the second one the panel budged, and her third desperate thrust sent the grating spinning and clattering into open space beyond.

"You first," she told Ufuk as she wiped the blood from her eyes.

In the dim light she saw him grit his teeth, seemed to snarl at her, but then turned on all fours and scurried through the opening. Jess waited a second, watched to see if Ufuk's body would explode in a hail of bullets or swarm of gnashing drones.

"Jessica! Are you okay?" came Giovanni's voice from above, echoing in the ventilation shaft. "We are coming."

"I'm fine. Hurry." Jess crawled forward through the opening.

Ufuk was on his feet, limping to lean against the wall, looking up.

Jess followed his eyes. On a metal gantry above them, a dozen of the insect drones perched, their sensor-eyes and antennae all pointed down at Jess and Ufuk. They didn't attack, but rocked back and forth, on the ready. Jess took her pistol out, her hand shaking. The room they'd entered was circular, about sixty feet in diameter with hewn rock walls. The smooth metal tube of what had to be a rocket rose through the middle of the chamber. They stood on a circular metal platform that ended with a ten-foot gap to the rocket that was twenty feet in diameter itself. Another hundred feet of open space below her feet to the bottom of the chamber.

"Ufuk, what are we doing here?" Jess hopped forward, leaning down to pull up the sodden and ripped fabric of her cotton pant leg to re-insert her stump into the prosthetic.

"Maybe he's already inside," Ufuk said.

"Inside what?" Jess wiped her stump, fit the suction cup into place, and stepped on her prosthetic.

"The crew capsule." He pointed up. "This is the only place he could be."

Thirty feet above them was the nose of the rocket, and thirty feet above that the circular gap in the domed ceiling where the silo doors must have opened. A double set of blast doors, each at least five foot thick. Beyond that, the open sky, with half of Saturn and its rings visible.

"The door isn't closed yet," Jess said. On the side of the top section of the rocket, a panel was open. "Let's get up there."

Another metal gantry ran from the rock wall twenty feet overhead right to the entrance of the crew capsule.

"Past them?"

The insect drones swayed menacingly ten feet above their heads.

A grunting roar of pain from the ventilation tunnel behind them, followed by curses in Italian. More thudding as bodies crashed one into the other.

"Get the rifles," Jess said to Ufuk, "we'll shoot our way—"

"Let go of me," a small voice screamed.

"Hector!" Jess yelled.

On the gangplank twenty feet overhead, Müller appeared. He dragged Hector behind him.

"Stop!" Jess held her pistol out, pointed it at Müller. Her hand trembled.

Müller looked down and winced. "We don't have time for this, Jessica."

"Let him go or I'll shoot you."

At those words, the insect drones leaned forward, their mouthparts quivering.

"I would be careful what you say," Müller said. "These are programmed as attack dogs. Keyed on defending me. You attack me, they attack you."

Jess closed one eye and sighted down the barrel of the pistol. It wobbled back and forth. Müller held the boy in front of him. She would have to make a head shot.

"Just let him go," she stammered. "What do you need him for?"

"Your American friends unleashed a volley of nuclear warheads twenty-five minutes ago. I doubt we even have minutes left before this place is incinerated."

"You're lying."

"Have I ever lied to you?"

Jess gritted her teeth, tried to steady her shaking hand. Had he ever lied to her? He'd tried to kill her, had tried to lay the blame for Nomad on her father's name. Müller was a bastard, but he was an honest one with a clear purpose that at least she could understand. The only person she'd trusted, and who continually lied, was the one standing next to her. Ufuk Erdogmus.

"Do you want Hector to die?" Müller shook the boy. "Where I am going, he will live. He will be a king. Humanity will be saved."

"What are you talking about?"

"You blame me for your mother and father dying, but look beside you," Müller said. "Ufuk was complicit, he knew as well. He just likes to play the good guy. At least I don't lie."

"Let him go!" Jess screamed.

Müller took two steps toward the crew capsule, holding Hector in front of him. "There's no time. Get out of here. When the rocket goes off, this chamber will be an inferno. That shaft you just climbed from wasn't just a ventilation duct."

"He's sort of right," Ufuk said quietly. "It is a venting duct, but—"

"What the hell is wrong with the two of you?" Jess screamed. She tried to steady her hand holding the pistol. Sweat and blood dripped into her eyes, stinging them. She tried to wipe it away with the back of her left hand. She heard Giovanni climbing out of the opening behind her.

Müller took two more steps, still holding the boy in front of him. "This is the only way, Jessica."

"Goddamn it." Jess lowered her pistol.

The edge of Saturn in the silo opening blotted out for an instant. A shape moved in the darkness. Something dropped from above, a body with its arms and legs spread-eagled. It slammed straight into the top of Müller, sending him splaying to one side and Hector to the other.

Massarra.

The Israeli bounced off Müller and hit the metal grating hard. Hector scrambled to one side, away from them. The insect drones swiveled their antennae to look up. Without thinking, Jess pocketed the pistol and took two bounding steps to the side of the chamber, spotting a rock outcropping five feet up she could leverage up from.

Müller got his feet, but Massarra was faster. She had a knife out, and spun around, about to plunge it into the German's chest, but the first insect drone got to her first, diving into her neck. She managed to lunge at Müller, knocking him backward. He tumbled and fell off the gangplank, spinning to crash into the grating below. All ten of the insect drones descended on Massarra as she tried to fight them off.

Jess planted her right foot and leapt up, her hands grabbing the grating ten feet above. With practiced ease of decades of mountain climbing and filled with a furious rage, she swung her entire body over the top to land on the metal floor.

Massarra screamed as the insect drones tore into her flesh.

Müller staggered to his feet, looking up at Massarra.

He didn't even see Jess coming.

She rolled and bounded to her feet in the same motion, driving her body forward. She wrapped her arms around Müller and shoved him, driving her legs forward into open space. They thudded into the side of the rocket, already falling, a hundred feet of open space below them.

A splitting white light opened in the skies above.

Jess's head slammed hard into something as she spun through open space.

PART FIVE

1

USS Carl Vinson
Arafura Sea
Ten miles north of Australia
May 2nd

Admiral Reynolds lit up a cigar, clamped it between his teeth and took a few solid puffs. A Cuban cigar for breakfast. That was his definition of a celebration. To the stern of the Carl Vinson, the southern sun gamely fought to shine its rays through the gauzy stratosphere, but the air did seem clearer down here. A beautiful cathedral of pink grew into the sky with the rising sun, replacing the indigo night. Even the marbled globe of Saturn, perched on its rings on the horizon, looked peaceful this morning.

"Coffee, sir?"

Junior Signalman Harris leaned out of the bridge door with a steaming mug in one hand, and a plate with a ham sandwich in the other.

"Thank you, Harris," Reynolds said, taking both, the cigar clamped between his teeth. He put the coffee down on top of the radar and held his cigar. "And I promise I'll eat the sandwich."

The Signalman beamed a smile from ear to ear. "Thank you, sir."

"It's a beautiful morning, isn't it, Harris?"

"That it is, sir."

Half an hour ago, it had been pitch black out here, his landing deck invisible save for some running lights at the edges. As the sun broke over the horizon, it slowly illuminated countless dots of light below him, the thousands of faces of the American refugees that had been forced below decks for weeks when war threatened. That storm was past. The thousands of people on his deck were absolutely silent. They came topside for a breath of fresh air, but more than that, to see their future.

The coast of Australia visible just on the horizon to the south.

And the rising sun didn't just illuminate the people on his deck. As far as his eyes could see into the misty distance, thousands of merchant and civilian ships plowed white wake into the seas around his battle group.

Three days ago, the world hadn't seemed so rosy. Two Chinese aircraft carrier battle groups and a hundred frigates and destroyers, with forty fast attack subs under the waves, had confronted his convoy. When the Trident missiles were launched, Reynolds thought that a conflagration of unimaginable proportions was about to be unleashed.

But President Donnelly wasn't quite the idiot Reynolds thought he was.

That volley of missiles had targeted Shanghai, a coastal city already devastated and wiped from the map by Nomad. There was nothing left of it, and precious few civilians in that area. The nuclear bombs had detonated at ten thousand feet, and had still obliterated and irradiated an area of China, but it was more of a cautioning.

The mother of all warning shots across the bow.

The wall of Chinese navy ships had parted soon after that to let through his convoy, with messages coming over the wire stating that the Chinese government had been shaken up. Chairman Zemin had been deposed, replaced by Chairman Chen Sheng who'd realigned himself with the remains of the government in Beijing, reuniting the country and defusing the conflict.

Was it Donnelly's blunt force message that had caused the change?

Reynolds doubted it.

Something else had happened. He suspected it was the secret mission into Sanctuary China that had tipped the balance, but he had no way of knowing. The spooks on board were keeping their mouths shut.

But it didn't matter.

For a few tense hours, they'd steamed past the Chinese blockade, but then a day later, they were in open seas. Another day and they passed the Solomon Islands, went south of New Guinea headed through the Torres Straits.

To safety.

In another day they would make the reconstructed port of Perth. They had two weeks until Saturn would arrive and unleash whatever hell it had in store for them, but that left Reynolds a week to disembark the millions of refugees, and then another week to

246

steam his battle group, and whoever wanted to come with them, to the deepest, darkest pit of the Southern Oceans on the furthest point away from where Saturn's rings would impact the planet.

He took a sip of his mug of coffee and felt its hotness slide down his throat, and then took another satisfied puff of his cigar. Some of the faces looked up at him and waved. He waved back. One of them held up a small girl. It was the red-haired-and-bearded man from the gate, the one he'd told Harris to go and let past the guards in San Diego. She waved. Reynolds smiled and waved back. It was almost enough to bring a tear to the old salty dog's eyes. Almost, but not quite.

Dorothy would be proud.

His wife had died of cancer three years before, more than a year before the horror of Nomad. At least she was spared that, but not the agony of the metastasizing evil that had consumed her body. He *had* cried then, in private, told her that he would stay by her side, that he would quit his command.

She'd told him, *no*, that he had something important still to do.

How could she have known?

She couldn't have.

But, she *would* be proud, his wife of more than forty years. Admiral Reynolds let one tear slip and wiped it away, then turned to smile at the rising sun.

2

Xing'an Launch Facility
Northern China
May 6th

"Come back," Jess called out.

The little boy ran ahead of her, just out of reach of her mittened hand.

Fat snowflakes drifted from a white sky. Jess turned to see her mother waving at her from the frosted window of their cottage. Smoke curled from the stone chimney, the delicious woody smell of the fireplace floating out over the slicked surface of the snow. It had been warm for March, this past week. The Catskills Mountains rose behind the house, the evergreens shedding their white winter coats in preparation for spring.

"Billy!" Jess squeaked. "Come back. We're not supposed to play by the creek."

Her brother laughed and ran harder, just evading her outstretched hand. He half-tumbled down the embankment and skidded out onto the ice to finally stop. He stood and stuck his tongue out, taunting her.

"Billy, come—"

A cracking sound, like a twig snapping, but louder. The smile on Billy's face vanished, his small mouth opening wide as he pitched back, slipped, and then fell. Disappeared into the white ice.

"Billy!" Jess screamed.

She darted forward down the embankment and threw herself stomach-first onto the ice, sliding across it—and there, the small boy's face in the black hole, ringed in white, slowly disappearing into the depths.

But this time, she reached out.

She grabbed the hood of his coat, and pulled with all her strength, the ice cracking and groaning around her. She pulled and pulled, but the ice held, and a second later there he was. Billy, coughing up a mouthful of water, rolled over onto the solid ice next to her, his face at first shocked, but then smiling.

Smiling.

"Her eyes are opening," said a soft female voice.

The dream of the boy on the ice faded.

Jess's eyes fluttered open, but then closed again from the painful white light.

"Turn off the light," the female voice said again.

Jess's mind swam. Where was she? Who was that? She'd seen green eyes. Short brown hair, but not brown skin like Massarra. Pale white. Angelic white.

She opened her eyes again, and the light was dimmer, but there was that face again. "Am I dead?" she said without thinking.

The woman laughed. "Not yet."

"The missiles, Müller said they were, what…"

"Everything is okay," the woman said in that soft voice, but heavily accented.

"Who are you?"

"This is Belenko," Zasekin said, coming to stand beside Jess's bed. "She is…ah…my friend, yes?"

"Your friend?" Jess had a pounding headache. "How long have I been out?"

"Five days."

"In and out," Ufuk said, also coming to the bed. "Not unconscious, but you've been slipping in and out. Had to dose you up with some pretty strong drugs."

Jess lifted herself onto one elbow. White plastic walls. The same design as the infirmary in Tanzania, when Massarra had been the one on the gurney. "Where's Massarra? I saw her fall onto Müller, those things, they…is she here?"

Ufuk's smile faded. "She didn't make it this time."

The air seemed to evacuate from her lungs and she gagged. "She's dead?"

"The injuries were too much, even for her, and there was a fight after you fell, we—"

"Jessica!" squealed a small voice, followed by a pitter-patter of footsteps. Hector appeared through the infirmary door and launched himself at Jess, halfway landing on the bed with his arms around her neck.

249

The jolt of pain from the boy's impact was nothing to the joy.

"Take it easy," Giovanni said, coming quick on the boy's footsteps. "You don't want to hurt her, Hector."

"I'm okay." Jess squeezed back with one arm as hard as she could.

She looked straight into Giovanni's eyes. "And Müller?"

"Dead."

"He's dead?"

Giovanni tousled Hector's hair and pulled him back. "You just need to rest. For all of us. We're safe, at least for now."

Jess surveyed the room. In the corner was Ufuk's mysterious canister, but now they knew it was his sample of human genetic material, fertilized eggs, millions of them, frozen in a tiny capsule.

Groaning, Jess lifted herself upright until she was sitting. She had pain everywhere—in her back and neck—but a sharp pain in her groin as well. Intravenous tubes snaked down from bags into her right arm. "Get me my leg. I need to see."

"You are one tough solider, you know that?" Giovanni helped her from one side, while Raffa supported her from the other. "You fell at least eighty feet, ricocheted off a railing, and ended up right on top of Müller."

Jess limped through the corridors, trying to put as little weight on her helpers as she could. She wanted to have the satisfaction of walking her way to see Müller's body.

"Years of mountain work paid off," she joked. "Teaches you how to fall."

"You have a skill for it," Raffa said, smiling.

Jess felt the teenager's solid muscles under his cotton shirt. In the time she'd know him, he'd become a man. Maybe not a teenager anymore?

"How old are you, Raffa?"

"Twenty."

"When was your birthday?"

"Last week, but didn't think was a good time to ask for a party."

They all laughed.

Each tunnel and corridor they walked through—some with lights flickering—there were blackened walls, bullet holes punched through them.

"It was quite a battle you missed while you were sleeping," Giovanni said. "Raffa saved my life more than once. Saved all our lives battling those last drones."

Raffa's face turned beet red.

They climbed two sets of stairs and entered a large hallway. A group of men in animal furs squatted around a fire, bits of wood crackling. They turned and smiled toothless grins but ignored them apart from that.

"Zasekin's Buryat people," Giovanni whispered. "Ufuk promised them a safe place to come to. They've already ransacked everything they can get their hands on."

"They might have saved our lives."

Past a set of twisted blast doors was the base of the silo, and there, lying in a twisted heap, he was.

Dr. Hermann Müller.

His eyes were open, clouded white. His lips blue. A black stain spread around his body where his blood had congealed. Jess lifted a hand to her face. He stank.

"We didn't want to touch him," Giovanni said. "Nobody does."

Jess looked up. The rocket, a hundred and fifty feet high, was battered with gaping holes in it. The silo roof was still open. Snow dusted the ground.

"The white light when I fell—was that my head hitting something?"

"That was the drones from outside. Once they finished off everything they could attack out there, they swept up here. Müller wasn't controlling them, he'd just left them on search and destroy—so they came straight in here and searched and destroyed."

Through the opening two hundred feet overhead, Jess saw gray clouds scudding past. "Can we close the doors?"

"We should get back."

Jess turned her gaze from the roof to the inert corpse of Müller, took a deep breath and nodded.

Jess managed to limp most of the way back to the infirmary by herself. Her head was still aching; a throbbing between her temples, and pain in her groin, but her mind couldn't stop circling around and around. They said the Carl Vinson battle group had made it to Australia, that millions of Americans had been saved, but that also meant that they weren't going to make it to Australia, didn't it? Nine days to Saturn. That was too short a time to run. Could they hide here? Nobody seemed to want to talk to her about it, told her to rest and take it easy.

That was never a good sign.

They reached the infirmary, but at the room before hers, she stopped in her tracks. Ufuk sat at a chair inside the room, holding the hand of someone on the table.

Massarra.

Her skin was almost as pale as Müller's, but at least her eyes were closed. She was arranged as if she was asleep, a fresh powdering of blush on her cheeks and red lipstick. Jess had never seen the Israeli wear makeup. She was dressed carefully, perfectly, by someone who loved her.

"You know, I think she was my best friend," Ufuk said. He'd had his head resting against the gurney, but turned to them. "She was the bravest person I ever knew."

"Me too," Jess replied quietly. "She never gave up."

A smile quivered on Ufuk's face. "We were lovers once, did I ever tell you that?"

"And yet you lied to her." Jess felt the indignation rising inside. "You never told her about the existence of the Sanctuaries, kept her and your Levantine council—your own people—in the dark. How many did you let die?"

"And how many did I save?" Ufuk said. "I lied to a lot of people, Jessica. I had to."

"I can't stay here," Jess whispered to Giovanni.

Ufuk's forehead returned to resting on the gurney, his left leg twitching.

Giovanni and Jess retreated quietly.

"The Americans are already at Perth, that ship has sailed in all senses," Giovanni said.

They'd come down a level to his quarters, a quiet room off the kitchens that had a pull-down bunk. He'd found some pillows and taken blankets from the infirmary. He held Jess in his arms and stroked her head.

"What about one of the trucks, those Russian amphibious things?"

"The soldiers that didn't die here took them, returned to Sanctuary China. The trucks that remained are destroyed."

"The American transport too?"

"Jessica, Australia is on the other side of the world from where we are."

"That didn't stop us before. How did Zasekin get here?"

"That Czilim hovercraft, you remember he talked about it? His Chestnut, he calls it?"

"And is it here?"

"Do you want to be outside when Saturn hits? Do you remember what Nomad was like? And this might be worse."

"But Ufuk says we're almost in the exact impact line with the rings at this latitude."

"You should stop listening to Ufuk."

Every muscle and bone in her body ached, it was painful to even shift her weight from one side to another. Giovanni mentioning Ufuk brought to mind the man bowed over the dead body of Massarra, the regret in his eyes.

She turned around, wincing. Giovanni was about to ask what it was that she needed when she leaned forward and kissed him hard. She pulled his arms onto her, ignoring the pain, guiding his hands around her broken body.

For one night, she would forget the world.

3

Xing'an Launch Facility
Northern China
May 7th

Jess found Ufuk Erdogmus by himself, on top of the hill above the complex of blue-roofed buildings, by the gaping hole of the silo doors. The sun was already high in the milky blue-white sky. The half-orb of Saturn hung in the horizon in the east, clearly visible even during the day now. It had been a week since Jess last saw it, and already it looked more than twice as big. About thirty million kilometers away, but closing at four million kilometers a day.

When it was on the other side of the sun, it was a full circle, reflecting the sun, but as it passed to one side of the sun and approached Earth, it was a half-Saturn, but would grow to almost full on the approach trajectory.

Ufuk said from now on, it would double in size each day, growing exponentially until it would fill the entire sky, from horizon to horizon. Saturn rose and fell in tandem with the sun each day, about thirty degrees away from it in the sky, the gap widening as Saturn approached.

Eight days. That was all they had. There was no stopping it, no escaping, and there was something calming in that. An end to petty squabbles, and perhaps, an end to secrets.

"You wanted to be up there, didn't you?" Jess said, seeing Ufuk's eyes on the massive ringed planet. She stuffed her hands into the pockets of the over-sized arctic parka she had on.

"I was supposed to be up there, yes." He wore a similar heavy coat and pants.

"Bugs you when a plan doesn't work, doesn't it?"

"This goes beyond mere bothering. The Mars First crew knew they were on a one-way mission—"

"But didn't know to where. An important detail, don't you think? If you're risking your life for something?"

"I had to lie to them, otherwise they wouldn't be there."

Neither would we, Jess thought, but didn't say. "Have you been able to contact them?"

"Even if I could, they might not speak to me, but it doesn't matter. The communications gear here is destroyed." He exhaled, let the breath go out long and slow. "They are doomed no matter what. I failed them."

"Did something go wrong?" Jess noticed that he said the communications gear was destroyed, yet he didn't seem intent on fixing it. The man was always on the move, always doing something, but now he was doing nothing.

"Not immediately, that's not what I mean. I expect they will live long lives."

"Then what *do* you mean?"

"My genetics package."

"The canister?"

"Even if my colony construction works technically, their gene pool is too small."

Jess leaned over to look down the open silo doors. "Don't you have any more rockets stashed away somewhere?"

Ufuk laughed, a big hearty guffaw that was infectious enough to bring a smile to Jess's lips despite the pain in her joints. "What's so funny?"

"You think I have infinite resources?"

"How did you communicate with Zasekin when you were locked up in Oman? I talked to him. He said he talked to you continuously. All the time."

"That wasn't me."

"Who was it?"

"Simon."

The artificial intelligence. Jess shook her head. "That's incredible."

"But there is an end to my surprises," Ufuk said. "You think I have a rocket here and there up my sleeves?"

"Seems to have worked for you so far."

"Seven launches to put all the equipment for Mars First into space, all like clockwork, but then the eighth—" Ufuk put his fingers in front of his face and blew on them, his fingers flying apart at the same time, "—poof, exploded, just like that. A tiny package, but critical. The genetic material. Me being me, I had a backup of course. Had a twin set of genetics hidden with the Levantine council, and even had three backup rockets at strategic locations.

255

One of them in America was destroyed, but then Tanzania, and then—"

"Here."

"The best laid plans, heh?" He looked up at Saturn.

She thought he was insane, planning a human colony in space, but she had to respect his intentions, if not the methods. "So there's no way to get up there? That canister is pretty small."

"A simple matter of physics is all that stops us. Newton. Action and reaction. To get into orbit, I need to accelerate to *only* twenty-eight thousand kilometers an hour—but to escape Earth's gravity, we need to go much faster, almost forty thousand kilometers an hour. When Saturn and Earth meet, they will flash past each other at a hundred-and-forty thousand kilometers an hour."

"You're losing me."

"Means we need a big rocket. This was the only one left that big."

The wind blew a swirl of snow across the ground. In the days since the fight, a few inches had fallen, a white carpet almost totally hiding the evidence of the anger and bloodshed in the valley below. The twisted remains of the Big Dog troop transport was just visible in the distance. Jess promised herself that she'd walk over there and bury the American soldiers, but it was going to be a job digging into the frozen earth. She wasn't sure if they'd come here to save her, or take over this facility, but either way, they were her fallen brothers and sisters.

"I owned more than a thousand buildings around the world, did you know that?" Ufuk said. "Six space launch facilities, a hundred factories producing the world's most advanced robotics, hundreds of thousands of people going to work every day at my beck and call." He laughed again, but this time a sad chuckle. "And now, just me."

The world had to look so different through the eyes of someone like him, Jess thought, and yet he looked so small today.

That morning, Jess had awoken in the arms of Giovanni, with Hector cuddled between them in a nest of blankets. Just like they did after Nomad, huddled in the caves of Castle Ruspoli after her parents died. Just like they did on that first drive down the Italian coast. It seemed a lifetime ago. It had felt like her and Giovanni were a family back then, and today, for the first time in longer than she could remember, it felt that way again.

In front of her, Ufuk pulled his knees into his chin and shivered.

She felt sorry for him.

At the end of all this, at least she had Giovanni and Hector. He had nobody, and even if Massarra had survived, would he be any less alone? Everyone close to him, he'd lied to, to get what he wanted. In his mind, it was for a greater good, and maybe he was right, but that just made him more alone. Not even Simon, the friend he'd created, was here anymore. Nothing Ufuk did was an accident—so was it by design?

Did he want to be alone?

Was anyone like him ever *not* alone?

There was more to it than that, though.

She took another look at Ufuk, and he seemed only half the person he saw before. Without Müller in this world, Ufuk became like a man without a shadow. Something unnatural. Even when he was locked up in Oman, tortured and beaten, he'd seemed perfectly at ease, meditating.

Now he jittered and shook restlessly.

"The work you did with the Levantine Council, that must have saved millions of lives. A lot of those people are heading into sub-Saharan Africa because of you."

"People I also lied to."

"And the American convoy probably only made it to safety in Australia because of you. That was your plan, right? Setting up the internal fight between Chen Sheng and Chairman Zemin?"

"Divide and conquer. We had to bring Zemin's special security forces outside of Sanctuary China so that Sheng could effect the coup."

"Clever."

"Clever of you to notice."

"More clever of you to set it up. And I know you had to have Müller take Hector into Sanctuary China, so that Zemin would let him in—and then so that the Americans would be forced to use you and me to get us inside."

"Thank you, Jessica. Thank you for—"

"I forgive you. For everything."

257

The words had an almost electric effect on Ufuk. His body convulsed, and he stopped himself halfway through what looked like a sob by catching his fist in his mouth.

"You can't save everyone, Ufuk. You know that, don't you?" Jess said the words softly, soothingly. She hadn't come up here to absolve this man. She hadn't meant to even find him. She just wanted to look at the silo blast doors. "The only person you can save, ultimately, is yourself."

"I know."

"I'm not sure that you do."

"I'm trying."

The wind whistled as it picked up, bringing with it a fresh flurry of snow.

"What I really need you to do now—"

"Anything, Jessica, you just tell me."

"Is for you to put that big brain of yours to work on keeping us alive through this Saturn impact."

"You were supposed to be in Sanctuary China. Safe and secure," Ufuk said. "Or failing that, in sunny Australia. I was supposed to be up there." He pointed into the sky.

"That's in the past. We're in the present. I need you to focus on the future."

"That's all I do."

"What about getting back into Sanctuary China?"

"Roger's dead, and so are many of my allies. I did manage to initiate the coup with Sheng, but I had to break a lot of promises—"

"You mean you had to lie."

"To a lot of people," Ufuk finished his sentence. "After the nuclear blasts over Shanghai, the new government is a little skittish. Would you let a scheming little Turk like me into your hiding hole before Armageddon? When I have nothing left that anyone wants? Or at least, nobody believes I do anymore?"

"So we're almost on the exact wrong latitude for what's coming?"

"The worst should be over the North Atlantic, but it will be bad here. The Earth is going to plow a straight line through two hundred thousand kilometers of rock and ice in an hour and half. The impact might strip away our atmosphere—or it might not—

258

but it will unleash a burst of energy of millions of Hiroshima-sized bombs spread across the world."

"Can't we hide here? Can we close these blast doors?"

"These doors weight ten tons each. The explosions fused some of the metal, cracked the rocks. Maybe. It was never designed to be a bunker."

"Better than being above ground."

"Not airtight, and no clean water—and we have three dozen Buryat nomads lighting camp fires in the corridors."

"We can get them to leave."

Ufuk raised his eyebrows and grinned at her. "*You* go ahead and get them to leave." At least the man had some humor left in him. "I'm going back inside to check on the communications gear. I put an antenna up on top of the ridge earlier. I'll see what I can do about sealing off part of the complex."

"Great."

Jess rubbed her shoulders as she watched him walk down the slope and disappeared behind one of the buildings. The billionaire was obviously having a hard time adjusting to his new—and smaller—place in the world, for as long as that would last. With Ufuk around, she was sure they'd stay alive, and that was important for her, to keep Hector safe even as much as she distrusted the man.

"You need a place that can survive an atomic bomb?" said a thickly accented voice.

Jess turned to find Zasekin smiling at her. "That would be nice."

Belenko was with him, holding his hand. Both of them were dressed in thin cotton tunics and pants from the infirmary, the Russians seemingly impervious to the cold and snow.

"And we can take all the equipment from this place to trade?"

"We can take anything we want. What are you getting at?"

"Cigarettes?"

Jess's brows knitted together. "I think there are a few hundred cases in the commissary. Ufuk told me yesterday to keep them secret from the Buryat."

"Then we might have a deal to make. My old regiment, we were the 103rd Missile Brigade in Ulan Ude. Very big bunker. Very old and reliable Soviet design."

4

Xing'an Launch Facility
Northern China
May 7th

"This is madness," Giovanni said. "We stay here."

"They have their own air scrubbing system," Jess said. "Zasekin, tell him."

"This is true," the Russian said. "One hundred feet of Siberian shield granite and double ten foot thick steel blast doors."

"And their own water recycling," Jess added.

"And why didn't you go there before?" Giovanni said to Zasekin.

The Russian's nose crinkled. "It is a little...how do you say...like a place where you bury people?"

"A grave?"

"I am not sure if that is the word."

"A tomb?"

"*That* is the word." The Russian's lopsided grin indicated he had no trouble with the idea of pits dug into the earth. "I will also say it is full of nuclear bombs." At this he shrugged, perhaps to indicate that this was neither here nor there, but thought it worth mentioning.

"It's an *operational* missile site? How is any of this supposed to be convincing me? This is too dangerous."

Giovanni paced the length of the hall. The four of them, including Ufuk, were alone in the main mess of the complex. Hector was with Belenko and Raffa. Jess didn't think he needed to see his uncle freaking out, which was exactly what Giovanni was doing.

"The weapons are perfectly safe when they're stored, isn't that right?" Ufuk said from the corner, away from everyone else. "It's not in full operation."

"I am not interested in any of your opinions," Giovanni said, halfway through turning back to pace the other length of the hall.

The overhead lighting flickered on and off. No smooth glowing walls here. Fluorescent tubes hung below plastic ceiling tiles. The two hallways doors were closed, but by hand, and only half-closed. The walls were blackened from fire and ripped with bullet holes during the fight, the ground littered with shell casings and the shattered body parts of insect drones. In the middle of the room, a pallet truck was loaded with crates with Chinese markings.

They were cigarettes, and Zasekin was excited by them.

"These will get us in." The Russian patted one of the crates.

"Those will get us into a Red Army nuclear site?" Giovanni said, turning again.

"Rizak isn't crazy. This will get us into the missile compound, but not the nuclear weapon facility." Zasekin's face was serious now.

"Rizak? That's your friend?" Giovanni stopped pacing.

"Very good friend. We grow up together."

"And you've talked to him?"

"A few times since we left Baikal. We did think of going there, but it was too dangerous at the time."

"Because Lake Baikal was exploding?"

"And because Major General Kovalenko was still there. The last time I talked to Rizak, half of the men had deserted, including the Major General."

"But Rizak stayed?"

"The last I spoke to him, perhaps two months ago. It was a good place to keep...as a..."

"A tomb?" Giovanni started pacing again.

"It's easy to get to," Jess said, standing to take hold of Giovanni's arm. "Six hundred miles straight across the Mongolian desert, and then up the Selenge river."

"Very easy in the Czilim hovercraft," Zasekin said, smiling his rotten-toothed smile.

The smile didn't seem to comfort Giovanni. "That is a thousand kilometers of deep snow and ice—"

"In a *hover*craft," Jess said, still holding onto his arm. "It hovers."

"We should stay here. We dig into the mountain, barricade ourselves. It will be like when Nomad passed. We survived that, under Castle Ruspoli. Don't you remember? We can survive the same way here."

"This won't be like Nomad—" Ufuk started to say.

"Shut up." Giovanni cut him off without taking his eyes from Jess.

"This won't be like Nomad, it might be worse, at least here," Jess said. "And Giovanni, I wouldn't ask you if I didn't think, with all my heart, that this was the right thing to do. To protect us. To protect Hector."

The Italian took a good long look at her. "And you think heading north, into the cold, is the solution?"

"This event will tend to warm things up, at least in the very short term," Ufuk said in a small voice from the corner.

Giovanni's jaw muscles flexed. "If this Czilim hovercraft is so fast, then why not go south? Get out of the way?"

"Because the Mongolian desert is perfect for it," Jess said, keeping looking straight into his eyes. "Smooth snow, flat for almost the whole way. South is industrial wreckage and mountains."

"Very difficult to go south," Zasekin said. "But we just came from the north, from Ulan Bator. That is more than half of the trip, and it was less than a day to get here."

Jess felt Giovanni's arm go slack in her grip. "We can't be outside when this happens," he said.

"Rizak?"

The radio hissed static.

The four of them had moved from the underground complex into the Czilim, now parked outside near the burnt out shells of the Russian tank-trucks that Jess and Giovanni had been transported here in. The first thing everyone did the moment they exited the building was to look up.

The milky-blue-white sky was striped with high stratospheric clouds and a few puffy, lower altitude cumulus. The bright patch of the sun was halfway to the horizon, about two o'clock in the afternoon, but straight overhead was Saturn. It had grown visibly even in the few hours since Jess came outside this morning.

"Rizak?" Zasekin repeated into the radio.

They had the hatches of the green-pained hovercraft open. The interior stank of equal parts engine oil, diesel and whiskey from an open bottle near the radio.

Zasekin scratched his head and smiled awkwardly at Ufuk and Giovanni. He tried the radio again, but after five minutes he shrugged. "Maybe we try again later, no?"

They had to use the Russian radio, encrypted and selected to one of the military frequencies.

"Privet?" crackled a voice over the radio.

Zasekin had his finger over a button on the radio, about to switch it off, and his grimace turned back into the broken-tooth smile. "Ah, Rizak," he said into the radio.

An excited exchange in Russian, followed by something Jess understood.

"RS-26 Rubezh?" Zasekin said, his voice picking up in tempo.

"RS-24."

"Still operational?" Ufuk said to Zasekin.

The Russian nodded.

"Why do you really want to do this?"

Giovanni kept his side of the small room he shared with Jess and Hector, deep in the bowels of the complex.

"I told you, because I think it's the best thing." Jess replied.

Hector sat on a chair at the corner the further away from the both of them, of course still stuck on his tablet. Giovanni had tried to take it away, but Hector was having none of that. He screamed and cried until his uncle gave it back. The night before, they'd felt like a family again, but not this evening.

"Now is not the time for lies," Giovanni said.

"I'm not lying."

"Then what is this RS-24? What Zasekin was talking about on the radio?"

"It's a missile."

"And this is for Ufuk, yes?" Giovanni managed to restrain himself from swearing while uttering the Turk's name.

"Not for Ufuk," Jess said gently. "For all of us. For all of humanity."

Giovanni leapt up from the bed and threw the sheets onto the floor. "I cannot believe you are buying into his bullshit."

263

"I just wanted to wait until we knew if this Rizak was there before talking to you about it, otherwise—"

"Now you sound like him, you know that?"

"Ufuk might be nuts, but he spent a decade trying to build a human colony in space, to keep some record of humanity. That little canister, he needs to get it up there."

"All I care about is in this room."

"This will get you what you want, and protect us at the same time. This place isn't as safe as that Russian bunker will be."

"How does it get me what I want?" Giovanni stood on the other side of the small room, his arms wide, palms facing up.

"Because Ufuk is going to strap himself to one of those missiles and launch himself into space. One way or the other, it will be the last time you'll ever have to look at him again. Ever."

5

"Everyone get behind the Czilim!" Jess yelled.

Raffa unspooled a line of detonator wire behind him and did his best to jog over the deep snow with the awkward Russian snowshoes. Jess took hold of Hector, and Giovanni covered the both of them. Everyone else—Zasekin, Evgeny, Lucca, and Belenko—was inside the giant amphibious machine.

"You ready?" Jess asked Raffa.

His chest heaving in and out, he finished attaching the leads of the unspooled wire to the detonator box, then looked at Jess and nodded.

"Cover your ears," Jess said, and used her hands to cover Hector's.

The six-ton mass of the Czilim rocked against their backs as the concussion of the explosion sucked away the air, and then the deafening boom followed by a shower of shrapnel of wood chunks and clumps of frozen mud. Black smoke wafted around the camouflage-painted metal edge of the Czilim, and with it the faint smell of tar from the exploded Semtex.

Raffa disconnected the detonator wires, while Jess released Hector and trudged through the thigh-deep snow to inspect their handy work. A mass of twisted and blackened tree trunks and debris remained, but they'd blown a fifty-foot gap through the worst of it. She glanced at the Czilim. With the spray skirt deflated, the giant machine only looked half the size it did when it was underway, sort of the way a dog looked twice as big when it barked, the hackles raised on its spine. The metal structure of the hovercraft angled at forty-five degrees with a front turret with windows for the driver, and two massive, ten-foot enclosed propellers in the aft for propulsion.

She looked at the hole they'd blown in the debris pile, then walked over to look through the middle of it. It dipped down ten feet and then back up.

"We should fit through," Zasekin said, coming up beside her. He picked at a sharp edge of a branch. "My Chestnut can get through that, but we might rip her skirt."

Again.

The day before they'd had to stop after traversing another pile of debris. The six-ton Czilim almost catapulted over a fault line that had appeared from nowhere as they rocketed across the undulating, snow-covered Mongolian steppes at sixty kilometers an hour—about forty miles an hour, Jess had to keep calculating in her head. The Russian machine was built like a tank, but like everything the Soviets ever built, it had had its weakness. They ripped the thick rubber skirt of the hovercraft, and it had spun around, limping in circles until Zasekin ordered them to stop. Evgeny and Zasekin had to spend the whole day with lumps of rubber and hole punches and wire repairing it.

Two days before, they'd left the facility, loaded everything they could pry away from the Buryat nomads' sticky fingers, including—most importantly—the cases of cigarettes. Those they'd stowed inside the Czilim's fairly voluminous interior. The rest of it, tinned goods and water, along with radios and any other working electronics they could unbolt or tear from the walls, they'd put into Buryat sleds that the hovercraft towed behind it.

There wasn't time for anything more elegant.

While the rest of them were packing the ammunition and explosives, Ufuk had hauled down something totally unexpected. A hibernation pod from the crew capsule of the rocket. He said this was the key to how he was going to get up to the Mars First mission, that he was going to freeze himself and wait for someone to come and collect him. He had his backpack on, the one with the mysterious canister, but not a mystery anymore. He was insane, in Giovanni's opinion, but Jess was happy to have the energy return to Ufuk's step. It might just be what would keep them alive.

Giovanni was enthusiastic in helping Ufuk load the hibernation pod onto the Czilim, an odd sight to behold. Jess knew it was because the Italian was barely contained in his glee at the prospect of Ufuk strapping himself to the top of a nuclear missile and launching himself into space.

Misha—one of Zasekin's men—had decided to stay behind. In the week he'd been at the facility, he seemed to have found himself a nice Buryat woman. He helped loading the Czilim, but said that he didn't want to go anywhere, that he would take his chances by hiding deep inside the facility. The real reason, Zasekin had told Jess in private, was that Misha was afraid to go back to Russia—that even now, he feared being arrested as a deserter.

Ufuk had done his best to show the Buryat how to seal parts of the facility. They'd used one of the tank-trucks they got working to shove a pile of rocks into the silo opening, collapse and fill that part of it. They had no idea if it would work, but it was the best they could do.

They left Massarra behind as well.

Jess had spent hours trying to dig a hole into the frozen earth outside, but in the end, had to settle for gently placing the Israeli's body beneath a pile of rocks, up on the hillside, with a view to the east. She buried the American Special Forces men the same way, all ten of them, what parts of them she could find. They held an impromptu and quick ceremony, where Ufuk had said a few words.

Hector had cried.

The problem of what to do with Dr. Hermann Müller resolved itself. After her first trip to look at him, Jess had passed his body a few times, but eventually had decided that she wanted to bury him as well. Some part of her wanted to forgive him, as much of a bastard as he was, but this was more for her own sanity. It would give her peace, more than anything else.

When she came to get his body, though, it was gone.

It had to be one of the Buryat.

Jess didn't ask.

They left at first light on May 8th, with a week to go before the arrival of Saturn. The first two hundred miles were smooth sailing, speeding over the low hills and shallow valleys of the Mongolian deserts and steppes, but all of that came to a crunching half when they hit the fault line and almost wrecked the hovercraft.

An earthquake must have opened it up.

Then they hit this line of debris. Something had heated the ice and snow, created a river that flowed down through a valley from the highlands, bringing with it masses of debris. A volcanic fissure further up, probably, and it wasn't there when Zasekin crossed the area two weeks before, but then this was a changing Earth.

Everyone worked with a manic intensity whenever the Czilim stopped.

Even Hector.

"That's it?"

Jess craned her neck forward and wiped away condensation from the Czilim's windscreen. The noise of the engines was almost deafening, but had a calming effect once you got used to it, as if it enveloped you.

"That is the Selenge," Zasekin said.

He maneuvered the controls of the hovercraft, slid them sideways to a gap in the trees at the edge of the frozen river. "She will take us all the way up to Ulan Ude. I told you to trust the Chestnut!"

He leaned on the throttle, and the roar of the engines increased in pitch. The hovercraft slid forward and into the channel. This river stretched all the way from Ulan Bator up into Russia, snaked hundreds of kilometers. It was perfect for hovercraft. Smooth snow and ice, clear of most obstacles, and a map-less, single track that would bring them to their home.

The painful knot in Jess's stomach eased just a little.

"We are about to enter Russia," Zasekin said, "but no worry, you are with the border guards." He laughed a hearty guffaw at his own joke, and leaned over to take out and light a cigarette.

Jess watched the hummocks of snow pass by the hovercraft, remembering the frozen river of her childhood.

"You know what I always thought freedom was?" she said.

"Blue jeans and rock and roll?" The Russian laughed again at his own joke. Being back in Russia seemed to have a positive effect on him.

"I always thought freedom was the ability to do whatever you wanted."

The Russian considered this and took a drag from his cigarette. "And this is not freedom?"

The knot of worry eased in her stomach a little again. "Not really. No. After all this, I realize that freedom is really to be free of fear, not just to do what we want. I think fear takes away our freedom."

"You know what I think freedom is?" Zasekin asked.

Jess shook her head, a smile already on her face. It wasn't easy being serious with this big bear of a Russian.

"A full stomach and a beautiful girl by your side." He smiled his big broken-toothed grin at her. "And this morning, I have both."

They laughed together this time.

Zasekin turned off the Czilim's engines, and with a roaring clatter they stopped, replaced with an almost painful silence after two days of its shaking their bones. A chain link fence appeared ghost-like in the hovercraft's searchlights. Not just a chain link fence, but a series of three of them, twenty feet high each and topped with barbed wire. The deep snow at the entrance looked untouched. Large signs in Cyrillic text warned of something in Russian.

For a day and a night they'd rushed up the Selenge River. The cold intensified as they ventured north into Siberia, and they didn't see a living thing—human or otherwise, through the windscreen of the Czilim. They didn't stop for eighteen hours, with Evgeny refueling what they had left in diesel while the machine was still running.

"Are you sure this is it?" Giovanni asked, crowding between Jess and Zasekin to get a look outside.

"I lived and worked here for five years," Zasekin said. "This is it. We go outside to the gate. Trust me."

Jess and Raffa collected their M4s just in case.

Zasekin opened the side door of the Czilim, and biting cold air rushed in. He jumped out into waist-deep snow and laughed, then began to wade his way around the side to the gate. He said that Rizak wouldn't turn on any lights until he saw Zasekin's face on the exterior camera. The man was worried.

Raffa went next, his rifle up, scanning back and forth. He turned to help Jess down. Giovanni stayed in the Czilim with

Hector and Belenko, ready to operate the hovercraft turret-mounted machine gun if need be.

Jess landed past her waist in the cold snow.

She looked at the horizon to their east.

Saturn was rising.

It was about three o'clock in the morning, and was almost pitch black outside except for a few of the strongest stars that managed to pierce the stratospheric gauze, but the massive almost-full globe of Saturn shone bright as it cleared the horizon, casting the snow and ice into a monochromatic version of sunlight. They'd made it to Ulan Ude with a bit more than three days to spare, and Saturn was less than thirteen million kilometers away now—closing the distance at four million kilometers a day.

A bright dot preceded Saturn.

Its moon Titan.

It was bigger than Mercury, and over a million kilometers closer to them than Saturn, Ufuk had explained when they took turns looking through the Czilim's windows. Saturn rose about three hours before the sun, the two of them arcing their way across the sky each day. Titan appeared before Saturn, and then a constellation of tiny dots appeared. Saturn had over sixty moons. The brightest of the bright dots was Enceladus, which Ufuk was the most excited in describing. He said it was the brightest object in the solar system, and this was due to it being covered in a fresh layer of water ice that welled up from massive subsurface oceans.

He said the oceans might even contain a form of life.

The lights atop the chain link fence blinked on, blinding Jess for an instant as her eyes adjusted. Metal scraped against metal and a hinge creaked.

"You see?" Zasekin said. He held aloft two cartons of cigarettes.

The Russian clapped Jess on the back and then turned to rattle off excited Russian at a half-open door on the other side of the triple-line of fences.

"He will open the gates," Zasekin said after a second. "My friend Rizak!"

6

ICBM Complex
Ulan Ude, Russia
May 14th

"You see, I told you everything would be okay," Jess said to Giovanni.

She folded a set of sheets and put them away in an overhead drawer, resisting but at the same time enjoying the feeling of being a homemaker. This was going to be their home, at least for the next few weeks or months until the effects of impact with Saturn's rings abated—if it ever did. Perhaps the atmosphere would be shorn away, the Earth flung into an uninhabitable orbit.

None of that mattered, not right now.

The desperate fear of the past few days was gone. The fear that she'd made a mistake, forced them into a terrible end, the feeling of exposure, pinned to the surface outside—but all that was in the past.

Now they were underground.

Whatever happened, they would be safe, at least for the time being, and that was all Jess could ask for. To be free of fear, for today and tomorrow. That was freedom, and she felt a bubble of optimism flow through her. She had her small family, her and Hector and Giovanni, tucked away deep in a corner of the missile bunker. It was a vast underground system that stretched hundreds of feet down into solid granite.

The place was designed for a complement of a hundred soldiers—and they'd taken what supplies they could with them when they left. Only Rizak and one other soldier had remained. They had no families, and nobody else dared to try and cross the razor wire in this abandoned corner of Siberia.

The Russians still feared Russia, even now.

Jess and Hector and Giovanni had their own four-room corner of the complex. It felt like pure luxury to have clean beds, a hot shower, and so much space—and security. The place was built as a super-fortress, and in a few hours they would be sealing it off from the outside entirely.

"What about when Ufuk is gone?" Giovanni said, sitting on one of the beds in the room across from where Jess was arranging their freshly washed clothes.

Jess couldn't help laughing. "This is the first time I've ever heard you having separation anxiety about being away from Ufuk."

"Trust me, I'm happy the idiot is going ride a nuclear missile into space. He wants to kill himself, I'm going to be very obliging to help him along. What I'm worried about is, what happens when Ufuk is gone? Can we trust these Russians?"

"These Russians want to get to Australia as much as we do."

"And you think the Americans will help?"

They'd been in touch with Colonel Hague on the radio last night—the commanding officer from Oman—who'd made it with the rest of the American refugees to Western Australia. He said they were heroes, promised to do everything the American government could do to help rescue them once Saturn had passed.

"They said they have a patch of land for us. I'm going to call it the Rollins Ranch, what do you think?"

Hector ran through the hallway between them with a metal tin he pretended was the Czilim hovercraft, buzzing a noise that imitated its engines. Giovanni was happy he was finally off the tablet and stopped playing with Ufuk's games.

"I think the Rollins Ranch is a great name."

Jess crossed over into the room Giovanni was in and deposited herself on his lap. She kissed him.

"What was that for?" he asked, bemused, kissing her back.

"I don't think I've ever told you this…"

His easy smile slid away. "What's wrong?"

"I love you. Thank you for everything."

The Italian's smile returned. "I love you, too."

Hector had stopped in the doorway and watched them.

Jess reached out to grab him and plant a few kisses on his forehead and cheeks. "Come on, you two, we better hurry or we're going to miss the show!"

"Is it safe?" Hector said.

272

The kid clung onto Jess's pant leg, his eyes wide at the enormous orb of Saturn hanging just over the horizon.

"I think so," Jess replied, but even she wasn't sure.

All nine of them stood in a group together at the edge of the wire fencing—the four Russians and Belenko, Giovanni and Jess and Hector, with Ufuk standing to one side, acting as their tour guide.

"It will be safe for another few hours," Ufuk said. "I suggest you don't take any chances and secure yourselves underground right after this. Amazing that we have clear skies this morning."

The sky was cobalt blue to the west, but pink and orange to the east with the sun rising but just over the horizon. Saturn hung brilliantly above them, the color of the striated brown bands of its atmosphere visible now, the massive rings seeming like they touched the Earth already. They were almost edge-on to the rings, so they saw a bright, sharp band—a knife that was about to cut into the Earth.

In the west was the spectacle Ufuk had urged them to come outside to see. Titan, Saturn's largest moon, was dropping through the indigo sky at an incredible speed. In the space of two seconds, it passed almost straight in front of the moon and then away.

"Titan is missing the Earth by three hundred thousand kilometers," Ufuk explained. "That's inside the moon's orbit."

It looked four times the size of the moon, but brownish in color and smooth.

"From the methane atmosphere," Ufuk said.

A few seconds more, and Titan dropped below the horizon.

"Amazing, isn't it? Watching the visible effect of a forty-three kilometer per second intersect? Saturn is less than a million kilometers away now."

"So the show's over?" Giovanni asked in a more-than-slightly-worried-sounding voice. He had Hector in his arms.

"The show is only just beginning, unfortunately, but no direct impacts with objects larger than a few dozen meters, unless we're very unlucky. And I think we've had about all the bad luck we can have so far."

"Let's get underground," Giovanni said to Jess.

Overhead, tiny sparklers seemed to light up the sky.

273

"Just one second," Ufuk urged. "Look there." He pointed at bright dots to the side of Saturn. "That's Rhea, the second largest moon, and there is Mimas, and Iapetus…"

"Jess, let's go." Giovanni's grip on her arm tightened.

"Okay, okay."

The view was terrifying but awe inspiring.

"And Enceladus," Ufuk said to Jess. "The brightest jewel of Saturn."

The dot he pointed at glowed brighter than any of the others.

"So you're going to freeze yourself in that?" Giovanni pointed at the hibernation pod crammed into the nose cone of the missile.

It looked like a coffin, and probably was one.

Jess and Giovanni stood next to Ufuk on a metal grating next to the top of the fifty-foot RU-24 intercontinental ballistic missile. The past two days, while everyone else was hauling in supplies from the Czilim and preparing their living quarters, Ufuk had been preparing his own.

He'd opened up the nose cone fairings—the covers—and took out the dummy warhead. It revealed a space not more than six feet high and four feet in diameter. Into it he'd crammed the hibernation pod that he'd salvaged from the Tangoing rocket in China, and filled the rest of the compartment with lithium-ion batteries he'd found, as well as some foam insulation. It looked decidedly non-high-tech.

"I'm not going to freeze myself," Ufuk replied. "I will be lowering my core temperature down to just above the freezing point of water, though. The insulation of the pod itself and the power I've daisy-chained in should be able to keep me alive for a few months."

"And then what?"

"One of the crew of the Mars First mission will pick me up and defrost me."

"And you think they won't just let you float by them?" Giovanni had heard what Ufuk had done to the crew of Mars First.

"Another risk in a long list of risks, but one I think is worth it."

Against the wall was the canister of genetic material, its light glowing.

"You're going to fit that in there with you?" Jess asked, pointing at the canister.

"It's happy at very cold temperatures, I'll stick that in as luggage."

The man sounded like he was going on vacation to the beach. He was fearless in his pursuits, Jess had to give him that.

"Mars First will end up in an orbit around the sun," Ufuk continued. "At the L3 Lagrange point, a position that is stable between the Earth and the Sun—but I don't need this rocket to accelerate me to interplanetary speeds to get there."

"And why is that?" Giovanni asked.

His question was more to humor Ufuk than really being interested. Jess could see that Giovanni was more than ready to be done with Ufuk, but was staying with Jess because she wanted to see the Turk off.

"Physics," Ufuk said brightly. "I don't need to accelerate to twenty-three thousand miles per hour to escape the Earth's pull, because I have Saturn to pull me. In seven hours, just as Saturn passes the Earth, it's gravity will be much stronger than ours just a little ways up. I just have to propel this capsule to fifty thousand kilometers straight up, and gravity slingshot will do the rest."

"And put you into orbit around the sun?" Jess frowned, but then the kinds of calculations involved went beyond what she could understand, and it wasn't her life he was risking.

"The RU-24 is a very stable, very powerful rocket," Ufuk replied. "Three stage solid propellant. It has just enough muscle to get the job done, but only because of the happy accident of Saturn being this close."

"Great," Giovanni said sarcastically. "Let's leave him to it."

Hector was busy prodding the missile.

Jess looked at Giovanni, then back at Ufuk. "I guess this is goodbye." She held out her hand.

Ufuk rubbed the back of his neck with one hand. "Giovanni, would you mind if I had just a moment with Jess, alone?"

"For what?"

275

"To apologize."

"Go ahead and do it now."

"Giovanni," Jess said softly. "It's okay. I'll just be a second."

The man was about to commit suicide, Jess figured, that or save humanity. Either way, she could make a second for him.

Giovanni took Hector's hand and led him away, along the gantry into the main building.

"Why?" Jess asked as soon as they left.

"Why am I going?" Ufuk replied. He began walking around the missile's circumference, inspecting it.

Jess followed him. "Why me? Why did you expend so much energy making me a focus of all your efforts?"

"You were just one part of it, Jessica." He patted the rocket.

"That's not answering the question."

"Because, without your father, humanity might be dead. Without his observation of Nomad over thirty years ago, we might have been caught unaware."

"Most of humanity *was* caught unaware."

"But your father gave me time to plan and prepare."

Jess walked past the genetic canister and noticed some odd. It was open, the secret interior part she'd never seen before, but it was empty. Maybe Ufuk had already taken that out and put it into the missile.

"I tried to help him, your father," Ufuk said. "Your whole family, I tried to intervene, but I failed."

He was on the other side of the missile now, and Jess took three quick steps to get him back into view. When she rounded the missile, though, something was odd.

Hector was there, sitting against the wall. He looked asleep.

What was he doing here? Didn't Giovanni just take him?

"I tried to help them, but I failed," Ufuk repeated. "But I will help you."

A sudden sickness fell through the pit of Jess's stomach. Hector wasn't asleep. He looked drugged. She took a step toward him, but too late realized it was a trap.

She spun around, ducking, and brought a fist up blindly. She caught Ufuk almost square in the chin, blood spattering from teeth she knocked out. He staggered back with something held out in one hand. Jess tried to steady herself, but Ufuk was incredibly fast. He dodged around her next blow and threw an arm around her back.

"Giovann—" Jess tried to yell.

A sharp prick in her neck as she scrabbled to take hold of Ufuk's hair.

Her vision swam and she looked at Hector.

What had she done?

What had *Ufuk* done?

Blackness descended as she fought to stay conscious.

7

Destiny Colony
Orbiting Saturn, near Enceladus
October 12th

The small boy's face in the black hole, ringed in white, floated in front of Jess. She tried to reach out, and screamed a silent scream into the endless night.

"Hey, I think she's waking up!" someone yelled, an echo beyond sight.

Jess blinked and then shut her eyes tight against the brightness. A soft beeping noise in the light. Beep. Beep.

Like a heartbeat.

She opened her eyes again. A woman with black eyes and black hair stared back at her. Jess tried to say something, but her throat was thick. She felt ill. Pitching forward, she vomited.

"Just get it all out," said the woman.

"You're going to feel terrible, but it will get better," said a man's voice.

Jess fell back against the bed. "Where's Hector?"

"He's safe. He's with you," said the man.

He appeared over her. Blue eyes. Caucasian features. The other woman was Asian, her brain realized as it pieced itself back together. She realized she worried that she'd been transported back to Sanctuary China.

What had Ufuk done?

"Hector," Jess gurgled.

Someone held her up and pointed.

And there he was—Hector's hair was matted down and he looked terrified, but he was wide-eyed and awake in a blue hospital gown in the gurney next to her. Alive. That was all that mattered.

"Where's Ufuk?" was Jess's next question.

"Gone."

"Gone where?" she gasped. She wanted as much distance between her and that animal as possible. What had he done? Her memory was fragmented. She remembered him attacking her. Struggling to keep him away. Hector slumped against the wall.

"You'd know better than us," the man replied.

"Who...who are you?" Jess stammered. She shivered and felt like she wanted to retch again.

"Commander Jason Rankin. You've been asleep for a long time. Just rest."

Jess's mind tried to understand what he was saying. "Asleep?"

"Just rest."

"Rankin?" A thought, half-formed, percolated up through her mind. "Wait, *Jason* Rankin?"

"That's right. You made it."

"Made what?"

"You made it up here. You're the only one."

Jess still felt like she was going to throw up, but she propped herself up onto her elbows. "Made what where? Where am I?"

The room was white, the same glowing plastic white that she'd come to despise in the Sanctuaries, and the same faint scent of new-car plastic, but as if the car was a year old. Or more. Beyond a large glass window, stars wheeled by.

And then.

Saturn swung into view. Massive. And crystal clear.

"You're on Destiny," Rankin replied. "Enceladus Station. In orbit around Saturn."

8

Destiny Colony
Orbiting Saturn, near Enceladus
November 2nd

The blue marble of the Earth lit up in a fiery glow as it plowed through Saturn's rings. The planet caught the ring system to the sunward side of the gas giant, and mowed a pencil-thick black line through the brilliantly-lit outer rings, plunged through the denser sets of middle B rings and into the inner rings. At twenty thousand kilometers from the top of Saturn's atmosphere, Earth made its closest approach, and then ground its way back out.

The first impact with the outer rings had been near the equator. A fireball twelve thousand miles long that half-encircled the world. Saturn's rings weren't more than a hundred feet thick, and mostly composed of ice crystals and snow-sized chunks of dirty snow, but in the aggregate—and at the impact speed of over forty kilometers per second—it unleashed a massive amount of energy. Over the next seventy-six minutes, the fireball has intensified as Earth dove through the outer into the inner rings, and razed from the equator most of the way to the North Pole.

A pencil-thick black gap through the rings, from Earth passing through them. A gap that was eight thousand miles wide. That was the diameter of the Earth, but it was hard to understand scale from this viewpoint, so Jess shifted the zoom on the tablet controls, and the image on the wall screen enlarged the Earth and scrolled back to the beginning of the recording to eight hours before the first impact.

At that point, Jess had still been on Earth.

She tried to zoom in to the area of northern Asia, to see if she could see a telltale flicker, anything that could identify the rocket launch, but the resolution of imaging system wasn't high enough. The recording played back again, and Earth tore through the rings. She played it over and over again.

Six months.

That's how long she'd been in hibernation sleep, cooled to near freezing, but kept barely alive—her heartbeat once per second.

Hector had been stuffed into the pod with her, his arms around her chest. For six months they'd floated in the vacuum of space until a drone from Mars First had picked them up on a looping orbit that brought them near the station.

She restarted the playback of the Earth-Saturn intercept, and then played back an audio recording. Static hissed, and then: "We are safe..." It was Giovanni's voice, followed by indecipherable crackling, and then, "...take...Hector..." They were the only words they'd been able to clearly identify as Giovanni's. Five words she played over and over again as she watched the Earth make its fiery passage.

The crew of Mars First had managed a few sporadic communications with radios on Earth as they sped past and away. One of the cargo pods had detached from Mars First and fired its engines to drop into Earth orbit. A cluster of communication satellites, Simon had told the crew. At least not everything Ufuk had said was a lie.

"Returning to Australia, I repeat, we are returning to Australia," said another voice, this time Admiral Reynolds. He'd managed to get a few communications out.

They'd been able to piece together that the Carl Vinson battle group had at least survived the Saturn encounter, but what had happened to Giovanni? What happened to Lucca and Raffa? Had they fought with Ufuk to try and save her and Hector? Did they have no idea until it was too late? Giovanni had survived at least the initial impact—that much she could infer from the static-filled message relayed by the Carl Vinson, but beyond that, she had no idea.

After a few days of sporadic radio messages, no communications had been heard from Earth since the impact. Now they were speeding toward the outer edges of the solar system. It was still possible they'd hear something, and Jess hung on to that possibility, but there was no possibility of return.

One more surprise.

When the medical system scanned her body on arrival, it discovered she was pregnant.

At first she was excited.

Then terrified.

"Hector, are you going to play on that all day?" Jess said.

"I'm not playing, I'm working," Hector replied. His fingers scrolled across the tablet in his lap. He sat cross-legged and looking out the window.

Beyond the glass window-wall of the mess, an insect-drone scuttled past, then released, its eight legs splaying out as it coasted away from the rotating habitation module of the Mars First spacecraft to the growing donut of the Destiny colony. In the distance below, Enceladus glowed—a soft-white snowball—and beyond that, the ever-present mass of Saturn, the center of this new universe.

Hector had some kind of connection to the drone swarms, something Jess couldn't understand. More than that, he was keyed into Mars First's systems as the backup to Ufuk Erdogmus. The entire electronic network here regarded him as the new superuser. Hector was the king of Destiny.

A thin cable unfurled from the insect-drone's belly. Commander Rankin had explained a little of how Ufuk Erdogmus's creations had been designed to work here. The wire coming out of the drone was an electromagnetic tether. In the massive magnetic fields around Saturn, the tethers generated what amounted to free energy. A thin-but-massive carbon nanotube tether—four hundred miles long—connected the growing Destiny spacecraft structure to Enceladus itself, and served as an elevator to conduct material up and down from it. This main tether generated hundreds of thousands of watts that powered the drones and everything else, including life support.

Enceladus was snowball-white because it was ice.

A liquid ocean of water dozens of miles deep covered the moon under the exterior frozen shell. Enceladus was tidally locked with Saturn, one side of it always facing the planet, but these same tidal forces generated heat energy that kept the subterranean ocean warm. An endless supply of water and oxygen and hydrogen for the growing space station.

Jess squinted to see a faint white plume erupting from the north pole of Enceladus. Regular geysers erupted, releasing pressure from below, but releasing pressure from *what* exactly was still a mystery. The best guess was that some form of alien life lived deep below the ice—another fascinating and terrifying prospect. In his ramblings, Ufuk had told her that the only other place that he thought life existed in the solar system was Enceladus. Alien life. Jess had to remind herself, though, that here, *she* was the alien.

She focused her attention on the wire-frame structure the drones were assembling in the near distance. The rotating habitat of the Mars First spacecraft was a hundred feet in diameter, but the slowly self-assembling shell of the Destiny colony structure was five times that size. It would be ready in just three months, by Rankin's best estimates, but the humans were secondary in this construction. It was the drones and the artificial intelligence of Simon that were the primary builders.

The humans' role would only come later.

To populate the colony.

It had at least answered one of Commander Rankin's questions when he'd been sent out on this mission—why it was a mostly female crew. The answer: because they'd be needed to gestate. The only problem was, the genetic package from Earth never made it up here. Jess had seen it opened, there was nothing there, it must have been ruined at some point, which led to another, more terrifying truth.

She wasn't just pregnant with one baby.

It was four. Quadruplets.

And all of them with vastly different genetics.

"Hector, come on, it's time for bed."

"One more minute?"

"One more minute."

Jess played the Earth-Saturn intercept again, and watched Earth crash into the rings, watched the fireball hit the atmosphere. For the past three weeks since waking up here, she'd had a lot of time to think. She'd been a pawn in someone else's game, but that didn't matter anymore.

Was Ufuk dead?

Even that didn't matter.

How long had Ufuk known he was going to do this to her? Make her his human genetic transport into space? He must have had Zasekin suggest going to the missile silo, make out like it wasn't his idea—otherwise they would have never gone. Anyway, if the crew here knew it was Ufuk in that pod, they probably wouldn't have retrieved it.

It was all a set up.

The pain she'd felt after being unconscious in the facility in northern China, after the battle when she'd killed Muller. Ufuk must have implanted something in her then, his package must have been damaged.

At first she felt violated. A visceral disgust.

Over the weeks, the feeling had dissipated as she watched the Earth collide with Saturn's rings over and over again. Millions of people had died, and here she was, warm and safe. She remembered what she'd said to Zasekin that morning—that freedom was the absence of fear. She didn't fear anymore.

And that made her free.

Over the weeks, she'd held Hector close, and realized that all she'd ever really wanted was there in her arms. To save the boy, to make her father proud. Ufuk hadn't given her what she wanted, but maybe he'd given her what she needed, in the end.

Saturn's orbit was going to take it far into the outer solar system, far out past even Pluto. It would be a hundred and fifty four years before Saturn made it back to the inner solar system, and someone from here might venture back to the Earth. Out of the window-wall, a bright star flashed, and Jess realized it was the sun. By the time Saturn returned to Earth, she would be dead. At least she had Hector, she could thank Ufuk for that, and that was the only thing that mattered to her now.

Jessica looked at the sun receding one more time before she scooped Hector into her arms, nuzzled his neck. She would probably live a long life out here in the stars—a life now without fear—but she sensed where her story was ending, Hector's was only just beginning.

"Come on, it's time for bed," she said, squeezing Hector, her heart blossoming. "Tomorrow is another day."

From the Author
A sincere *thank you* for reading!
This is where the Nomad series comes to an end—or is it?
One day I will revisit this series, when Saturn swings around in its
orbit back to Earth in about two hundred years, and the descend-
ants on Destiny Colony return to a new Earth.

But until then,
can interest you in one of my new releases?

NEW RELEASE—POLAR VORTEX

A routine commercial flight disappears over the North Pole.
Vanished into thin air. No distress calls. No wreckage. Weeks
later, found on the ice, a chance discovery…the journal from passenger Mitch Matthews reveals the incredible truth...
Search for *Polar Vortex* on Amazon.

NEW RELEASE—THE DREAMING TREE

Described by readers as The Girl with the Dragon Tattoo
meets Black Mirror. A new breed of predator hunts on the streets
of New York—chased by Delta Devlin, the NYPD detective
whose gift and curse are eyes that see things only she can.
Search for *The Dreaming Tree* on Amazon.

AND PLEASE...

If you'd like more quality fiction at this low price, I'd really appreciate a review on Amazon. The number of reviews a book accumulates on a daily basis has a direct impact on how it sells, so just leaving a review, no matter how short, helps make it possible for me to continue to do what I do.

OTHER BOOKS BY MATTHEW MATHER

CyberStorm

Award-winning CyberStorm depicts, in realistic and sometimes terrifying detail, what a full scale cyberattack against present-day New York City might look like from the perspective of one family trying to survive it. Search for CyberStorm on Amazon.

Darknet

A prophetic and frighteningly realistic novel set in present-day New York, Darknet is the story of one man's odyssey to overcome a global menace pushing the world toward oblivion, and his incredible gamble to risk everything to save his family. Search for Darknet on Amazon.

Atopia Chronicles (Series)

In the near future, to escape the crush and clutter of a packed and polluted Earth, the world's elite flock to Atopia, an enormous corporate-owned artificial island in the Pacific Ocean. It is there that Dr. Patricia Killiam rushes to perfect the ultimate in virtual reality: a program to save the ravaged Earth from mankind's insatiable appetite for natural resources. Search for Atopia on Amazon.

CPSIA information can be obtained
at www.ICGtesting.com
Printed in the USA
LVHW040928221119
638065LV00005B/2109/P